City of Secrets

Christine Jordan

Published in 2014 by FeedARead.com Publishing

Copyright © The author as named on the book cover.

First Edition

A CIP catalogue record for this title is available from the British
Library.

Cover Art work by Diana Chitulescu

This book is dedicated to my soul sister.

Chapter 1

The scriptorium stood empty, a stillness in it.

The study carrels, twenty eight in all, lined both sides of the long building. Thick damask curtains, normally pulled across each one to cloister the novices, were drawn back, exposing their oak desks, displaying a neat collection of ink wells, pen knives and quills. Leather-bound books and manuscripts lay open, exposing the vellum, like crisp linen, the background to letters and illuminations, waiting to be meticulously crafted. More books and manuscripts were stacked on shelves along the centre of the room. At one end was the Prior's study area, set apart to show pre-eminence. The friars had long since retired from their studies.

A sharp October wind blew through the unglazed windows. The bells of St Peter's Abbey began their hourly chime. On the second chime, the luminous edge of a passing dark cloud revealed a full moon whose light shone through each window, casting shards of shadows across the wooden floorboards. The curtains rustled softly.

On the floor, eyes staring upwards at the finely crafted, scissor-braced oak roof lay a young woman, mouth slightly open, lips tinged with blue. Her fair hair, streaked across her face, hid her fine features. She lay at an awkward angle, her body twisted. The claret and plum-coloured marks appearing on her neck were the only evidence of her violent and disrespectful death.

***

Emmelina moved with the stealth of a fawn grazing in open fields at dawn. Limb by limb, she edged her way to the outside of the bed so as not to disturb her sleeping husband. Moving the covers to form a lump beside his heaving hulk, she lowered her left leg till her toes touched the cool, wooden floor. Humphrey made a grunting noise and turned onto his back. Emmelina stiffened. Every muscle in her body tensed. Surely, after drinking several flagons of beer in the Fleece Inn, he would not wake. The Fleece, situated on the opposite side of the street was newly built and packed full of pilgrims visiting the abbey and had become a nightly haunt for Humphrey. Still, she held her breath, closed her eyes and waited until he settled.

Certain he was asleep; she raised herself from the bed and tiptoed across the floorboards. Her shoes, made from the finest Cordovan goat leather and imported by her husband from Spain, had been tucked under the chair and her clothes were draped across the back. While keeping a watchful eye on Humphrey, she pulled on her under-garments and barefooted tiptoed out of the bedroom and down the creaky stairs. She made her way to the fore-hall where her husband kept a large wooden chest in which he stored his old documents. He rarely looked in there, which was why she had chosen it to hide her faith garments and the wooden pattens she wore when walking through the streets late at night.

Tying the dark-brown woollen over-garment tightly at her small waist, and securing a leather bag to her belt, she covered her head and shoulders with a scarf made from the same material and slipped her stockinged feet into the pattens. She paused at the bottom of the stairs to make a final check on her sleeping husband, listening for the slightest sound. His thunderous snores could be heard all through the house. Satisfied he wouldn't wake before morning, she lifted the metal latch on the heavy wooden door and stepped out into Maverdine Lane. A quick glance along the lane, in both directions, confirmed no-one was about. Only then did she make her way towards The Cross, an intersection where East, West, North and South Gate streets converged. Here stood the octagonal shaped High Cross towering above the nearby buildings and higher than any of the many smaller preaching crosses scattered about the city. Elaborately carved with the statues of Kings John and Edward, standing proud and upright in their crocketed niches and topped with a spire, it was a visible landmark. She looked up at them and crossed herself.

Continuing down East Gate Street, she stopped just before the city gate and ducked into an alleyway. It reeked of stale urine and dog mess. She knew the porter would be entertaining his lady friend at this hour, which would make it easier for her to slip past him and out onto the fields, which lay beyond the city's defences. Listening out for the familiar sounds of their raucous love-making, and, hearing them, she walked through the East Gate with a confident stride and over the wooden drawbridge, which spanned the old Roman moat, immediately turning left to trace the outer walls of the city towards Gaudy Green. The evening had turned decidedly wintry. She hurried along in the dark, pulling her scarf across her mouth in response to the burning sensation at the back of her throat from the searing cold air.

Now almost a mile from the city she heard the bells of St Peter's Abbey chime twice. On the second chime, the clouds thinned and a full moon illuminated her way. In the stillness of the night, the only other sound to be heard was the swishing of her skirts and the occasional screech of an owl as she made her way upwards to Robin Hoodes Hill. Emmelina strode along the worn footpaths leading her to higher ground. With each step she became more alive, more invigorated. She thought of her fat lump of a husband lying in his drunken stupor and in that moment, a stronger resolve rose within her to carry her along what had now become a steep and thickly forested hill.

Since giving birth to a stillborn daughter three years ago a sombre change had occurred within her. At the same time a hidden facet of her character had emerged. The part that had no feeling and no thought of consequences. It was a cold inner core she retreated to, each and every time Humphrey violated her. When he forced himself upon her she would lay there with her eyes tightly shut and her head turned away from him, listening to his laboured breathing, smelling his sour skin and feeling the touch of his sweaty flesh. Worst of all, was the feel of him inside her, thrusting without tenderness into the delicate parts of her she had not given him permission to enter. She always lay without movement waiting for him to finish so she could turn over and pretend to be asleep. It was at these most vulnerable times she would tell herself, over and over, that one day she would be free of him. She said it to her true self, not the cold shell she became when lying with Humphrey.

During the first few months of living under Humphrey's roof she had made every attempt to stop him but soon realised it was hopeless. He was bigger and stronger and it only hurt her more. The only consolation was the act itself lasted but a few minutes. She longed to be free of the burden of her marriage but she could see no way out. Her secret faith had carried her through the last four years, since her parents had died and given her an outlet, beyond the confines of the home she shared with Humphrey.

As she reached the summit, the trees thinned out until eventually she came upon a clearing in the undergrowth where her fellow followers stood in a circle wearing the habitual dark robes, their bare feet on the cold dark earth. She rummaged in her leather bag and brought out a candle, which she lit from a bank of candles arranged on a makeshift altar on the ground, then took her place. Surrounded by a circle of oneness, of understanding and trust and of knowingness, Emmelina breathed in deeply and closed her eyes. The essence of calm and belonging enveloped her, warming her deadened heart. This was the one time Emmelina was true to herself, her authentic self.

A deep, male voice addressed her as she took her place in the circle.

'Welcome, Saoirse.'

She recognised his voice. It was Finn, his bleached, white hair standing out in the dark night. He looked younger than his years, the kindness in his eyes twinkling in the moonlight.

'Let us begin.'

Blackfriars Priory

Guido, the novice friar, entered the scriptorium from the east wing, carrying a roll of cloth. His movements were quick and furtive. Laying the cloth out on the floor beside the young girl, he knelt down and rolled her lifeless body onto it. He struggled with her tiny frame, then, seeming to change his mind, he unwrapped her and ripping at her neckline exposed her firm breasts. He gave them a rough squeeze. She didn't protest. Good, he thought. That's how it should be. Feeling the rage welling up within himself he allowed the baser side of his nature to surface. He put his hand under his black cappa and began to rub himself. He looked at her pretty face, her full breasts. She was silent now, completely in his power. He looked down at the growing bulge underneath his cassock. He quickened his movements and, with a loud gasp and racking of his body, came over her beautiful and innocent face. He noted, with perverse satisfaction, she didn't squirm or balk when the fluid hit her lips. She accepted his gift graciously. Wiping himself on the sackcloth, he finished wrapping her body and, picking her up with some difficulty, put her over his shoulder and made his way down the western staircase out into the cloister. The moon had disappeared behind the clouds. All was dark and quiet.

'Excellent,' Guido hissed, as he entered the monks' refectory.

From there, he made his way to the narrow lane the monks called a 'slype', which led from the priory down to the banks of the River Severn where the friars had a mooring from which some of their supplies were delivered. Now very out of breath, Guido staggered onto the wooden pontoon. With a mighty effort, he lifted the sack from his shoulder and heaved her body into the fast flowing river, trying to throw her as far out as he could manage. Her body hit the blackness of the water like a sack of discarded butcher's bones. Guido watched as the sack was swept along with the lunar tide making its way out towards Bristol and the sea beyond.

As he walked back to the dormitory in the grey light of dusk the familiar feeling of utter self-loathing and disgust returned. Whenever those feelings surfaced he pushed them to the back of his mind, the memories of his childhood, at the hands of his overbearing father, too painful to bear. A cold and feverish sweat consumed him. He quickened his step and thought about Lauds.

Robin Hoodes Hill

To the east of the hill just above the black horizon, a thin line of pale grey sky could be seen cracking the darkness. Dawn was breaking.

Emmelina lay in the centre of the circle. Her bare legs were intertwined with someone else's; her head lay upon the naked breast of another woman. Her mons was being gently stroked from behind by the man she knew only as Tegan. Completely relaxed and warm, despite the coldness of the ground, she lay there half asleep feeling the fine hairs covering her skin standing on end, as if all her nerve endings had been ignited. Her legs were trembling as they often did after intense pleasure.

She had spent the night being touched tenderly in the most intimate of places, her sacred union with God fulfilled here on earth. Ending in a cosmic sensation of oneness, her body racked with the cascading spasms of a prolonged orgasm unlike any she could produce herself, she had drifted off into a heavenly slumber. A playful tug at her pubic hair woke her and, noticing the imminent dawn, she knew she must hurry home before her husband woke. Removing Tegan's hand, she extricated herself from the twine of bodies and walked over to the heap of clothes she had left at the edge of the circle. Tegan watched her as her naked body moved with the grace of a fawn, the muscles in her shapely legs taut, her flat stomach going in at the waist. Her breasts were full, the nipples dark and hard, her skin pink and in parts red where some of the more impassioned lovers had left their mark. Her long hair fell over angular shoulders to the small of her back. It was the colour of winter sloe berries. Her eyes were the shape of almonds and black as charcoal.

No-one spoke. No-one ever spoke. Not in the normal way of conversation. Only to make announcements about the next meeting or recite the sacred words of their faith. It had to be that way. Anonymous. Not only was it safer but Emmelina had found it to be more lascivious. They knew only their names, not their real names but their faith names. Hers was Saoirse, meaning freedom and independence. She hoped one day she could truly become a free spirit. It was her dearest wish.

Wrapping her cloak around her she left without saying goodbye and began the weary walk back home.

Treadworth House

The grass between Maud's toes was wet and bracingly cold as she walked barefoot to the edge of her garden to pick herbs to make her early morning brew of fennel and peppermint. She looked up at the sky, leaning backwards and stretching her old bones to ease the stiffness that was always there on first waking. The sky was beginning to brighten in the east and yet the moon was still visible, a much paler version than the night's full moon. Break of day, for Maud, was a most magical time, not yet day, no longer night. A time of stillness and solitude before the dawn chorus.

As she bent down to break off a few stems of fennel she heard a noise. Expecting to see a family of rabbits hopping about in the field beyond or perhaps a hungry fox she was surprised to see a young woman dressed in dark clothing hurrying along the worn pathway that led towards the city's East Gate. She straightened up to get a better look. The young woman turned her head and looked over at Maud. Aware Maud was looking at her, she dropped her head, pulled her hood further down over her face and hurried on by. Maud continued to watch as the figure grew smaller and disappeared into the layers of morning mist.

She bent down again and gathered a few more stems and a clutch of peppermint before returning to her kitchen where the embers of the previous night's fire were feebly glowing in the hearth. She took some twigs from a basket on the floor and placed them on top of the embers, blowing gently to re-kindle the fire. The dry twigs crackled and an orange flame sparked into life. She quickly placed more twigs and several small pieces of wood on top. The fire began to take hold.

Maud separated the seeds from their pods, the leaves from their stems and placed them in a metal pot with some weak ale from a jug. She placed the pot on the metal peg above the fire to make her first drink of the day then eased herself into a large wooden chair by the fire, warming her toes and waiting for her brew to boil.

Pomfrey, her cat and companion jumped down from the window seat where he had been patiently watching the proceedings, stretched himself and sidled up to her. Sitting at her feet, he looked up as if waiting for permission. Maud patted her lap and Pomfrey, taking the hint, took up his favourite position on her warm lap in front of a now roaring fire. The kitchen smelt of aniseed. Maud smiled while Pomfrey purred loudly.

'She has become a beautiful young lady, Pomfrey.'

Chapter 2

Guido sat through the daybreak service of Lauds with the most devout of expressions upon his face. He sat at the front of the chapel next to Osburne and Wilfrid who always sat together and often, Guido had noticed, shared each other's bed. They were novice monks, like him, who had joined the priory at the same time. The monks were not supposed to enter into relationships with each other but since joining the priory Guido had soon realised many of the monks did so, even the older ones. At first, he had thought this shocking but soon realised it was considered quite acceptable as long as it was not openly acknowledged.

He had been approached by a number of monks in his first year and had been sorely tempted. Only once had he succumbed. The monk in question was no longer at the priory, having been sent up to Oxford to study. There had been something quite womanly about him. His body was slim and delicate and his lips, Guido recalled, pink and soft when he kissed them. The sex had not been as successful or as pleasurable as he had imagined it would be. Guido had become aroused very quickly in response to the monk's gentle touch but when it came to the actual act of penetration he had turned rough and forceful so Guido had decided it was not an experience he wished to repeat. He was relieved when he heard the monk would be going to Oxford. It had taken him longer than usual to rid himself of the feelings of disgust on that occasion.

Guido listened intently to the words of Sub Prior Gervaise. He seemed to be speaking directly to him.

"Wash me ever more from my guilt and cleanse me from my sin."

The words resounded throughout the chancel, the monks' private chapel.

9

"For I know how guilty I am; My sin is always before me, Against you, you alone, have I sinned, And I have done evil in your sight."

A grey light filtered through the east window onto the stone flags upon which Sub Prior Gervaise stood in his leather sandals and black cappa reciting the morning prayers in his distinctive monotone. There were thirty nine monks gathered in the chancel. Only two were missing. Prior Vincent had been summoned to Rome on church business and would not be back for several months. In his absence, Sub Prior Gervaise had been left in charge. He was a small man with a stout frame. When he spoke the jowls at the side of his mouth flapped in and out like a pair of bellows. His face looked grey and drawn this morning and his eyes were heavily lidded as if he had been awake all night. The other missing friar was Brother Paulinus, the infirmarian, responsible for the running of the hospital. He had been excused from Lauds to attend to a sick woman who had been admitted to the infirmary the previous evening. She was not expected to last the night.

There was a sluggish feel to the service this morning. Guido looked around him at the other monks. They appeared half asleep. He looked across at old Brother Jacquemon. His chin was resting on his chest and Guido guessed, as usual, he was napping. Sub Prior Gervaise had excused this behaviour from Jacquemon not only because of his great age but because he had proved himself to be a most loyal monk.

Guido's attention drifted back to the words of the Sub Prior. He needed absolution and to know he was on the right path. Gervaise continued in his monotone.

"You will sprinkle me with hyssop, and I will be made clean; You will wash me, and I will be whiter than snow. You will make me hear the sound of joy and gladness; The bones you have crushed will rejoice. Turn your face away from my sins, And wipe out all my transgressions; Create a pure heart in me, God, Free me from the guilt of bloodshed, God my saviour."

10

The fires of guilt subsided within Guido as he listened and was given absolution. He made a mental note to pick some hyssop from the priory's garden.

As soon as the service of Lauds had finished, the monks filed out of the cold chancel in silence. They left by the night stair that led to the monks' dormitory. They would be allowed to sleep for a short time before being woken again to attend Prime. Guido could hardly keep his eyes open. He lay down on his mattress and pulled the coarse woollen blankets tightly around his body to keep out the chilly draughts. He lay for a few moments listening to the noises of the monks as they settled into their beds and within a very short time he had drifted off into a deep and restful sleep.

After Prime the monks were allowed into the refectory to break their fast. They stopped briefly at the lavatorium in the cloister to wash their hands and face. Guido could already smell the freshly baked bread and the weak, warm ale that was about to be served up. His stomach rumbled loudly.

The grey, dull morning had brightened and light now shone through the south facing, triple lancet window, which dominated the long refectory room. The monks sat around an oak table, which stretched the length of the room. Sub Prior Gervaise sat at one end, Jacquemon at the other. The monks ate as if it were their last meal, stuffing chunks of bread into their mouths and washing it down with weak ale.

Breakfast was usually a fairly quiet affair, not because of any order of silence but because the frequently interrupted sleep rendered the monks weary beyond speech. Guido valued his time in the refectory in the winter months. The room was warm and the smell of bread baking or pottage stewing wafted in from the kitchen next door. It reminded him of home. He thought of his mother, warm and loving and of the Italian countryside he loved as a child but, as always, his thoughts became too painful and he put them to the back of his mind.

As breakfast neared an end Gervaise stood and reminded everyone to go to the Chapter House as he had an important announcement to make.

Chapter 3

'Emmelina,' shouted Humphrey from the bedroom.

She had barely got through the door and changed out of her night clothes. His voice startled her. The familiar tightening in her solar plexus and the early morning feeling of dread at the thought of another day spent in the company of her husband returned, drawing down her spirits.

Emmelina's parents had died in a fire, which demolished their home when she was just thirteen. With no siblings and no other living relatives she had been taken in by Humphrey Pauncefoot, then a wealthy bachelor, who had made his money as a cordwainer, making fine leather shoes for his affluent clients. From her first night under his roof as his charge, Humphrey had forced himself upon her. Months later, when she found herself pregnant, Humphrey decided to make an honest girl of her. They had been married for almost four years and Emmelina had, as yet, not borne him a living heir. This time she heard something different in the way he spoke. Moving towards the bottom of the stairs, she raised her voice, the fluttering of fear in her stomach ever present.

'Yes, husband.'

'Here,' he replied.

His voice sounded strange. What could be the matter? She climbed each step slowly, going over in her mind what he might be calling her for. Had she slipped up? Had she left a clue as to where she had been all night? Did he suspect anything? She began to concoct excuses in her mind. The fearful sickness churned her insides as she opened the bedroom door. He was still in bed, lying on his back. For a moment she thought he might be interested in having sex with her. That she could cope with but not the truth of where she had spent the night.

'What is it, husband?' she asked from the safe distance of the door.

'Fetch the physician.'

His speech was slurred and she noticed his right hand was hanging over the side of the bed, twitching, his fist clenched and strangely twisted. Realising she was free from any suspicion or the submission of her wifely duties, she approached him. His face was bloated but his skin, frequently flushed from the drink, was unusually grey. His pale blue eyes were watery and bloodshot, like the eyes of piglets ready for slaughter. Although she could hardly bear to touch him, to do so made her flesh creep, she leant towards him and touched his forehead. It was cold and clammy with no evidence of fever.

'Perhaps you drank too much last night. Would you like me to prepare you some Milk Thistle?' Emmelina asked, placating him.

'Don't treat me like a fool,' he slurred.

'I know the effects of drink only too well. Now go and fetch the physician or would you prefer me to lie here and die?' He studied her face for signs of agreement. A crooked smile crossed his face. 'You'd like that wouldn't you...for me to die?'

'Don't talk nonsense. Of course I wouldn't. I'll fetch the physician straight away if that is what you desire, husband.'

She had become very good at playing the part of the dutiful wife. Humphrey grunted at her answer. Relieved that she was not under suspicion, Emmelina left the bedroom and hurried downstairs. She grabbed her overcoat of deep burgundy damask, slipped on her pattens and went outside into the pale grey of the morning. Emerging into West Gate Street, she crossed in front of St Mary de Grace church and dipped into Pinch Belly Alley, so called because of its narrowness. She slipped her slim figure past the stone protruding from the side of the wall. It had been placed there deliberately to prevent errant animals straying into the lane. Relieved to get to the end of the dark and dank alley, which smelt strongly of urine, she turned left into Old Smith Street. The rhythmic noise of metal being hammered into shape by ironmongers, blade smiths and pewterers, together with the smell of burning charcoal was a stark contrast to the quietness of the alley. Emmelina could never understand why Physician Teylove chose to live in such a noisy street but then she supposed the rents were cheap and that would suit a man such as Teylove.

A few doors along she stopped in front of a small house sandwiched between the workshops of a spoon-maker and an ironmonger. She knocked loudly on the wooden door. Humphrey's physician was a small, weasel-like creature and Emmelina didn't much care for him. He had been treating Humphrey for pains in his feet with foul smelling poultices. Emmelina suspected it had more to do with Humphrey's excessive drinking as his attacks nearly always followed a heavy bout at the Fleece Inn. Physician Teylove opened the door.

'Yes, what do you want?'

He spoke through his teeth, hardly moving his thin lips, his weaselly eyes looking her up and down.

'It's Humphrey, Physician Teylove, he says he's not feeling well and to fetch you.'

There was a pause. Emmelina had the impression he was about to refuse but then she saw him change his mind. Motivated by money, rather than a desire to heal and, knowing Humphrey would pay him well for his time, he answered.

'Very well. Wait here a moment while I get my medicine chest.'

He closed the door then re-appeared some minutes later, clasping a wooden box under his arm. He pulled on a dosan brown cap and wrapped a heavy cloak around his small frame. Emmelina followed behind him as they walked, with great haste, back to her house.

Humphrey was still in bed when they arrived. The physician placed the box on an ornate oak dresser by his bedside.

'What seems to be the trouble?' he asked Humphrey, his tone cold and unsympathetic.

Humphrey turned his head towards Teylove. Emmelina noticed his mouth seemed to be twisted and there was a bubble

15

of saliva at the corner. Without waiting for a reply Teylove leant over Humphrey and undoing his night shirt pressed his ear to Humphrey's heart and listened. The room became still and quiet. Only the faint noise of the stall holders from the market in West Gate Street could be heard through the half open window. He listened for some time then straightened up and asked Humphrey if he was in any pain.

'Head hurts,' Humphrey slurred, 'here.' He lifted his good hand and pointed to his temple.

The physician looked puzzled for a few moments then turned to Emmelina.

'I believe he has a serious imbalance of all four humours. He will need to be given an emetic to expel the excess fluids in his head in order to take away the pain. Fetch me some warm ale so I can prepare a tincture.'

He opened his box to reveal several small compartments each containing a powder of some description. From the front box he scooped up a small amount of lustrous grey powder and emptied it into a small silver cup, placing the troy spoon carefully back into its holder. He turned round to face Emmelina.

'Well, are you going to bring me that ale?'

Once again, he spoke through gritted teeth, making Emmelina jump at his sharp tone. She hurried from the bedroom and went down to the kitchen where she expected to see Fayette but the kitchen was cold and empty. Usually, her maidservant would be awake by now, pottering around the kitchen preparing Humphrey's breakfast and seeing to the fire. She found the fire unlit and no Fayette.

Emmelina and Fayette were more like friends, than mistress and maidservant. Humphrey disapproved of her friendship and frequently reprimanded her for it but she had long since been unmoved by his reproaches, many that they were. She enjoyed helping Fayette in the kitchen. They would talk about the young boys in the city who had shown interest in her. At seventeen, Fayette was old enough to be married, and

16

yet, so far, she had resisted the temptation, despite, it seemed from their chats, an abundance of interested parties. Emmelina harboured a secret but benign jealousy of Fayette. She had fine features for a peasant girl, with hair the colour of summer straw falling to her waist in an abundance of curls. It shone with the lustre of sunshine and her eyes were an arresting turquoise blue, the colour of a summer sky. It wasn't hard to see why she had so many admirers.

Last night, after dinner, Fayette had been tidying away the remains of the roast pigeon she had prepared for them whilst Humphrey was in the back room going through his accounts and finishing the bottle of red wine, which had accompanied the meal before he left to go to The Fleece. Emmelina had invited Fayette to sit with her by the fire but she had declined. Thinking about it now, Fayette had seemed in a hurry to be away.

Fleetingly, she wondered whether Fayette had crept out in the night to meet up with one of her many admirers and perhaps fallen asleep in the arms of her lover. She would ask her all about it when she saw her but for now she needed to concentrate on getting some ale. Teylove had asked for warm ale but she could see this would be difficult. She went to the larder and poured a small amount of cool ale into a jug from the flagon, which was always kept topped up and, collecting a wooden cup from the dresser, returned to the bedroom.

She found Teylove standing by the bed scratching his head and murmuring to himself. He didn't inspire confidence in her.

'Hurry now. Put it over there,' he ordered, pointing at the dresser.

Emmelina did as she was told and the physician then poured a small quantity of ale into the silver cup.

He tutted. 'I asked for warm ale. This is not warm.'

'I know. The fire remains unlit. I'll attend to it now.'

She turned to leave.

'You can do that later. I need you here. Help me raise his head so he's able to drink this.'

He stirred the concoction using the small silver troy spoon he had used to measure the quantity.

'What is that?' Emmelina enquired.

She had strong views on the methods physicians and monks used to heal people. From what she had learned from her mother, the treatments administered were more likely to kill than cure.

'It's an emetic called antimony. We use it to cause the patient to vomit and expel any rank humour.'

'How does that help?'

Personally, she couldn't see how making an ill person vomit would make them feel better but it was probably unwise to question his methods just now.

'If a patient has an imbalance of the four humours, and in your husband's case, I have diagnosed an excess of black bile in his skull causing his symptoms, then an emetic such as antimony should be used to expel the bile and thus restore the patient to health.'

It was the first time Teylove had showed any interest in conversing with her. Emmelina could see it was an opportunity for him to show his superior knowledge rather than any desire to speak with her.

'And if that doesn't work?'

Teylove's interest was short lived. He took Emmelina's question to be a slur on his achievements as a physician and snapped back at her.

'I see no reason to doubt the efficacy of this treatment.'

She opened her mouth to explain she was merely making enquiries and was in no way doubting his skills when he held up his hand and indicated for her to move towards the bed.

'Lift his head so I can get him to drink as much of this as he can manage.'

Emmelina placed her hand beneath the thick, damp neck of her husband and with some effort lifted his head off the

18

pillow.   Teylove placed the cup to his lips and entreated Humphrey to drink. With a swift movement he tipped most of the contents into Humphrey's mouth.   The effect was instantaneous.   Humphrey started to gag.   The taste alone, thought Emmelina, must be enough to make him sick.

'Fetch a pail to catch the bile. I fear it will not be long before we have a result.'

Emmelina returned to the kitchen to look for a wooden pail. There was still no sign of Fayette. She could do with a kind word or a squeeze of the hand to reassure her this morning but just now she could do with some help. A strong foreboding hit her as she looked around the empty kitchen. Something wasn't quite right.

Chapter 4

It had been late when John Sawyer and his young daughter, Dulcina arrived at the New Inn. They had entered the city by the West Gate, trudged across the wooden footbridge between the two bridges and on into Ebridge Street. As they made their way to The High Cross they passed a number of timber-framed merchant's houses and many inviting taverns. The streets were busy with market traders, some shouting at passers-by, encouraging them to sample their wares. Dulcina found it such a contrast to the bucolic quiet of the Forest of Dean, which was all she had known. The smell of roasting pig and boiled onions wafted past and reminded her she had not eaten since breakfast.

At The High Cross they turned left into North Gate Street where they were greeted by a large sign advertising the inn. Dulcina marvelled at the sheer size of the building, with its carved oak dragon posts at each corner, depicting angels. They walked under a wide archway, which brought them into an enclosed courtyard. Several families were making their way up some steps in the far left hand corner to the open galleries on the first and second floors. Dulcina had never been outside her village of Newent and there was nothing of this scale or grandeur there. She took her father's hand and held it tight. Most people were emerging from a doorway on the right. Her father suggested they go through this door to enquire about a bed for the night. They entered a large room, lit by candles and the warm glow of a crackling fire. The room was filled with the chatter of pilgrims of all ages, sizes and social classes. Dulcina noticed small children asleep on bench seats whilst their parents ate, drank and made new friends.

Having walked from Newent that day they were weary and famished and the warmth of the room compared to the cold chill of early evening seemed to have an immediate effect on her father. He stumbled, pulling hard on Dulcina's hand and before she could act he had fallen heavy like a sack of bricks on the stone flags of the tavern pulling her down with him. The innkeeper, Thomas Myatt, along with several others, rushed over to help them both to their feet. Thomas, of large size and ruddy complexion, was well known for his appreciation of the drink but he was equally well known for his kind- heartedness. He suggested they take a seat by the fire while he brought them some food.

Dulcina panicked for she knew her father had very little money and she feared he would bring food beyond their means.

'Just a jug of ale and some bread and cheese,' she shouted after him as he hurried off to the kitchen.

She looked across at her father who in the light of the fire looked frailer than ever. He had long dreamed of coming to Gloucester to visit the tomb of King Edward II. The king's body had been brought to the Abbey by Abbot Thoky for burial following his brutal murder in Berkeley Castle in 1327. Abbot Thoky had been the only Abbot in the country brave enough to accept his body for burial. All others had been afraid of the consequences since it was widely rumoured his wife, Isabella and her lover, Roger Mortimer had murdered the King. As the King had been divinely anointed so his bones were thought to heal ills and create good luck for those who came to see them. Thousands had already made the pilgrimage and her father had heard tales of miracles taking place, right there at the King's tomb.

He had been ill for some time and was barely able to carry on his job as a woodworker in the Forest of Dean. For years he had toiled, sawing great oaks into straight beams for the builders of Gloucester. Most of the modern buildings in the city had been made from timbers growing in the forest. In fact it was very probable, she thought, the very building she sat in now had timbers in it her father had personally crafted. Once a strapping young man in his day, he was now much thinner with a hacking cough that would not go away.

Thomas, the innkeeper, returned with a pewter jug full of strong ale and a large platter with a few rough chunks of bread and a single lump of Double Gloucester cheese.

'Get this down yer and yu'll feel much bett'rrr,' he said, rolling his 'r's and speaking in the local Gloucester twang. 'Is there anything else yu'll be needing?'

'We'd like a bed for the night if you have room?' Dulcina asked him.

'Go up on the second floor. There's still room up there. You can settle up in the morning. Looks like your father could do with a good night's rest.'

She smiled at him. 'You're very kind.'

Thomas winked at her and moved on.

They sat in silence whilst they ate. Dulcina noted her father only picked at his food even though he had eaten nothing since breakfast. Her appetite had waned with the worry for her father's health. She had never seen him collapse and wondered if it had happened before and whether he had kept it from her.

'How are you feeling now, Father?' she asked him when they had finished eating.

He raised his weary head and smiled at her. 'A little better, thank you. I'm very tired. I'd like to go up to the room now if you're ready? I want to feel refreshed for tomorrow.'

His eyes brightened and she knew he was thinking about the miracle he had dreamed of these past years. Dulcina looked around her to check no-one was looking before producing a cloth from her basket in which she hurriedly wrapped the remains of the bread and cheese.

'That will keep for the journey home tomorrow. Come, I'll help you to your feet.'

They made their way out, Dulcina holding onto her father's arm. It was a struggle to climb the steps up to the second floor, her father stopping every few steps to catch his breath. They followed other pilgrims into a large, dimly lit room where more than forty beds were crammed together, all but a few taken with sleeping bodies. She was shocked to see one couple fornicating in the far corner. They appeared fully dressed but she knew, from the animal-like grunting sounds coming from the entwined couple, exactly what they were doing. She averted her gaze and concentrated on finding two beds close enough together for her and her father, keen to see him settled for the night. By the time she had helped to lay her father's frail body onto the straw mattress, the grunting had ceased. So too had the sound of men who Dulcina had seen urinating in communal chamber pots scattered around the place. The sound was not unlike a horse pissing in the street. She sighed as she lay her head down on the well-used mattress. This was to be their accommodation for the night. A fetid smell filled her nose and she was glad of the strong ale, which sent her to sleep as soon as she laid her head down.

Chapter 5

The monks took their seats around the walls of the chilly Chapter House. Sub Prior Gervaise squeezed his substantial bulk into the central stone-arcaded seat at the east end of the room. He began by reading out the Rules of Order by which all chapter meetings were governed. The monks sat quietly, some nodded off, not many paid attention while Gervaise read out the rules they had heard countless times before. Gervaise liked 'holding chapter'. He could show off his importance. The monks were a captive audience and he could tell them what to do, how and when to do it and no-one would argue with him.

'As you know I have a very important announcement to make. God has seen fit to send to us a very generous benefactor. Many of you will already know him. He and his family are regular attendants at our public services. His name is Gilbert Garlick, a wealthy cordwainer in this city, and he has most generously donated a substantial sum of money to the priory's funds.'

Washed, fed and watered, the monks' weariness left them. Alertness overtook their drawn faces. He had mentioned the word 'generous' twice and 'substantial' in the same sentence. An excited buzz passed along the circle of monks.

'How much?' asked Brother Enoch, the Clerk of Works in charge of all building projects at the priory.

Gervaise raised a dark and straggly eyebrow. 'Enough to put in place our plans for building the window in the north transept and to build new lodgings for the prior.'

Enoch beamed. Building work had been thin on the ground of late, mainly due to lack of funds. A big project like this would keep him busy. In his excitement he forget himself. 'I am well aware of the plans for the north transept window, Brother, but I have no knowledge of any plans for the Prior's new lodgings. Prior Vincent said nothing about this before he left for Rome,' he queried.

Gervaise glowered. Prior Vincent was an irritating man. They had both joined the priory at around the same time. That was in 1464 when they were both young men. Brother Vincent, as he was then, was not an ambitious man but he was clever and pious and always seemed to get the attention and praise of the old prior. It didn't seem to matter how hard Gervaise worked and prayed he could never triumph over Vincent. When the old prior died in 1488 both monks stood for election. Despite Gervaise's best efforts and enticements the monks elected Brother Vincent. It had rankled him ever since, ate away at him. Everything Prior Vincent did or said was met with derision from Gervaise. Every opportunity that came his way to countermand him, he took. In short, he hated him with a passion that over the years had consumed him and taken away his focus from the true work of God.

Vincent had progressive ideas about how the order should be run, which he brought back from foreign priories he visited when on church business. Gervaise didn't agree with his methods and detested seeing his rules reverted when Prior Vincent returned. Gervaise always looked forward to Vincent's trips abroad and this trip had proved to be the longest so far. He had been absent for many months. When left in charge, Gervaise liked to run a well ordered and highly disciplined priory based on the ancient principles of absolute obedience. He could see no reason why anything should be changed. As soon as Prior Vincent had left the grounds of the priory, Gervaise had overturned the prior's newly implemented rules and procedures. Prior Vincent infuriated him. He dreaded his return. In all likelihood, within days Prior Vincent would undo all the changes he had made and Gervaise would be left resentful and brooding. He missed having total power over the monks and ordering the day to day running of the priory. He longed for a time when he could make changes and plans on a permanent basis. He was marking time, waiting for the day when Brother Vincent was no more.

'You question me, Brother Enoch?'

Enoch looked around at the silent monks, each one averted their gaze and bowed their heads. 'No, Sub Prior,' he replied, lowering his gaze to the tiled floor, realising his mistake.

The monks had learned not to question Gervaise in the absence of Prior Vincent. Those monks that had challenged him in the past had soon found themselves demoted or made to do repulsive tasks, like cleaning out the latrines. Still with their heads bowed they whispered amongst themselves. It was foolish to openly challenge the sub prior but they could not help gossiping. The whispering grew louder as one by one the monks joined in.

'Silence,' commanded Gervaise, 'I have not finished.' He paused until the room fell silent. 'Brother Enoch, you must organise your men and make an immediate start on the building programme.'

Enoch nodded his assent. It would be foolish to do otherwise.

Gervaise continued. 'Master Garlick will be attending Sunday's public sermon and I must prepare an appropriate thanksgiving service. At the end of the service we must say special prayers for his generous soul. We have much work to do. I will see you all at Terce.'

Gervaise held out his hand and made the sign of the cross.

'*Dominus Vobiscum*'
'*The Lord be with you.*'
In one voice the monks responded.
'*Et cum spiritu tuo.*'
'*And with your spirit.*'

They emptied out of the Chapter House and into the central cloister. Gervaise's words were still echoing in Guido's head.

"*You will sprinkle me with hyssop, and I will be made clean.*"

This time, he made his way straight to the herb garden to pick hyssop before settling to his studies in the scriptorium.

Chapter 6

Despite her unfamiliar and strange surroundings, Dulcina had slept well with the help of the ale. She was woken by the sound of coughing close by. Her immediate thoughts were of her father. She leapt from her bed, having slept in the clothes she had travelled in, and went to her father's assistance. The coughing always seemed worse first thing in the morning but by breakfast he usually seemed better. She raised his frail body into a sitting position. He too, was fully dressed. A plump woman who was suckling a small baby at her breast in the next bed enquired after her father and asked if she could help.

'Thank you. You're very kind but I can manage.'

The baby began to cry, having unlatched itself. 'There, there, my babber. There you go.'

She offered her breast once more and the baby latched back on, sucking hungrily. The woman closed her eyes and went back to sleep, the baby still at her breast.

As they gathered their meagre belongings together Dulcina noticed a man pouring the contents of piss pots into a large pail. He must have seen her puzzled look.

He shouted over. 'We sell's it to the tanners over the way by St John's church, look. I get's good money. Be a shame to waste it,' he added as he carried on emptying the pots.

Dulcina wondered what they used it for but didn't ask. What an odorous occupation, she thought, turning away from the man as if that would help with the smell invading her nostrils. After a while, her father's coughing ceased and he was able to gather his few belongings and go downstairs for some breakfast and settle their bill before their pilgrimage to the Abbey.

The Abbey was a short walk away, down a narrow lane, which led to St Michael's Gate. From there they would continue across the Abbey precinct and enter through what had become known as the Pilgrim's Door. As they approached the lane their progress was halted by a solid throng of people, fellow pilgrims, waiting their turn to pray and ask for miracles at the King's tomb. They joined this thread of believers making slow progress towards the gate. Several beggars passed along the line, looking pitiful, rattling their begging bowls. Some were holding wooden clappers, which they rattled loudly at the hopeful pilgrims. Dulcina noticed people turned away or stepped back from these beggars and wondered why. An old woman standing next to her kindly explained the reason.

'Theyms lepers, deary. Best to keep your distance,' she warned, her watery eyes, opaque with age.

Dulcina had never seen a leper in her life but had heard of the terrible disease. She clutched her father's hand and looked in the other direction as the lepers got closer. Her father did the same but more likely, she guessed, because he had very little money left and could spare nothing.

Yesterday was the first time Dulcina had seen the Abbey. Even though they were miles from the city it dominated the skyline, standing on the Eastern side of the River Severn towering above all other buildings in Gloucester. The only other building, which had caught her attention, was an odd conical structure close to the West Gate Bridge. She had asked the porter at the gate what it was and discovered it was a kiln for making glass. She couldn't imagine living in a house with glass in the openings. Now she was standing in front of the Abbey she looked up at the perpendicular tower built for Abbot Seabroke. Faced with such magnificence she could finally begin to understand her father's obsession.

They passed through St Michael's Gate and into the Abbey precinct, walking in a straight line through the lay cemetery and entering the Abbey through the pilgrim's door. The inside was just as magnificent, perhaps more so, than its exterior. Dulcina gazed up at the fan vaulted nave and the stained glass windows. Everywhere she looked, there were candles burning in tall, ornately crafted silver candlesticks. In slow procession, they approached the exquisitely carved tomb of King Edward with a sense of awe. An effigy of the king,

28

carved in alabaster, lay on top of a stone plinth itself elaborately carved and decorated with saintly figures. The king held a sceptre in his right hand and supported a globe in his left. He was clothed in a robe of ruby red. A golden-maned lion sat at his feet and a pair of golden-winged angels sat at each shoulder, staring upwards as if gazing at the halls of heaven. On his head he wore a golden crown, encrusted with precious gem stones of red and blue. He looked regal and at peace. On the side of the plinth sat a small ship of solid gold. It shimmered in the early morning light, now sieving through the great east window. Floating motes of purple and blue danced upon the gleaming tomb.

Dulcina sank to her knees, crossed herself and prayed. Overwhelmed by the beauty and opulence of the tomb she prayed for her father's health to be restored. John Sawyer was already on his knees his lips mouthing the most devout of prayers. It was not long before Dulcina's prayers were interrupted. Her father had begun to cough and this time when she opened her eyes to look at him she could see droplets of blood on his lips.

'Father! What's the matter?'

John Sawyer clutched at his chest and looked at his daughter with a terrified expression upon his face. He was struggling for breath and didn't seem able to answer her.

'Someone help him, please, someone help him,' she screamed, forgetting she was in front of the venerable tomb. One of the monks hurried towards them eager to put an end to the commotion.

He spoke softly. 'I'll take him to the infirmary. He is in need of great care.'

Dulcina managed a weak smile and, without replying, followed him along the fan-vaulted cloisters turning into a short passageway that led to the infirmary hall. It was not unlike the nave of a church, with its high vaulted ceiling, but for the long line of beds occupied by the poor and infirm on both sides of the hall. Her father was still struggling for his breath as the monk laid him on a straw mattress. Another monk approached and spoke to Dulcina.

'How long has he been like this?'

'He's had the cough for almost a year now but nothing as bad as this. Is he going to be all right?'

'Only God can know that, my child.'

The kind monk took her hand and squeezed it gently, leaving her alone with her father. He returned moments later holding open a tattered and well-read book. He began reciting a passage in Latin.

"In manus tuas, Domine, commendamus spiritum Eius."

(Into Thine hands, Lord, we commend his soul.)

Dulcina watched as her father gasped for his breath. He looked frightened. His face had taken on a grey pallor while his skin glistened with the dampness of a fever. He looked very small and vulnerable. He reached out his hand to her and she held it tightly.

Moments later, his hand went limp in hers. He had taken his last breath.

Chapter 7

It was not long before the emetic took its hold on Humphrey. Emmelina was shocked at the ferocity of its effects. Poor Humphrey had been violently sick but it had also caused him to empty his bowels. Teylove had left shortly after administering the medicine promising to return in the afternoon so she was left on her own to deal with him. With no Fayette to help her she was exhausted by midday. The sheer weight of her husband made it difficult to move him. She did what she could to clean up his foul smelling mess and make him as comfortable as possible. By lunchtime it seemed like the worst was over when he fell into a deep sleep.

Tired and hungry she went downstairs to the kitchen. The fire was still unlit. The cold dampness of the day had crept into the room displacing its usual warmth and cheeriness. Fayette's kind and reassuring smile was nowhere to be seen. She poked the greying embers, hoping to spark the fire back to life. Her thoughts once again turned to Fayette. Where could she be? If she'd stayed out with someone surely she'd be home by now? Then she thought the unthinkable. What if she has met someone and decided to run away with him and kept it a secret from her because she knew how much it would upset her to be left alone in the house with Humphrey?

She slumped down on a chair by the kitchen table, pulling at her hair in a gesture of frustration. Was this God's punishment for not loving her husband, for sneaking out at night and following her faith? Amidst this self-recrimination she thought she heard a knock at the door. Thinking it was Fayette she ran to open it. At the door stood Severin Browne. She had seen him once or twice from a distance when Humphrey had brought him home for supper but her husband had always made it clear she was not welcome to join them. All she knew about him was that he was a member of her husband's guild.

'Oh,' she gasped, 'I thought you were someone else.'

She realised what a mess she must look and wiped the damp straggles of hair from her face with the back of her hand.

'Are you all right?' he inquired.

'Yes. I'm fine, really. It's my husband...'

'That's who I've come to see. Is he unwell?'

'I'm afraid he is most unwell and...' Her voice broke and to her shame tears welled at the back of her eyes. She sniffed, drew in a deep breath and smoothed her hair. 'I'm so sorry. I don't know what you must think of me. Fayette, my maidservant, is nowhere to be seen and the physician has been fetched to see to Humphrey and the fire is not yet lit,' she explained in babbling fashion.

'Perhaps I can help?' he offered.

Emmelina was somewhat taken aback by his kind offer and without thinking she stood back and allowed him to make his way past her, across the threshold and into the kitchen.

'Please...' Severin entreated, pulling a chair from under the table. 'Sit down. I'll fix the fire for you but first, by the look of you, I think you're in need of a strong drink.'

He strode to the larder and came back with the remains of the bottle of red wine from last night's meal. It was good, strong wine from Gascony. He poured it into a pewter goblet, which he took from the wooden dresser.

'Here, drink this while I see to the fire.'

Emmelina joined him by the fire and took a large gulp of the wine. As she hadn't eaten all day, the strong alcohol was swift to take its effect. She was aware of a swimming sensation of light headedness, followed by a warmth that travelled from her throat all the way down to her empty stomach. She studied her visitor as he bent down to gather up some wood. He appeared to be in his early to mid-twenties. It was hard to tell as his skin was weathered and creased with laughter lines. His hair was the colour of glossy raven's wings, the curls touching the back of his neck. He was wearing a thin woollen shirt and a well-worn apron made from pieces of leather, which came down to his knees. His sleeves were rolled up revealing well developed muscles in his upper arms. They became taut as he leant over to tend to the fire. He looked over his shoulder at her and smiled.

'Feeling a little better now?'

'Much better, thank you.' She smiled back at him, feeling a little self-conscious at the thought he may have caught her studied appreciation of him. 'Actually, I feel a little light headed. I've had nothing to eat today.'

'Well, we'll have to remedy that. Let me fetch you something.'

Emmelina raised herself up from the chair to help him. He put out his hand.

'No, you stay there and rest a while.'

Her gaze followed him as he walked to the larder. He was tall and broad shouldered. His apron was tied tightly at his slim waist. When he re-appeared, holding the remains of a loaf and the leftover pigeon from the night before, he was grinning.

'This is all I could find,' he said, placing the food on the table.

She realised he was teasing her about the food. Pigeon was rarely eaten by someone of his lower social position. She didn't mind. To the contrary, she was rather glad he was there, feeling in desperate need, just then, of some amiable company. His kindness was comforting if not a little surprising. The surprise was not an unpleasant one.

'Tell me. What ails Humphrey? Too much revelry?'

He laughed out loud. Most people who knew Humphrey knew of his weakness and his love for frequenting the city's taverns.

'I'm afraid I think it's more serious than that.'

Severin stopped laughing. 'I'm sorry. I had no idea. I was only trying to cheer you up.'

She nudged her food around on her plate as she spoke. 'The physician has given him some medicine but I fear it has made him worse.'

'Can I see him?'

She looked up at him. He was leaning across the table towards her. His eyes were dark and brooding, his skin brown like the leather he worked with. His mouth showed a mischievous streak. His gaze lingered a little longer than it should have. Only a moment, but it was enough to make her feel embarrassed. She looked away.

'He's asleep just now. He's had a terrible morning.'

She didn't really want anyone to see or smell the mess that remained in the bedroom.

'Sounds like you've had the same kind of morning.'

'I'm not normally like this. I'm worried about Fayette.'

He gave her a strange look.

'Obviously, I'm worried about my husband,' she added.

It was an afterthought and an obvious one. She hoped Severin had not noticed her lack of concern for Humphrey. For the second time since the arrival of this man she found herself feeling embarrassed.

'Of course.' He spoke without conviction. 'Well, if you're feeling better, I…'

She interrupted him, not wanting him to go, not just yet anyway. 'What business did you have with my husband?'

'I came to take Humphrey to the Tanners' Hall. But it can wait.'

Her husband had mentioned Severin's name but she had not taken much notice of him until now. A thought crossed her mind. Perhaps she could take more than a passing interest in her husband's leather business now he had taken ill. The Tanners' Hall was on the other side of St Peter's Abbey not far from the house and easily within walking distance. Humphrey would need her help until his health improved.

'Are you sure it can wait?' she asked him.

'I'm certain of it,' he said, this time with conviction.

There was a knock at the door.

'That's probably Humphrey's physician. He said he would return to see how he was.'

Emmelina shot out of her chair and went into the hallway. Severin followed her. She opened the door and there stood Physician Teylove in no better humour than when he had left earlier. He looked at Emmelina, then past her at Severin. Teylove's eyes narrowed with suspicion but he said nothing.

'Severin works with my husband in the leather trade, Physician Teylove,' Emmelina explained, her cheeks colouring.

Teylove grunted and pushed his way across the threshold. As he did so, he knocked Emmelina into Severin. It was only for the briefest of moments but her breast brushed against his chest. She was so close she could smell the leather in his tunic, mixed with a pleasant muskiness. But she dare not look up at him. Severin bid her a polite but hasty good day and stepped into the lane. Emmelina turned back to Teylove and, with a resigned inner sigh, resumed the drudgery that was to be the rest of her day.

Chapter 8

Dulcina sat for a while, holding her father's hand. She noticed how quickly it became cold. Lost in her grief, she was unaware how long she had been sitting there until the kind monk put his hand on her shoulder.

'He's gone. There's nothing more you can do for him. He's with the Lord.'

'What should I do now?' she asked, bewildered and lost.

'We'll see to him,' he answered kindly.

The monks took away her father's body, washed it and wrapped it in muslin cloth. He was buried in the same lay cemetery they had not long walked through to reach the King's tomb. Dulcina's sobs grew louder as she stood by his graveside, remembering how she had held her father's hand as they walked, full of hope, towards the tomb. The Abbey bells tolled three times throughout the brief service, accompanied by a boy monk who held a small hand bell, which he rang in slow rhythm, its sound slightly muffled and morose. The monks said prayers in a language Dulcina could not understand and then left her by the graveside to say her final farewell. Before they left, Dulcina thanked the monks for their kindness. She stood by the freshly dug grave weeping and saying her prayers until she realised she could not stay there forever. She would have to leave her father. The tears still falling down her cheeks, she made her way through St Michael's Gate and back towards The High Cross. The further she walked from her father's grave the more forlorn and fearful she became. The streets were busy and full of chatter. She sat down on the stone steps of the High Cross and gazed into the space ahead of her. An emptiness had crept into her stomach, a feeling she was unfamiliar with. She was used to the gnawing pain of hunger but this went deeper, sapping her spirit.

The youngest of five children, her mother and four brothers had all died before she had reached the age of three. Her father was all she had in the world. She wondered what was to become of her now. She had no idea where to go or what to do. Her father had always been there to look after her, keep her safe, feed and clothe her. They had very little but Dulcina had never wanted for anything. Now she had a deep longing to feel her loving father's arms around her to comfort her and tell her everything would be all right. She remembered the scraps of bread and cheese she had put in her basket the night before and wondered how long that would last. She turned over in her palm the few coins the monks had found on her father's body and knew that would not last long either. She had to do something.

Her thoughts were disturbed by a commotion on The Cross. Two women, dressed in rags, their faces covered in sores had begun a fight. A small crowd had gathered around them, cheering them on. The women were swearing at each other and pulling at their matted hair. The taller of the two had managed to get the other woman on the floor and was slamming her head on to the hardened earth. Two men in uniform approached them and, with some difficulty, pulled the women apart. Dulcina heard one of the men tell the women they were being arrested and if they were so inclined could carry on with their differences within the walls of the castle's goal. A cheer went up as the women, still struggling and trying to attack each other, were dragged away. The crowd dispersed and the familiar noise of the bustling city returned. The gate streets were full of people but Dulcina gained no comfort from them. She was headed for a life on those very streets just like those women. She was certain of it. Her thoughts continued in this vein convincing her all hope was lost when the kind face of the innkeeper from the New Inn came into her mind's eye and gave her an idea. Perhaps she could get work at the inn. He might take pity on her. They had seemed busy enough. She rallied at the thought of finding work and hopefully a roof over her head.

With a weariness beyond her years, and with a good deal of trepidation, she walked into the bar where she had eaten with her father the night before. It was much less crowded but still as she walked past the occupied tables she was aware of men's eyes upon her. Her desperation pushed her on until at last she saw Thomas Myatt standing at the bar pouring a pitcher of ale. He greeted her with a full smile. At least he had remembered her.

'I just came to ask if you had any work.'

She bit her lower lip and waited for his reply.

'Can't say I have lass. Just took a young 'un on yesterday, look. How's that father of yours?'

Dulcina's lip quivered. 'He's dead, sir.'

Chapter 9

There seemed to be little improvement in Humphrey's illness. If anything, he had become much weaker since the physician's visit. His speech was still slurred, his mouth remained slightly crooked and one of his eyes drooped. His right arm had stopped shaking but the fist remained clenched and strangely twisted. Humphrey was too ill to object when she suggested she should sleep in the spare room. She secretly wished Humphrey would not improve too soon so she could stay there longer. This way it would be easier for her to sneak out and attend her faith meetings on the hill.

She had been so busy since Humphrey took ill she had not found the time to leave the house let alone make enquiries about Fayette who had still not returned. Emmelina's time had been taken up with the endless tasks of cleaning, cooking and lighting fires, none of which she was particularly skilled at. It was only since Fayette's absence she realised just how much there was to be done to keep a large house going. It seemed more likely now Fayette had run away with a handsome young man. Still, it was unlike her not to mention her plans to Emmelina. Perhaps she felt bad about leaving her alone with Humphrey.

Physician Teylove called again mid- morning. He seemed satisfied his diagnosis of an imbalance of humours was the correct one. Examining Humphrey again, he decided a treatment of bloodletting with the use of leeches was in order. Emmelina was not convinced. Teylove lifted a jar from his wooden box and placed it on the side table. It contained several slimy creatures, like flat worms, squirming around each other. Some were creeping up the sides of the jar with the use of a sucker-like disc, trying to escape. Emmelina shuddered as she watched the doctor remove the leeches and place them on the fleshy arms and barrel chest of her husband. Humphrey appeared oblivious to the procedure. Whatever was ailing him seemed to have rendered him a timid and sleepy hulk.

'These leeches need to be left for several hours to be fully effective. I'll return later today to remove them. Don't touch them,' Teylove instructed as he packed up his things and left.

Emmelina called out to thank him but he was in no mood to be thanked. She heard his footsteps clattering on the wooden steps and then the door slammed. She was left alone with her husband. She watched as he lay on the bed, helpless and covered in leeches. Her mind wandered to Severin's visit yesterday. She had caught herself thinking about him, even the smell of him had remained with her. Every time she thought of him or called to mind the sound of his deep brown voice she experienced a strange fluttering in her stomach. Her feelings for Humphrey were at best indifferent. Her day dreams were disturbed by the noise of Humphrey grunting. She noticed how the folds of skin around his neck rippled. Recoiling at the sight, she realised she had nothing but revulsion for him.

She had been going through in her mind how she could get to see Severin again and had thought of a very good way without alerting Humphrey's suspicious mind. In his new state of feebleness he would need help in the business. There was no-one else who could help him except Emmelina. Humphrey had no living relatives she knew of and since the death of her parents she was alone in the world even though married to Humphrey. Whilst he lay there with leeches sucking his life blood she decided to broach the subject.

'Husband...?' she began.

He half opened his eyes and looked at her.

'Severin Browne called upon you yesterday. He said you had a business meeting with him at the Tanners' Hall.'

She waited, half expecting him to cut her off like he usually did but this time he was listening. She found the courage to go on.

'Would you like me to go to in your place and report back to you?' she suggested. Without waiting for his reply she added. 'Physician Teylove says he doesn't know when you'll be able to resume your work. I should like to help you.'

She gave him a kind smile. He didn't speak but she thought she saw his head nod in agreement with her.

'Perhaps I should go now and let you rest. Then I can report back to you on my return?'

He nodded again, blinking his cold eyes. She could hardly believe it. She resisted the urge to drop everything and run from the room. Instead, she deliberately fussed around her husband, plumping his pillows, much to his annoyance and straightening objects on the dresser. She looked across at him and, seeing his eyes were closed, she tiptoed out of the room.

Once outside the bedchamber, she flew down the stairs, grabbed her winter cloak and, with heart racing, ran to the door. Just as she grabbed the latch to open it a loud knock jolted her. Irritated by the possible delay she flung open the door.

'Mistress Pauncefoot.'

It was Gilbert Garlick, a business colleague of Humphrey's. An off-putting prurient man, Emmelina had never taken to him.

'Yes,' she said, with more force than she had intended.

'I've come to see how Humphrey is. Physician Teylove tells me he's not well.'

'That's right. He's not well enough to receive visitors.'

Garlick looked affronted. He was a tall, lean man, with a neatly trimmed moustache and a beard, which hid his rather long and pointed chin. His unsettling gaze made it difficult for Emmelina to maintain eye contact.

'I'm sorry but my husband is most unwell and can't be disturbed.' When Garlick showed no sign of leaving she mollified him by adding. 'But perhaps you could call back in a few days' time to see how he is?'

'I was hoping to see him today. That's very unfortunate.'

He paused giving Emmelina the impression he was waiting for her to change her mind. She stepped across the threshold to hurry him along.

'I'm just on my way out to an appointment.'

41

'Very well,' he said. 'I can see you're in somewhat of a hurry but please be sure to tell him I called.'

'Of course. Now I must go or I shall be late.'

Despite the fact she was now standing in the lane poised to close the door behind her, Garlick had not moved. He appeared intent on engaging her further in conversation.

'If there's anything my wife or I can do to help?' he offered.

'That's very kind but I'm sure I can manage,' she replied, pulling on the door handle, hoping he would take the hint.

'And what pressing business causes you to be in such a hurry. Perhaps I can assist you wherever it is you're going?'

Emmelina could feel a kind of pressure building inside her. How rude of him to ask such an intrusive question. He would not have dared ask Humphrey where he was going. It was only because she was a woman. The urge to push him out of her way and shout something rude was tempting but she remained outwardly calm. He was standing far too close, for her comfort, peering down at her, making her feel trapped and suffocating her with his oppressive presence. There was something about the way he was looking at her that made her feel uncomfortable. She took hold of her cloak and pulled it tighter underneath her chin as if she were protecting herself from an invisible threat.

'No thank you,' she answered him back.

She had the distinct impression he was fishing for information but she had no intention of telling him where she was going. She knew, for once, Humphrey would have agreed with her but not for the same reasons. Garlick looked like he was going to delay her further and ask another intolerable question when he turned on his heel and bid her good day. She watched him take long, determined strides, till he reached the end of the lane and turned into West Gate Street. Only then did she hurry in the opposite direction towards the tannery.

Maverdine Lane skirted the Abbey's precinct wall, which bordered the monks' cemetery. On her left stood its tall and imposing tower, the stone appearing dull next to the creamy, freshly carved stone of the recently built Lady Chapel. The large bells of the abbey began to toll. Three long, dull peals signifying someone had died. She thought she heard the muffled sound of a hand bell close by on the other side of the wall and the sound of a woman sobbing but she thought little of the deep sadness of the grieving mourner. Like a bird freed from its cage she ran along the alleyway, her excitement at being free, albeit temporary, left her breathless. Within a few minutes she had reached the narrow side street known as Upper Tanners' Yard close to the River Twyver. She hadn't given much thought as to what she was doing until now. What would she say when she got there? What would people think of her walking into a building full of working men? Although these considerations entered her head she dismissed them almost immediately. The only thing she cared about was seeing Severin Browne again. Besides, she told herself, she had a very good reason to see him. She needed to make sure her husband's business affairs continued, despite his illness.

The stone building had two floors and was fronted by several arched openings, similar to the windows at Blackfriars Priory. As she neared the entrance, the rankest of smells assaulted her senses. It was worse than any of the city's cess pits and she balked. She took out a square of cloth and pressed it to her nose and tried to concentrate on the delicate smell of rose petals on the damask cloth. She took a deep breath, straightened her back, tilted her head upwards slightly and walked into the building trying her best to look confident even though she didn't feel it. The floor was tamped dirt with several sunken vats facing her as she entered the building. A rather scraggy looking young boy, no more than ten was standing waist deep in one of the vats stamping about in a vile looking and acrid smelling concoction. Another equally scraggy, older man was carrying lengths of stripped oak bark and emptying them into the pit next to the boy's. The older man turned to her and looked rather surprised.

'Can I help you, mistress?'

'I was looking for Master Browne. Is he here?' she asked.

'No, mistress. We haven't seen him today. You could try his workshop round the corner in North Gate Street...'

Emmelina did not think it a good idea to call on him at home. Disheartened, she thanked the old man and re-traced her steps back to her cold and unwelcoming home.

Chapter 10

Emmelina was sorely disappointed not to have seen Severin at the Tanners' Hall. She had wanted to ask William the Tanner where she could find him but she did not want to draw attention to herself. Full of elation on her walk to the tannery, she had returned home with the feeling she had been cheated somehow. Determined to see him again, and having been given permission by her husband she set out early the next morning to the Tanner's Hall. She had only just arrived when she heard a deep and somewhat gravelly voice behind her.

'Mistress Pauncefoot...'

She recognised it immediately and swung round. Emmelina was holding the perfumed cloth to her nose. Severin stood before her, his hands on his hips, looking cocky as usual but a little tired.

She removed the cloth from her face to speak. 'Master Browne,' she said, blushing with embarrassment, like a bride on her wedding night.

'This is indeed a pleasure,' he said, a broad grin widening into a mocking smile.

'My husband has asked me to speak to you about your business with him.'

'Has he?' Severin said, raising an eyebrow in surprise.

'Yes,' she flustered, 'As you know, my husband is not well and he's asked me to carry on his business with you and he wants me to report back to him.'

She didn't know what else to say and began to feel out of her depth. Perhaps her expression had given her away because Severin stopped grinning.

'Please, this is no place for you. Let me walk you back home.'

She nearly accepted his suggestion considering the vile smell she was being subjected to from the sunken vats ahead of her but thought otherwise. If she was to involve herself in her husband's business and see more of Severin she would have to put up with such things.   The smell, which became much worse when she removed the cloth to speak, caught at the back of her throat.

'Thank you for your kind offer,' she coughed, 'but I can assure you I am quite comfortable here.'   She thought she detected a slight smirk on Severin's face but pressed on.   She pointed to the scraggy pair.   'What are these men doing?' she enquired, trying to give the impression she was not at all bothered by the smell.

Her voice sounded superior.   She didn't want to sound like that but it was coming out all wrong but she couldn't think of anything else to say.   Severin walked past her towards the vats.   She followed.

'This is William Tawyer.'

William nodded but didn't stop what he was doing.   He was a wiry old man with kind eyes and large hands, which were the colour of brown earth.

'He's making up a fresh dying solution using oak bark to tan the leather and this,' pointing to the boy, 'is his son, Young Will.'

The young boy looked as miserable as anyone ever could.   His body bent over, his eyes dull and joyless.   Emmelina pitied him.   He glowered at her when he heard Severin say his name.   Emmelina responded by smiling at him but he didn't smile back.

'Young Will's in charge of the drenching process.'

The boy looked away and carried on stamping his bare, brown stained feet on the hides, his legs immersed to knee height in the vat of foul smelling liquid.   He remained sullen, ignoring Severin's attempt to praise the boy by intimating he was in charge.

Severin pressed on, explaining in some detail how they arrived at the finished product.

'When William gets delivery of the carcasses from the butchers he has to immerse them in a warm infusion to remove the fat and hairs from the hide.'

'Is that why it smells so foul,' she asked him through her sleeve.

'We have to make the solution as acidic as possible so all of the hair and fat is removed. If it isn't the hide rots and we can't use it. We use dung from pigeons, dogs, chickens and of course piss from the piss pots,' he told her, pointing to a number of large ceramic pots, finished in a greenish glaze lined up just inside the entrance.

'Oh,' she replied, gagging into her sleeve.

Severin took her by the arm. 'Come with me, I think it best if I explain everything in pleasanter surroundings.'

He led her down Tanners' Street past St John's church towards the North Gate. They stopped outside a small timber framed building.

'This is my house...and also my workshop,' he announced, pulling on the wooden latch and opening the door wide. 'Come in.'

Emmelina remained outside as did Severin.

'Didn't you say Humphrey wants you to carry on his business with me?' Severin pointed out.

'Yes...but...' she began.

'And didn't he want you to report back to him?'

'Well, yes, but...' she stammered.

'Well then, we can't conduct business in the street,' he was mocking her again. 'Besides, I have something to show you and once I've explained what it is, you'll be able to report back to him, won't you,' he concluded.

Emmelina looked about her before stepping inside. It wouldn't do to be seen going into another man's house unaccompanied. The street was busy with strolling pilgrims, street entertainers and the familiar sight of the mendicant monks from nearby Whitefriars in their distinctive white habits. Confident she could not be seen by anyone she knew, she stepped inside.

The smell of new leather filled the room. A large work table dominated the space. On it was a selection of leather hides

47

of different colours. She walked over to them and ran her hand across them. Soft to the touch, she picked one up and smelled it. The finished hide had a deeply satisfying, earthy smell, nothing like the vile stench involved in producing it.

She looked about her. On one wall hung a variety of hand tools. Awls of different sizes and shapes for making holes, a strange half-moon shaped tool and several sharp knives. On another, hung a row upon row of leather sword sheaths embossed with a coat of arms and pictures of fighting soldiers. A leather trunk on the floor caught her eye and she walked over to it. The rich brown leather had a lustrous shine and had been delicately worked with an interlocking triangular pattern at the edges. The central pattern consisted of circular petal shapes. She recognised it as the Star of Epiphany. She had seen a pilgrim carving such a pattern on the stone of the chapel at the leper hospital she often visited. An ornate metal clasp finished the design.

'This is gorgeous,' she exclaimed, bending to her knees to get a closer look. 'Did you make this?'

Severin looked pleased with himself. 'My first commission for Lord Malverne. It's for his wife. I wanted Humphrey to see it before I deliver it to his Lordship.'

Emmelina was familiar with Humphrey's leather work but he had produced nothing so fine or with such precise and delicate working.

'May I look inside,' she asked.

Severin joined her, and kneeling by her side opened the chest. He had created separate compartments for storage.

'I've divided it up so Lady Cecily can store necklaces in one, rings in another, perhaps pendants or buttons in another and so on.'

She was keenly aware of how close he was to her. She noticed the dark hair on his forearms, his chipped fingernails and the scarring on his hands from using sharp tools. She consciously breathed in, savouring the moment while it lasted.

'You have a great talent,' she told him, breaking the spell she was under. 'This chest is a fine work of art, fit for a King. It must have taken you a long time?'

Severin stood up. 'Once I'd worked out the pattern, it only took a matter of weeks to complete. Lord Malverne wanted to celebrate his wedding anniversary by presenting his wife with a gift. I suggested a chest she could use to store her valuables in. Do you think she'll like it?'

Emmelina vaguely knew Lord Malverne's wife. Humphrey had introduced her following a Sunday Service at Blackfriars Priory. Humphrey patronised the priory and attended services there regularly. As his wife she also had to attend though she hated sitting there listening to the monks preach sermons about things she did not believe in. Humphrey, like most people she knew, was a religious hypocrite. Although he never admitted it, she was convinced he only attended services to further his position in certain helpful circles. Lord Malverne was a very important customer of Humphrey's. When she was first introduced to Lady Cecily the woman had treated her with such haughty disdain, she had taken to avoiding her. Remembering now, her rather plump figure and unattractive demeanour she wondered how such mean spirited women had husbands who honoured and cherished them so, lavishing upon them such beautiful and expensive gifts. It seemed so unfair. She had never received presents from Humphrey, not even at Christmas or for her birthday. Annoyance and jealousy crept into her voice.

'If she has any taste... she'll adore it.'

'You really think so. I value the opinion of a woman in these matters.'

'You should have more belief in yourself,' she replied, surprised at his reticence.

He smiled at her, returning to his unabashed cockiness that she found so alluring. He picked up a large piece of parchment and laid it out on the table.

'When I have an idea in my head, I have to make a sketch of it before I forget it. I need to see how it would look and then I transfer the pattern on to the hide.'

Emmelina noticed how excited he had become whilst explaining to her how he created such expertly crafted items. He obviously loved his work and showed great passion for it. She wondered whether the same passion extended into other areas of his life. As she studied his features and saw his dark eyes fire up she thought it probably did.

'Was this what your meeting with my husband was about?' she asked him, conscious of the time.

He became more animated, moving over to the pile of hides on the long table.

'Not entirely. I wanted to show him the improvements we've been making in the tanning process. At the moment we have to import hides from Cordova in Spain to get the best quality and the softest leather. That adds higher costs to the finished product. I've been working with William to produce a leather hide that comes close to the quality and pliability of the Spanish goat leather. If we can produce leather of a similar quality to theirs we can lower our costs and make higher profits.'

'Are these Cordovan leather?' she asked, following him.

'No. These are hides William has produced.'

He smoothed the dark blue leather hide with the flat of his hand.

'I haven't seen this colour before,' she said, feeling the edge of the hide and deliberately placing her fingers so they touched his. Engrossed in his work, he didn't seem to notice.

'That's something else I've been working on. I've been experimenting with the use of different plants and materials. This was dyed using black grape skins from Abbot de Staunton's vineyard at Over. Mixed with Indigo it gives a much deeper blue.'

'I like the colour. What will you make with this?'

'I haven't decided yet. Perhaps I'll make a small trinket box for a lady to keep her jewels in. What do you think I should make?'

He was teasing her again.

'I've no idea but I'd like to see it when it's finished.'

'It might take some time. I'm working on a big order for Lord Malverne.' He pointed to the sheaths hanging against the wall. 'But I'm more interested in creating objects of real beauty.'

He stared at her so intensely she dropped her gaze. He moved closer and tilted her chin upward with the tip of his finger so she was forced to look at him.

'You shouldn't do that,' he said. 'Put your head down and hide your face.'

She weakened and knew, if he made an improper move, she would not object but he didn't. Feeling awkward, she extricated herself from his touch and moved away.

'I must be getting back. Humphrey will be wondering where I am and I don't like to leave him on his own for long when he's so unwell. Thank you for showing me your work and for explaining about the leather. I'm sure Humphrey will be very interested when I tell him.'

'Must you go?' he entreated, closing the gap she had created between them. She stepped further back in response and found herself up against the door. She heard herself saying, 'I really must...'

He placed his hand on the door, preventing her from opening it. She looked up at him, his face close enough to kiss. She closed her eyes. She could smell him. Once again a physical connection, like a pulse of energy between them was present. She wondered if he sensed it too. She wanted to ask him but that would have been sheer foolishness. Her overwhelming desire was to kiss him. She thought he might be going to kiss her but she was wrong. He moved away. She opened her eyes to find him grinning at her.

'It would be good if you didn't mention what we've been doing,' he said, ruffling his hair.

51

'What,' she exclaimed, misunderstanding his meaning.

'We're not supposed to get involved with the tanners. The guilds like to keep things separate. It could cause trouble for me and your husband if this got out.'

'Oh right,' she replied, relieved he was only referring to business matters. 'I'm glad you warned me. I wouldn't have known. I obviously have a lot to learn.'

'I'd be happy to teach you?' he offered.

'I'd like that.'

She thanked him and left the house quickly before anything more transpired. Nevertheless, she couldn't help feeling cheated. She had half expected him to kiss her and he hadn't. Of course she would have been incensed if he had dared to do such a thing but secretly and inwardly she would have been enthralled.

Chapter 11

Severin fingered the smooth, soft leather of the chest, before wrapping it in lengths of woollen cloth. Pleased with the finished piece it was time to deliver it to Lord Malverne in time for his wedding anniversary. He would need to leave early if he was to reach the manor house in good time. Strapping the chest securely behind his back, he set off along Tanners' Lane towards Alvin Bridge, another toll bridge, which spanned the River Twyver. From there, he followed the road towards Tewkesbury.

It was a bright and crisp November morning, the blue sky peppered with white sweeping clouds. Still the wind cut through his woollen coat despite wearing several layers. Severin walked with quick determination, keen to reach his destination and deliver the chest safely. He passed by a wayside cross, one of the many scattered around the city, without dropping to his knees to pray. What was the point, he told himself. Bad things would still happen. After the crossroad, Tulwell Court appeared on his left, a large manor house belonging to St Oswald's Priory. He could see several monks working in the grounds, heavily wrapped up against the cold. A few miles further and he would reach Lord Malverne's manor house.

He had visited only once before when he was summoned by his lordship to discuss the anniversary present. Lord Malverne was a good customer to have and he hoped he might open more influential doors to him. Humphrey Pauncefoot had done it that way, many years before. Now it was time for the next generation to make their mark.

Severin admired Humphrey Pauncefoot. He had a good business head on him and was not afraid to take on new challenges. He could be difficult but then that was what made him a good business man. He wasn't afraid of upsetting anyone. Then there was his wife. She was something else. They were an odd couple. Clearly, he was a lot older than her.

He wondered how they had met and why, someone as comely as Emmelina, had married him. He supposed it was his money. Women were attracted to money. But then again, women were attracted to him, even though he had none. Not yet anyway. He couldn't be certain but he had an inkling Emmelina Pauncefoot was attracted to him. But he couldn't be sure. Women were difficult creatures to work out.

Still occupied by thoughts of Emmelina, he arrived at the narrow lane off the Tewkesbury Road, which led to the manor house. The smoky smell of a wood fire on a cold day reminded him of home as he approached the stone, gothic porch, weary and glad to remove the chest from his back. The opening led to an inner porch, not unlike that of a church, which in turn led to a metal-studded gothic door. He pulled hard on the bell pull. A few moments later, an old woman who was cleanly dressed answered the door. Severin smiled at her and told her he was expected. The old woman did not return his smile. She led the way into a large, stone flagged hallway, which was partly oak panelled. An open wooden staircase leading to the upper floor was finished off with a skilfully carved balustrade of heart shaped insets. A roaring fire blazed in the stone fireplace, its flames flickering across the walls, creating dancing shadows in the dimly lit north-facing room. She told him to wait and disappeared through a door on the right, only to emerge seconds later to show him into the same room. The Great Hall.

Lord Malverne sat at a long oak table in front of an imposing stone fireplace, which was belting out heat from a roaring fire. The table was strewn with more food than Severin had seen in one place before. Roasted meats, bread, cheeses and wine. Severin stared up at the raftered ceiling above Lord Malverne and at his hunting trophies and his display of weapons around the stone-faced walls. As a young man Lord Malverne had fought at the battle of Tewkesbury on the Yorkist side. An angry purple scar across his left cheek acted as a constant reminder to all who knew him of his fighting days. Severin could see he had been a handsome man. Still was.

Lord Malverne greeted him with his loud boom of a voice. 'Severin, come join me. Have some food,' he said, gesturing for him to take a seat at the table.

Severin hesitated. It was unheard of for a Lord to invite someone of Severin's social position to his table but Lord Malverne was not a man who was bound by custom. He was unorthodox in many ways, including the upbringing of his daughters.

'I insist. You've had a long walk, no doubt. You must be hungry?'

'Thank you, your Lordship. I have indeed worked up an appetite on the way here.'

With the greatest of care Severin placed the chest on the wooden floor, took off his heavy woollen cloak and joined Lord Malverne at the table.

'Help yourself. There's plenty.'

A half-eaten lark, chunks of cheese and loaves of wheat bread lay upon the table.

He barked an order at a young girl who was standing at the far end of the room. 'Pour my guest some wine.'

The girl rushed over to the table, poured a goblet of red wine and placed it in front of Severin. He took a sip. It tasted of hedgerow berries. Lord Malverne reached for a chunk of bread and stuffed it in his mouth.

'So, you've finished the chest?' he said, speaking with his mouth full of food.

'I have, your Lordship.'

'Would you like to see it?' Severin asked, standing up.

Lord Malverne motioned to him. 'Sit down. Eat something first.'

Severin sat back down.

'And the other matter? Do you have it with you?'

Severin dug under his shirt and pulled out a package, wrapped in the same kind of cloth as the chest. He passed it to Lord Malverne who took it from him and tucked it into the waistband of his breeches.

'Don't you want to check it?'

'I'm sure it will be fine,' Lord Malverne replied, tearing at the delicate leg of a roast lark.

The two men ate in polite silence. The food tasted good and Severin made the most of it by piling his plate with a bit of everything from the table. Lord Malverne reached over and cut a large piece of cheese, stabbing it with the knife and dropping it onto his plate. 'Try some of this,' he suggested, replacing the knife.

'Thank you, I will.'

Severin picked up the knife and helped himself to the cheese. The young servant girl approached the table and without speaking filled Lord Malverne's goblet from the jug filling Severin's before returning to her place in the corner of the room. Severin took another long drink. The silence between them was awkward. He tried to think of something to say.

'I trust Lady Cecily is well?' he asked.

'She's very well, thank you.'

'And Lady Alice?'

Lord Malverne had four daughters and no sons. Lady Alice was his youngest. Severin had caught sight of her, only momentarily, on his last visit. She looked headstrong and independent, something he admired in a woman.

'Lady Alice is also very well...as are my other daughters,' he added, a wry smile upon his face.

'Of course,' Severin replied.

'In fact, Lady Alice will be joining us soon.'

Severin's head shot up at the mention of Lord Malverne's daughter.

'She's keen to learn the sport of falconry and I've agreed to teach her,' he told Severin. 'Against the wishes of Lady Cecily of course.' He laughed. The door opened and without turning around, he announced. 'Ah and here she is.'

A young girl of no more than thirteen, walked into the room wearing a tightly-bodiced gown, made from ruby coloured belainge, a popular woollen cloth. She wore a simple cream coloured wimple upon her head. Her hair had been swept up underneath the wimple with only a few amber coloured wisps framing her pale face. She flung her arms around the thick neck of her father as he sat at the table, not seeming to notice Severin was in the room.

'Oh father, I'm so excited...'

Lord Malverne prised her arms from around his neck. 'We have a guest, Alice.'

Alice turned to Severin. She blushed. 'I'm sorry father. If I'd known...'

'No harm done. This is Severin. He's made something for your mother for our wedding anniversary but you mustn't say anything to her about it.'

'Ooh, what is it?' she replied, becoming excited once again.

Severin stood up and walked across to the chest, still concealed under the cloth. He picked it up, placed it on the table and with the care of one revealing something of great value, he unfolded the cloth, exposing the decorative leather.

'This is exquisite,' she exclaimed, running her delicate fingers over the raised pattern. 'Mother will love it.'

Severin found his eyes wandering to her small breasts, pressed flat underneath her tightly laced bodice. But he could only look. She was a girl, not yet a woman with a boyishness about her. It was mere fantasy to think he could contemplate an alliance with someone from such an esteemed family. He was a journeyman, she was a lady. But he had ambition. And it was obvious he had talent or why else would Lord Malverne commission him. Maybe, one day, he could set his sights on such a woman. No sooner had the thought entered his head, another image flashed across his mind. That of Humphrey Pauncefoot's wife. To his embarrassment, his member twitched. He returned to the table before his indiscretion could be noticed and sat down.

'Severin, you must join us. Come see how the Lady Alice fares at falconry. We've picked out a small hawk for her.'

'I must be getting back...' Severin told them, standing to leave, his hands covering his subsiding indiscretion.

'I do hope you'll come back and see us again. Perhaps father has more work for you. It's my birthday soon,' she said, looking over at her father and widening her eyes in impish mischief.

'Be gone with you,' her father replied, not a hint of reprimand in his voice.

He turned to Severin. 'She's going to be trouble for any man that wants to take her on.'

Chapter 12

Fayette had been missing for almost two days. Emmelina was beginning to lose all hope that she would return. With all of the extra domestic chores she had to take on she had not had time to go into the city and ask after her. She knew from conversations she'd had with Fayette that she often drank in the New Inn and for that reason she was now making her way there. It was her last hope. She stopped opposite the inn in North Gate Street and watched as people came and went, building her nerve to go in alone. The New Inn had been built by the Abbey in 1450 on the site of an older inn to accommodate the thousands of pilgrims the city now attracted. She had passed the inn many times before but had never actually gone inside. She entered the open courtyard and pressed through the throng of pilgrims and into the tavern. Thomas Myatt stood at the bar holding court with a group of young men who had obviously been drinking heavily. She coughed loudly hoping to get his attention. One of the young men looked her up and down as she stood waiting. She knew that look. She coughed louder. The man nudged Thomas's elbow and he turned to look at her.

'Might I have a word?' she asked him.

'Certainly. What can I do for you?'

He took her aside, distancing her from the group.

'I'm looking for Fayette Cordy. I understand she drinks in here from time to time? Have you seen her recently?'

'Fayette Cordy,' he repeated, rubbing his left ear vigorously and looking vague. She noticed it had a piece missing and wondered if he had lost it in a brawl.

'She works for me,' Emmelina went on to explain, 'and she didn't come home last night. I'm worried about her.'

'Ah, yes. I know who you mean now. A fine looking young woman,' he grinned, cupping his hands to his chest. Emmelina smiled at the gesture, not taking offence. She was well aware of Fayette's formidable endowments.

'Was she here last night?'

'Yes, now I think of it she was in here with that Severin Browne. Sitting over there they were. Thought they made a handsome couple.'

For a moment Emmelina thought her heart might stop beating as if a malevolent spirit had ripped it from her chest and was stomping on it with force. Severin had been with Fayette the night she disappeared but he had said nothing of this when she told him of her disappearance. She composed herself quickly and made to leave.

'Mistress? If I may be so bold? If you are in need of a new maidservant I know someone who could fill that position?'

Emmelina stopped. She was in desperate need of someone to help her and if Fayette had been seeing Severin she didn't much care to keep her job open.

'That's very kind of you, innkeeper. Who is it?'

'Why she's over there, miss' he said, pointing at a young woman sitting alone. 'She came to me yesterday looking for work but I can't take her on. I let her sleep upstairs last night but I can't keep doing that or I'll lose business.'

Emmelina looked over at her. She was no more than fourteen at most. Her pale skin was streaked with tears. She had a beautiful mass of ringlets, the colour of autumn leaves and she had the sweetest sweetheart lips. Emmelina approached her.

'Master Myatt tells me you're looking for work?'

'Yes, mistress. I am,' Dulcina replied, dabbing at the corner of her eye with the hem of her skirt.

'What's your name?'

'Dulcina, miss. Dulcina Sawyer.'

'Do you have any experience?'

'No, mistress but I'm quick to learn and a hard worker,' Dulcina assured her, adding, 'I won't let you down.'

Emmelina studied her. She looked small and vulnerable.

'You've been crying. Why?'

'My father died yesterday morning.'

Emmelina's heart went out to her, remembering the night she lost her parents.

'What about the rest of your family?'

'My mother and brothers died of a sickness when I was young.'

'Have you nowhere else to go?'

'No.'

Dulcina's bottom lip quivered and she burst into tears. Emmelina remembered the night she fled from her burning home, not knowing whether her parents were safe and later being told they were both dead. Her first feelings were those of shock but they were swiftly followed by a cavernous emptiness at the loss, and numbing fear at the thought of being alone with no-one to care for her and no-where to go. She never wanted to feel that crushing desolation again. She looked down at Dulcina who was still crying into the hem of her skirts. Only her large, viridescent eyes could be seen above the cloth, wide and staring. She saw the same fear, the same desolation and her heart shrank with a pain that rose up, uninvited, from her past.

'Very well,' said Emmelina, 'you must come with me.'

Dulcina gasped in surprise and buried her face in her skirts and sobbed.

Thomas said. 'Well, what do you say to the mistress?'

Dulcina composed herself and wiped her nose with the hem of her skirt. 'Sorry, miss. I didn't mean to seem ungrateful. I just can't believe anyone would be so kind.'

Emmelina held out her hand.

'Come with me, Dulcina. I have a fire that needs lighting and plenty of chores to be done. In return you shall have a room of your own, food to eat and a friend when you need one. How does that sound?'

Dulcina burst into tears once more but this time it was from unexpected kindness.

Chapter 13

Emmelina and Dulcina left the inn together. Conversation was difficult as the streets were noisy with pilgrims, traders, journeymen looking for work and itinerant musicians. Emmelina told Dulcina to follow her and keep close. As they turned into Maverdine Lane, Emmelina saw an old woman standing by her door.

'Damn it,' she cursed to Dulcina, 'I don't need a hawker now. I'm not in the mood.'

Getting closer, she could see the woman did not look much like a hawker or a beggar. She was dressed plainly but her clothes were of good quality. She wore a dark-green woollen surcoat with a cream coloured smock underneath. Her arms and upper chest were exposed showing a preponderance of small brown moles. She had a kind face, although, it too, was covered in brown freckles, which matched her kind russet-coloured eyes. She looked like the sort of person who worked outdoors yet she was not dressed like a peasant. Emmelina puzzled over this, wondering who she was and why she was standing outside her house. She was even more surprised when the woman addressed her by her name.

'You know me?' Emmelina asked, her eyes widening.

'You probably don't remember me. I knew your parents.'

'You knew my parents?'

Emmelina could hardly believe it. A connection to her past, her childhood and someone who knew her family. She studied Maud's face, hoping to dredge up a memory from her past.

'Did you visit my mother at our old house?' she queried.

Maud smiled broadly, her kind eyes sparkling. 'I did. Many times.'

'Did you sometimes drink mint tea?'

'Always,' Maud laughed, throwing her head backwards. 'We used to sit in the kitchen, drink peppermint tea and talk for hours.'

Emmelina had always associated the smell of peppermint with happy memories. She was momentarily transported back to her mother's kitchen in the old house. In her mind she saw her mother sitting at the table with another woman, laughing, happy and carefree. She was a small child skipping around the kitchen table, making them laugh. The house was warm, welcoming and safe.

'Is your name Maud?' she asked, pulling the name from a long forgotten memory.

Maud smiled. 'You remember. Yes. Maud Biddle.'

'You must come in,' Emmelina told her, opening the door and showing the two women into the kitchen.

'Please sit down. I'm sorry. The place is in a mess. My maidservant went off a couple of days ago and she hasn't come back.'

Emmelina's mind was buzzing. She had a million questions to ask this woman. She also had to see to Dulcina. Perhaps she should start by making them a hot drink. She looked across at the unlit fire.

'I would offer you a hot drink but...'

'I'll see to that,' Dulcina announced, walking over to the unlit fire. 'I may be new to this house but I'm not completely useless and I do know my way around a kitchen so you sit down miss and I'll light the fire and make the drink.'

Seeing the puzzled look Maud gave Dulcina, Emmelina explained.

'Dulcina and I have only just met.' Then she added. 'Dulcina lost her father yesterday. She's no family left so I've taken her on.'

'I'm very sorry to hear that, Dulcina but I'm sure you've done well to meet up with Emmelina,' Maud remarked.

Dulcina wiped away a tear as she busied herself finding her way around the kitchen. Emmelina, relieved at not having to light the fire, sat down at the table opposite Maud.

'How do you know my parents?' Emmelina asked, anxious to know all Maud could tell her.

'Your mother, Sabrina, was a good friend of mine.'

Emmelina hadn't heard her mother's name mentioned since hearing her father's last words when he called out to his wife the night they died. She was shocked at her own reaction. Memories of her mother. Her smell, the way she looked; the kind words she said to her at bedtime or when she fell over and hurt herself. A familiar but unbearable ache in her chest surfaced, overwhelming her. The tears began to well.

'Are you all right?' Maud asked her, adding. 'I didn't mean to give you a shock.'

'I'm fine,' she said, widening her eyes hoping the tears she could feel welling up would not spill out onto her cheek and give her real emotions away. 'When did you last see my mother?'

'Up on the hill.'

Emmelina shot Maud a wary look. She had never told anyone about her visits to the hill. If she were ever found out she would be accused of heresy and lose her liberty and very probably her life. It was her secret and no-one knew. Thankfully, Dulcina was pottering around the kitchen, opening cupboards and searching for things. She had found an apron and already looked the part of housemaid. She seemed oblivious to the conversation.

'You know about that?' Emmelina whispered back, glancing over at Dulcina to make sure she wasn't eavesdropping.

Maud nodded. 'I stopped going when my husband died. It was a long time ago and you were only little. I didn't think you'd remember me.'

'I do remember you at the house, not anywhere else.'

'What was my mother like?' Emmelina asked, moving away from the perilous subject of the hill.

'Your mother was a caring, loving soul and a good friend to me. She would do anything to help anybody.'

The pain in Emmelina's chest remained and at the mention of her mother seemed to go deeper, like a hot knife.

'Your mother was a very wise woman. She knew a lot about how to use herbs to heal sickness. She would spend hours in the kitchen making up potions from herbs she had picked from the fields or powdered herbs your father brought back from his travels. When people who were sick came to the house she would give them tiny bottles of her potions to take away with them.'

'I can remember lots of people visiting the house and my mother was always in the kitchen brewing some potion or other from plants she picked from the garden but I never really knew what she was doing.'

'Did you know she was also a gifted healer and very well read? She would ask your father to bring back books from his travels abroad on healing and medicine.'

'I remember those books,' Emmelina exclaimed, another deeply buried memory surfacing.

Her mood brightened for a moment, but then the dark shroud that wrapped itself around her heart like a tourniquet, keeping the memories from her, loosened.

She was woken from her sleep by sounds outside her bedroom window. The sound of men's voices. She could smell something burning. Then her room filled with black, choking smoke. She opened her door to go in search of her mother, only to be met by a wall of thick smoke and intense heat. There was nowhere to go but to turn round and escape through the open window.

Something shifted inside her, like the unravelling of a tight knot of wool. 'I expect they were destroyed in the fire,' she said, looking down at her hands resting on the table.

Maud reached out and took hold of Emmelina's hands and held onto them without speaking, then she gave them a squeeze and let go. Dulcina approached with two wooden cups filled to the top with weak warm ale. She placed them on the table, spilling some of the contents. Dulcina used the corner of her clean apron to wipe up the spillage, apologising over and over for her clumsiness.

'Sorry, miss. I don't know how that happened.'

Maud lightened the situation. 'If you rub that table any more, you'll rub a hole in it.'

Dulcina didn't know whether to laugh or be fearful. 'It's all right Dulcina,' Emmelina re-assured her. 'Just don't fill the cup to the top next time.'

'Thank you, miss, I'm ever so sorry.'

'Why don't you go into the larder and see what you can find to make us some dinner?' Emmelina suggested.

Dulcina disappeared into the larder to find some food. Maud reached over and took hold of Emmelina's hand again.

'Did you know just how special your mother was?'

'She was special to me.'

'I know,' Maud said, turning Emmelina's palm upwards.

She studied it for some time before she spoke. 'I can see you were much loved as a child.'

Emmelina stared into her hand, wondering what it was Maud could see. She had heard of people who could tell things about you from reading your palm but she had never met anyone who could. Dulcina emerged from the larder carrying an un-plucked chicken that Fayette had hung in the larder some days before. She sat down by the fire and began to pluck it, throwing the feathers onto the flaming fire.

Maud continued to study Emmelina's palm, occasionally tracing her fingers along the lines. 'You have much pain in your life. Much unhappiness.' She looked into Emmelina's eyes. 'Was there a child?' she asked.

Emmelina drew back her hand as if she'd been burned by a flame. The question shocked her. Was Maud referring to the child she lost? How could she know about that? Maud took back her hand and stroked it. The tenderness in her touch and voice melted something inside her. She answered the question.

'Yes, but it was born dead.'

'I'm sorry.' Maud stood up and came to Emmelina's side and hugged her. 'I'm very sorry,' she repeated.

The pain in Emmelina's chest became almost unbearable as the rawness of her grief surfaced, remembering the tiny, lifeless child in her arms. She had lost so many people in her short life, people she loved and who loved her. She breathed in deeply, in an attempt to remain in control, but it didn't work. An oasis of grief, long held and unresolved, engulfed her and she let the tears fall. Like the breached banks of a river they were unstoppable. Surprised at the ferocity of her pain, she wept, sobbing into Maud's shoulder. As if grief were an infectious disease, Dulcina, having just lost her father, also set about crying. Only Maud seemed resistant to it. She beckoned Dulcina over and held both women until the violent sobbing subsided.

'I think I'd better make another drink for all of us,' Maud announced.

The fire had taken hold, warming the kitchen and brightening the gloom. Dulcina had placed a small pot of weak ale on top of the flames to warm. Maud now took a cloth and picked up the pot of simmering ale by its handle and poured it into three cups made from elder wood.

She turned to look at the shelves on the dresser. Scanning them, she noticed an odd shaped bottle on the top shelf. She reached up and brought it down. Uncorking it, she carefully poured a tot of syrupy mead into the ale.

'I wouldn't normally…' she grinned, hoping to lift their mood.

Emmelina sipped the warm concoction in between sobs. Just as she was beginning to feel better she heard a knock at the door and the tightness in her chest returned.

Chapter 14

'That's Physician Teylove,' Emmelina sighed.

Maud gave Emmelina a questioning and worried look.

'He's come to see my husband. He's not well,' she explained. 'He took ill last night and the physician says he has an imbalance of the humours in his head. He's been treating him with leeches and emetics.'

'What are his symptoms?' Maud asked, her interest piqued.

'His speech is slurred and his right arm is twisted and shakes sometimes.'

Maud looked concerned. 'I don't know about you but I'm not convinced the use of leeches or emetics does much good?'

There was another knock at the door, this time impatient, much louder.

'I'd better answer the door.'

Emmelina, already on her feet, hurried out.

'I don't like to be kept waiting. I'm a busy man and it's cold out here,' Teylove greeted her.

He pushed past her and climbed the stairs. She followed with Maud at her heels leaving Dulcina alone in the kitchen. Humphrey lay there looking pale and very weak, his right arm twisted at his side. The leeches, now fully engorged had turned a dark blood red. He began detaching the bloated leeches from Humphrey's skin and dropping them back into the jar with the others. Maud stepped forward.

'Do you think that's doing him any good?' she enquired of him.

'And who are you?'

'I'm a friend of Mistress Pauncefoot's.'

Teylove huffed, dismissing her.

Maud persisted. Well?'

'Of course I think it is doing him some good or I wouldn't be doing it if I thought otherwise,' he snapped back.

'How can you tell?'

Teylove turned to her. 'What a ridiculous question.'

'I don't think it is. How do you know?' she asked again. 'What signs do you look for, which tell you the patient is getting better after a course of bloodletting?'

'I should think that's obvious.'

'I was just wondering what your thoughts were and how you came to your diagnosis and subsequent treatment?'

Emmelina looked on in admiration. She would have liked to ask him the same questions but didn't have the pluck Maud was now demonstrating. Besides, it wasn't her place. Humphrey would be furious with her. She glanced at him, lying there helpless and her fear of him lessened. Maud seemed unfazed by the acerbic physician. Perhaps it was the effect of the mead on an empty stomach but Emmelina looked on in awe and found she was enjoying Maud's inquisition of the irascible physician. Teylove hurried to the bed and started ripping the leeches from Humphrey's skin. Humphrey winced.

'Can't you see I'm busy?'

'What do you think is the cause of his illness?' she pressed. Maud was like an angry wasp refusing to go away until the sting had been delivered.

'I have told this man's wife what the problem is and as his physician I shall treat him as I see fit.'

Teylove had travelled to the other side of the bed to get away from her but still she pestered him. He remained silent busying himself by packing his things back into his medicine chest. Maud was not finished with him.

'Has there been any improvements in this man's condition since yesterday?'

She turned to Emmelina for the answer. Emmelina wished the conversation had never begun. What should she say? If she said 'yes', that would please Teylove but not Maud. She agreed with Maud's view on the use of leeches and did not want to go against her own principles. If she said 'no' that would please Maud but not Teylove. She looked from one to

69

the other. They were staring back at her, waiting for her answer.

'N...not much,' she faltered, fearing the consequences.

Teylove slammed his box shut and stood very upright, puffing out his sunken chest.

'It is obvious to me, Mistress Pauncefoot, that you no longer require my services. I shall expect to be paid for my time here. I will now take my leave. Good day to you.'

With that he left the room and clattered down the stairs. They heard the door slam. The two women were silent for a moment, the only sound, Humphrey's laboured breathing. Maud shrugged her shoulders, a mischievous grin upon her face. Emmelina started to giggle but before long she was laughing. Laughing in front of Humphrey and he could not say a thing. Laughing as only women can when they share such moments.

Maud recovered herself and rolled up her sleeves. She walked over to Humphrey who seemed to be sleeping. Closing her eyes she laid her hands on his head, keeping them there for a while. Humphrey stirred. With slow movements, she moved her hands onto his chest, then his arms and then back to his head, keeping her eyes closed throughout.

'He's very weak,' she said, opening her eyes and covering Humphrey with a blanket. 'If you like I can call in tomorrow and give him some more healing. It will build up his strength. Then we need to get him out of bed and moving around. His muscles will weaken further if we don't exercise them.'

'What's wrong with him, Maud?' asked Emmelina.

'I can't say for certain but I've seen similar symptoms before and I know bleeding and emetics don't help. He needs rest now.'

They went back downstairs and into the kitchen. Emmelina hadn't laughed out loud in her own house since she moved there four years ago at the age of thirteen. And never in

70

front of Humphrey. The energy in the house had changed. It had somehow become lighter and less oppressive.

Back in the kitchen Maud took her aside. 'I need to speak to you,' she whispered, 'in private?'

Emmelina nodded.

'Dulcina, I'm going to get some things from the market. I won't be long. You'll be all right? Won't you?'

Dulcina was half way through plucking the chicken she had found. 'Don't worry about me, miss. You run along and do what you need to do. I'll keep an eye on your husband and make a start on supper.'

Chapter 15

Outside, Maud stopped her in the quiet lane.

'I came to warn you.'

'Warn me? About what?'

'I think you may be in some kind of danger. I'm afraid for you.'

'I don't understand.'

'I saw you the other morning coming from the direction of the hill. I recognised you straight away.' She touched Emmelina's cheek. 'So like your mother.'

Emmelina softened at her touch. It had been such a long time since anyone had touched her in that loving, maternal way. Her husband never touched her like that. Only when he wanted her but she didn't consider that loving.

'That night I had a dream. I had a similar dream the night your parents died.'

The hairs on Emmelina's arms bristled and she shuddered. 'What did you dream about?' she asked, fearing the answer.

'It's not really a dream, more like a vision. I was wandering around on top of a hill, searching for something but I can't remember now what I was searching for...'

'Robin Hoodes Hill?' Emmelina interjected.

'I don't know. Just a hill. I was wading through thick white fog. An icy fog was swirling around my ankles but I couldn't see my feet. As I put my foot down I couldn't feel the ground beneath me. Such a strange feeling. Then the fog thickened and I couldn't see anything, just whiteness. I panicked. But then I heard your mother's voice calling out to me. I took a few small steps towards the sound of her voice. The fog began to clear a little and ahead of me your mother appeared. She said one word to me before disappearing back into the fog.'

'What did she say?' Emmelina asked, full of trepidation.

'She called your name.'

Emmelina went cold. Was her mother communing with her friend from the other side? What did this all mean? It was all very disturbing. Then she had another thought.

'Your dream, last night...you dreamt about me didn't you? Was I *the* one calling out?'

Maud hesitated, then swallowed hard. 'Yes.'

'Are you saying I'm going to die?' Emmelina asked, aware her voice was rising but unable to control it.

'I can't say. It may be nothing more than a strange coincidence.'

'My mother used to say there was no such thing as coincidences.'

Maud took hold of her hand. 'Listen, I just think you need to be careful, that's all.'

'I'm always careful.'

'That's good to hear.'

Maud kept hold of Emmelina's hand to comfort her. Two men dressed in uniform walked past, eyeing them with suspicion. Maud let go of her and they moved on, out of earshot.

'Your mother had quite a reputation for healing the sick but, sadly, some people didn't always appreciate her efforts.'

'Why not? Who didn't appreciate her?'

'People who had something to lose...'

Emmelina thought for a second. Vague memories from the past were beginning to form pictures in her mind. She could see her mother's face, happy and glowing with health. She wanted to hear more about her from Maud. It gave her a sense of pride to know how her mother had helped the sick but she couldn't stop the niggling feeling that something wasn't quite right. It bothered her. She couldn't pin down her thoughts and give them a more concrete form. Who wouldn't appreciate her mother? Who had something to lose? And then...

'Do you mean people like Teylove?'

'Exactly. Physicians like Teylove didn't like their patients going to Sabrina. For one thing she didn't ask anyone for money. She did it out of love. Men like Teylove don't understand that kind of thinking. And what was worse the sick came away from your mother's house feeling better. Some people started to talk of miracles. Then the monks heard about her. They didn't like it that a woman appeared to be performing miracles. People started talking about your mother, spreading nasty rumours.'

'What kind of rumours?' Emmelina asked.

They were walking past The Cross. Emmelina stopped on the corner of St Michael the Archangel's Church. She turned to Maud.

'What kind of rumours?'

Maud pulled her into the arched porch of the twelfth century church and whispered in her ear. 'The word went round your mother was a sorceress.'

'What! But that's absurd. My mother was the kindest, gentlest...'

Maud stopped her.

'Your mother was an angel.'

Another thought took hold and Emmelina blurted it out.

'Is that what the fire was about? Did someone deliberately set fire to our house? Was my mother murdered?'

'I don't know. But it's something I've wondered about all these years. The questions have never gone away and I've never managed to get answers to them. It's one of the reasons I didn't keep in touch with you after they were gone. I thought you'd be safer.'

A boiling rage consumed her. Had her mother been burnt to death for healing and helping people? Who else knew about this? Her husband? Teylove? Was that why Teylove was so horrible to her? She thought *she* was the problem. That he didn't like her because she wasn't good enough to be the wife of Humphrey Pauncefoot. The rage continued to roil, like boiling pitch.

'I'm sorry, Emmelina. I would never have told you any of this but for the dream. I had to warn you.'

Emmelina took hold of Maud's mottled hands. 'I'm so glad you came to see me. You've brought my mother back into my life. And I'm glad I know more about her even if it is painful. Please don't feel bad.'

'I wish I'd never said anything but then if I hadn't and something did happen to you I would never be able to forgive myself. Not a second time.'

'I understand. You don't have to explain. But what I don't understand is how this has any bearing on me. No-one has accused me of being a sorceress. Surely the same fate is not to befall me?'

'Probably not. I just wanted to ask you… Does anyone know about your visits to the hill?'

'No,' she replied, her voice strident, meant to convince. 'No-one. I'm very careful and I haven't told a living soul.'

'Does Humphrey know?'

'Absolutely not.'

'How do you know?'

'He drinks a lot and he's a very heavy sleeper.'

'Good. It's probably nothing. I've probably over-reacted. Perhaps seeing you yesterday brought back some old memories and they surfaced in a dream. I'm just a foolish old woman, frightening you like this. You better go back. Humphrey may be asking for you. I'll call in tomorrow and bring him a tonic. Just be careful.'

'I'd like that. Perhaps you can tell me more about my parents?'

Maud smiled and stroked her hair. 'Take great care.'

The two women hugged like mother and daughter before parting.

Chapter 16

Emmelina watched as Maud made her way through the throng towards the East Gate. Her head was buzzing with the events of the last two days. Although late, she decided to go for a walk instead of going back home. She needed to walk off this pent up energy, fuelled by a rising hatred towards those people who had been cruel to her mother. She knew the type. Narrow minded, superstitious bigots.

She headed towards the South Gate. Once clear of the city walls, the countryside opened out into an expanse of brown winter fields. She took a few deep breaths. The air seemed fresher than within the city walls and with each breath the tightness in her chest loosened. Walking always helped to unravel her thoughts and calm her down. It seemed to have a healing effect upon her. She followed the bank in a southerly direction away from the city. The pathway led her to the muddy banks of the river to a point where the grey water eddied and swirled at a sweeping bend. Stopping for a minute to take in the view she could see in the distance the single tall tower of Llanthony Secunda Priory, bordered by its red brick walls. Travellers, pilgrims and foreigners formed a thin trail like an army of ants in the far distance, towards the queue forming at the city's South Gate.

As she walked her mind begin to un-muddle itself. So much had happened, but the one thought that dominated the muddle was Severin. She had gone to the New Inn to inquire about Fayette's whereabouts only to be told by the inn-keeper that Severin had been with her the night before her disappearance. The thought of him with Fayette had thrown her feelings for him into utter confusion. There were many unanswered questions. Who was he? What was his relationship with Fayette? Were they in love? Did he know where she was? But more worrying. Why didn't he say anything to her when she told him she was missing? Thinking about it now, he had reacted oddly when she said she was worried about Fayette but perhaps she had misread him, having felt guilty at her own lack of care for her husband. Still, he could have said something to her but he didn't. Why? And... she could hardly bear to let herself even think this. What if he had something to do with Fayette's disappearance? What if something terrible had happened to her? Her theory about running off with a lover didn't hold water any longer now she knew who the lover was. It was all too much. Her head ached with the mess of it all. Whatever theories or excuses she came up with concerning Severin and Fayette, none of it helped. She had to concede, however unhappy it made her feel, he was not what he seemed to be. But then who was? Thoughts of her mother, her husband, Teylove, Fayette and Severin were all swirling around in her head banging into each other like the logs in the river causing her to have an almighty headache. It was no good, she concluded, she needed to know more about what had happened to her mother and she would start with her husband. As far as Severin was concerned she resolved to keep away from him and to report Fayette's disappearance to the bailiff, Richard Bliss. And the danger to herself, which Maud had come to warn her about she decided was the foolishness of a kind old lady.

Soothed somewhat by these thoughts she was unaware quite how far she had walked. She found herself by the Cockayne, the monks' fish weir by Llanthony Quay. It had been given to the Llanthony monks by their benefactor, Miles de Gloucester. A thin layer of fog floated just above the surface of the water. As she scanned the weir hoping to see a large fish flip to the surface her gaze stopped at something else caught in the lattice work protruding above the water. She squinted to focus on the strange object. There was something familiar about whatever it was she was staring at. She walked to the edge of the bank. Holding onto a wooden stake and placing her full weight against it she craned her neck to make sense of the object floating in the water. As if knocked by an invisible force, she jerked backwards when she finally realised what it was she was staring at. A bloated corpse, snagged by the wooden stakes of the fish weir was bobbing up and down in the gentle ebb and flow of the river's current. She realised with gloomy certainty the cause of the familiarity, which presented itself. She recognised the clothing and the long golden hair swirling in the current. It was Fayette's body, bloated and face down in the cold, murky water.

Emmelina ran back the way she had come. Within a short time she was back at the South Gate. Her skirts were torn and muddy and her legs were badly scratched by blackthorn bushes she had trampled through. The first person she saw was the gate porter, one of the constable's men. Flying through the gate house door, she fell onto a low wooden bench. Out of breath and in shock, she sat for a moment and tried to gather her thoughts. The porter, an inexperienced young man looked on perplexed but prepared, his hand covering his leather sword sheath.

Eventually, she got her breath back and shouted out to the guarded gate porter. 'Fetch the constable at once. There's a dead body in the river.'

Chapter 17

The next few hours were a blur to Emmelina. The porter sent one of his men to fetch the constable from the castle. He arrived with Bailiff Bliss and more men. They crowded around Emmelina in the confined space of the gate house. Constable Rudge took charge. He was a solid man, broad shouldered, with a large purple-pitted drinker's nose. He looked at her with suspicion as he entered the gate house.

'You told my gate porter there was a body in the river?'

'That's correct, sir. It's my missing servant, Fayette,' Emmelina replied.

'And who are you?'

'Emmelina Pauncefoot, sir. Wife of Humphrey, the cordwainer.'

Constable Rudge said nothing. He stared at her, looking her up and down for quite some time before he asked his next question. His voice was deep and authoritative.

'How do you know the body is that of your servant?'

'I recognised her clothes, sir. She was wearing them the last time I saw her.'

Once again, Constable Rudge remained silent. He seemed to be formulating his next question. He stared straight at her making Emmelina feel so unnerved she didn't know where to look.

'When did you last see her?'

'Two nights ago, sir.'

'Did you report her missing?'

'No. I haven't had time.'

Constable Rudge gave her a questioning look. Emmelina explained that with Fayette gone and her husband ill she had been too busy to do anything.

'Your husband is ill?'

Emmelina wondered why he was interested in her husband's illness and what that had to do with Fayette's dead body in the river but she answered all the same. 'He took ill a

79

few days ago, the same morning I discovered Fayette was missing,' she explained.

Constable Rudge gave Bailiff Bliss a look of concern. He didn't say anything but Emmelina could tell he was suspicious of her. But why? Surely, he didn't think she had anything to do with Fayette's death. Maud's words of caution came back to her.

'Take me to the spot where you say you found this body.'

Emmelina didn't like the way he phrased his last question but she didn't say anything. She raised her weary body from the bench and led them back to the Cockayne. She did not want to see her friend's body again but she knew she had no choice in the matter. They would need to recover the body and the coroner would need to ascertain, if possible, the cause of her death. And, of course, Fayette would need to be buried and laid to rest.

Word had got round there was a dead body in the river and this brought a pack of morbid onlookers. The grey light of the afternoon had quickly faded to the murky light of dusk and the fog had thickened, making it difficult to see. The constable ordered firebrands to be lit. He asked Emmelina to point out the exact spot where she had found the body.

'Over there,' she informed him, pointing towards the fish weir.

The flickering firebrands were held over the weir. The sound of the tide sloshing against the wooden stakes and the crackling of the firebrands only emphasised the unreality of the scene before Emmelina. There, in the eerie mist, bobbed Fayette's lonely body.

The monks from Llanthony Priory had also turned out to see what was causing such interest on the banks of their fish quay. Constable Rudge called upon them to provide a boat so that his men could row out to where Fayette was snagged and recover her. Two of his men clambered into the small boat and rowed out to the weir. Emmelina watched as the body of her dear friend was hauled into the boat like a harpooned whale.

The men rowed back to the bank. Emmelina watched on as they took hold of poor Fayette by each arm and with an unkind roughness, hauled her body onto the ground, flipping her over, like a gutted fish, face upwards. The throng of onlookers now crowded around her body. In the glowing light of the firebrands, Fayette's skin appeared translucent. Her once beautiful face, now bloated, had been nibbled away at the cheekbone by hungry fish leaving flakes of greenish, rotting flesh. Her eyes were still open but the sparkle had gone replaced by orbs of watery grey. Emmelina gagged and turned away. She ran to the river bank and was violently sick.

By the time she had composed herself, Fayette's body was being thrown on the back of a cart, which had been brought to ferry her back to the Booth Hall. Emmelina took one last look. She wished she hadn't. Fayette's mouth had opened slightly and a voracious lamprey slithered from the blackness of the opening. That single image would remain with her for the rest of her days and haunt her dreams.

Chapter 18

It was late evening when Emmelina finally arrived home. When she walked into the kitchen her spirits lifted as the warmth of the glowing fire and the smell of something savoury bubbling in a pot greeted her. Dulcina seemed organized and happier than earlier in the day.

'Has my husband asked after me?' Emmelina enquired, more from fear than concern.

'No, miss. I've been upstairs a few times to check on him but he's been asleep most of the day. Is anything the matter, miss? You look a bit done in.'

Emmelina slumped into a chair by the fire.

'Here, miss. Have some o' this.'

Dulcina poured a large cup of strong ale and handed it to Emmelina. She did not pour herself one or join Emmelina by the fire. Instead, she carried on her preparations for the next day's meal.

'Thank you, Dulcina. I do feel tired.'

Emmelina gulped the ale whilst staring into the fire. She wondered whether she should mention Fayette's death to Dulcina. On balance, she decided to say nothing, not wanting her to worry, or worse, leave. She was glad Dulcina was there when she arrived home. It made such a difference just to have someone else in the house. Someone other than her husband. She knew she ought to go and check on him but the longer she sat, the more ale she drank, the less energy she had to climb the stairs. Her cheeks flushed from the warmth of the fire and the strength of the ale, which she wasn't used to drinking. Dulcina busied herself about the kitchen as if she had been born in it. She wasn't trying to make conversation either, which was a relief and she didn't seem particularly concerned to know where Emmelina had been all day. Emmelina didn't feel much like talking. Something was worrying her and it wasn't something she could discuss with anyone. When Constable Rudge had questioned her about Fayette she hadn't mentioned

82

anything about Severin.   She hadn't been asked a direct question about him but then she hadn't mentioned he had been drinking with Fayette the night she disappeared. Why? Was she protecting him? Who was he to her? She was so confused and uneasy about her feelings towards him. There was a strong attraction, on her part at least. She couldn't be certain what his feelings were towards her. Did she want him to be innocent? Was he even guilty? After all, just going for a drink with someone didn't mean you had murdered them. Oh God. She had said it now. Was Fayette murdered? If so, did Severin do it? Was he the sort of man capable of such a thing? Her thoughts, like butterflies on summer hogweed, were leaping from one thing to another. Perhaps she should go and look in on Humphrey. That would stop all this nonsense. There was a knock at the door. Emmelina stood up to answer it. The vein at her temple began to throb with the start of another headache.

'Sit down, miss. I'll go.'

Emmelina didn't protest. She slumped back down and took another gulp of ale. She heard voices at the door, and then Dulcina appeared in the kitchen.

'Someone to see you, miss.'

Emmelina looked up to see Severin Browne standing in her kitchen. He looked agitated. Dulcina in her naivety had shown him into the kitchen.

'I've just heard about Fayette,' he said.

Emmelina stared at him. She didn't know what to say. She wanted to say something cutting to hurt him like he had hurt her. Nothing came into her head. She was never any good at the quick retort. It was always later she thought of something she could have said, particularly after an argument with Humphrey.

'Have I come at an inconvenient time? Perhaps I should come back tomorrow? You look upset?'

There it was again. The sound of genuine concern in his voice as if he really meant what he was saying. What a charmer, she thought, bitterly. Why did men disappoint her so much? Humphrey was a selfish, cruel man, devoid of emotion and tenderness. He was not easy on the eye, in fact, Emmelina found his features repellent. She would not have been concerned about his looks had he been capable of showing kindness towards her. But he was not. Severin, on the other hand, was very pleasing on the eye with an alluring personality. Standing in her dimly-lit kitchen like a dazzling cynosure, she couldn't keep her eyes off him. Against her better judgement she found herself hugely attracted to him despite the nagging doubt in the back of her mind. She could not be sure he was who he appeared to be. Her experience with men had been jaded by her relationship with Humphrey. She couldn't trust her instincts anymore.

'Yes, perhaps tomorrow would be better,' she heard herself say.

He turned to go, looking thoroughly miserable.

'No wait...'

Dulcina had already returned to her preparations and was standing between them at the table.

'I'll finish that, Dulcina. You've had a long day. I'll see you in the morning.'

'Are you sure, miss? It won't take me long to...'

'I'm quite sure Dulcina.'

'I haven't finished...' Dulcina began.

'That can wait till morning.'

She spoke a little too sharply to Dulcina than she had meant to but it had had the desired effect. Dulcina had finally got the message.

'I think you're right, miss. I can finish that in the morning. Goodnight, miss. Goodnight, sir.'

She bowed and left them alone in the kitchen. The fire crackled. Neither spoke. Despite her better judgement she had not let him go. That feeling was there again. Like an invisible thread pulsating between her body and his. She wondered if he could feel it too.

'Why are you here?' she asked him, not looking at him but swirling the remaining dregs of ale around in her cup.

'I heard about Fayette.'

'What have you heard?' she said, fixing him with an accusatory stare.

'That's she's dead. I thought you might be upset.'

'I am upset. Very upset.'

Perhaps it was the effect of the ale or just the unusual circumstances she found herself in but she wasn't in the mood for observing the usual niceties of small talk and social politeness. She needed to know what happened to Fayette and it seemed Severin was the last person to see her alive.

'Why didn't you tell me about you and Fayette?'

She searched his face for signs of guilt.

'What do you mean? There's nothing to tell.'

'You were seen in the New Inn with her the night she disappeared.'

Severin looked uncomfortable, like a small child caught telling lies. 'How do you know about that?'

'Thomas, the innkeeper told me.'

He leaned across the table, splaying his long fingers against the grain of the wood.

'I was in there with her earlier that night but I can assure you she was most definitely alive when I left her at The Cross.'

'Then why didn't you tell me you were with her when I first mentioned she was missing?'

He paused. Was that a sign of guilt, she wondered or something else?

'I didn't say anything because I didn't want you to know I was with her that night.'

'Why not?' she shot back at him.

She heard her voice, shrill and accusatory.

'I didn't want to give you the wrong impression of me and I thought, like you, she'd gone off with someone and she'd be back. I never imagined they'd be fishing her body out of the river.'

85

He pushed himself away from the table, lacing his hands together on the top of his head in a gesture of frustration. Emmelina saw something primal in him. His pupils had dilated causing his eyes to look as black and fiery as those of a wild stallion. The cockiness she found so appealing in him had been replaced by a rawness she found even more seductive. Drawn to him she went to his side.

'Why didn't you want to give me the wrong impression?'

'I don't know…maybe I was…Look, I don't know…' he faltered.

She wanted him to kiss her. Wanted more than that from him. She wanted to feel his strong hands on her body and for that brief moment she wished he would take her right there in the kitchen under the same roof as her ailing husband. The thought of it raised her pulse.

'I only know that whatever ill befell Fayette it had nothing to do with me. You do believe me, don't you?'

She looked into his wild eyes, this time searching for innocence not guilt. She so wanted to believe him.

'I believe you,' she breathed.

There was a perceptible shift in his mood. He seemed less tense as if he had gotten away with something. Emmelina's feelings were lurching from impure thoughts to suspicion in a matter of moments. She really did not know what to think of the man standing before her. Just when she thought she might be able to trust him he asked her questions that fuelled her suspicions once more.

'Does anyone else know? Did you tell the constable?'

Wantonness quickly turned to anger as his only concern seemed to be whether anyone else knew about his tryst with Fayette. Her growing trust in him dissipated in an instant. The doubts re-appeared and she found herself questioning him, looking for inconsistencies in every word he spoke, but desperately needing consistency, transparency, and above all the truth.

'Why so concerned about who knows? Have you something to hide?'

'No. But you know what people are like in this city. They jump to conclusions. Just like you tonight. If the constable knew about me and Fayette he'd probably lock me up first, ask questions later. I don't want to spend my time in the castle gaol waiting for them to find out I'm innocent.'

Emmelina saw his point. It was a small minded community fed by a need to mete out justice in the most horrible of ways. The powers that be would be quick to point the finger of guilt. She had known of people languishing for months in the city's gaol awaiting trial only to die there before their innocence or guilt had been proven. She wouldn't want that to happen to anyone and certainly not to Severin. It was an irrational thought but she would not want him taken from her. Even though she had only known him for such a short time, the thought of him being removed from her life so soon left her feeling bereft. Just one more person to be added to the list of people loved and lost.

'I didn't mention it to him. He didn't ask,' she said quietly.

'Thank you. I've no right to ask it of you but thanks all the same.'

They stood close to each other, the silence between them throbbing with many unsaid words. Emmelina longed to fill the silence and the space between them.

'What do you think happened to Fayette? Do you think it was an accident?' he asked, jolting her out of the moment.

'I don't know. If it wasn't an accident then what did happen to her?' Before Severin had time to reply, she added, 'I can't really think about that at the moment.'

'You're tired. I should go,' he said, picking up his cap from the table and turning to go.

Emmelina knew if he didn't go she might do something, which could never be undone. She let him go.

'I am very tired,' she said, yawning.

'It's been a rough few days for you. How is Humphrey by the way?'

The sound of her husband's name jarred on her nerves and the vein at her temple throbbed with renewed force. She put her fingers to her temple hoping to halt the pounding in her skull.

'Are you all right?'

'Yes. I'm just really tired and the shock of seeing Fayette's body.'

'You were there?'

'Yes. Didn't you know? I was the one who found her.'

Fayette's lifeless body bobbing gently in the mist-covered water formed a picture in her mind. Her hand went to her stomach as it churned with repugnance.

'Are you sure you're all right. You look pale.'

He stood in front of her, looking uncertain as to whether he should leave or stay. A simple, primal need to be comforted, like she was a small child again overcame her. She wanted nothing more from him than to have his strong, comforting arms around her. She closed the gap between them, detecting for a moment, in his look, the same primal need in him, as a man, to comfort her. But the promising moment of intimacy was cruelly denied her as she heard footsteps from behind and swinging round, out of self-consciousness, she saw Dulcina appear at the top of the stairs, dressed in her night clothes.

'Oh sorry, miss,' Dulcina apologised, turning on the stairs to go back to her room.

'That's all right, Dulcina,' Emmelina replied, 'I was just seeing Master Browne to the door.'

Severin, looking relieved from his awkward dilemma, backed away from her. 'I'll say goodnight to you both,' he said, putting his cap on and tucking his curly black hair behind his ears.

He left them sharing an embarrassed silence but for different reasons. Dulcina because she was improperly dressed; Emmelina because she had acted improperly. Dulcina joined

Emmelina at the open door. They watched him walk down the lane.

'He's very handsome, miss, if you don't mind me saying.'

'I do mind you saying,' Emmelina scolded in jest, 'but you're right, he is handsome.'

The two women returned to the kitchen. Emmelina picked up the iron poker and stabbed at the dying embers.

'I'm going to make some peppermint tea, would you like some?' she asked Dulcina.

Emmelina expected her to refuse but to her delight Dulcina joined her by the fire. Speaking to Maud about the past had kindled an interest in making peppermint tea. Fayette had dried some mint leaves from the garden earlier in the summer and they had been stored somewhere in the larder. She went in search of them. When she returned with the mint and some weak ale in a jug she found Dulcina putting more wood on the fire. The young girl looked up and smiled. She reached over to the small pot and held it out for Emmelina to pour out the ale and add the mint leaves. The pot was placed back on the flames and the two women sat in silence watching the embers mutate and the flames lick round the small charred iron pot. It was an easy silence. The smell of peppermint filled the room accompanied by the comforting sound of bubbles popping as the tisane came to the boil. They had both had a gruelling day. Emmelina reflected on the capricious nature of life. How it could change in an instant sometimes in a good way but, more often than not, for her, in a bad way. A bond of sorts was forming between her and Dulcina, one of sorrow.

Chapter 19

Guido sat at his desk looking out of the window onto the cloister below. He had been working on a manuscript, meticulously penning an elaborate coronet into the margin beside the letter 'E', which he had scripted in ochre-coloured ink the day before. The text was in Latin, a language he was more at home with than the native language he had to learn when he came to England.

The scriptorium had an air of suppressed silence. Each of the study carrels was occupied with studious monks applying themselves to the task at hand, only a drawn curtain separating them. The only sound Guido could hear was the purposeful scratching of quills on parchment. He found it stifling and longed to get out. Unable to leave, his mind began to wander. He couldn't help himself. Like an addiction, his thoughts focussed on his favourite topics. Women and sex. The face of the young woman, laid upon the scriptorium floor, entered his head. For some reason he couldn't get her out of his mind. Every time he thought of her the inevitable stirring of his loins began. He picked up his pen knife and began chiselling the outline of her face in the stone slab framing the window. It took some time as he had to be as quiet as possible. The Sub Prior would probably be asleep in his carrel as usual but still he didn't want to wake him.

He looked at his efforts and decided it was amateur and not worthy of the subject. The image was too small and did not do justice to her large eyes and straight nose. He began again, this time making the image much larger and adding more detail. He imagined it in colour. He gave her a jewelled necklace around her throat to replace the image he had of the dark marks upon her pale skin. To honour her and give her the respect he thought she deserved he added embellishments to her wimple. A stitched embroidery pattern in golden thread interspersed with cerulean jewels at her throat to match her eyes. He gave her high cheekbones and a solemn downturned mouth. He hadn't seen her smile and in any case it seemed inappropriate to give her a happy demeanour. He began to get aroused. His erection intensified. He looked down at the growing bulge under his cassock and knew from previous experience he would have to relieve himself. Drawing the curtain back, he crept out of the scriptorium and went upstairs to the privacy of the monk's dormitory.

When he had finished he made his way to the lavatorium in the cloister. As he bent to wash his hands he heard voices. He twisted round to see Gilbert Garlick walking with the Sub Prior across the cloister. They were making their way towards the Prior's private lodgings and they appeared to be having a disagreement. He hoped they wouldn't notice him but then he heard Gervaise's familiar bellow.

'Guido.'

Guido shook the cold water from his hands. He would be in trouble again for not being where he should be.

'Come here.'

Guido wiped his hands on the front of his cassock and ran towards them.

'Where should you be now?'

'In the scriptorium sir, but I...'

'Never mind that. I could use your help. I want you to fetch Brother Jacquemon.'

Guido stopped; glad to be sent off in search of Jacquemon.

'Where will I find him, Sub Prior?' he shouted after them.

'In the infirmary helping Brother Paulinus. And be quick about it,' Gervaise snapped back.

Guido quickened his step and headed towards the infirmary. Once inside, he scanned the sick beds on either side of the room as he made his way to the very far end. He spotted Brother Paulinus first, standing by the bedside of a young woman. She had lost all her hair and her face was covered with pustules. She appeared to be ranting in a foreign tongue whilst writhing about on the mattress. Brother Jacquemon was holding her down whilst Brother Paulinus applied an ointment, made from mercury, to her face. Guido noticed her gown had become loose, exposing part of her ample breasts. His loins stirred involuntarily. Paulinus saw Guido staring at the poor woman. He re-adjusted her gown before addressing him.

'Yes Guido.' His tone was terse. 'What do you want?'

'The Sub Prior wishes to see Brother Jacquemon at once.'

Paulinus tut-tutted. 'Can't it wait? You can see I'm busy.'

Guido could tell Brother Paulinus didn't like him much. It didn't matter what he said or how he said it, Paulinus would always be curt with him.

'I don't think so. I was sent in haste.'

Paulinus sighed heavily. 'Very well then. Take over from Jacquemon.'

'But...'

'Just do it.'

He glared at Guido. Guido knew that look. Paulinus was not to be crossed. Jacquemon shuffled out of the infirmary leaving Guido to restrain the sick woman. Taking hold of the woman's arms, Guido set about pinning her to the bed. His grip was far stronger than old Jacquemon's. He leaned in closer to her feverish body and found himself repulsed by the rank smell upon her damp skin. Still, he thought, he might be able to touch her when no-one was looking. A twitch between his thighs urged him on but when he looked into the woman's putrefying face his ardour dampened.

Paulinus worked on in silence. When he had finished applying the ointment he spoke.

'You can let go now. I'm finished. I have no more need of your services.'

Paulinus waved him away and picking up the vessel of ointment turned his back on Guido. Guido could not ignore the opportunity, which had presented itself. With the deftness of a pickpocket, he slipped his hand underneath the sick woman's garment, grabbed her breast and squeezed it hard. She cried out in pain. Paulinus swung round and glared at Guido.

'Get out,' he shouted in disgust. 'Have you no shame?'

Guido was already on his feet, heading for the exit. As he left he heard Paulinus muttering to himself. Something about bad apples.

Guido crossed the cloister and instead of returning to the scriptorium decided to go straight to the monks' private chapel to ask for forgiveness for his latest sin. The door leading to the Chapter House was ajar when he arrived and he could hear Sub Prior Gervaise talking, his voice raised in anger. He crept to the opening and listened.

'Why do I need to sign this document? Is my word good for nothing?'

It was Gilbert Garlick. Gervaise answered him in an exasperated tone.

'You don't seem to realise the seriousness of the situation you're in my friend. Have you forgotten what I've done for you?'

'No,' Garlick replied, like a contrite schoolboy, 'but you are asking too much of me. I have responsibilities.'

'You have responsibilities to God,' said Gervaise. Not being one to miss an opportunity to preach to the fallen, he launched into one of his Sunday sermons.

'*The sinner who desires to resist the Devil's temptation on this sun-filled day of grace must be armed with the sharp sword of confession, the piercing lance of bitter contrition, and the shield of required satisfaction...*'

Garlick interrupted. 'Yes, all right. I've heard enough.'

Guido leaned against the door so he could hear. The door, recently oiled, swung open and he fell awkwardly into the Chapter House and onto the tiled floor. Keeping his head down, afraid to catch the eye of the Sub Prior, he picked himself up but before he could stand Garlick had gotten hold of him and wrenched him to his feet.

'Are you in the habit of eavesdropping?' he demanded of Guido, shaking him violently. Now on the defensive, he turned to Gervaise. 'Is this the obedience training you give novices at this priory?'

Guido knew Gervaise would be furious with him and kept his gaze lowered in false shame. When he did look up he saw a red-faced Sub Prior. The spidery veins on his face seemed about to burst.

'Forgive me, I was...' began Guido in an attempt to offer up a lame excuse.

Garlick still held his arm tightly and it was beginning to hurt.

'Don't say another word.' Gervaise held up his hand to silence him. 'How long have you been standing there?'

'Not long, Sub Prior.'

'How long?' Gervaise bellowed back.

'Not long at all,' Guido stammered. 'Just a few moments.'

He tried to release Garlick's grip but the man held tight.

'What did you hear?'

'Nothing, I swear.'

He let out a cry as Garlick twisted his arm. Gervaise recognised Garlick's violent mood and thought it wise to caution him.

'That's enough, Garlick. You can let him go now.'

Garlick pushed Guido away slamming him into the back of the door.

'Get back to your work,' Gervaise ordered. 'I'll deal with you later.'

Guido backed out of the room, his head bowed in fear, not deference and hurried down the covered walkway, which led to the scriptorium. His absolution would have to wait till the sacrament on Sunday.

Chapter 20

The vast aisled nave of Blackfriars Priory was full of worshippers for the Sunday Service. Gilbert Garlick stood with his wife and four young children at the front of the congregation directly opposite the stone pulpit. He wore a navy woollen cap with a mantle of sapphire blue velvet and sturdy leather boots. His eyes were a striking cobalt blue and when he looked at you they had a disquieting intensity about them. He held himself upright with an air of superiority. His wife, Hazel stood next to him, looking small and vulnerable. She wore a loose fitting, full length gown of embroidered damask and a wimple of cream silk. The children fidgeted and squabbled amongst themselves. Gilbert ignored them. Instead, he scowled at his wife when they became overly boisterous. She reacted by immediately scolding them.

To their left stood Teylove with his wife. She was much taller than him but had the same mean spirited, pinched expression. Next to them were several merchants and members of the city council whom Emmelina recognised. Behind the regular members of the congregation stood a rag bag of people. Journeymen, paupers, foreigners, travellers. All eager to hear what the Sub Prior had to say. The Blackfriar's sermons were very popular in the City, raging against sinners and heretics such as the Lollards. Sermons were held in English and not in Latin and so even those with little education could understand what was being said. They reached out to the ordinary man in a way the Abbey did not. The Abbey stood for ostentation and royalty whereas Blackfriars stood for a simpler way of life, reflected in their architecture and form of worship.

Emmelina stood with Dulcina. Since her husband's illness she had not been to church and probably would not have gone had it not been for Dulcina who wanted to pray for the soul of her father and didn't want to attend church on her own. Emmelina had agreed to go with her. Besides, in a community like Gloucester her absence would be noted and her life made more difficult once Humphrey was well again. She hated the hypocrisy of the clergy preferring her own simple faith. Her own hypocrisy in attending church services she despised, sickened her but she came to terms with it by telling herself it was a question of self-preservation rather than any false religious conviction.

Gervaise entered the cavernous nave from behind the pulpitum, a screen erected to separate the nave from the monks' private chapel. Well attended and popular masses were held in the nave every day. As he made his way to the rectangular, stone lectern, a reverential hush descended upon the assembled worshippers. The lectern was carved with the ancient monogram of Jesus. IHS, meaning, 'in the name of God'. When she thought about the terrible things, which had been done 'in the name of God', her soul wept with despair. The crusades, instigated by the Roman Catholic Church, were one example. How could anyone call themselves Christian when they urged the faithful to go on 'armed pilgrimage'? It was beyond comprehension. The very phrase was a contradiction.

Gervaise placed his podgy hands firmly on the plinth and then, having inspected his flock for several seconds, began his sermon.

'God wants us to walk in love but Satan wants us to walk in lust. Lust corrupts the most faithful of our flock.'

He looked up from his prepared text and scanned the room to check he had their attention.

'Unless there be a true and hearty confession of our sins to God, we have no promise that we shall find mercy through the blood of the Redeemer.'

Gervaise paused to allow a few murmured 'amens' to pass amongst the congregation. Garlick's children were fidgeting at the front. Gervaise scowled at the older boy, who immediately looked as though he were about to be struck by a bolt of lightning and sent to eternal hell. He looked away from the Sub Prior and buried his head in his mother's skirts.

96

'So rise, miserable one, from the night of sin, open the windows of your heart and let in the light. Through this you can see the specks of your conscience, the ugliness and impurity of your life.'

Emmelina listened to the first few minutes of his sermon but found her thoughts drifting. How often had she stood in the nave, next to Humphrey and listened to the Prior talk about sin. Why were the monks so concerned with sin? Was it because they were immersed in it themselves?

'My text this morning consists of three words, "I have sinned."'

She watched the faces of the congregation as Gervaise spewed out his doctrine of a vengeful and hateful God. A mixture of terror, guilt, hopelessness and confusion showed. Only the monks' faces remained impassive. An occupational skill. Her attention was drawn back to Gervaise when she heard Gilbert Garlick's name.

'And so, let us give solemn thanks and praise, with one heart and one voice, to our gracious benefactor, Gilbert Garlick, who by his generosity has surely secured his place in heaven. Glory be to God. Amen.'

Sub Prior Gervaise then asked the congregation if anyone wished to receive the Sacrament of Unction although he kept his gaze on Gilbert Garlick. Gilbert Garlick left his wife's side and strode with purpose to be the first to receive the sacrament. Jacquemon approached him with the silver chalice containing the blessed oil. Making the sign of the cross Gervaise anointed his forehead with the oil saying:

'As with this visible Oil, thy body outwardly is anointed...'

Several more sinners moved forward and formed a queue.

'...and send thee release of all thy pains, troubles, and diseases, both in body and mind and to pardon thee all thy sins and offences committed by thy bodily senses, passions, and carnal affections.'

And that was it, thought Emmelina. Go forth and commit sinful acts and then anoint yourself with oil while the Sub Prior says a few words to you and all your sins are washed away. Until you sin again and then you'll have to repeat the ritual. The hypocrisy of the church had no bounds and this thought sickened her. She considered her own 'carnal affections' and had no pressing need to be pardoned of any sin or offence against God. Her conscience was clear. If she did not commit sin and led a blameless, loving life, every day of her life, then she would have no need to be absolved of any wrongdoing. The church had invented the notion of eternal damnation to frighten people and make them go to church. It seemed to her the church was obsessed with sin. No matter how often they preached against it, it hadn't stopped people from sinning, otherwise confession would not have been invented. She looked around her. What would they all think of her if they knew her thoughts? But they didn't and nor would they. It was her secret. Her life depended on it.

Maud had warned her not to go to the hill but as she stood watching the city's sinners walk up to the Sub Prior and be freed of all sin she developed a pressing need to go there again.

Chapter 21

That night Emmelina resolved to visit the hill despite Maud's cautionary words.   Her greatest fear had been Humphrey waking in the night and finding her gone. Now he was ill, and she slept in the other room, she was able to leave the house undetected. This new opportunity, which had opened up was too great a temptation to ignore. As she passed Humphrey's bedroom, she stopped, putting her ear to the door to listen. Confident he was asleep; she left the house and made her way to the hill.

The night sky was clear and free of cloud and awash with twinkling stars. The moon shone bright enough to help her pick her way through the overgrown grassy path.   She was particularly careful as she passed by Maud's house. Maud kept odd hours and it wouldn't have surprised her to see her wandering around in her garden enchanting plants or whatever it was she did. Thankfully, Maud's house was quiet and no light could be seen. Emmelina quickened her pace. Her heart thudded like a tabor drum as she reached the higher ground and the clearing where she knew she would find her sanctuary.

The need to cleanse her soul of the poisonous preaching's of the church, consumed her. She longed to purge herself of the hateful, religious doctrine. The notion of a vengeful God who would inflict eternal suffering in the fires of hell and damnation to those unfortunate souls who failed to renounce their sins was objectionable to her. It seemed the church assumed sin was unavoidable; to Emmelina it seemed the church was immersed in sin. Was it not possible to live a sinless life here on earth, she pondered.   Emmelina believed in a loving God.   Her faith taught her it was possible to achieve oneness with God in this life.

Emmelina's faith was based upon the teachings of Marguerite Porete. She had been burned at the stake in 1310 in the city of Paris as a heretic because she had refused to withdraw her book, the Mirror of Simple Souls, or recant her views. Emmelina supposed one of the main reasons she was put to death was because she suggested we no longer needed to seek God through any Sacrament or Scriptures of the Holy Church. The church would be against such works for it threatened their very existence and authority. But it wasn't just her apparent criticism of the church that had got her into trouble. It was her references to the soul having no anxiety or fear about sin and feeling no reproach for doing the Soul's pleasure and expressing that desire nakedly. God is *"Lover, Loved and Love"*, she had written in her book, not hateful, vengeful and cruel and this made a lot of sense to Emmelina.

Emmelina had first met Finn the day after her parent's funeral. He stopped her in the street and told her he knew them well and asked her to meet him on Robin Hoodes Hill that night and he would explain more. Intrigued and eager to get away from Humphrey whom she was now living with she did. When she got there Finn was alone. He told her about her parent's faith and how they would want her to carry it on. She met him several times more, always on the hill where he told her that in France, in the region of Hainaut, where he came from, women had been allowed to live together in religious communities and practice their faith freely until the Catholic Church had decreed their principles perverted and banished them from the church. To Emmelina, Marguerite Porete was a heroine. Since then she sometimes fantasised about leading a religious life in an all-woman community where she could escape from Humphrey for good and spend her days in peaceful contemplation. It was pure fantasy, she reminded herself. No such communities existed in England and if they did the Catholic Church would soon see them banished.

Then one evening Finn told her she was ready to meet the other members of the faith and to undergo an initiation ceremony. Finn was so kind and everything he told her made such a lot of sense. She couldn't wait to belong. To belong to something.

When she arrived fully clothed at the appointed time she was taken to one side by a group of women who undressed her, washed her whole body with a solution mixed with the herb Rosemary, which was used for spiritual purification, then pulled a white slip made of soft silk over her naked body. There was an air of excitement as everyone's attention was upon her. Emmelina burned with anticipation. Finally, the women placed a veil of sheer silk over her head, which covered her face. Like a bride of God, she walked back to the clearing where Finn and the other men awaited her.

Finn welcomed her into the circle where a bank of candles burned in the centre. He beckoned her to stand in front of him and began the ceremony. After a few words welcoming her into the faith, Finn began to speak the words of his faith, which Emmelina repeated. Although she didn't understand the sacred words fully they impregnated within her a heightened sense of aliveness. When the time came he peeled her robe from her shoulders and kissed her on the lips. It was a tender kiss of love. The circle began to chant as Finn picked her up and laid her down on the ground, which had been covered with animal skins and thick woollen covers. Even now, remembering that night she can still feel the cold seeping into her spine as she lay expectant and trembling. She watched as he took off his robe and kneeled beside her. She had never seen a naked body before and never a man's even though Humphrey had by now violated her he never removed all his clothes. She closed her eyes as Finn climbed on top of her, caressing her body with his soft, tender hands. She had a powerful need to give herself to him, to be consumed by his maleness, so she could attain the zenith of God's love.

Her initiation ceremony had been the most exciting evening of her life. Intense feelings had been aroused within her, altering her in some permanent way. She had visited the hill regularly ever since.

Tonight, as always, Finn stood tall at the far side of the clearing. His white hair showing vividly against the darkness of the night sky. He nodded to her as she approached the circle. Emmelina nodded and smiled back at him. She had brought candles with her as always in her leather pouch, which she now lit and placed on the makeshift altar, returning to her place in the circle. More than twenty followers now stood in the circle of faith, more women than men. She glanced around. Everyone was barefooted and dressed in dark clothing, their faces, serene and loving. Her gaze lingered upon Damiana, a curvaceous woman in her twenties. Emmelina had passed by her in the street once. They had recognised each other, but carried on without speaking. It wasn't safe to acknowledge a follower of the faith. But now Damiana caught her gaze and smiled, openly acknowledging her.

Finn never prepared his sermons but spoke from the heart and from long and committed study of the Porete text, which he had himself translated from old French to English. It would be dangerous to carry around such a book. If caught, he would be found guilty of heresy, a crime punishable by death. Finn began the service. He spoke English with a foreign accent, having arrived in Gloucester some years earlier from northern France. He spoke in a lilting, almost poetic voice.

'Welcome. Let us begin.'

A light breeze blew through the forest, rustling leaves and swaying branches. The altar candles flickered but remained lit. Emmelina closed her eyes and concentrated on her breath, clearing her mind of its busy daily chatter. Emmelina listened to Finn's hypnotic voice.

"*Beloved, let us love one another, for love cometh of God. And every one that loveth, is born of God, and knoweth God. He that loveth not knoweth God; for God is love and he that dwelleth in love, dwelleth in God and God in him.*"

She could feel the stresses of the previous few days flow from her body as she relaxed. Finn continued.

'*Your Soul must give up Reason for it cannot fully comprehend God and the presence of Divine Love. When your Soul is truly full of God's Love it is united with God and thus in a state of union which causes it to transcend the contradictions of this world. In such a divine state you cannot sin because you are wholly united with God's Will and thus your Soul is incapable of acting sinfully. This is the effect of Divine grace, overcoming your sinful nature. It is in this state of being, united with God through Love that your Soul returns to its source. The presence of God is in everything.'*

'The presence of God is in everything,' they repeated.

As Emmelina's hips swayed back and forth, the divine energy entered her body, filling her with a sense of being connected to everything and everyone, something beyond her comprehension, something unknown. Finn walked along the circle, touching each person's forehead with the flat of his hand while repeating:

"Our Souls have the light of Faith and the power of Love as our mistresses. We have permission to do all that pleases us, by the witness of Love. Our Souls give to Nature whatever she asks."

Finally, he reached Emmelina. As soon as his hand touched her forehead a hot rush of blood to her head left her feeling faint and woozy.

"Let our Souls go forth to the ravishing Farnearness where we will find peace upon peace of peace and our souls will be free and noble and unencumbered."

Emmelina crossed over into a higher dimension of consciousness. An annihilated soul whom God was honouring with the glimpse of the glory of her Soul.

'The presence of God is in everything,' she breathed.

The chanting became louder and more feverish. Finn returned to Damiana. She was swaying fervently, her eyes closed, her dark hair strewn across the pale skin of her face. She stopped swaying and closed her eyes when Finn cupped her face and kissed her lightly on the lips. His hands moved down her body to the rope around her waist and untying it he placed his hands inside her woollen cloak and gently removed it from her shoulders. It dropped to the earth, exposing her large breasts, the curve of her belly and the thicket of dark hair between her legs. Damiana moaned. Her eyes remained closed. The chanting increased in fervour. Finn's hands moved across Damiana's smooth body, touching her shoulders, breasts, belly, back and finally thighs. By this time he was kneeling on the ground, his hands cupping her taut behind. He buried his face in her mons. Damiana's moans increased. She grabbed Finn's hair to steady herself. After a while, he traced his tongue upwards to her navel, lingering a while at her breasts and finally kissed her again on the lips. Every movement, every touch was done with the utmost tenderness and respect. Finn turned to the others.

"Let us dissolve, melt, join and unite with one another so that we may go forth to the ravishing spark and light of the annihilated Soul."

There were no words, just sounds. Finn led the chanting. Others joined in, chanting and swaying.

Emmelina turned to face a woman she knew only as Rowan. They smiled at one another and then kissed. Emmelina tenderly re-enacted Finn's moves, removing the woman's cloak to reveal a boyish body. Angular and shapeless, she had small breasts and fine sand-coloured pubic hair. As Emmelina traced her hands across Rowan's body she could feel her bony skeleton. Rowan gave out a low moan as Emmelina tasted the saltiness of her mons. Her caress ended as Finn's had done with a kiss on Rowan's lips. An ache in between her legs intensified and was now pulsating, presaging her urge to be united in bliss with those present. She had not to wait long. Finn gave the signal to hold hands and come together in a close huddle in the middle of the clearing.

"We have honoured our bodies. Now let us conjoin in a blissful union of Souls without sin."

Behind her, a hot hand parted her thighs and searched with fevered enthusiasm for her cleft of Venus. She almost buckled with the sensation. She didn't turn to see who it was. The anonymity added to the pleasure. He worked on her for a few moments, then gently brought her to her knees and entered her from behind. He continued to work on her, bringing her to her first orgasm of the night.

Chapter 22

In anticipation of Maud's visit Emmelina had set a pot of weak ale to boil on the fire and added some clumps of dried mint. She missed the company of Fayette and hoped Maud would have more time to spend with her this morning. Maud was always so cheerful and positive. It made Emmelina realise just how miserable she had become living under the same roof as Humphrey. She had sent Dulcina out to do some shopping at the market and told her to take her time.

'That's a welcoming smell,' Maud commented as she walked into the kitchen.

Emmelina beamed. 'Can you stay and drink some tea with me?'

Maud placed her bag on the table. 'I'm not in any rush today. A cup of tea is just what I need after my walk here.'

She sat down by the roaring fire and waited for Emmelina to hand her a cup of steaming tea. Emmelina had already set out the cups and she now carefully poured the peppermint tea. She joined Maud who had stretched out her legs and was warming her feet by the fire.

'You talked about my mother yesterday but said very little about my father. What was he like?'

Maud continued to warm her feet, flexing her toes up and down. 'I didn't know your father as well as your mother. He was away for months at a time.'

'That must be why I don't have any strong memories of him.'

'He was a good man. Well educated and he loved your mother. He taught her to read and encouraged her to use her gifts. Not many men would do that.'

Emmelina thought about Humphrey. His lack of encouragement and his increasing indifference to her. Her mother had taught her to read but Humphrey had not looked upon the accomplishment with any pride. He seemed annoyed with her whenever she glanced at his business documents. A growing sense of respect for her father was matched with her wish for more memories of him.

'What did he do that took him away so often?'

'Your father was a wine merchant. He imported wine from somewhere in France.'

'Was it Gascony, by any chance?' Emmelina asked, thinking of the many barrels of wine that lay in the cellar.

'I think your mother mentioned he travelled a lot to a place by that name. I thought you couldn't remember much about your father's work?'

'I can't but there's an awful lot of wine down in the cellar with the word Gascony printed on the barrels.' A thought entered Emmelina's head. 'My father must have been a very wealthy man, mustn't he?'

'I suppose so.'

'So where did all his money go when he died? Who would that have gone to? He didn't have any family. At least no-one came forward to claim me as kin.'

'Do you know if he made a will?'

'Well if he did, he would have left everything to me. There was no-one else.'

For a moment she allowed her thoughts to run riot. She imagined a life of financial independence, without Humphrey. A life she could live on her own terms. But it was no use, she realised, even without Humphrey she would never be allowed to live a life like that. No woman would be left alone. A husband would come along and there would be no guarantee her life would be any different than it was now. Maud's voice brought her thudding back to reality.

'I don't suppose it's something you could ask Humphrey?'

'I've never really thought about it until now.'

Emmelina's loathing for her husband found a new level. Not only had he stolen her virginity, he had, in all likelihood, stolen her inheritance. She thought of the barrels of wine in the cellar he never shared with her. Her lack of freedom, like a prisoner without bars. The sour bile of hatred curdled at the back of her throat. Maud had no idea of her true feelings for her husband and she might not understand if she tried to explain so she decided it was best to change the subject. She made a mental note to look in Humphrey's chest for evidence of her father's will.

'What about your husband, Maud. What was he like?'

Maud smiled, as if she were remembering something pleasant. 'He was a good man, but very different to your father. He used to make me laugh a lot. Always happy, always in high spirits.'

'Do you miss him?' Emmelina asked.

'It's been ten years since he passed. I still miss him. But...' she said, placing her empty cup on the table. 'I have my cat Pomfrey to keep me company and I keep myself busy.' She stood up and poured out the tonic. 'I must be getting along. You stay here and finish your tea. I'll see to Humphrey. I won't be long.'

Emmelina detected a false cheeriness in Maud's voice but she didn't press her. Glad to accept any excuse not to see Humphrey, she let Maud attend to him on her own. She was still thinking about her father's will. She waited till Maud left the kitchen, finished her tea and went to the chest in the fore hall where Humphrey kept his old documents. She knelt beside the chest and first removed her outer garments and laid them on the floor. She had never shown any interest in the rolls of parchment, dry and brittle, that lay in the bottom of the chest. She lifted them all out and placed them on the floor, next to her clothes, then, one by one, unfurled them, looking for her father's name or for any reference to him. She worked quickly as she didn't want Dulcina or Maud to see her and ask awkward questions. It was not long before she came across what she was looking for. Unfurling the parchment and sitting on the floor, she read:

"*In the name of God, Amen. On 31 January 1483, in the first year of the reign of Richard III, King of England, I, Edmund Dabinett, citizen and wine importer of the city of Gloucester, being of sound mind and memory, make and set out my testament concerning my moveable possessions, in the following manner.*

First, I leave and commend my soul to almighty God, my creator and my saviour, to all the saints, and my body to be buried in the nave of the parish church of Holy Trinity, Gloucester, of which I am presently a parishioner.

In the event of the death of my wife, Sabrina Dabinett, I bequeath, to my only daughter, Emmelina Dabinett, each and every pearl that I own, or whatever sort it may be, large or small."

Emmelina read and re-read the passage where her father had clearly intended to leave everything he owned to her. The bile at the back of her throat returned. She was supposed to feel grateful to Humphrey for taking her in. How many times had he reminded her of that? A murderous anger filled her up to bursting. How had Humphrey gotten hold of this document? Had her father entrusted it to him for safe-keeping? It seemed odd it had not been destroyed in the fire. Perhaps her father had suspected something? She would never know now, unless she confronted Humphrey? The thought terrified her. There was no telling what he would do. She thought it through some more, staring at her father's words written on the parchment. What could she do? Nothing, she thought, laying down the document on her lap. She was a married woman and, as such, any wealth she possessed would belong to her husband. There would be no point confronting Humphrey. She would come off worse. A noise from the top of the stairs made her jump. She rolled the document up and threw it back in the chest, along with the other documents and her clothes. She closed the lid just as Maud appeared at the bottom of the stairs.

'He's asking for you,' she said, holding the empty cup of tonic.

'I'd better go,' Emmelina said, making her way past Maud on the stairs.

'Are you all right, Emmelina? You look upset.'

'I'm fine,' she replied, touching Maud's shoulder in a gesture of reassurance, whilst trying her best to smile.

'I'll call in tomorrow, then,' Maud told her, unaware of the seething anger consuming Emmelina as she climbed the stairs.

Before entering the bedroom, she took several deep breaths to calm herself. Being angry at Humphrey served no purpose and would only make her life more unbearable than it already was. As she told herself to forget the will and concentrate on making her life with Humphrey as palatable as possible, her inner spirit died another small death. With every small death, she became more downcast and dispirited. It was not a new feeling. There had been many small deaths. One thing she was certain of. There was nothing to be gained in dwelling on matters she had no control over. Her only chance of survival was to endure. One way she knew she could do this was to engage with him about the business. His illness had given her the perfect opportunity to immerse herself in something that would take her mind off the miserable circumstances of her life. She had not had chance to recount her meeting with Severin and so, determined to rise above her despondency, she opened the door with a well-practiced smile. Humphrey was propped up on a pillow.

'You were asking for me, husband?'

'Yes. I wanted to know how you got on at the Tanners' Hall.'

Relieved to hear that Humphrey wanted to see her to discuss business and not reprimand her for some misdemeanour, she sat by his bedside and recounted her visit with Severin. She hoped he would not detect anything in her demeanour or speech that would give anything away about her feelings towards him. Her feelings for her husband were well hidden for she had become well-practiced at hiding them. Even though he lay virtually helpless in his bed, the memory of his dark moods and rages played on her mind and still managed to paralyse her with fear. Fear replaced anger as she carried on her conversation with him.

It seemed strange talking to Humphrey about his business. He had never involved her and she didn't resent that because it would have meant spending more time with him, a prospect she did not relish. But here she was having a business-like conversation, albeit one-sided. One thing she could not take away from Humphrey was his good business head. Even though he was weak and his speech had been affected, his mind still appeared to be as sharp as ever. Although nothing had been said between the two of them Emmelina knew he was painfully aware of his predicament. He needed to carry on his business as best he could and there simply was no-one else but Emmelina. Perhaps that was why he was tolerating her, for the moment. They spent some time discussing the duties she needed to undertake on a daily basis to keep the business running smoothly, such as the accounts and the ordering of supplies. His mood had brightened, even though he was struggling to make himself understood. Occasionally, drool trickled from the side of his mouth and like a good wife she wiped his chin dry and dabbed at the corner of his twisted lips with a clean cloth. At any other time, this would have been met with wild irritation but like an injured animal who instinctively knew his captor was being kind, he lay propped up on his pillows and allowed her to tend to him. The change in his mood gave Emmelina the courage to venture on to less prosaic matters.

'Master Browne told me to tell no-one about your business with him. Why is that, husband?'

She needed to know more about Humphrey's business interests if she was to help him. It was as much in her favour as his to keep the business going during his illness and she needed to know if anything he was doing was in any way illegal.

'It has to do with the guilds,' he mumbled, 'such powerful organisations, they're supposed to protect members' interests but instead they're rife with politics, rivalry and power struggles. If anyone from the guild heard I was getting involved with work that was the business of the tanners it would provoke outrage. For the time being it's best kept quiet.'

'What guild do you belong to, Humphrey?'

'I'm a member of the Honourable Guild of Cordwainers. The Tanners have their own guild.'

The latter was said with an air of condescension as if he were superior to the tanners.

'So you aren't doing anything illegal?' she asked, relieved.

Humphrey gave out an exasperated but weak snort of laughter. 'Is that what you were thinking?'

Emmelina looked down at her hands. It was foolish of her even to ask the question.

'No, not really.' She lied. 'What guild is Severin in?'

It had been asked before thinking. Mercifully, Humphrey had not read anything into her interest in Severin Browne.

'He's a journeyman in the Cordwainer's Guild, thanks to me. He has some interesting ideas and he's a damn fine leatherworker.'

'I know...'

Again her words were out of her mouth before she thought. If she wasn't careful he would know she had been to Severin's house. She had to think of something to say. 'He told me about his work,' she said before he could question her further, 'when I went to see him at the Tanners' Hall.'

She waited for his reaction but there was none. Feeling more confident she continued. 'Would I need to be a member of the guild with the work I'm going to be doing for you?' she asked in all innocence.

His mood changed. 'Over my dead body,' he said with hateful menace. 'The day I see a wife of mine at a guild meeting is a day I hope never to see.'

He spat the word 'never'. He might as well have spat at her. The words hurt like birds pecking at her fleshy insides. She trembled with the force of them.

'You're tired. I've taken up enough of your time. I'll let you rest,' she said curtly and stood up to go.

Humphrey said nothing. Emmelina excused herself and left.

Chapter 23

Emmelina woke to the sound of a terrific storm. The rain, persistent and heavy, had woken her several times in the night with a start. The incessant hammering on the roof tiles and the howling of the wind, rattling through the creaking rafters, worried her. At times she thought the roof would fly off, such was the force behind the wind.

She had hardly slept when she heard someone knocking. She opened her eyes to a darkened room and the sound of the relentless rain. She lay there, waiting for Dulcina to answer the door. Whoever was knocking was not going away and seemed determined to be let in. Dulcina must be fast asleep, thought Emmelina. Begrudgingly, she dragged on some clothes and made her way downstairs. It was barely dawn. Opening the door, Emmelina was surprised to see Maud. She looked agitated.

'I'm so sorry to disturb you this early in the morning but I have to ask you something.'

'Could it have waited?' Emmelina asked, half asleep.

'Does Humphrey own any cattle?'

'Yes. They're grazing on common land over at Castle Meads. Why?'

'You need to move them.'

'What?' Emmelina was still half asleep. She was not much of a morning person and not in the best of moods. 'Did you come all this way just to tell me to move my cattle and at this hour?'

'I've had one of my visions.'

Emmelina wasn't quite sure what she meant but from Maud's tone of voice it sounded serious. She showed her into the kitchen where Maud began pacing the floor. Not like Maud at all, thought Emmelina. She was normally a paragon of calm.

'You have very little time. You must get your cattle to high ground as soon as you can.'

113

'Sorry but you're not making much sense. You've had a vision and I must move my cattle. Why?'

'There's going to be a terrible flood. By nightfall the river will have burst its banks and any cattle or livestock grazing near the river will be swept away by the force of the flood and that includes yours. Buildings and people with them. All will be destroyed.'

Maud was sounding more like one of those toothless soothsayers on The Cross prophesying doom and the end of the world. She sat down wearily as if burdened by a heavy weight. An uneasy silence followed. Emmelina decided to stoke the fire realising she had probably been a little sharp with her friend.

'I know it sounds bizarre and you probably think I'm some crazed old woman...'

'I don't think that at all. It's just a lot to take in and I haven't really woken up yet. I'm much better in the morning after a drink and something to eat.'

She turned to Maud and smiled. Maud smiled back, the friendship repaired. An easy flow returned to their conversation. Emmelina disappeared into the larder emerging with some thick slices of bread and cold boiled ham. Pouring them both a cup of weak ale, she took a few bites of her bread. A gulp of ale later and she was beginning to feel more awake and less irritable.

'Tell me about your visions. I don't really understand them. Have you had them before?'

'They started when I was very young. I thought they were just nightmares at first. They became so frequent, some nights; I didn't want to go to sleep. I didn't want to know what was going to happen the next day.'

Emmelina studied her friend's worried face. 'What do you mean? You didn't want to know what was going to happen the next day.'

'Because whatever I saw in my dreams happened in real life.'

114

An unnerving tingle at the back of her neck made her shudder as though a ghost had walked behind her.

'I used to think it was a curse when I was younger but now I realise it's a gift.'

'Did my mother have visions?'

'No. She was blessed with the gift of healing.'

'Oh,' she said. A vision of her mother smiling and tending to the sick came into her mind. 'So, what did you actually see in this dream, this vision, last night,' she corrected herself.

'I was stood on West Gate Bridge looking down at the river. The water was dark and murky with swirling grey mist. From under the bridge floated the dead body of a woman, horribly disfigured.'

Emmelina went cold. She remembered Fayette's body.

'As I stood there a deluge of water swept under the bridge, flushing the body towards me. The dead body came alive, reached up and grabbed me, pulling me into the water. The arches beneath the bridge crumbled and fell into the river. Then the bridge collapsed and I was swept away in the water. I was carried further and further down the river and all the time I was struggling to make my way to the bank. But then the water rose to the level of the bank and then cows and sheep and people started to fall into the water with me and we were all being swept away in the strong current. I woke up covered in sweat and knew I had to warn you.'

Maud drained her cup of ale.

'Whose dead body was it?' Emmelina asked, fearing the answer.

Maud remained silent.

'Who was it, Maud?'

'It was you, Emmelina.'

Emmelina held onto her cup tightly and stared into the fire.

'What do you think that means, Maud? Am I going to die?'

She looked up at Maud, wide awake now.

'I don't know.'

'But that's the second dream or vision or whatever they are you've had about me. None of it good.'

'I know and I don't know what to make of it.'

The women sat a few moments longer in silence, neither daring to voice their dark thoughts.

'I think it's all this business with Fayette,' Emmelina suggested. 'That's what the dreams mean, nothing more.'

'You're probably right,' Maud replied, in an attempt to reassure her.

'But what about the cattle?' Emmelina asked, deflecting the attention away from her. 'You think...'

'I don't think,' Maud cut in, 'I know. It's not just a bad dream. It's the feelings after the dream. I can't shake them. That's what's bothering me now. I only feel like that when something terrible is about to happen...' Maud saw the look on Emmelina's face. 'But if we act quickly, we can change the outcome. You must trust me, Emmelina.'

'I do trust you, Maud. You're about the only...no... you *are* the only person I do trust.'

'Then you must move your cattle,' Maud repeated.

'Do you have any idea how difficult that would be?'

'No. I have no idea but something is telling me it has to be done.'

Emmelina was never her best in the morning and her disturbed sleep hadn't helped her mood. She propped her elbows on the table and massaged her forehead forcefully. 'I wouldn't know where to start,' she groaned.

'Try,' was Maud's curt answer.

Emmelina's face softened as it crumpled into a smile as if she were laughing at some internal joke.

'You're a crazy woman. I mean that in the most respectful way. I admire your sense of conviction but I can see one problem. Well, two, actually.'

'What's that?'

'Where would I move them to and how?'

'That's not a problem,' Maud answered, batting the air as if shooing a fly. 'I've already thought of that on my way here. We'll move them to Painswick Common. Good high, grazing land.'

'We can't move cattle just like that?'

'Yes, we can. Why not?'

Emmelina tried to think of a reason why but couldn't come up with one. 'I suppose you're right. But how am I going to get them up there?'

'I'll help you. I'm not averse to herding cattle and I'm sure Dulcina will help.'

She rolled up her sleeves as if to demonstrate her willingness.

'How would we get them there? Would we have to drive them through the centre of the city?'

'Yes. That's the quickest way. Over the bridge, down West Gate Street to The Cross and out through the North Gate.'

'I can't do that,' Emmelina protested.

Maud rolled her eyes to the ceiling.

'I never thought a daughter of Sabrina's would be so difficult about everything.'

Emmelina gasped. 'Don't bring my mother into this,' she replied, tetchily.

'I'm sorry. But can't you see what you're doing? You're putting obstacles in the way of everything and looking for reasons why you can't do things instead of finding ways to do what's needed.'

'It's probably living with Humphrey for so long. I'm sure I was never this bad,' she sighed, in an attack of self-awareness.

Maud spoke in a soft, calming tone.

'I apologise. That really was cruel of me to say that. I'm just getting frustrated and we don't have time to sit here and argue. We have to get going and quick.'

117

'Humphrey,' Emmelina exclaimed, suddenly remembering him. 'What about Humphrey. What's he going to say?'

'What about Humphrey?' Maud answered, dismissing Humphrey as a problem in the same way as she batted the fly. 'You don't need to tell him, not yet anyway. Besides, he should thank you when he hears about the flood.'

'What if there is no flood?'

'Listen to that,' she said, pointing at the door.

They listened to the rain hammering against the outside door and the wind howling through the rafters above them. Emmelina went to the door and opened it. Raindrops were bouncing high off the ground and already the lane had become a puddled, muddy mess. Looking at the spread of the water now lying in the lane she began to see there might be something to Maud's vision. She turned to her.

'Let's do it.'

Chapter 24

'We'll have to drive them through the centre of the city and preferably before the market traders start setting up,' Maud announced.

Emmelina had forgotten. It was Wednesday, market day in Gloucester when the city would be packed. She heard hurried footsteps on the stairs. Dulcina was awake.

'So sorry, miss. I didn't think I'd slept in. I'll get breakfast ready now.'

'No need, Dulcina. We're going out.'

'In this, miss?'

Dulcina looked at the lashing rain.

'Yes. Grab some food from the larder. You're coming with us.'

'I'm coming with you?' she questioned, giving Emmelina a bewildered look.

'I don't have time to explain. Just hurry.'

The three women set out to walk to Castle Meads. Market traders were already streaming across the two bridges. A steady line of carts and pack horses were queuing in the rain to pay their toll to enter the city. As she crossed over the wooden bridge, it swayed beneath her. A panicky feeling took hold as she contemplated Maud's vision and wondered whether they would have time to get the cattle over the bridge before it collapsed. The thought of being stuck on a flood plain with no way of getting back home filled her with dread but she did not share it with the others.

When they reached the swollen river on the other side, Emmelina looked down at its banks. The water was already lapping over the side. She glanced at Maud. Maud simply raised her eyebrows as if to say 'Now you believe me'.

Once out in the open fields, the wind became fierce, whipping against their cheeks and swirling around their rain sodden skirts, making it hard to walk. Already, the ground beneath had become a squelching bog and several times they stumbled in the yielding mud.

They found Peter Brattle, Humphrey's cattle man sitting in front of a meagre fire in his cottage eating a piece of dry bread, blithely unaware of the impending danger to him and his small home. Emmelina had been thinking how she could get him to help them without stirring up too much suspicion. She knew if she said it was Humphrey's idea to move the cattle he wouldn't bother arguing with her or asking any awkward questions. She was right. She told him that he was in charge, they had come to help him and he must tell them what to do but that they had to move fast. Peter didn't object. He took three staffs from the side of his fireplace and handed them to the women.

'You'll need these. Once they get going they generally follow one another and won't be much trouble but we must herd them up first.'

They followed Peter across the field to a group of willow trees where the cows were sheltering from the driving rain. He shouted a few unintelligible commands at them, gave one or two a slap on the rump with his hand and, like a well-trained army, the cows moved slowly in the direction of West Gate Bridge. Peter led from the front with Maud on one side, Dulcina on the other and Emmelina taking up the rear. A few strayed out of line now and again but the women mimicked Peter by shouting and waving their sticks at them. By the time they reached the bridge the cows had formed an orderly queue.

The bridge had become busy, despite the rain, and was full of traders with heavy carts full of goods. Emmelina was mindful of the extra weight placed upon the bridge by the traders and her herd of cattle. She prayed they might cross without incident. The traders seemed oblivious to the danger they found themselves in and idled across the bridge. Emmelina could not contain her impatience. She wanted to be across before it gave way and tipped her into the cold rapids of the Severn just like in Maud's vision. She began shouting incomprehensible commands to the cattle in front of her, and waving her staff, giving the odd slap here and there to drive them on as fast as she could. A few of the traders shouted at her to stop before she trampled them down but she did not heed their warnings. When she finally reached the city side of the river and planted her feet on the solid ground of Ebridge Street, she said a silent prayer and thanked God for keeping her safe.

Emmelina was aware of everyone watching them, wondering what they were doing herding a bunch of kine through the city on market day. A few bad tempered comments were hurled at them as Peter shook his stick at the milling throng and shouted at them to move out of the way. Walking past her house with a herd of kine was something she thought she'd never be doing and it all seemed unreal. She looked up at the bedroom window, shielding her eyes from the driving rain and thought of Humphrey, lying in his sick bed, completely oblivious to the scene below him. What would he think of her walking through the street in full public view, the wife of Humphrey, the cordwainer, wet and mud spattered? Then she thought of Severin. What would he think of her if he saw her looking like a common peasant? That seemed to bother her more. She bowed her head and pulled her rain soaked hood over her face just in case she bumped into him.

Battling their way through the gauntlet of traders they finally reached the North Gate. Once outside the city walls their journey became easier. They kept to the road until they crossed the River Twyver. From there Peter took them across country. The road climbed steadily until they arrived at Painswick Common. The rain had not let up and the four of them were weary and soaked to the skin. They sat and ate the food Dulcina had taken from the larder before setting back down the hill. Emmelina asked Peter to stay away from his hut that evening using the excuse he would need to be close by to keep watch on the cattle. She gave him a few coins to find lodgings for the night in Painswick and having said their goodbyes, the three women then made their weary way back home.

They had been gone a few hours and in that time the River Twyver, a tributary of the River Severn, had already burst its banks and flooded the fields leaving the women no choice but to wade, thigh high through muddy water before they could re-join the road. The journey back was quiet. No-one had the energy to talk. They were soaking, hungry, cold and tired.

When they finally reached the city gates, they were a sorry sight. Like a band of vagrants, their clothes heavy with mud and their step weary with hunger they made their way down North Gate Street. Passing Severin's house, Emmelina once again hid her face and prayed Severin would not see her looking like a tramp. Despite the rain, the city was still busy with market traders and pilgrims. The streets had turned into nothing more than ankle-deep, muddy lanes. Grateful to arrive home, the women set about lighting the fire and preparing something to eat. Too weary to talk, they bustled around the kitchen with silent efficiency. They worked as a team, Dulcina lit the fire, Emmelina brought food from the larder and Maud helped prepare the peppermint tea. Once the fire was lit, Maud removed her outer garments and placed them in front of the fire to dry. She looked around her and noticed neither Dulcina nor Emmelina had removed theirs.

'Aren't you going to take those wet clothes off?' she asked. There was no reply. Sensing reluctance, on their part, to remove their clothes in front of each other, she added, 'We're all girls together. I'm sure you haven't got anything I haven't seen before.'

Dulcina blushed and Emmelina laughed. It had the desired effect of removing the awkwardness from the situation. Emmelina removed her wet clothes but Dulcina, still unsure, remained guarded.

'In a moment, you're going to look like the odd one out,' Maud coaxed her, as she draped her woollen clothes over the back of a chair and joined Emmelina by the fire.

'Don't look then,' Dulcina replied, turning away from them.

Maud rolled her eyes at Emmelina, in a good humoured way, and concentrated on pouring the tea, which had just come to the boil. Emmelina held out the cups to her. Moments later, Dulcina joined them, wearing only her undergarments.

'Now tell me that doesn't feel better to get those wet clothes off,' Maud teased Dulcina.

Dulcina giggled with embarrassment. Nothing more was said as the women sipped their tea in the steaming kitchen and listened to the rain pounding on the walls outside. The warm glow from the fire matched the warmth of their deepening friendship. It was the closest Emmelina had been to a family since the death of her parents.

Chapter 25

Emmelina slept well that night, despite the relentless battering on the roof above her by the lashing and unceasing rain.

When she woke the next morning she dressed hurriedly and after breakfast made her way to the river to see for herself whether Maud's vision had come true. The rain had turned to drizzle but as she walked along West Gate Street, the damage caused was easy to see. There was a smell of wet earth mixed with the sour smell of putrefaction. The streets leading to the river were eerily empty for the time of day. As she neared the Foreign Bridge she noticed a commotion taking place up ahead. She quickened her step. It seemed like the whole city had turned out to see the damage done by the storm. The city burgesses were standing around issuing orders. Carts piled high with lengths of wood were being ferried between the two bridges. Pushing her way through the crowd she finally reached the bridge. In every direction all that could be seen was flood water. Battered trows lay trapped under the bridge where they had been swept by the force of so much water trying to pass through such a narrow channel. Castle Meads, where her cattle had been grazing beneath willow trees only yesterday was under several feet of water. Peter Brattle's hut was nowhere to be seen, probably drifting out to the Bristol Channel by now. Bloated animal carcasses floated past her in the murky flood water. The small body of a young child, still wearing what looked like her night clothes, drifted past her before she had chance to look away. She remembered Maud's vision about the bodies in the flood and regretted not being able to warn anyone. Perhaps she could have saved that poor child.

She turned away and joined a crowd of people. Listening to their chatter she heard that several buildings and their inhabitants had been swept away in the early hours of the morning, whilst people had been asleep in their beds. Old Walter Bridgeward had been one of the victims. Emmelina had seen him only days ago, sitting outside his cottage, enjoying his retirement. It was too early to tell but it was likely hundreds more people, cattle and livestock had perished. Both bridges had taken a severe battering. The Foreign Bridge had completely collapsed and the West Gate Bridge had been dangerously undermined. They had been closed for safety reasons but the burgesses, as usual, were up in arms because of the effect this would have on local trade.

Maud's vision had come true. She was pleased she had trusted her friend and moved the cattle. At least Humphrey would be grateful, for once. But she could not shake her troubling guilt at not being able to save more victims of the flood. It would have been impossible, she knew, to warn anyone. What would she have said? She couldn't tell them about Maud's vision. Whilst she stood on the bridge watching the pandemonium an irate Gilbert Garlick approached her.

'Mistress Pauncefoot,' he greeted her curtly.

'Morning, Master Garlick,' she replied, equally formally.

'I hear you were seen herding cattle over the bridge yesterday with two other women. That seems a very strange occupation for a wife of a cordwainer. Did I hear that correctly?'

'You did, Master Garlick,' she answered him, 'Is that a crime?'

'Not in itself. But people are saying you must have known about the flood before it happened. But that wouldn't be possible would it?'

His right eyebrow lifted independently of the other, twisting his face into an unattractive, inquisitive grimace. His piercing eyes, once again, drilled into her.

'No, that wouldn't be possible,' she said, not elaborating.

She took a step back and bumped into an old woman leaning on the bridge. The woman turned around and swore at her. Emmelina stepped sideways in the other direction. Garlick moved his foot across, preventing her from moving away.

'A fortunate coincidence for you?'

'My mother always said there were no such things as coincidences. Did you know my mother?'

She studied his face.

'What happened to your parents was very unfortunate.'

He bowed his head in mock reverence. Emmelina made to leave but found she was trapped between the old woman, the wall and Garlick's foot which blocked her way.

'Please, let me pass,' she demanded, 'I must get back to my husband.'

'Ah yes, Humphrey. How is he these days? No-one has seen anything of him lately. Physician Teylove informs me you have dispensed with his services.'

Emmelina didn't like the way this conversation was going and didn't want to answer any more of his intrusive questions. Garlick unsettled her.

'My husband is improving, thank you, Master Garlick. And he'll be expecting me back soon so I'm sorry but I will have to be on my way.'

Garlick's foot remained in place. He stood a full foot taller than Emmelina, staring down at her with those eyes.

'Garlick. There you are. Alderman van Eck wants us to go with him to the Booth Hall to discuss the closure of the bridge.'

It was Bailiff Bliss, an acquaintance of Garlick's. Garlick looked momentarily annoyed at the interruption, then turned to Emmelina and smiled obsequiously.

'I'll call round to see Humphrey if I may now he's getting better. I take it he's well enough to see me?'

'I'm sure my husband would be delighted to see an old friend.'

He moved his foot allowing Emmelina to pass and moved off in the direction of the Booth Hall with the Bailiff. Emmelina took one last look at the devastation caused by the flood. In the distance she could just make out herds of cows on the far side of the river wading through the flood water looking lost and incongruous. She pulled her cloak tight around her and made her way back home through the mud. She crossed to the other side of Ebridge Street and walked slowly so as to keep well behind Garlick.

By the time she reached home Maud had arrived to attend to Humphrey. . Although he had improved, he was still too weak to make it down stairs and so remained bedridden. Maud was alone in the kitchen.

'People are talking about us,' Emmelina revealed.

'What do you mean?' Maud looked up from the fresh herbal mixture she was stirring.

'They're saying we must have known about the flood and that's why we moved the cattle.'

'Who's "they"?'

'That Gilbert Garlick. I don't like him. He makes my flesh creep. He asked me how I knew about the flood.'

'You didn't...'

'Of course I didn't say anything about your vision. I don't trust that man. I think he could cause trouble. He'll spread rumours about us I know it. I just get a bad feeling about him,' she paused. 'He wants to come and see Humphrey.'

'What's wrong with that?'

'I don't know. I just don't like him interfering. I just want to be left alone.'

'I'm sure it's nothing. Things will die down, you'll see.'

Emmelina wanted to share Maud's optimism, but all she was left with was an intense sense of dread mixed with sorrow and regret at the number of lives she wasn't able to save.

Chapter 26

The flood waters remained high for several days. Each day brought sad news for someone as the bodies of their loved ones were discovered. As the water began to subside, the bloated and rotting carcasses of kine, sheep, oxen and horses were exposed as well as those of men, women and children. Although she told herself it was wiser to stay away from the flood, her curiosity got the better of her and she decided to go down to the riverside to see the extent of the devastation. As she neared the bank she saw a murder of crows pecking at the flesh of a dead cow and further along she thought she saw the body of a small child but she turned away before the image set in her mind. The powerful torrent of water had ripped trees and bushes from the ground, smashed buildings and huts into driftwood, leaving many homeless, dead or missing. Peter's small dwelling was still nowhere to be seen. Those animals lucky enough to reach higher ground were now being rounded up and herded back towards Castle Meads. Bales of hay were being carted in to feed them. The riverside was busy once more with builders and tradesmen repairing the collapsed bridge and clearing away the debris left behind. Several people Emmelina knew were still missing, in all likelihood swept from their beds as they lay asleep so sudden was the torrent of water that swept through the city that night.

Maud had been right about the flood. Thank goodness she had listened to her and spared her cattle from such a terrible fate and saved the life of poor, sweet Peter. They were safe on Painswick Common and for the time being Emmelina resolved to keep them there.

The first signs of illness in the city's surviving cattle came a few days after the flood. Cows became unsteady on their feet and trembled as if cold. This was followed by laboured breathing, a lack of appetite and convulsions. The final stage, which came swiftly, was the appearance of blood leaking from the eyes, nose, ears and anus. Death was inevitable.

Within a matter of days, alarm bells began to ring amongst the city's farmers and traders when the animal death toll rapidly rose into the hundreds. Worried about the effect this would have on trade and visitors to the city the burgesses called an emergency meeting. Emmelina decided she would attend. Humphrey's outburst the other day when she had suggested to him she should go to the guild meetings during his illness had made her all the more determined. She also made the decision to keep this from Humphrey. Her interest in all matters of business had grown. She thought she knew enough about her husband's affairs to hold her own in a meeting of the city's burgesses. When Emmelina told Dulcina of her plan to attend the meeting she was surprised at her reaction. It seemed Dulcina agreed with her husband.

'They won't let you over the threshold,' Dulcina exclaimed, deftly plucking the feathers from a goose.

'They can't stop me. I shall tell them I'm attending at my husband's insistence.'

'But you aren't,' Dulcina said, adding naively, 'are you?'

'Well, no, but that's what I shall be telling them if they ask,' Emmelina countered.

'Do you think you should ask the master's permission?'

Whether it was the reference to Humphrey being her master or just frustration at Dulcina's lack of support, Emmelina snapped back at Dulcina. 'I think you should keep your thoughts to yourself if you haven't got anything encouraging to say.'

Even as the words left her mouth, she regretted them. Dulcina said nothing but kept her head down and concentrated on preparing the pasty-looking goose. Emmelina, furious at her diffidence stormed out of the kitchen.

She crept back upstairs and slipped into Humphrey's bedroom. He was asleep, breathing heavily. Carefully, she rifled through her clothes chest for something suitable to wear. Something which would convey her importance, her high status and hopefully make her feel more confident than she was feeling. She chose a heavily embroidered dress of scarlet cloth, trimmed with grebe, together with a high bonnet.

So engrossed in her search for suitable clothing, Emmelina had not noticed Humphrey's breathing. Fearing he might have died, she went over to check on him. Holding her breath, she bent her ear towards his mouth. She listened, watching for any signs of the gentle rise and fall of his chest. There was none. For a second, she thought he had gone. Then, without warning, he sucked in air, making a sound like a pig being slaughtered, grunted a few times then went back to sleep, breathing evenly. She studied his face, the thick neck, the hairs growing out of his bulbous nose. He revolted her.

She went back to the chest and picked through a few more things before creeping out of the room taking her clothes with her. She dressed in her bedroom, her thoughts lingering on the words she had just had with Dulcina. In a moment of self-awareness, she realised she was taking out the anger and frustration towards Humphrey on poor, sweet Dulcina. That was unforgiveable of her. Dulcina was a naive, young girl from the country who had no family. She would have to apologise to her before she left.

Fully dressed in her finery, she walked past Humphrey's door.

'Emmelina,' he shouted.

She jumped.

'In here now and don't send that girl in your place.'

Emmelina hesitated. He was bound to notice she was dressed in her fine clothes and ask what she was doing and where she was going.

'Emmelina,' he bellowed.

She could tell from the tone of his voice that he was getting impatient. It wouldn't be fair to send Dulcina in to him. He would probably throw something at her. She took off her hat and laid it outside the door. She gave up a silent prayer that her husband wouldn't notice anything different about her.

'Yes, husband. Did you want something?' she asked, putting on her sweetest voice and opening the door a crack.

'Here,' he growled.

She walked over to the bed, conscious he was glaring at her. A spark of pure anger appeared in his eyes.

'Where are you going dressed like that?' he demanded.

The terror and sickness Humphrey triggered within her resurfaced. For a second she didn't know what to say.

'Well?'

'Nowhere special,' she said, unconvincingly.

Humphrey stared at her, his piggy eyes flitting up and down, taking in what she was wearing. Humphrey was no fool. She only wore these clothes for special occasions.

'Wherever you are going I forbid you to go.'

'I'm not attending a guild meeting Humphrey. You have made your views on that quite clear.'

'Where to then? You're meeting someone?'

'No,' she protested. 'Nothing like that. If you must know I'm going to a town meeting to discuss what's to be done about the repair of the bridges.'

'That's for burgesses. Not a place for a woman. You're not going.'

Emmelina heard Dulcina's words. Perhaps she should have asked her husband's permission. But what would be the point. He would only have said no. Just like he was now. It seemed to her everyone was against her. Trapped, suffocated, repressed. Humphrey was controlling her from his sick bed and her own maidservant was castigating her in her own house. Something snapped inside her.

'You might be able to stop me from going to a guild meeting but I don't think it's fair to stop me from going to a meeting that concerns me. I am a citizen of this city and am entitled to go.'

'You are my wife and entitled to only what *I* say you are entitled to.'

131

Emmelina looked at her helpless husband. What would he do if she walked out and left him lying there, stewing in his own vituperative bile? He could hardly run after her. She wanted to tell him how she felt about him; how she hated him; how she despised him; how he repulsed her. But she didn't. She knew when he was well again she would suffer as never before. She took the middle road.

'I am entitled to be treated like a human being with respect. I'm sorry Humphrey but the meeting is important to us both and I am going to attend. If you like I'll report back to you in the morning.'

Emmelina had never seen her husband lost for words. He lay on the bed, his mouth half open to speak but no words came. She walked over to the door, halted and spoke over her shoulder.

'I'll send Dulcina in later to settle you for the night. Good night, Humphrey.'

Still no word from him. She closed the door behind her and went downstairs. Her heart was racing but this time she did not feel the accompanying tightness in her chest. She had raised her voice to him. The first time ever. A mixture of terror and triumph rose within her as she made her way down the stairs.

She found Dulcina in the kitchen, stuffing the goose with a deliciously smelling mixture of spices, quince and pears. Dulcina had turned out to be an excellent cook. Remembering her harsh words, she decided to apologise.

'I'm sorry, Dulcina. I shouldn't have shouted at you.'

Dulcina's innocent, sweet face brightened but all the same she didn't look up. 'That's all right, miss. I shouldn't have said anything.'

'I know you're only thinking of me but you don't have to worry. I'll be absolutely fine.'

Dulcina gave her a questioning look. 'I hope so, miss.'

Chapter 27

The Booth Hall had a number of uses. Its main use was as an exchange or guild market for the sale of wool and leather but it also doubled as the Assize Court. Above the entrance was the city's colourful coat of arms. In the top two corners were the red and white roses of York and Lancaster. Beaming rays of sunshine radiated from them towards the picture of a boar, a red quince lodged in his jaws. The boar represented the King, Richard the Third, who had given the city its charter in 1483. Below these were the horseshoes and nails, symbolic of the trade of ironwork and smithery in the city. Positioned in the centre was a red-handled sword, its tip pointing upwards and piercing the fur-trimmed, purple `Cap of Maintenance'. The hat was traditionally worn by the nobility under their coronets. It was also a symbol of authority for the mayor.

Emmelina found the Booth Hall packed with prominent burgesses, traders, and farmers. All men. The hall was long and lofty, being supported by a double column of substantial chestnut timbers. A set of weighing beams used for weighing packs of wool and leather hung incongruously above the assembled gathering. The clay floor had been strewn with dried stalks of barley that morning. When she walked in, the hall was buzzing with the sounds of animated conversations between several, but clearly, separate groups of men. Separate in terms of trade and status within the community. All talk ceased when Emmelina appeared and those with their backs to her turned round to stare, the shock clearly visible on their faces. No-one spoke and for several seconds, the only sound was the swishing of her skirts across the barley strewn floor. She seemed to glide past the assembled men until she arrived at her chosen point, by the chestnut beams.

At the end of the hall sat Mayor Rawlings, Bailiff Bliss, Alderman van Eck, Constable Rudge, Gilbert Garlick and Lord Malverne. Lord Malverne had lost a great number of his herd to the disease and word was he was not best pleased. They were having a heated discussion but this now stopped as they noticed her arrival in the hall. Gilbert Garlick's eyes burned through her. Constable Rudge rose to his feet but was pulled back down by Lord Malverne who looked angry and impatient. He then spoke sharply to Rawlings and with that the mayor took hold of his gavel and called the meeting to order.

Fearing the worst, Emmelina pressed her back against the massive chestnut beam waiting for them to say something to her. She was conscious of her bonnet balanced on top of her head and she began to regret her choice of clothes. She was noticeably over-dressed. Surprised she hadn't been frog marched out immediately on entering and wondering whether it would have been better for that to have happened rather than what she feared was about to happen, she stiffened readying herself.

'Mistress Pauncefoot,'

She pressed hard against the solid wood until the bony parts of her spine hurt.

'Are you lost?'

The men held nothing back and loud laughter filled the room. Mayor Rawlings blasted the sounding block. Garlick smirked. Emmelina stood her ground, despite being aware of the colour rising in her cheeks.

'No, sir. I am not lost. I'm here representing my husband who is unable to be present due to his ill health but nevertheless wishes to have some input into this meeting through his appointed representative. That is me,' she added at the end of her prepared speech.

The men mumbled in their little groups. There was more discussion at the bench and then Lord Malverne spoke impatiently to the mayor.

'Just get on with it, for God's sake.'

Relieved she was not to be questioned further or worse thrown out, she straightened up and, adjusting her bonnet stood to listen to what everyone had to say. The main worry was that news of the sickness had spread beyond the city walls and traders were beginning to take their business to other markets like Worcester to the north, and Bristol to the south. The danger was once trade was lost to these cities it would never return. If that happened, the city's fortunes would decline and trade would go elsewhere. The wealthy burgesses, threatened by the loss of income and wealth generation were on edge. Instead of constructive discussion aimed at resolving the problem all Emmelina witnessed was arguing and attacking amongst the various members representing different vested interests. Corn from the Vale of Gloucester, to the north and east of the city, would have to be transported as far as Bristol by cart, adding greater expense to the exporters of corn, whereas cloth from the Stroud area could more easily be taken to Bristol and loaded onto boats there without too much additional cost. However, importers of wine would have to have their cargo unloaded at Bristol and carted to Gloucester. The trow men were up in arms over this as they would go out of business altogether if they could not bring goods between Bristol and Gloucester. It seemed to Emmelina everyone kept moaning and complaining but no-one so far had come up with anything constructive about what to do. The mood of the room changed, however, when old Brother Jacquemon, who had been standing at the back of the hall with Sub Prior Gervaise, moved forward.

'The Lord, Jesus Christ has placed a curse upon this city,' he announced in a deep, doom laden voice, holding above his head a copy of the Bible and waving it around. 'The Lord has sought to cast upon us a grievous murrain as prophesised in the Book of Exodus.'

He opened the book at a page he had bookmarked and began to quote from it.

"*Then the Lord said unto Moses; Go in unto Pharaoh and tell him. Thus saith the Lord God of the Hebrews. Let my people go, that they may serve me. For if thou refuse to let them go, and wilt hold them still, behold, the hand of the Lord is upon thy cattle which is in the field, upon the horses, upon the asses, upon the camels, upon the oxen, and upon the sheep: there shall be a grievous murrain.*"

Everyone remained quiet as Jacquemon, his eyes wide and staring continued.

'God sees everything, he sees there is sinfulness here and God has sought to punish us all. This is the plague as prophesised in the Bible and we must endure.'

He crossed himself and everyone in the room followed his gesture, murmuring 'Amen'. For several more moments, no-one spoke. All eyes were upon the old monk. Gilbert Garlick stood up.

'Not everyone has been affected by the flood.' He fixed his stare upon Emmelina. 'Is there not someone here whose cattle were spared? Someone who drove their cattle to high ground only the day before the flood came?'

People muttered amongst themselves.

'Aye, that be true,' a farmer could be heard to concur, nodding his head. Others nodded in general agreement.

Emmelina's throat and chest began to constrict as if some unseen energy, demonic in nature, were pressing down against her. The men continued staring and pointing at her.

A small commotion started at the back of the hall as the men stood aside to let someone through. It was Severin. Her sadness at Fayette's death remained raw but her concern regarding Severin's involvement or otherwise in her death, had not waned. It was made all the more bewildering by her feelings for him. The same old questions kept going round in her head. What was his relationship with Fayette? And the worst one, which she dared not form fully in her mind. Did he have anything to do with her death? Every time she thought about it she tried to tell herself it was all innocent and he had told her the truth about his evening with her. She so wanted to believe he had told her the truth.

He was wearing a pair of tight leather breeches, which were tucked into high boots and despite the coldness of the evening he wore only a coarse woollen shirt, open at the neck and tucked into his trousers, which were held up by a wide leather belt. Emmelina's heartbeat quickened and the colour in her cheeks rose for a second time that evening but this time for quite different reasons. He stopped in front of Jacquemon.

'This is no plague. I've seen this disease before.' He addressed the old monk. 'With respect, Brother Jacquemon this is not a plague being visited upon us by God. It is as a result of the flood and nothing more.'

The shock, fear and despondency caused by Jacquemon's outburst was quickly replaced by rising hope. The accusation made against Emmelina forgotten, for the moment. Feverish questioning of Severin by almost all of those assembled ensued. Mayor Rawlings interrupted the chaos by striking his gavel soundly, several times upon the sounding block, his voice barely audible above the racket.

'Order, order. I call this meeting to order.'

No-one was listening. Severin raised his hand in a calming gesture. The crowd quietened, eager to hear more. Severin held the floor.

'As some of you know, I came here from Italy. Whilst I was working in the leather trade by the River Adige one year, a terrible flood hit the city. A few days later the cattle started to get ill and die. I'm sure this is the same thing.'

'How can you be so sure?' Lord Malverne asked impatiently.

'The cattle had exactly the same symptoms, my Lord.' Severin answered in a reverential tone.

'And what did they do to stop it?' asked Lord Malverne impatiently.

'They had to burn everything.'

Severin scanned the room for their reaction. It was a drastic solution but he knew from experience it was the only one.

'Burn everything?' Lord Malverne repeated, his eyebrow arched in disbelief.

'Yes, my Lord. They burnt the carcasses of all the dead animals. Any animal showing signs of the disease were killed and burnt. Huge pyres burned, day and night. They also burnt the ground the cattle grazed on, my Lord.'

'We can't do that. It would ruin us,' shouted one of the burgesses.

Others joined in.

'It's the only way,' Severin added solemnly, 'if you don't, it will spread from the cattle to us.'

Jacquemon rifled through his bible, alighting at last on the passage he was searching for.

'He's right,' he shouted, tapping his hand on the page and holding his bible aloft. '*Exodus 9:10. "And they took ashes of the furnace...and it became a boil breaking forth with blains upon man, and upon beast."*'

The meeting descended into a chaotic shambles, each vested interest group remonstrating with whoever would listen. No-one had considered the illness affecting the cattle could spread to humans. The consequences were grave. No-one present in the Booth Hall had been around when the Great Plague hit the city in 1349 but many still talked about it. Back then, when the citizens of Gloucester started leaving the city in large numbers the civil authorities ordered them to be fined for every day of absence. They feared there would be no-one left to run the city. They also ordered no travellers from Bristol should be allowed to enter the city. Despite these precautions, thousands died, reducing the city's population by two thirds. It decimated trade.

Emmelina kept her eyes on Severin but not once did he look at her. Lord Malverne spoke up.

'You are asking us to make a decision, which has far reaching consequences for the city and everyone's livelihood. How sure are you about this?'

Severin appeared to falter momentarily. Emmelina intervened.

'My Lord, if I may speak?'

She waited for his permission before proceeding.

'Very well,'

He nodded his assent.

'As you know, my husband's cattle have been moved to higher ground where there is no flood water and they are as healthy as before the flood, despite having grazed on the same land only days before. This surely gives some credence to Master Browne's theory and his proposal for dealing with it,' she gestured.

Garlick stood up.

'That's what I've been trying to...'

Lord Malverne cut him off. 'Be quiet, Garlick. Sit down. Let's stick to the facts.'

Garlick, having had the wind blown out of his sails, reluctantly sat down. He fixed Emmelina with a gut boiling stare. Lord Malverne continued.

'Are you supporting Master Browne's proposal, Mistress Pauncefoot as to the possible cause of this disease?'

'I think it very possible, my Lord. And if Master Browne is right, we, that is, the city, must act swiftly to prevent it spreading from them to us.'

'Does anyone else have anything to add as to the cause of this terrible affliction?' the mayor asked, not acknowledging her contribution.

There were a few murmurings from the floor but no-one spoke up.

'Very well. Master Browne has proposed that to deal effectively with this problem we must begin burning all affected cattle and livestock, including their grazing land. I suggest we put Master Browne's proposal to a vote. All those in favour, raise your hand.'

Emmelina, not certain whether she was allowed to vote, raised her hand anyway.

'I'm sorry, Mistress Pauncefoot. Please lower your hand. Your vote cannot be counted. You're not a burgess or a member of a guild,' Mayor Rawlings addressed her.

'Oh, for God's sake,' yelled Lord Malverne, 'let her vote. Count it as a proxy vote on behalf of her husband.'

Emmelina, who had lowered her hand, now thrust it proudly in the air to be counted. She looked around the room and from the show of hands it was obvious Severin's proposal had been carried. She had not only survived the meeting, she had been allowed to speak and vote. She couldn't help but smile to herself as she turned to leave, her head tilted upwards in a triumphant pose. She walked past Severin without looking at him but aware of his presence and out into the night air before anyone could spoil the exhilaration swelling in her chest. She understood now what Humphrey meant about power struggles and politics.

Before the meeting ended, Garlick approached Gervaise. He drew him into the corner of the hall and spoke quietly to him. Loyal Jacquemon stood close by.

'Something must be done about that woman. I don't trust her. Do you know her husband is unwell and no-one has seen him for days? Physician Teylove tells me she has dispensed of his services and is allowing some old woman to treat him.' He was aware his voice was getting louder. Looking around to make sure no-one had overheard him, he leaned in closer to Gervaise. 'She was seen leading her husband's cattle through the city to higher ground the day before the flood. Her cattle are free from disease whilst everyone else's will have to be burned. How do we know this affliction has been caused by the flood? Perhaps she's put some kind of a hex on them?' he whispered.

'I am inclined to agree with you. These matters you speak of are of concern to me. Leave it with me. I shall pray upon it tonight at Vespers. We need to keep a watchful eye on anything, which smacks of heresy. The church is quite clear on this.'

'I think it would be prudent to have her followed,' Garlick suggested, the idea inspired by Gervaise's reference to "a watchful eye". 'We need to know where she goes and who she sees. You never know what she might do next.'

Gervaise had attended many of the burgesses meetings and not once had a woman been present or been allowed to speak. It was against the natural order of God's work.

'Leave it with me. I must go now or I will be late for Vespers.' He turned. 'Come Jacquemon.'

Chapter 28

Gervaise and Jacquemon returned to the priory in time for Vespers. Jacquemon, as usual, slept through most of the service. During the winter months, it was usual for the monks to retire to their beds, weary from lack of sleep and from their day's toil. Tonight was no exception. They filed out of the cold chapel in silence. Gervaise waited for them to leave. Old Jacquemon was last. Gervaise watched him as he shuffled slowly towards the door and noted how his stoop had become more pronounced. He listened to his faltering footsteps as he made his way back to the dormitory. Satisfied he was now alone in the candle lit chapel, he made his way to the altar. He needed time to reflect and to pray.

Since the meeting and the audacious presence of Mistress Pauncefoot, he had been troubled. Never had a woman attended a business meeting of the burgesses. It was wrong. He remembered Emmelina's mother, Sabrina Dabinett. She had made herself unpopular by meddling in the affairs of the city's physicians and questioning the good work of the monks. That hadn't ended well. No good could ever come of such meddling on the part of a woman. It was not the natural order of things nor was it God's will.

He knelt down, with some difficulty, on the stone step. His knee caps gave way and made a clicking sound from the burden of the weight they were being asked to bear. Gervaise crossed himself and kissed the gold crucifix he wore around his neck. He closed his eyes and began to pray in Latin.

"Deus, in adiutorium meum intende. Domine, ad adiuvandum me festina."

(O God, come to my assistance. O Lord, make haste to help me.)

As he knelt there in the silence and the flickering light, he remembered a book Prior Vincent had brought back with him some years ago when on church business in Cologne, Germany. Prior Vincent had put it away at the back of his private

142

bookcase in the scriptorium muttering something about never wanting to see the day when he would be called upon to use it. Gervaise saw it as a sign from God. Thanking Him for his divine intervention, he heaved himself up from the step. Crossing himself again, he took a lighted candle from the altar and with great haste made his way to the scriptorium by the night stairs, stopping briefly at the top to catch his breath.

Gervaise held the candle up and ran his hand along the top shelf, disturbing decades of dust as he did so. The dust filled his nose and throat, making his chest wheeze and his nose itch. Not able to get close enough to read the book titles, because he was too short and, getting increasingly frustrated, he set the candle down and dragged a wooden stool over to the shelves. Despite the cold, Gervaise was sweating. Standing on the stool, holding the candle in one hand and steadying himself with the other, he scanned the books until his gaze landed upon an unassuming dark, leather-bound book. He could make out the familiar orange tint of the animal hair edges. He reached up to the book, lost his balance and spilt the hot candle wax on his hand. The flame flickered and the candle almost went out. Gervaise cursed. Gradually, he steadied himself and climbed down from the stool. He placed the book on top of Vincent's study desk by the window, opened it, and squinting, read the metallic, dark brown ink on the first page of the parchment. His eyes widened and a smug smile appeared on his thin lips as he read the introduction.

"Hence, Lucifer has also caused a certain unusual heretical perversity to grow up in the land of the Lord – a Heresy, I say, of Sorceresses, since it is to be designated by the particular gender over which he is known to have power…This heresy also consists of losses that are inflicted in the form of daily misfortunes on humans, domestic animals and the fruits of the earth through the permission of God and the co-operation of demons."

Gervaise closed the book and, tucking it under his arm, whispered aloud to himself.

'Opus dei. Opus dei. There is much work to be done. '

Chapter 29

Emmelina had been feeling unnerved since her encounter with Gilbert Garlick on the bridge and her sense of unease had deepened last night at the burgesses meeting. Waiting for his knock on the door and dreading it, she found herself moving around the house in an agitated fashion. The cold December weather did not help her mood and having heeded Maud's warning about visiting the hill it now seemed like a very long week. Sunday had, once again, consisted of listening to hateful preachers telling her how sinful she was. Friday's town meeting had been eventful in that she had seen Severin but that had only intensified the unsettled feelings she was now experiencing.

There was no real change in Humphrey's condition as he still lay upstairs, unable to get out of bed, unaided. The more she tried to busy herself, the more suffocated she became by the constraints of her life. Unable to bear it any longer, she gathered together some old clothes in a basket and some pennies from Humphrey's chest and, shouting a hurried goodbye to Dulcina, flew out of the house intending to visit the women's leper hospital on the London Road.

She had not gone far when she spotted Severin emerging from his house with a young woman she had not seen before. The dreadful sickness returned as it had done when she found out from Thomas Myatt Severin had been in the New Inn with Fayette the night of her death. Only this time the sickness was overlaid by an angry jealousy towards the young woman who was now walking towards her. An anger of a very different sort was directed at Severin. The feelings came from nowhere, she had never experienced them before and she was shocked at their ferocity. She slowed down and watched them turn into the New Inn as she had suspected. Her heart still beating, she stood for a moment thinking what she should do. She was behaving like a jealous wife, but she had no right to behave like one. Who was the young woman he was with? She was dressed in much finery, like a lady. Too good for him, she thought, petulantly. A reckless thought crossed her mind. Should she follow them into the inn and confront them? Or should she act as if it were a perfectly normal thing to bump into him in the New Inn? Or should she go home and forget about him. Get on with her life as wife to Humphrey?

In an instant, before she fully realised it herself, she had walked into the courtyard and through the tavern door. There were the usual drinkers at the bar. She noticed Thomas Myatt serving an old man from a barrel of cider. He looked surprised to see her but nodded and smiled. Over in the corner, sat Severin with the young woman. They appeared to be well acquainted. She had time to study the woman. 'Girl' would probably be a better description. She could not have been more than fifteen at best. Emmelina found herself making comparisons between her and the girl. Her breasts were smaller and her figure skinnier. She had a boyish quality about her, like Rowan in the circle, sexless and bony. Severin spotted her and stood up sharply as if he had been caught out doing something he shouldn't have been. Perhaps he was.

'Mistress Pauncefoot,' he announced, 'this is a pleasant surprise.'

His neck flushed red as if he were embarrassed. What had he to be embarrassed about thought Emmelina?

'I hadn't expected to see you in here,' he added.

'Obviously not,' Emmelina replied, staring at the girl whom Severin had not yet introduced.

For a second, he looked awkward and unsure of himself. She had not seen a hint of this side of his nature before. He always seemed so cocksure of himself when in her company.

'Mistress Pauncefoot, let me introduce you to Lady Alice, Lord Malverne's daughter.'

The young girl smiled back, a mischievous glint in her eye, almost mocking her as if she knew what was in Emmelina's heart. Lord Malverne's daughter. It wasn't enough for her to be snubbed by the wife now she had to endure the mockery of his daughter.

'Lady Alice called in to see me about a commission.'

Lady Alice piped up. 'Yes, he's making me a chest for my birthday.'

'How old will you be?' Emmelina asked her, curious to know what age she was but at the same time meaning to put the young girl in her place.

'I'll be fourteen next month,' she announced proudly, 'and father has promised me a chest like the one he made for mother.'

'Yes, that was a lovely chest Severin made for your mother. Exquisite.'

Emmelina was acting up. She wanted to show this little rich girl she wasn't the only one who had been in Severin's workshop, although why she should let people know that when she was a married woman, she didn't know. She was being foolish and uncharacteristically catty. Severin seemed to bring out the worst in her.

'You've seen it?' the girl asked, looking slightly abashed. Emmelina was triumphant in the face of the young girl's deflation. 'Yes, I had a business meeting recently with Master Browne and he had great pleasure showing me his work.'

Emmelina deliberately made her remark ambiguous. Lady Alice could make of it what she wanted and Emmelina hoped she would make much more of it than there actually was. She was jealous of another woman. An emotion she'd never experienced before. It was making her mischievous.

Severin, acting like an arbitrator between two warring factions tried to restore some sense of calm. 'Mistress Pauncefoot is taking over her husband's business whilst he recovers from an illness.'

Emmelina was furious with him. Now the girl would know she was married and therefore, unavailable and in no position to be a threat to her in the attentions of Severin Browne. It was time she left. She had made enough of a fool of herself and hadn't placed herself in the best of lights in front of Severin. No doubt he was highly amused at the sight of two women vying for his attention.

'It was nice to meet you, Lady Alice. I must be going. I must get back to my husband.'

'I'll see you out,' Severin offered.

'No, please attend to your companion.'

She turned and left, pleased she had not given him the opportunity to explain himself.

Once outside, her thoughts turned to her husband. He would be wondering where she was. The dread at the thought of being enclosed in the house with him for the rest of the day returned like a dead weight pressing upon her heart. The thought of returning home to him, lying like a fetid carcass on his bed extinguished all thoughts of Severin and his conquests.

As she turned the corner into Maverdine Lane she saw the tall figure of Gilbert Garlick talking to Dulcina at her door. The nausea deepened and she slowed her steps. She could see he was engaging Dulcina in conversation. Dulcina's nervous laugh echoed down the lane. By the time she reached the door, Dulcina looked embarrassed. Her cheeks were flushed and her gaze directed at the floor away from the gimlet eyed Garlick. He turned to Emmelina and bowed. Ignoring Garlick momentarily she spoke to Dulcina.

'Thank you Dulcina. You may go inside and finish off your chores.'

'Thank you, miss.'

Dulcina bowed her head and stepped back into the house.

'I see you have a replacement for Fayette,' Garlick said, his eyes following Dulcina as she made her way back down the hall.

'I'm sure you haven't come here to discuss my choice of maidservant?'

He turned his attention to Emmelina, looking at her in the same way he had looked at Dulcina as if he could see what

147

they looked like underneath their clothes. She shuddered in response and pulled her cloak tighter around her neck, covering her chest, which seemed to be of particular interest to Garlick. For a moment he threw her off her stance. She had meant to be cold and business-like but, as always, she found him unnerving. She tried to get past him and into the safety of her house but he blocked her way. A sickening feeling of repulsion mixed with hatred overwhelmed her. Something in her snapped. She was sick of being bullied by men. For once, she determined to stand up to him. She straightened and looked directly into his eyes.

A few seconds passed whilst they both stood their ground. Emmelina stared defiantly into his cold, black eyes. Could he have had something to do with the fire her parents died in? Did he conspire with her husband to steal her inheritance? It was time to find out...

'Perhaps then you have you come to tell me about the fire my parents died in?'

A look of astonishment passed over his face before he composed himself. Was that proof of his involvement or was he just surprised because he had not been expecting such a question. It was hard to tell.

'Were you there the night they died?'

Garlick took a step back. 'Why are you asking about that now?'

'I have reason to believe it was not an accident. That perhaps the fire had been started deliberately?'

'And who has given you reason to believe such nonsense?'

Emmelina was not about to reveal her source. She eyed him with suspicion.

'Surely, you cannot believe such mischief making?'

'I don't know what or who to believe,' she told him, 'I'm beginning to wonder about Fayette's death and whether that was just a dreadful accident.'

She searched his face for a reaction and thought she saw a moment of fear in his eyes.

Garlick took another step back, bowed to her and said. 'I'll call back another day to see Humphrey. Please tell him I called.'

She watched him stride down the lane until he turned left towards The Cross. Then she ran inside, to the kitchen, her heart beating so fast she could feel it pulsing in her veins. She poured herself a cup of wine and drank it down in one. Dulcina stood by, silently watching her.

'That man makes my flesh creep,' she said, shuddering once more. 'What was he saying to you Dulcina?'

Dulcina looked nervous. 'Nothing much. He wanted to see Humphrey but I told him you weren't at home and he should come back when you were in. Did I say the right thing?'

'Yes, of course. Sorry, I didn't mean to snap. It's just… that man…he's vile. If he comes back and I'm not in, don't let him in the house.'

'Don't worry, miss, I won't.'

'I don't trust him.'

'Why not, miss? Who is he?

'He's a cordwainer, like my husband. But they are business rivals and I don't trust him.'

The explanation seemed to satisfy Dulcina who carried on preparing the meal. Emmelina poured herself another cup of wine and drank that with equal swiftness, slamming the empty cup on the table. Why were men so vexatious? They were either cold and cruel, like Humphrey, or cunning and deceitful like Garlick, or they were just plain vexing and troublesome like Severin. Was this all her life would ever consist of, having to deal with such men, she thought. She'd rather be in a convent. She drained the bottle, slamming it down with equal ferocity. Dulcina stared at the empty bottle but did not say anything. She didn't have to. Emmelina caught her meaning.

Chapter 30

The grey light of a winter's day had begun to fade and a damp chill could be felt in the air when Dulcina left the house on her evening off. The first of the cattle to be burned had begun earlier in the day and the acrid smell of animal flesh burning on huge pyres outside the city walls now drifted into the city's streets. The air was thick and choking; the smell, unlike anything she had smelt before.

In the few weeks since her father's death, she had settled into a comforting routine of visiting his grave. She would spend an hour or so standing or kneeling by the graveside recalling memories of her time with him and offering up prayers for his soul. She hoped one day to join him and the rest of her family but until then she had to content herself in this life. Afterwards, to console herself, she would wander around the city's streets until quite late then return to the house, worn down by melancholia and creep upstairs to her lonely attic room where she cried herself to sleep.

It was a dark and moonless night by the time she left the cemetery and the coldness of the evening had seeped into her very bones. She pulled her cloak tight around her neck and quickened her pace. Most food stalls had packed up for the day but the pork man was still there waiting for the last few scraps of meat to be bought. The smell of roast pork and boiled onions greeted her as she neared the old man's stall reminding her of the day she had walked into the city with her father to visit the king's tomb, full of hope. A powerful sadness, like a physical pain, wrenched at her heart and instantly lowered her mood. She seemed to have no control over it. Whenever she thought of her father, she yearned to be back by his side, back home in the forest. Her glum thoughts took the edge off her appetite.

She stopped for a moment to warm herself, gazing at the glowing embers in the brazier. A hand touched her shoulder and for a foolish moment she thought it might be her father. She swung round, beaming, only to be shocked and disappointed to see Gilbert Garlick. She knew Emmelina's thoughts on this man and, although it was none of her business, she wondered why her mistress was so against him. He had been nothing but charming to her. Garlick gave her a broad smile.

'Good evening, Dulcina. How lovely you are looking. I trust you are well?'

Dulcina blushed slightly at the compliment upturning the corners of her sweetheart lips. She was wearing the new clothes her mistress had bought her and he had noticed. It was rare for her to get any attention and never from someone as important as Garlick.

'Would you like some of that?' he pointed to the remains of the whole pig roasting on the spit.

'Oh no, I couldn't,' she protested.

'Nonsense. It would give me great pleasure to buy something for such a pretty girl.'

Without waiting for her assent he paid the old man and handed Dulcina a piece of bread covered with thick slices of pork, boiled onions and her favourite, crispy crackling. She thanked Garlick and bit into the crackling. It made a loud crunching noise. Embarrassed, she apologised.

'No, please. There is no better way to eat such a tasty treat.'

He took her arm and led her away from the stall and towards The Cross. Dulcina tried to eat without making too much mess but it was hopeless. She could feel the pork fat running down her chin but had no free hand to wipe it away.

'Here, let me do that for you,' Garlick offered.

He took out a cloth from his pocket and began wiping the fat from Dulcina's mouth and chin, all the while, his piercing eyes drilling into her. She took another bite, this time dripping the fat onto the front of her dress. Garlick wiped it off, his hand brushing against her breast as he did so. Dulcina stepped back a little. He didn't seem to notice her silent objection.

'You must be thirsty after that. Let's go in here and I'll get us some refreshment.'

They had reached the entrance to the Fleece Inn. Dulcina tried to object but he led her firmly by the arm into the Fleece's dimly lit undercroft. Barrels of beer and cider were stacked next to each other forming a bar of sorts. Several drinkers, their faces florid from the drink and sporting the customary 'grog blossom', the drinker's bulbous, purpling nose, sat along both sides of the undercroft at long rectangular tables, talking loudly and laughing at each other's jokes. Garlick ordered a flagon of Longney Russet cider and led Dulcina to a table at the end of the narrow, but lengthy undercroft, where it was dark and shadowy beneath the ancient tunnel-vaulted ceiling. The tables were sticky from spillages and there was a dank smell of stale beer. Dulcina sat on the end of a wooden bench, next to one of the rounded Norman arches, which supported the roof. Garlick sat next to her and poured them both a generous measure. He watched her as she took a sip.

'How do you find it, working for Mistress Pauncefoot?' Garlick enquired.

'I like it. The mistress has been very kind to me, taking me in.'

Dulcina was aware he was staring at her. This only made her more nervous, which in turn made her drink more than she was used to.

'Um, yes,' Garlick replied, seeming uninterested in what she had to say.

'And Master Pauncefoot? How is my good friend, Humphrey? I haven't seen him in a long time. Every time I try to visit him your mistress tells me he's too ill. Is he still alive?'

This last question was spoken in jest.

'I don't have much to do with him. The mistress and Maud attend to him mostly.'

'Yes, I'm sure,' Garlick said, rubbing the point of his chin. 'I hear Physician Teylove is no longer in attendance. Is that right?'

Dulcina took a few more sips. She was beginning to feel light-headed and a little flirtatious. She wasn't used to receiving male attention and she had never been taken to a tavern and had drink bought for her. Her father was very strict with her and had practically never let her out of his sight. He would even take her with him to the forest in the better weather so he could keep an eye on her.

'That's right, sir. They had words,'

'What do you mean? *They* had words,' Garlick answered, becoming interested in the conversation.

She swallowed a mouthful of cider and dribbling some of it down her chin; she quickly wiped it away with the back of her hand, hoping he hadn't noticed. 'The mistress, sir and her friend, Maud. I heard them upstairs in the Master's bedroom. Asking lots of questions. Next thing I heard him thundering down the stairs and I haven't seen him since.'

'Does the old woman visit him every day?'

'Almost every day.'

'What does she do when she visits?'

'She mixes up this special tonic, in the kitchen and takes it up to him and he drinks it. She's very good with him.'

Garlick edged along the bench closer to Dulcina, turning towards her and leaning in slightly, a move that had not gone un-noticed by Dulcina. She shifted, by very small increments, away from him until she was perched on the end of the bench, trying not to make it obvious what she was doing.

'And what's in the medicine?'

'All sorts 'o things. She brings herbs from her garden and mixes them up in the kitchen.'

'What else does she do when she visits?'

'Well, it's a funny thing…'

'Go on,' he urged, inching nearer.

'After she gives him his tonic, she puts her hands on his chest and moves them around different parts of his body and he drops off straight to sleep he does. Like a new-born baby,' Dulcina replied, her tongue loosening with each nervous sip.

153

'That's interesting. Have some more. You've hardly touched your drink.'

'I think I've had plenty enough, thank you all the same.' She laughed nervously, trying to create more space between her and Garlick. She could feel the heat from his thigh, which was now pressing against hers but she was unsure what she should do. She sat there, unable to move any further along the bench to get away from him. He then did something, which alarmed her. He placed his hand on her knee and gave it a squeeze. The novelty of Garlick's attention ended there. She began to understand why Emmelina didn't care much for him. It wasn't just his eyes, she decided, that bothered her, although they did have a tendency to look at her chest rather than at her face. It was his seeming lack of a sense of anyone else's personal space. She started to feel crowded in and the need to escape from the attentions of Garlick sobered her a little.

He topped up her cup without asking. Dulcina took another small sip to humour him. She was beginning to regret accepting the pork but then she hadn't had much choice in the matter. She sat with her knees firmly clenched together and her eyes staring down at the table.

A group of men at the table opposite roared with laughter at some lewd joke one of the men had just told. Dulcina caught a few snatches of the joke and flushed with embarrassment. She had never been in the company of so many men on her own before. She had no idea that was the way they talked about women. Her father would not have approved. She tried to stand up but his hand remained firmly on her knee.

'I must be getting back. My mistress will be wondering where I've got to.'

'Have another drink before you go.'

'No, really. I've had quite enough.'

'Just one more sip won't do any harm?' he said, removing his hand and placing the tankard to her lips.

'Just one more sip then.'

154

Her eyes flitted from Garlick to the other drinkers. Garlick looked around him. They were beginning to attract far too much unwanted attention. 'Very well,' he agreed.

Relieved, Dulcina took one more sip and stood to go.

'I've enjoyed our little chat,' Garlick told her, as he finished his cider, 'and your company. We must do it again, soon.'

He patted her behind as she stood up. Dulcina did not react to his impertinence but hurried outside. He followed her out into the cold night air. West Gate Street was quiet and empty of traders. The church of St Mary de Grace stood between her and the safety of Emmelina's house. She thanked him and pressed on.

'Don't be in such a hurry to go. You haven't thanked me properly?' he leered, taking her arm once more, and pulling her towards the darkened recess of Pinch Belly Alley.

Dulcina struggled. With an unknown strength, fuelled by fear, she wrenched her arm from his grasp and ran. Garlick pursued her and catching her around the waist, dragged her into the black shadows of the church porch where they could not be seen.

He pushed her against the wall of the inner porch like he was corralling an animal. His hand found her ample breast and squeezed hard, whilst forcing his leg in between hers. His rough cheek was pressed against her soft face. She could feel the day's growth of bristle rubbing against her skin, burning her. He lifted his face to kiss her. She tried to turn her head away to avoid him but he twisted her face to his and his hot breath suffocated her, taking her breath away. The swelling between his thighs, pushed hard against her body. He pressed his mouth against her unyielding lips. He was breathing heavily and his arm was now pressing against her windpipe making it impossible to breathe. She was pinned to the wall by the weight of his body with no hope of escaping, any scream now muffled by his mouth. She felt him grappling with the fastenings of his trousers. She tried to press her thighs together,

155

terrified at the thought of what she was about to endure. He lifted her skirts and pulled down her underclothes. With his other hand, he took out the swelling from his pants, which she could now feel, hard as a rock pressing against the soft flesh of her inner thigh. Still unable to scream, she said silent prayers for her safe deliverance. These were disturbed by the sound of footsteps approaching. Garlick heard them too. He still had his mouth pressed against her lips. Hearing the footsteps and aware this might be her only chance of escape, she dug her teeth into the inside of his lip. He let out a yelp.

'Everything all right in there?' asked a voice.

Dulcina took her advantage and pushed Garlick aside emerging from the shadows of the porch.

'Dulcina?' the voice said.

It was Severin. He looked on as an irate Garlick emerged from the porch, wiping his lower lip with the back of his hand, his clothes in a state of disarray.

'Can I help?' he asked.

Garlick pushed past him, grunted something under his breath and hurried away from them.

'What's wrong with him?' Severin turned to ask Dulcina but he knew the answer before she spoke. 'Come, I'll see you get home safely.'

He placed his arm around her shoulder in a protective way and walked her back down Maverdine Lane in silence. Emmelina answered the door.

'Dulcina?'

Severin answered. 'Dulcina's had a bit of trouble.'

'What's happened? Where have you been?'

The question was addressed to both of them.

'*We* haven't been anywhere. Can we come in? It's cold out here.'

Emmelina stood back to let them pass. Once inside the kitchen Severin sat Dulcina down and went into the larder returning with a bottle of wine.

'You don't mind, do you?' he asked Emmelina, holding up the bottle, 'I think Dulcina's in need of a drink.'

This was said as he poured out a cup of wine, not waiting for a response and placed it in front of a silent, trembling Dulcina.

'Here, drink this. You'll feel better.'

Dulcina pushed the cup away.

'If you don't mind, I'd like to go to my bed.'

She stood up and wobbling slightly, walked to the door.

'What's the matter, Dulcina? What's happened?'

'I don't want to talk about it. I just want to go to my room.'

Emmelina stood with her hands on her hips, looking from one to the other.

'Let her go,' Severin said, making a gesture with his hand that implied 'better left alone'. They watched as Dulcina climbed the stairs to her attic room, leaning heavily on the balustrade.

'What's happened? Why is Dulcina in such a state?'

Her tone was accusatory.

'If you mean, have I done anything to upset her, then no. I came across her in the porch of St Mary de Grace with Gilbert Garlick.'

'With Garlick,' Emmelina gasped.

'Something *was* going on but I don't think it was something Dulcina was agreeing to.'

'Was he forcing himself upon her?' she asked, the repulsion she felt for Garlick rising like sour bile in her throat.

'It looked pretty much that way.'

'Poor Dulcina. I should go and speak to her.'

'Leave her. I don't think she wants to talk about it right now. Leave it till tomorrow.'

'Perhaps you're right. She did look like she'd had a terrible shock.'

Emmelina sat down at the table and poured herself a cup of wine. 'Would you like some?' she offered.

She hadn't seen him since she caught him drinking with Lady Alice. She had made a fool of herself and afterwards had given herself a good talking to. She was, after all, a married woman and should know better than to behave as she had. Up until now, her efforts at self-discipline had gone well but in his presence her resolve weakened. He was an enigma to her. One day, she had him down as a philanderer, entertaining young ladies; the next he was the noble and courteous King, like Alexander from Porete's book, saving Dulcina from a fate worse than even death itself. She thought of Fayette. His actions tonight were not those of a man who would do harm to a woman. Perhaps she had misjudged him. 'I think I should go,' he said.

Against her better judgement, she hoped he would stay a little longer. She wanted to ask him to stay but she knew she couldn't. There was an awkward silence. Severin filled it.

'How is Humphrey? Is he improving?'

Damn this man, she thought. Why spoil the moment by mentioning her husband. He had to be the most vexatious person she had ever known but also the most beguiling. She resigned herself to a conversation about her husband and tried to put thoughts of an intimate moment with him aside.

'He's doing well, thank you, now I've dismissed Physician Teylove.'

She took a sip of wine and smiled to herself, remembering the scene in the bedroom when Maud got the better of Teylove.

'Was that wise?' Severin asked.

'My mother's friend, Maud, is attending to him now and he's getting a little better every day.'

'I'm pleased for you. I hope he makes a full recovery. Be sure to give him my regards, won't you? I really must be going.'

'Must you?' she asked, instantly regretting the disappointment evident in her voice.

'I think it best.'

He was behaving absolutely as he should in the circumstances, which was annoying but very sensible.

'Very well. I'll see you to the door.'

She followed him out.

'Thank you for helping Dulcina this evening. I dread to think what might have happened to her if you hadn't come along.'

'It was nothing.'

'I…' she hesitated. 'I want to apologise.'

'For what?'

'I think I may have judged you wrongly.'

'In what way?'

'My suspicions about you and Fayette…'

'Oh that. I told you. I left her at The Cross.'

'I know but I couldn't be sure. I didn't know you then.'

'You don't know me now,' he grinned, a hint of lustful suggestion.

Emmelina blushed.

'Well thank you. I appreciate your apology.'

He remained standing by the door. Emmelina wondered if he, like her, did not want to leave. She waited for him to speak, certain he would make some move toward her or say something which would cement their secret, unspoken attraction to each other.

'They've decided to go ahead with the Boy Bishop celebrations, despite the flood damage. I was just wondering if you and Dulcina were planning to join in this year?'

Damn him, she thought. He had to be the most frustrating man she had come across, not that she had known many.

'When is it?' she asked, vaguely remembering last year's event.

'This Tuesday. They say there's to be a special celebration on account of Robert Fayrfax being in the city.'

Emmelina had no idea who Robert Fayrfax was. She hated feeling inadequate and stupid in front of anyone,

159

especially Severin. For a simple leather worker he had an urbane quality she admired. It made him even more attractive in her eyes.

'The King and his mother have favoured him and made him a Gentleman of the Chapel Royal. He's on his way to Snodhill Castle over in Herefordshire to take up his Chaplaincy. They say he's going to perform in St Peter's Abbey.'

Emmelina was still no wiser and embarrassed at her lack of knowledge of what was happening in the city and beyond.

'I'm sorry. Who is this Fayrfax fellow?'

Severin laughed. 'He's a composer of music at the king's court.'

Emmelina had no idea Severin was interested in music. She didn't know much about him at all come to think of it.

'Oh. Does he know the bridge has collapsed?'

'I dare say he doesn't but I'm sure he'll be able to pay someone to take him across the river. I might see you there then. You and Dulcina that is.'

'My husband normally goes to these kind of events. I'll have to see what he says.'

'Of course. I think it would do both of you a lot of good. Help cheer you up in this gloom of winter.'

Emmelina smiled but did not reply. She was already thinking about how she could sneak out and attend the feast without Humphrey knowing.

'Well, I'll bid you goodnight.'

She watched him as he walked down the lane until he turned into West Gate Street all the while thinking about the next time she would see him. Hopefully at the Boy Bishop's feast. It was only when he disappeared round the corner she closed the door. She wondered whether she should go and see how Dulcina was after her ordeal at the hands of that odious Garlick but decided against it. Dulcina, she was sure, would feel better in the morning and open up to her when she felt able.

160

Chapter 31

For all the affected superiority evident in his face, the young choir boy, dressed in his ill-fitting bishop's robe, holding erect the heavy crozier, looked comical as he peered from underneath the oversized mitre placed upon his head. This was possibly one of the strangest customs of the catholic church Emmelina had ever witnessed. Every year, on the sixth day of December, the feast day of Saint Nicholas, the patron saint of children, a chorister from the Abbey was elected bishop. The real bishop would step aside and allow the boy to reign for three weeks or more. As he was paraded past all those who gathered in the Gate Streets to watch the procession, he nodded as if blessing his worshippers, making the best of his time as honorary bishop.

Emmelina had decided not to mention the Boy Bishop ceremony to Humphrey. He had spent most of the day asleep and she knew what his answer would be if she asked. She had tried to persuade Dulcina to come with her but without success. Whatever had happened between her and Garlick had affected Dulcina quite markedly. Instead of her usual cheery disposition, she had withdrawn into herself, getting on with her daily tasks in a sombre, uncommunicative way. By the end of the day, Emmelina had been glad to leave the house.

The streets were packed with onlookers, revellers, travellers, merchants from within the city and beyond, all to see the church dignitaries bowing and kneeling in subservient obedience to a mere boy. Emmelina had to admit to herself, it was amusing. She pushed through the crowds towards the High Cross hoping to see Severin but wasn't very hopeful with so many people around. The Cross steps were strewn with bodies, most of them worse for wear after a day of merry making. She stepped in between them trying her hardest not to step on someone until she reached the top step. From there she had a better view. It was not long before her efforts were rewarded. Coming towards her from North Gate Street, she saw him, his slight swagger and black, curly hair marking him out from the crowd. Her insides flipped over at first sight of him. She waited for him to get nearer before shouting his name but she realised when he didn't acknowledge her that her voice could not be heard over the noise. She pushed her way back down the steps, this time not overly concerned whether she trod on anyone. A drunken youth, who had been sleeping it off, woke up when Emmelina's pattens pinched his leg. He lashed out at her sending her toppling off the step and crashing into the melee of people below. The commotion must have alerted Severin because within seconds he was helping her to her feet.

'Are you all right?'

'I think so,' Emmelina replied, patting down her skirts.

Severin took hold of her hand. 'Let's get out of this. It's getting a little crazy on the streets.'

He led her along West Gate Street in the direction of home but didn't stop. Instead, he carried on, heading towards the Booth Hall. Emmelina's heart began to race as she sensed the prospect of an unexpected adventure. The streets were so crowded, no-one would notice he had hold of her hand so she didn't release it from his warm grip. They reached the narrow part of the street where St Mary de Grace church stood in the centre of West Gate Street. Their progress almost came to a stop there were so many people trying to push through the narrow passageway. Occasionally, Severin shouted back at her to ask if she was all right. When they reached the next log jam in the street at Holy Trinity church, the crowds were beginning to thin out. Without any warning, Severin stopped and Emmelina almost slammed into him. She heard him say something but it was lost in the hubbub. He wrenched his hand from hers as she heard the name 'Alice'. She looked past him to see Lord Malverne and his daughter, Lady Alice standing before them.

Lord Malverne was grinning at Severin in that way men do when they suspect infidelity. His daughter had her hand on Severin's arm, in a far too intimate greeting. The resentment she felt toward this young woman returned like a jealous lover.

'How lovely to see you again,' Lady Alice was saying to Severin. She turned to her father, ignoring Emmelina. 'Isn't it father?'

Lord Malverne replied. 'Always a pleasure to see Severin. And Mistress Pauncefoot. What a surprise to see you. I trust your husband is feeling better.'

Emmelina's neck and cheeks coloured up. 'Thank you for asking Lord Malverne but I'm afraid he's no better.'

'Sorry to hear that. I'm sure he'll rally.'

The conversation stopped, the unsaid words and truths hovering in the space between them. Severin broke the awkwardness.

'I was just seeing Mistress Pauncefoot home. She was having difficulty pushing her way through the crowds.'

'But aren't you going in the wrong direction? Master Pauncefoot lives in Maverdine Lane does he not?' Lady Alice asked him, giving Emmelina a sideways, disparaging look.

Emmelina's breathing stopped. Her face was burning with embarrassment. She looked away praying no-one had noticed her extreme discomfiture.

'We were just going to the Booth Hall Inn if you would both like to join us?' Lord Malverne announced.

'I must get back,' Emmelina announced, turning to go.

'Nonsense,' barked Lord Malverne. 'You must join us. I insist.'

'No really...'

Lord Malverne took her arm. 'It's my daughter's birthday today and I promised to take her to the Boy Bishop celebrations. She'd love you to come, wouldn't you Alice.'

Alice's face burned with the fires of jealousy.

'I'm sure Mistress Pauncefoot needs to return to look after her husband?'

'Nonsense,' Lord Malverne replied. 'I'm sure she's been doing enough of that. No doubt your maidservant is home to look after him?

'Well...'

'Yes, Dulcina will watch over Humphrey. Why don't we go?

She could not believe Severin had said 'we' like they were a married couple. The embarrassment she felt was unbearable. She began to feel sick.

Lord Malverne pulled her toward him.

'Tonight is the night of fools. Why don't you be foolish? Just for tonight,' he whispered in her ear.

Something in his tone and the gentle insistence of his arm on hers changed her mind. He was right. She had few opportunities in her life to enjoy herself. Besides, she thought, looking at Severin standing with Lady Alice it was obvious she wanted him to herself and she was not inclined to allow that to happen.

'I suppose it can't do any harm...'

'Excellent,' Lord Malverne said, pleased with his persuasive skills. 'I haven't been in the Booth Hall Inn since I married your mother,' he joked. 'Best place to be on a night like this.'

'Why is that father?'

'It's a favourite haunt of Constable Rudge and his men. They regularly pop in for a drink after the Assize Court. It won't be full of the fools that are out tonight.'

Emmelina's nerves were fraying fast. She had already encountered the heartless constable when she found Fayette's body. What on earth did she think she was doing? They made their way through the dwindling throng, Lady Alice on the arm of Severin and Emmelina with Lord Malverne. Rather than being empty as they had predicted it was full of people. A group of musicians were playing in the corner and men and women were holding hands in a circle dancing.

'It's a party,' Lady Alice squealed. 'Just what I wanted on my birthday. Do you mind if I dance, father?'

Lord Malverne laughed. 'Don't mind me. Go ahead and enjoy yourself. This is the one night when the normal rules don't apply. Remember, it's the Feast of Fools when everything is turned on its head.'

She grabbed hold of Severin's arm and without asking pulled him away to join the other dancers. Emmelina could not believe what she was seeing. She stared open mouthed at the retreating couple.

'She means no harm, Mistress Pauncefoot. It's my fault. I've brought her up to be far too headstrong. Her mother is always telling me I'm to blame. She says I've indulged her and treated her like the son I never had.'

He laughed again and Emmelina got the impression this was not the first tavern he had visited that night.

'Follow me, we need a round of drinks.'

She followed him to the bar where he was greeted by the landlord. He ordered cider and passed her a pewter tankard so large she had to hold it in both hands. After a few large gulps she began to relax and the awkwardness of earlier disappeared. Lord Malverne was very amiable company. He had the knack of putting people at their ease for which she was grateful. Perhaps he had learnt to be more at ease from his time on the battlefield when he would have faced death several times over, she thought.

The music stopped and Lady Alice returned, her face flushed with exertion. Severin was grinning and out of breath. He had obviously enjoyed himself. Emmelina pushed down the hostile thoughts surfacing towards Lady Alice and now Severin. Was he enjoying her company more than hers?

'Mistress Pauncefoot, may I be so bold and ask you to dance with this poor old wreck of a man?' Lord Malverne asked, pulling a pathetic face.

Emmelina laughed at him. She looked at Severin as though asking his permission. He shrugged his shoulders. Reluctantly, she left Severin alone with Lady Alice and joined Lord Malverne in the dance. When she returned she noticed Severin and Lady Alice standing close together, talking and laughing. The laughter was bawdy and she wondered what it

165

was Severin could have said to her. When she bumped into them at the New Inn it was obvious Lady Alice was flirting with Severin. Tonight, she couldn't be sure if it was mutual. She picked up her tankard of cider from the nearby table and took a long draught, emptying it.

'Mistress Pauncefoot, for one so young you drink like a man.' He laughed again and finished his drink. 'More drink, we need more drink. This is turning into a most delightful evening with, may I say, delightful company.'

He disappeared to fetch more drink and left Emmelina standing on her own. She stared at the two 'lovers', the cider coursing through her veins, giving her false courage. She watched as they ignored her and carried on flirting in front of her. When Lord Malverne returned with the cider, she took another draught, almost emptying the tankard and slammed it on the table. This was indeed the night of fools. She lurched towards the pair, fortified with false courage and hell bent on breaking up their private moment. She stood between them, her back to Lady Alice, putting an abrupt halt to their conversation.

'I'd like to dance,' she announced, looking at Severin with a defiant stance, her hands on her hips.

Severin, at first taken aback, grinned at her. Emmelina could tell from the way he was grinning that he was enjoying having two women vie for his attention. For some reason this made her even madder than before. Mad at him.

Severin looked past her. 'Excuse me, Lady Alice. I must dance with Mistress Pauncefoot.'

Lady Alice was not about to be brushed aside. She placed her hand on Emmelina's shoulder. Emmelina turned to face her.

'Severin was just about to dance with me,' she pushed Emmelina to one side, 'weren't you Severin?'

Severin had been put into an intolerable position. Who should he choose? Both would be insulted. He was beginning to think his idea of going to the inn was a bad one, especially when two headstrong women were involved. The two women stood in front of him waiting for his answer. He ran his fingers through his black curls, trying to summon up a solution to his dilemma. The answer came from Lord Malverne.

'Alice, my dear, I haven't had the chance to dance with you this evening,' he said, taking his daughter's arm firmly in his grasp and leading her away.

As he left, he looked back at Severin and winked. Relieved to have been spared, and out of sight of the jealous eyes of Lady Alice, Severin took Emmelina's hand and swung her round, pulling her close to him. She smelt his musky odour, felt the warmth of his body through his thin woollen shirt.

'Mistress Pauncefoot, you surprise me. Do I detect a certain ill will towards Lady Alice?'

'I don't know what you mean,' she protested.

'I think you do,' he said, letting go of her and gesturing for her to go ahead of him to join the circle of dancers.

Lady Alice stood with her father waiting for the dance to begin. She gave Emmelina a snide look. Emmelina returned with a look of triumph.

Severin held the hand of the woman next to him. Emmelina held the hand of the man to her right. The stranger's hand was clammy and his grip weak. Severin took hold of her hand, his grip was tight and his hand was on fire. His touch sent a quiver between her thighs, up and through her body. If they were alone now, she thought, she could not be held to account for her actions. Whether it was the drink or the Bacchanalian atmosphere of the Boy Bishop's celebrations she could not say. She wanted to kiss everyone around her except Lady Alice. Most of all she wanted to kiss Severin. Dare she? The music stopped. The man on her right let go of her hand. She turned to Severin and moved closer. His eyes burned into her with a knowing look.

'Severin,' Lady Alice called out from behind Emmelina. 'My father is tired. He wants to leave.'

167

Damn her, cursed Emmelina. The unseen thread between her and Severin had been cut. The spell broken.

'I should be going too,' Emmelina announced.

'I don't want to go yet,' Lady Alice said, taking hold of the neck of Severin's shirt. 'I haven't had my birthday kiss.'

She lunged towards him, unsteady on her feet, and tried to plant a kiss on his lips.

'Whoa,' Severin exclaimed. 'I think someone's had too much to drink.'

'Nonsense,' she said, straightening her skirts and obviously embarrassed at the rejection.

Lord Malverne joined them and summing up the situation like a man of the world that he was he took hold of Lady Alice by the arm.

'I think it's time we went home,' he said, looking slightly bemused.

Outside, they bid father and daughter goodnight. Emmelina watched as Lord Malverne walked, arm in arm, with his daughter towards Abbey Lane. She was rather skinny thought Emmelina.

The night air was cold and the streets were full of rubbish and pools of sick. Revellers were making their way home, holding each other up in a drunken huddle. Attempts at singing, which sounded more like shouting resounded along the gate streets. Bawdy jokes were being told ending in lewd, raucous laughter. The odd drunkard lay collapsed on the floor, having drunk so much they could not make it home.

They walked side by side in silence. It was as if the moment in the inn had not happened. Already, the whole evening seemed so unreal as if she had dreamed it. When they reached Maverdine Lane Severin bowed politely and bid Emmelina goodnight. He had become a stranger once more.

Chapter 32

Guido sat at the window of his study carrel watching the flurry of activity in the cloister below.

Brother Enoch was talking to the Sub Prior. He was pawing over an intricate drawing and pointing up at the north transept of the nave where the new window was to be built. The Sub Prior nodded his head in agreement at something then patted Brother Enoch on the back before turning to make his way across the cloister towards the scriptorium. Guido ducked away from the window opening in case the Sub Prior spotted him. He was supposed to be working on the priory's liturgical calendar for 1498 but instead he had been scribbling images of animals on a scrap of parchment in lead point. Today, memories of his childhood, when he lived with his mother in the wilderness of the Italian countryside occupied his daydreams. As a child it was a common sight to see alpine ibex, chamois and bearded eagles and these were now expertly drawn from memory. He had been happy there until his father took him to the city of Turin and left him in the care of the stonemasons at the Duomo di Torino at the age of thirteen to work on the building of the cathedral. He hated working on the rough stone and he wasn't suited to the work. It was only when Prior Vincent came to visit and noticed his drawings and asked permission to take him to England with him to learn the art of illuminating manuscripts he had escaped his father's career plans and the dusty work of a stonemason. He had never seen his mother again. She never came to say goodbye to him even though she must have known he would not be coming back. After he arrived in Gloucester, he would draw pictures of his mother from memory but over the years her face had become blurred and he found it harder to remember her features. He was so engrossed in his daydreams and scribblings, that the approach of the Sub Prior went unnoticed. When the curtain of his study carrel was swept across, he jumped, spilling the ink well and spattering his drawings.

'You clumsy oaf,' cursed Gervaise, annoyed at the mess but conscious the boy had been idling again. 'Clear up that mess and meet me in the Chapter House when you've finished and mind you come straight there.'

Guido assured Gervaise he would, as he went about mopping up the ink with a piece of cloth, sad to see his drawings ruined. Some minutes later, he arrived at the Chapter House where he found the Sub Prior sitting in the central stone-arcaded seat, concentrating on the pages of a brown, leather-bound book. Gervaise looked up when Guido entered, closing the book.

'Have you been following Mistress Pauncefoot as I asked?'

'I have, Sub Prior.'

'And you have not mentioned this to anyone?'

'No, Sub Prior. I have done as you ordered.'

'So what can you tell me about where she goes and who she meets?'

'She has visited the New Inn.'

'Did she meet anyone there?'

'I don't know.'

'What do you mean, you don't know?'

'I didn't follow her in. I would have been noticed.'

'Where else has she been?'

'To the market,' Guido replied. 'She bought candles and some fish,' Guido added.

'I'm not interested in what she bought but where she went and who she saw. Have you nothing else to tell me?'

'No, sir,' Guido answered, dropping his gaze to the floor and keeping it there.

He dare not confess to joining in the Boy Bishop celebrations and falling asleep in the Ram's Head Inn when he should have been following Mistress Pauncefoot.

'Have you actually been following her or using the time to malinger?' Gervaise snapped.

170

Guido had taken a vow of obedience when he joined the priory but he knew other monks did not always keep this promise. He wanted to tell the truth but he couldn't face the wrath of his sub prior. He decided to give a version of the truth.

'Yes, sir. I have been following her when I've been able to.'

'What do you mean, "When you've been able to"?'

'Well, I have my studies and I must attend the services.'

'Didn't I tell you that you were excused from those duties?'

'But, Sub Prior. Brother Jacquemon…'

'Brother Jacquemon is not in charge of this priory,' Gervaise bellowed. 'I am. I want you to follow this woman for the next seven days. Do not let her out of your sight. I shall clear your absence with the other monks. Report back to me, immediately, if you see anything suspicious. Do you understand?'

Guido brightened at the thought of being excused from the daily routine of the priory but wondered how he was going to get any sleep in the next seven days. Wisely, he did not think this the most opportune moment to ask Sub Prior Gervaise the answer to his quandary. He was not best pleased with him and, above anything, in the time he had been at the priory; he had learnt when to keep his mouth closed. It seemed he regularly upset the monks, especially Brother Paulinus. He left it at that, grateful that he would gain a little freedom if only for a few days.

'I understand, Sub Prior.'

'Very well. Go now and make sure she doesn't see you.'

171

Chapter 33

For the next few days, Emmelina tried to coax Dulcina into telling her what had happened with Gilbert Garlick. She refused to talk about it. Dulcina's sullen mood, together with her husband's continuing ill health and bad temper was enough to drive Emmelina out of the house. She hadn't seen Severin since the strange night of the Boy Bishop's evening. His behaviour with Lady Alice troubled her. A mounting frustration with her life and those in it made her want to scream her lungs out. Maud had warned her not to go to the hill but she could not stay away. Her soul yearned to be nourished; her body yearned to be touched.

Once she was sure it was safe to leave the house, she gathered her things and made her way to Robin Hoodes Hill, taking her usual route through the East Gate, across Gaudy Green, picking up the path close to Maud's house and then taking the steep trail up to the clearing at the top. The night was cold and inky dark, the moon and stars cloaked by thick black clouds. A fierce wind gusted through her woollen clothes, chilling her. The eerie sound of the trees swaying and creaking above, unnerved her. She half thought about turning back.

She stopped to untangle her skirts, which had managed to wrap themselves around her legs and to peel the hair from across her face, which was flailing in all directions despite her attempts to fasten it beneath her hood. As she did so, she heard a loud whack like someone falling to the ground. She turned. The path behind her was narrow and either side tall weeds grew, shadowed by mature horse chestnut trees. She strained her eyes and looked along the path as far as she could see. There was nothing. Even the animals were somewhere cosy on such a night, she thought. She lifted her skirts and carried on. As she neared the clearing, she could hear voices. They did not sound like the usual hushed tones of the members of her faith. She stopped again to listen. They were coming from the path to her left. The path she would have taken if she had left the city by the North Gate. They were men's voices. Whoever it was sounded drunk.

''Ere, up 'ere,' she heard one of them say.

'Can you see 'em?' another said.

'No nothing yet,' was the reply.

The words Emmelina heard next confirmed her worst fear.

'I hope we 'ant come up all this way for nothing. I's in the mood for a bit 'o cunny.'

Ribald laughter came from behind a thicket of bushes close by. They were a bunch of black-hearted drunkards from the city, hell bent on causing trouble. The voices were getting louder and closer. Emmelina lost no time. She ran to the clearing and began waving her arms above her head to warn the others. Finn was stood by the makeshift altar. As soon as he saw Emmelina, he kicked the lighted candles, dousing their flames.

'Run, everyone, run,' he shouted.

The assembled flock ran in all directions like frightened sheep. Emmelina ran into the bushes to her right, hoping to make her way back to the path she was familiar with. Frantic, she thrashed through the brambles, her arms stinging from the thorns pricking at her flesh. She saw the path ahead of her, but instead of rushing toward it, she stopped dead in her tracks. A monk dressed in the familiar black cappa of Blackfriars Priory was making his way up the path towards the clearing. She couldn't make out who he was because of the pitch night but it was unmistakeably someone from Blackfriars. What was he doing out here in the middle of the night, she wondered. Then it dawned on her. She did not know why but for days she had thought she was being watched. Was this the person who had been following her? But why would a monk from Blackfriars want to follow her? Was he in the habit of following women? Who was he? She could only hope he had not heard her and that he would continue up the hill to the clearing. She watched as he ambled along, seemingly oblivious to the mayhem taking place further up the hill. Once he was out of sight, she emerged from the bushes and flew back down the path. By the time she reached home, her clothes were torn, her lungs ached and she was exhausted. A deepening concern gnawed away at her insides, followed by a sickening unease. She closed the door behind her and for the first time was relieved to be home safe within its walls.

She crept into the fore hall and was just slipping off her pattens when she heard movement coming from upstairs. She stood very still, not daring to move and listened. The next sound was a loud thud. It sounded like Humphrey falling out of bed. Then she heard him call her name. Still she did not move. The best she could hope for was that he was having a nightmare and would fall back to sleep. There was a momentary silence, broken only by Humphrey bellowing her name and calling for her to attend to him. The sound of his voice, bellicose and threatening made her jump. She didn't know what to do. If she went straight up to see to him, he was sure to notice she was dressed. If she didn't go up to see him, he would wake Dulcina and, either way, her secret would be out. Humphrey's tone became more belligerent the longer she left it. She would have to do something. She took off her cloak and shoved it into the chest quickly removing her shoes and throwing them in. She would have to go up and see to him. If he noticed she was dressed and asked her why she would have to make something up.

As she reached the top of the stairs she heard the sound of the latch on Dulcina's bedroom door at the top of the house. He had woken her. Dulcina would catch her coming up the stairs and know she hadn't come from her bedroom. How was she going to explain this to either of them. She was trapped, unsure whether she should continue or turn back. The decision was taken out of her hands when Dulcina appeared, holding a candle. The two women stared at each other for what seemed to be an age. Emmelina thought her luck had finally run out. She was sure to be found out and would have to suffer the consequences. To her surprise Dulcina placed her finger to her lips, then nodded in the direction of Emmelina's bedroom. Without saying a word, she opened the door to Humphrey's room, disappeared and closed the door behind her.

An unspoken understanding had just passed between the two women. The tension in Emmelina's chest melted away. Dulcina must have guessed what was going on and chose to cover for her. As she crept past the door, she stopped to listen. She could hear Dulcina soothing and calming Humphrey and helping him back into bed. She heard Humphrey ask where she was. Dulcina told him his wife was not feeling well and was unable to get out of bed.

Emmelina headed for her bedroom before Dulcina re-emerged. It would be awkward trying to explain to Dulcina where she had been. She undressed in a hurry, dropping her outdoor clothes to the floor and kicking them out of sight under the bed. Her night clothes were folded at the end of the bed. She pulled them on and jumped into the cold bed, wrapping the blankets tightly around her. She lay for a while listening for Dulcina and wondering whether she would knock on her door. She heard Humphrey's door open and close, then the soft padding of footsteps up the stairs to the attic room. She owed such gratitude for Dulcina's unexpected loyalty and discretion. She would have to find a way to repay her. She wondered what Dulcina would say to her in the morning but, to her relief, the incident was never spoken of again.

Chapter 34

Like an irresistible, gravitational pull Emmelina found herself outside Severin's house. Her encounters with him were all too brief. Like a hunger, she wanted more. Her thoughts were never far away from him. If she wasn't thinking about Severin she was thinking about going to see him. Each time her mind wandered, she told herself to forget about him and concentrate on her husband's business. He had inadvertently saved her from Garlick at the burgesses meeting making sure any unwanted attention concerning her timely relocation of the cattle had been forgotten. He had saved Dulcina from Garlick but she had caught him flirting with young Lady Alice. And as for Fayette – well she wasn't sure what had happened there. And yet, here she was, against her better judgement, walking along North Gate Street towards his house.

The street was crowded as usual but instead of the familiar and varied smell of the market stalls, the over-riding odour was the burning of flesh. They had begun to burn the dead carcasses. She crossed to the opposite side in case he saw her; worried it might look obvious she was hanging around to catch a glimpse of him. As she walked excuses came to her about what to say to him if she bumped into him. She would tell him she was on her way to the leper hospital to take some old clothes. She had even packed a few items of good clothing in her basket just in case. Stopping on the corner of St Aldem's Lane, opposite his house, she rummaged in her bag to make it look like she had a reason for stopping. She casually looked across. His door and the workshop shutters were closed. Should she be grown up and go over and knock on the door? What would she say if he answered it?

A begging monk from Whitefriars approached her dressed in his traditional white garb and held out a begging bowl. Emmelina rummaged in her purse for a few coins. They tinkled into the bowl joining a meagre collection. The monk remained standing in front of her as if to say 'I want more than that'. When he realised she wasn't going to give him anymore he made an exaggerated bow in front of her.

'Bless you,' he said, not looking up.

She thought she detected an edge of sarcasm in his voice, which was neither charitable nor Christian. As she stood on the street corner trying to decide what to do a large group of people came towards her from the direction of the North Gate. A pot-bellied man with ruddy cheeks, a balding pate led the group. Behind him staggered a small, thin woman being dragged along by a rope which was attached to an iron branck. A common sight in the city, brancks were used to deal with quarrelsome wives or brawling women. A metal piece would be inserted into the woman's mouth. Then a metal ring was placed each side of the jaw to the back of the head. The nose came between two metal upright bars and the conjoint bar went over the woman's head where, with the other ring, it was fastened by a padlock. A rope was attached to the front ring to lead the poor woman along like a pig to market. A crowd had gathered and were taunting and jeering at this unfortunate wife. Emmelina saw herself as an unfortunate wife but she didn't think Humphrey would subject her to such a public and embarrassing ordeal. His punishments were private and carried out in the secrecy of his own home. Still, she was acutely aware of the fact that, but for the grace of Humphrey, she might be in that poor woman's position as the woman stumbled past her on her way to The Cross.

Pre-occupied with the spectacle before her she hadn't noticed Severin emerge from his house. Her immediate thought was to run and hide. She looked around to find such a place, ducking into John the Draper's shop a few yards from the corner hoping he hadn't seen her.

Bolts of scarlet cloth hung over oak beams in hues of carmine red, cream, blue, green, and brown. The smell of newly dyed cloth, clean and unworn, filled the shop. John and his wife sat at a long table at the back. They were cutting out patterns and folding them neatly on the table, ready to sew later.   John looked up from his cutting and welcomed Emmelina.

'Are you looking for a particular colour miss?'

'Thank you but I'm really just looking.'

Emmelina perused the bolts of cloth. A deep, velvety voice from close behind asked her what she was looking for. It was Severin. She turned to see him beaming at her, his eyes sparkling with devilment.

'Oh it's you,' she said, feeling her cheeks colour, not knowing what else to say.

He had obviously seen her and like a naughty child stealing sweetmeats from a market trader, she had been caught out. Now she looked very foolish. Flustered, she turned to John the Draper and thanked him before walking out of the shop with Severin.

'Were you looking for me?' he asked her when back in the street.

They began to walk in the direction of the New Inn.

'No why? Why do you say that?'

She spoke without looking at him hoping he would not detect the falseness in her voice.

'I've been watching you from my upstairs window. You looked like you wanted to cross over and call on me. Was I wrong?' he teased.

'Don't be ridiculous. I was on my way to the leper hospital,' she replied, in a business-like manner, showing him her basket of clothes.

'You're going in the wrong direction, then.'

She stopped, realising her mistake. Why did he have this effect on her? Why couldn't she be herself when she was with him?

'I have some shopping to do before I go there.'

She hardly recognised the stuffy, arrogant person she became in his presence.

'So that's why you went into the draper's shop when you saw me?' he joked.

178

'I didn't, I...'

'You were just making a detour?'

He was making fun of her but she was too annoyed with him to laugh at herself. They had stopped in front of the New Inn. Severin took her arm.

'Let's go in here for a drink and talk?'

'No, really, I...'

The feel of his warm hand upon her arm and the closeness of his body weakened her resolve and clouded her judgement. He led her into the New Inn where there was the usual crowd of hardened drinkers standing around the bar. Thomas looked up and seeing them together winked at Severin. Emmelina felt cheapened by the gesture and wondered how many other women he had taken there. She knew who two of them were and began to wish she hadn't agreed to go with him. He led her to the same corner she had caught him sitting at with Lady Alice. It was set back in an alcove and not visible to anyone standing at the bar. That's probably why he chose it, she thought. Without ordering, Thomas appeared and brought with him a flagon of ale and two cups and set them down on the table. Emmelina thought to herself if he winked one more time she would get up and leave. Much to her relief he didn't.

'Is this where you bring all your women?' she asked Severin once Thomas had left.

She regretted it instantly. She was acting like a jealous lover again. What's the matter with me, she thought. Feeling in need of a drink to settle her, she took a large gulp of ale. A vision of her and Severin naked and entwined came into her head. Lovers. I wonder? No. She pushed the thought from her mind. Her husband lay gravely ill not yards from where she was sitting. Why did she torture herself with such thoughts? Why was she here? What a foolish girl, she chided herself relentlessly.

'No. I don't bring *all* my women here.'

He said it as if there were more women in his life. Was he teasing her? Whatever his intention, he was enjoying it by the twinkle in his eyes.

'But what about...'

He interrupted before she could say her name. 'Lady Alice?'

Emmelina said nothing. She was already feeling very awkward and foolish.

'Lady Alice is the daughter of a very wealthy, very influential client. I indulge her, and, yes, before you say, she has a bit of a crush on me and I suppose I flirt with her a little bit but that's all,' he said, convincingly.

'And Fayette?'

Severin's face changed and he became serious for a moment. 'I told you, I asked her to meet me for a drink that one time, that's all.'

'Were you lovers?'

It was an impertinent question and she shouldn't have asked it but he seemed to be opening up to her and there was a pressing need to get at the truth, whatever that may be.

He laughed and shook his head. 'No. We were not lovers. I only met her that once and as I told you I left her at The Cross, alive and well.'

He didn't elaborate but she wasn't going to let it go. She took another large gulp of ale.

'What were you then?'

He sighed deeply. 'She came to my house a few weeks ago with a message from your husband. I invited her in and we got talking. She seemed nice enough so I asked her if she would like to go out sometime. I thought she'd say no but she didn't. Actually, she seemed quite keen.' He smiled to himself and took another drink. 'I suggested we meet in here. That was the first and only time I met her. Then...Well, you know what happened then.'

Emmelina looked into his black eyes and tried to read them but she saw nothing. He took a swig of ale and wiped his mouth with the back of his sleeve.

'That's the problem. I don't know what happened next.' She glared at him. 'All I know is she was here with you that night and then I found her in the river. What happened to her in between is a complete mystery to me.'

She slammed her cup on the table, rather more forcefully than she meant to. A few of the men at the bar looked over. She glared back at them and they looked away.

'You think I had something to do with her death, don't you?'

'I don't know what to think.'

'Well I didn't. I already told you. I left her at The Cross.' He sighed again, putting his head in his hands. 'You must know how things can get out of hand. What these people are like. As soon as they found out I was with her the night she disappeared I'd be arrested and before you know it I'd be strung up for something I didn't do.'

Emmelina thought about what he had said. It was true Constable Rudge would not think twice about hanging an innocent man or woman if there was the least suspicion. She so wanted to believe him. So wanted to believe there had been nothing between them. That they were not lovers.

'I'm sorry. I thought you were hiding something.' Worried he would see her concern as a sign of inappropriate feelings for him, she countered, 'I need to trust you if I'm going to be working with you.'

'Of course.'

He was back to mocking her and not taking her seriously. They sat for a while, an uneasy silence between them. Emmelina realised there was very little she knew about this stranger who had ambushed her thoughts and inveigled himself into her dreams. She broke the silence by asking him a non-contentious question she was curious to know the answer to.

181

'I was just wondering whether you're from Gloucester originally.'

He seemed relieved a tacit truce had been reached. 'No. My mother was Italian from the city of Verona. My father was English, from a village near Gloucester. You might know it. Tidenham?'

Emmelina looked blankly at him.

'It's in the Forest of Dean on the other side of the river. I was on my way there some years ago to look up my father's family but never made it. I ended up staying here.'

'Are your parents still in Italy?'

Severin wrapped both hands around his cup and looked deeply into its contents as if he would find the answer to her question therein. 'Both my parents are dead.'

'Oh, I didn't mean to...'

'My mother died in childbirth, giving birth to me. My father eventually died of a broken heart.'

Emmelina saw the pain of his loss, still raw, even now. She had the very same pain. She realised they had something important in common. He was an orphan and an only child like her. She had a deep desire to hold him, stroke his hair and take the pain away with soft words. Instead she sat there feeling the intensity of the invisible pulse between them.

'How did they meet?' she asked.

'My father travelled to Verona on business. He traded in iron ore. My mother was the daughter of one of my father's buyers. My father asked him for her hand in marriage. They struck a deal of sorts and the marriage was agreed upon. I was born the following year.'

'That was quick,' she responded, laughing in an attempt to lighten the mood.

'And what about you?' he asked, his expression becoming serious. 'How did you meet Humphrey?'

His question threw her off balance. She wasn't in the habit of talking about Humphrey or her marriage. The question made her realise how distasteful the subject was to her.

Concerned to keep this from Severin she answered in an offhanded manner, hiding her face from him in case he saw through her falseness.

'I married Humphrey after my parents died.'

'Now it's my turn to apologise…'

She smiled. 'No need.'

'How old were you when your parents died?'

'Fourteen. Just.'

Severin was quiet for a moment. 'So you married Humphrey when you were fourteen?'

Emmelina didn't like where this conversation was going. She was not used to being questioned about her personal life. Most people already knew the truth of her situation and didn't pry. 'Not exactly,' she replied, her voice hesitant.

Severin did not press her further as he could see by her uncomfortable expression she was reluctant to open up on the subject of her marriage. He changed the subject. 'Would you like another drink?'

'No, really. I must go…'

She rose to leave. Severin stood up with her and followed her out. North Gate Street was busy as usual. Emmelina turned to say goodbye when a commotion on the other side of the street caught her notice. It was William, the tanner, pushing his way past the throng of people towards them, a grave look upon his face.

'Severin,' he shouted, waving his arms to attract his attention.

'What's the matter, William?' Severin asked.

William was out of breath when he reached them and his scrawny frame shook from fear.

'It's Young Will. He's collapsed.'

Chapter 35

Severin sprinted across the road, followed by William and Emmelina. The boy had collapsed whilst stamping around in the vat of hides. When they reached the Tanners' Hall, Young Will was lying on the dirt floor next to the huge vats he spent his days trampling around in, his skinny frame, all raggedy, and quivering like a shot rabbit. His clothes and hair were wet, he was shivering violently and the boy's eyes were half open. Severin touched his forehead.

'He's on fire. We need to move him.'

Severin picked up the boy effortlessly and carried him to his house. His father walked beside them, giving commentary.

'He said he wasn't feeling well this morning but I thought he was shirking again so I made him come in and work. He kept on complaining but I just ignored 'im like I usually do and then he just went 'un collapsed in the vat. I had to fish him out before he drowned. He's never 'bin ill like this afore. His mother won't be too pleased. I can't afford to pay someone else to do his job'

Severin placed the boy carefully on a mattress on the floor in the corner of his workshop. He took off the boy's shirt and pants and asked Emmelina to bring him some cool water. When she returned Severin was asking the boy's father about the purple marks on his body.

'Never noticed them,' William replied, taking a closer look at the purplish bruising covering his body.

Emmelina wiped the boy's face with the damp cloth, rinsed it and placed it back on his forehead. Young Will muttered deliriously, swinging his head from side to side.

'What do you think's wrong with him?' Emmelina asked Severin in a low voice so William couldn't hear.

'I'm not certain but I've seen these marks before.' He turned to face Emmelina and whispered, 'In Italy.'

'Do you know what it is?'

184

'I have an idea but I'm not a physician,' he said, wiping his brow.

'I'll fetch Maud. She'll know what to do.'

She rushed back to Maverdine Lane, hoping Maud would still be there. She found her sitting at the kitchen table, talking to Dulcina and drinking one of her potions. When Emmelina explained about Young Will, Maud grabbed her things and left without finishing her drink.

When they arrived back at Severin's they found the boy lying on the mattress with his mother by his side, holding his hand. Maud leant over the boy and examined him. She felt the glands in his neck then pressed the purple marks on his body.

'Bring me a candle. The light is poor here.'

Severin lit a candle and took it over to Maud. She seemed interested in a large ulcerous lump on his ankle. The skin in the centre was blackened and necrotic. She held the light up and bent down to get a closer look.

'What does this boy do?' she asked his mother.

'He works in the tannery with his father.'

'Tanning leather?'

'That's right.'

'Do you know if he has cut himself recently?' she asked William.

'We're always getting cuts on us,' he answered, phlegmatically.

She thanked William and moved away from the boy.

'What's the matter with him, Maud?' Emmelina whispered, concerned about her silence and fearing the worst.

'I think he has the Black Bane.'

'The Italians called it "Carbonchio". I recognised the symptoms,' Severin added.

'Is he going to be all right?' Emmelina asked in her naivety.

Maud looked across to his mother who had remained at his side and was once again holding the boy's hand. Maud shook her head.

185

'Is there nothing that can be done?' Emmelina implored.
'Nothing. There's no cure. Just pray for a swift end.'

Chapter 36

Young Will did not last the night. He died with his mother, Ruth, at his side. Maud stayed with the boy till the end administering herbal tinctures to ease his pain and swabbing his febrile body. Severin's fear the disease would spread to humans had come to pass. Young Will became its first victim. Although the city had started to burn all the infected carcasses they had not acted soon enough for Young Will.

Emmelina returned early the next morning to find Young Will's body being laid out by his mother and Maud. His father had spent the evening in the New Inn with Severin drowning his sorrows and had been snoring loudly in the corner of the room when his son took his last breath. William now sat at the table with Severin at the back of the room, drinking weak ale and tearing at a loaf of fresh, warm bread fetched from John the Baker's bake house. Maud had strewn hyssop on the floor around Young Will's bed, an aromatic herb used to cleanse and disinfect. Emmelina ignored the men and approached Maud and Ruth who were working silently and reverently.

'Is there anything I can do to help,' she asked them, speaking in whispers.

Maud turned to her. She looked drawn and weary.

'Bless you,' she said, 'I could do with a glass of ale.' Nodding her head towards Ruth, she added, 'and I dare say, this poor soul could do with some refreshment.'

Ruth raised her head. Her eyes were red and swollen, her face grey and lined. She smiled weakly at Emmelina. Emmelina smiled back then crossed over to the table where the men sat. She picked up the jug of ale and as she did said to Severin.

'Do you mind?'

He didn't speak, just nodded his assent. Emmelina looked around her for some cups.

'Over there,' he said, acknowledging her unasked question.

His voice was deep and gravelly. He nodded towards a small dresser against the wall. Upon it was a selection of utensils. She took three cups and returned to the table, searingly aware he was watching her every move. Once again, in the silence of the room and amongst others, the invisible thread pulsated between them, bonding them in a secret of some sorts. To her, it was palpable. She hoped no one else was aware of it. She stood close to him now as she poured the ale feeling his eyes upon her. Glancing at him she saw in his expression a raw and urgent hunger. A strong, but unspoken connection passed between them. A secret and silent tryst set in motion. Her stomach flipped and her heart beat so fiercely she hoped it could not be seen underneath her tunic. Flustered, she returned to Maud.

'Here, let me finish this. Go and sit down.'

Maud straightened up and took the cup from her. Ruth remained at her son's side and started to wrap his body in a roll of muslin cloth.

'Let me help you,' Emmelina said, tenderly touching the woman's hand. The skin was dry and cracked from years of hard work in the tanneries. What had she to show for it, thought Emmelina? One dead boy and a husband who, from the look of him, was no use to her when she needed him most. As always, she reflected, it was the women pulling it all together and supporting one another. She helped Ruth wrap the cold and lifeless body of her son. The dark purple patches now covered every part of the boy's body. She was careful not to touch the blackened cyst on his leg. She remembered his sad little face and undernourished body when she first called at the Tanners' Hall and reflected on his short, miserable life. When they had finished Maud re-joined them. She placed her hands on Ruth's shoulders.

'You won't be able to bury him, Ruth.'

Ruth swung round. 'What do you mean? Why not?'

'He had the Black Bane. The burgesses will insist his body be taken outside the city walls and burnt. I'm sorry.'

188

Ruth started to weep. Maud put her arms around her.

'I know it's hard but we have to do it and it must be done straight away. Does your husband have a cart?'

She nodded through her sobs. Maud stroked her back, in an attempt to soothe away the pain.

'Emmelina, can you wake William.'

Emmelina looked across at William. His head lay upon his arms on the table snoring loudly. Severin was still watching her. He dug his elbow into William's side.

'Wake up, you're needed.'

William remained half asleep, his head on his arms, muttering curses under his breath. Severin gave him another dig, this time much harder. William sat up, rubbing his hands through his tatted hair.

'Go and get your cart.'

'What would I be needing that for?' he growled.

'Your son needs it,' Severin told him, draining the last of his ale.

William looked across at his son who now lay wrapped in his funereal cloth. He looked at his wife. Nothing was said. He stood up and left the room, his head bowed in shame.

When he returned, more awake now he had sampled the cold morning air; he loaded his son's body on to the back of the cart. Ruth climbed in the back beside her son. Before they left, Maud said a few words over the body to commit his soul to the Lord.

Emmelina, Maud and Severin stood together and watched in silence as the sad little troupe trundled down the empty street towards the city's North Gate. The stench of roasting animal carcasses had lain in the air for days. Even though the pyres had been lit outside the city's walls, the smoke could still be seen billowing skywards. Maud, exhausted from her vigil, hugged Emmelina goodbye and set off back to her warm kitchen and the comforting purr of Pomfrey. Emmelina turned to go. Severin stood before her.

'Don't go.'

His face bore the look of someone in need. She knew that look. Her stomach flittered as he silently took her hand and led her into the house, closing the door behind him and locking the catch. Still holding her hand, she allowed him to lead her upstairs. Every sense she possessed was pulsing, bristling with anticipation. She was keenly aware of his thick curls resting on his collar, the smell of his leather, the feel of the warmth of his hand. The only noise was the sound of their footsteps on the wooden stairs.

At the top, the stairs opened out into a single room, sparsely furnished and dominated by a large bed. He led her to it and sat her down. Still holding her hand he knelt in front of her and buried his head in her lap. She touched his hair, the glossy curls wrapping round her fingers, soft and thick. He moaned softly. He raised his head to look at her.

'You are hauntingly beautiful,' he breathed, reaching up to kiss her.

She gave herself to him body and soul.

***

Sometime later, she woke to the feel of Severin's touch. He was kissing the back of her neck and stroking the inside of her thigh. She said nothing and did nothing to stop his explorations of her body. In response to his touch, she turned to him and, consumed with need, pulled him towards her. He kissed her lips, gently at first then with an intense hunger. Their bodies moved in total harmony with each other, seeming to know, instinctively, where to place a leg or where to touch. A sexual dance of sublime bliss.

***

Emmelina woke first. Her first thought was to wonder how long she had slept. Severin lay next to her, his hair wet with sweat. She sat up. He stirred.

190

'I have to go,' she said, pushing his hand away from her waist.

As much as she would have liked to spend the rest of the day lying with him she knew it was impossible. Humphrey would kill her if he found out. Strangely, that thought held no fear for her. A reckless but empowering thought. She realised, with an absolute, undeniable knowing that nothing was more important to her right now than being with Severin. She was energised, intoxicated. It was as though she had been freed from an internal prison of deathly coldness. The bubbling, fizziness of life surged through her body, racing along her veins, causing her heart to pump anew. Severin's hand moved back to her waist, pulling her close to him. Once more, he was inflamed with passion. She could smell his damp skin and wanted more than anything, to be consumed by him, annihilated by him, conjoined with him as one.

Chapter 37

It was late in the afternoon when Emmelina returned home. She walked through the crowded streets like an ethereal being, floating not walking, past familiar people and buildings, seeing them afresh. The colours were brighter, the sounds more melodic, the smells more intense. Her step was light and springy. Her face was flushed and her hair dishevelled but it was of no concern to her. A group of musicians were playing a merry tune by The High Cross. She threw a few coins in their collection box. As she neared Maverdine Lane she realised the usual dread that accompanied her return home was not present. She worried for a moment whether she would give herself away by her changed demeanour for she could not suppress the inward smile of joy swelling inside her.

She walked into the kitchen still humming the tune she had just heard and was surprised to see Dulcina and Maud sat at the table in sullen silence. She greeted them with a beaming smile.

'What a lovely surprise to see *you* here Maud.'

She squeezed Maud's shoulder as she flounced past, making her way to the larder. When she didn't get a response she turned back round.

'What's the matter with you two?' she asked, standing in the larder doorway.

Dulcina remained silent.

'Humphrey's dead,' Maud announced, solemnly.

Emmelina stopped floating. Her chest tightened and her stomach clenched.

'He's dead?' she asked, needing confirmation, not quite believing what she had heard.

Maud nodded.

'He's really dead?'

'Yes, he died a few hours ago.'

Without saying another word Emmelina walked into the larder, emerging a few seconds later with a bottle of her

192

husband's finest wine. She placed the bottle on the table and crossed over to the dresser where she took down three of her husband's finest wine goblets. Silently, she placed those on the table, uncorked the bottle and poured out the wine. Maud looked curiously at her as if she were checking for noticeable signs of madness.

'You have no idea how often I've dreamt of this day. I've thought about how I would feel and now it's come and you know what...' she paused and looked up at the ceiling as if she were talking to her dead husband in the room above, 'I feel nothing but relief.'

Dulcina could not take her eyes off Emmelina. Wide eyed and speechless she watched as her recently widowed mistress picked up her wine, raised the goblet to the ceiling and took a long draught.

'May God strike me dead for what I am about to say, but...' she bit her bottom lip, 'good riddance.'

Dulcina gasped in horror and quickly crossed herself.

'I know I shouldn't speak ill of the dead and I know you think I'm a terrible woman...a terrible wife but I don't care. You have no idea what it's been like living here with that man all these years. No idea.'

She sounded slightly hysterical.

'You're upset...' Maud began.

'I'm not in the least upset,' Emmelina cut her off. She finished off her wine and poured herself another glass. 'Come on, you're not drinking. Join me in a toast. To Humphrey. May he rot in hell for what he's done to me and the life he's led me.'

As she uttered this last sentiment the fire flared up fiercely in the hearth, fed by an unseen force. The larder door slammed shut, the metal latch landing with a final clunk. Dulcina crossed herself again and whispered a few holy words under her breath.

Maud raised her voice. 'Emmelina!' 'You're upset. You don't know what you're saying.' She turned to Dulcina. 'She's beside herself with grief. That's why she's carrying on so.'

Dulcina didn't look convinced. She pushed aside the goblet without drinking from it and stood up from the table.

'Please, miss. If it's all right with you, may I be excused?'

Emmelina came to her senses, momentarily.

'I'm sorry, Dulcina. I don't mean to frighten you. Maud's right. I'm just upset. Don't take any notice of me.'

Dulcina fled from the room. Maud stood up to go.

'Are you leaving me as well?'

'It's been a long day.'

'Don't go. Please. Stay and talk?'

Maud sighed and sat back down.

'You really ought to be careful what you say around other people.'

'Dulcina's *not* other people. She knows how I feel,' she halted, 'felt, about Humphrey. I didn't have to say anything. It was obvious what kind of a man he was. Even as ill as he was he could still put the fear of God into you from his sick bed.'

'I know it hasn't been a happy marriage but he's dead now and you really should have more respect for your dead husband.'

'He had no respect for me,' she spat back, gulping the wine. 'I'm glad he's dead.'

'Promise me, Emmelina you won't repeat any of this to anyone outside of this room.'

'I wouldn't be that foolish.'

'I'm only saying this as your friend. I'm worried about you.'

'No need. I'm fine.'

'I'm not so sure.'

'Why, have you had another one of your premonitions?' she asked, almost challenging Maud.

'No. Not this time. Just a bad feeling.'

194

'I've told you. Don't worry about me. I'll be fine now. I'm free. Free of him. It's what I've wished for all these years. God has been good to me. He's answered my prayers.'

Chapter 38

The nave of Blackfriars Priory smelt strongly of incense as Emmelina walked behind Humphrey's coffin, flanked by Maud and Dulcina. Even in mourning she looked elegant and mysterious, her dark features contrasting starkly with the heavily embroidered white funeral gown she now wore. The train floated eerily from the rolls of cloth wrapped around her head, topped by a high conical bonnet, her face, hidden by a veil of the sheerest white silk.

As they entered the nave, closely followed by the mourners, dignitaries, business associates of Humphrey's and fellow members of the Cordwainer's guild, the monks were singing Guillame Dufay's funeral composition 'Ave Regina Cælorum', popularised since the monk's death in 1474.

Humphrey, Emmelina discovered from the Sub Prior, had made all the necessary arrangements for his funeral years before he took ill. He had left detailed instructions, which included endowing a chantry so his soul's passage through purgatory would be hastened, setting aside a burial place and even choosing the music to be sung. Dufay had included a personal reference in his composition.

"Miserere supplicanti Dufay sitque in conspectu tuo mors eius speciosa."

(Pity your supplicant Dufay and may his death be lovely in your sight.)

Humphrey had requested Dufay's name be replaced with his so that the words now being sung in the nave made a personal reference to him.

"Pity your supplicant Humphrey and may his death be lovely in your sight."

In return, he had paid the priory handsomely.

The monks placed Humphrey's coffin on the funeral bier at the front of the nave. It was covered by the Honourable Guild of Cordwainer's own pall of blue silk having a chevron of yellow silk and depicting the heads of three white goats with yellow horns. Whilst Sub Prior Gervaise took his place behind the pulpitum, Brother Jacquemon walked up and down swinging the smoking and pungent thurible. The chanting continued whilst the mourners filed into the nave. Gilbert Garlick stood with his wife as did Physician Teylove. Members of the Cordwainer's Guild were in attendance along with many more wealthy burgesses. When the chanting stopped, Gervaise cleared his throat and began the service.

"The life of man, born of a woman, is short and full of trouble, evanescent as a flower, swift as a shadow. Upon such a one has God opened his eyes and brought him into judgement. Who can make a clean person out of one who is conceived of unclean seed, except God? He has determined his number of months and fixed the limits which he cannot pass. Let him have peace until the day he desires comes like that of a hireling's."

Emmelina listened as Gervaise and the monks continued to say prayers to ensure Humphrey's soul would not remain in purgatory for long and he may have everlasting peace. She didn't much care whether his soul lingered in excoriating flames for eternity but she had not shared these thoughts since her outburst in the kitchen. She had decided it was more fitting if she played the grieving widow. Truthfully, she could not wait to get the funeral over with and get on with the rest of her life unencumbered by her loathsome husband.

One of her first thoughts since learning of Humphrey's death was how divine justice had played a part in her life, a life, which up till now, she had seen as an unhappy and unlucky existence. Her father's inheritance, denied to her by Humphrey had now reverted back to her. Everything belonged to her. All of Humphrey's wealth. And no-one could take it away from her.

Another precaution she had taken was not to see Severin. Though she ached to see him and feel his touch she could not take the risk. Even though she had not set eyes upon him since they had lain together she could still smell him on her skin and it had seen her through the last few hours. Their time would come. She just needed to be patient. Gervaise droned on.

"We are not created like dumb animals to suffer eternal death. As we have lived here we shall be judged in the hereafter so that we shall either receive punishment for our sins or be rewarded for our good deeds."

Emmelina didn't believe in the notion of hell but if she had she would be in no doubt Humphrey now dwelled there to pay for his earthly sins against her. Hell, she had discovered in her short life, was most definitely here on earth. Her faith taught her the soul was capable of ecstatic union with God in this life and not the next. When united with God in perpetual joy, sinfulness was not possible. It followed hell was just a place thought up by the church to make sure they had high attendance at services, so they could tell people what to do, absolve them of their sinfulness and collect tithes to put into the church's coffers. She kept these heretical thoughts to herself since the church was not noted for their tolerance of freedom of speech, requiring instead absolute and unquestioning devotion. Those who deviated paid with their lives like the founder of her faith and heroine, Marguerite Porete.

Eventually, after what seemed to Emmelina a tedious age, Humphrey's coffin was carried outside to be buried in the monks' cemetery. The day had turned grey. A dreary mizzle rained down on the mourners. They watched, in silence, as the coffin was lowered into the newly dug, muddy grave. Emmelina showed no emotion as she watched the soil being thrown on top of her husband's coffin. Not daring to look up for fear of meeting a raft of judgemental eyes upon her she kept her eyes firmly fixed on the grave. For effect she took out a square of silk cloth from underneath her garment and dabbed at her dry eyes beneath the veil. She had not shed one tear for Humphrey.

After what she considered to be a respectable length of time by the graveside, Emmelina turned to go. Dulcina and Maud followed her. She had not gone more than a few steps when she heard Gilbert Garlick calling her name. She shuddered at the sound of his voice.

'Mistress Pauncefoot,' he shouted again as he quickened his step to catch her up. Emmelina did not stop but instinctively started to walk faster. Garlick grabbed her arm to detain her. Emmelina pulled away from him.

'Please, Mistress Pauncefoot, I just wanted to say how sad I am for your loss. You must feel very alone now.'

Emmelina thought this an odd thing to say. She half turned to him.

'I have Dulcina to keep me company.'

'Yes, indeed. I was thinking more about how you are going to manage now Humphrey has gone?'

Again, Emmelina thought this a strange comment and her feelings of apprehension returned.

'I assume someone from Humphrey's family will come and take over the running of the business.'

So this is what he is up to, she thought. 'I'm afraid my husband has no surviving relatives and neither do I as you well know so that being the case I will be taking over my husband's affairs.'

'But...' Garlick began.

Emmelina cut him off. 'I shall look forward to attending the next Cordwainer's Guild meeting. I have a lot to learn. No doubt I shall see you there. Good day to you.'

She took hold of Dulcina's hand and, pulling hard, marched off leaving Garlick to digest her news.

Chapter 39

In the days following Humphrey's funeral Emmelina occupied her time going through Humphrey's business papers. She needed to know everything there was to know about all of his business dealings. If she was to attend the next guild meeting she had to be in possession of all the facts. Men like Garlick would do their best to try and make a fool of her. She already knew quite a lot from her bedside talks with Humphrey before he died but she was sure he kept secrets from her, especially about how much money he had.

Her spirits had lifted considerably. The oppressive mood that had pervaded the house dragging her down had now been replaced by a lightness and new sense of freedom, which permeated her soul. She caught herself humming tunes as she went about the house.

Her thoughts kept wandering to Severin. She hadn't seen him since they had lain together the morning of Humphrey's death. Although she longed to see him again she knew it was foolish so soon after her husband's funeral. It worried her he hadn't called to pay his respects, as was customary. And he hadn't attended the funeral. She wondered whether it was because, like her, he also thought it unwise so soon after Humphrey's demise. It had also crossed her mind, that, maybe, he didn't want to see her. She dismissed that thought. Whatever the truth of it, it was probably for the best as any hint she was involved with another man when her husband was barely cold in his grave would not bode well for her. Although it was hard she had to be patient and hope Severin felt the same.

She was a business woman now and had to think, and act, like one. Although she didn't mourn for Humphrey she did feel the loss of his financial support. When he was alive she had no worries in that respect. Humphrey had provided well for her materially. Now her future depended on her wits, her own hard work and her business acumen. The Cordwainer's guild meeting was in two hours' time and she needed to prepare.

Emmelina had commissioned John the Draper to make her some new clothes. Clothes more fitting to her elevated position. Humphrey never understood the importance women attached to buying clothes. He saw the whole affair as tedious, frivolous and unnecessary. One or two outfits were enough to fit most occasions in his opinion. So she found it seductively sinful to purchase four outfits in one shopping expedition. A sudden pang of guilt attacked her. Even from the grave he still had an effect on her.

She chose a heavy gown of brocade in a rich plum colour with a high neck and funnel shaped sleeves. Her skirts were fur lined as was the fashion and she had upon her head a hood, the front of which was stiffened and turned up to reveal a wired and jewelled under-cap.

Dulcina had not made a secret of the fact she did not think it wise for Emmelina to involve herself in the workings of the guild on account it was the business of men and not women. No good could come of it in her simple mind. She had previously expressed similar views about the town meeting. Emmelina couldn't help feeling cross with her. It was as if her dead husband was exerting his pervasive influence through the porous mind of Dulcina. Emmelina entered the kitchen, partly to say her goodbyes but also so Dulcina could see her in all her finery. She hoped to persuade her all would be well. She also had the need for a nip of wine to settle her nerves.

'I'm ready now Dulcina. What do you think?'

Dulcina looked up from her baking. 'You look well enough, mistress,' she replied, continuing with her work.

'You could sound a little more interested.'

'I'm sorry, miss, but I'm afraid for you.'

'You know you're far too old fashioned and superstitious for a woman of your age,' Emmelina commented, trying to make light of Dulcina's concerns.

Emmelina took a bottle of wine from the larder and returned to the kitchen. Dulcina gave her a disapproving look.

'Do you think that's a good idea, miss?'

'I hardly think that is any of your business, Dulcina,' Emmelina admonished, pouring the rich ruby liquid into a wine goblet and jamming the cork back into the spout.

'I'm sorry, miss. I spoke out of turn.'

'Why are you so against me going to the guild meeting?'

Dulcina wiped her hands on her apron and walked over to the bubbling pot by the fire and checked on its contents.

'My father always said women were best kept at home and away from the affairs of men and that no good ever came of an interfering woman. My father was a simple man but a wise man. I just don't think any good will come of it and that's all I'll say.'

Emmelina expected more of Dulcina. Her old friend, Fayette, would have encouraged her, not diminished her. Her reaction to Dulcina's comment was quick and explosive.

'I have spent the last four years of my life living in fear, afraid to speak my mind because of one man, my husband. I shall not live the rest of my life in the shadow of his or anyone else's fear,' Emmelina insisted.

Shocked at Emmelina's outburst, Dulcina bit down on her knuckles, looking genuinely afraid of her. Emmelina finished her drink and left, slamming the door with such force she caused the dresser to sway, dislodging a number of pewter bowls. They fell to the floor with a clatter, spinning and wobbling until finally coming to a stop long after Emmelina had gone.

***

The guild meetings were held in the Booth Hall after the court sessions and the wool and leather markets had ended. It was a short walk from Emmelina's house and usually a pleasant one, past the market stalls on market day, the bustling taverns and

202

the traders and merchants' houses displaying their various wares on drop down shelving from the frontages of their homes. Today was different. The streets were almost deserted apart from the last of the dwindling traders who were packing away their goods. Emmelina stepped over rotting fruit and vegetables and half eaten scraps of food, the usual detritus, which was evidence of market day. A few brave rats were nibbling at the remains in the diminishing winter light of the late afternoon.

She had not reached the Booth Hall before the full horror of the flood presented itself. Outside the premises of Alfred the Butcher a cart was being loaded with carcasses. It occurred to her that it was a little late to be doing meat deliveries. As she got closer she realised the carcasses were not those of animals but the bodies of Alfred and his oldest son. Their bodies were being dumped onto the cart like the animals they had once butchered. As Emmelina stepped closer she could see the tell-tales marks of purple bruising and the black necrotic boils upon their greying skin. Like Will, they had died of the Black Bane. Young Will had been the first human casualty of the Black Bane but he was not going to be the last. There seemed to be a connection just like Severin had said between those who had close contact with animals or their skins and catching the disease. She feared for Severin. His work meant he was often in close contact with the skins of animals. It was impossible to know whether it was the animals themselves, their hides or the flood water or something else. Maud seemed to think it was a combination of all three.

Alfred's wife was wailing, consumed with grief, her arms held up to the heavens, questioning the wisdom of the lord and asking him out loud how he could take a father from his children, a son from his mother. A gaggle of smaller children were hanging onto her skirts, crying and demanding her attention. Emmelina could not help but reflect upon the pitiful scene before her. Her own life seemed to be engulfed by death, dying, funerals and grief. First her parents, then Fayette, Will, then Humphrey, the flood victims and in increasing numbers those struck down with the Black Bane. She sympathised with the butcher's wife. What would she do now the main provider for her family was dead? The woman's grief reflected on Emmelina's mood, her own grief, not from the death of her husband but the death of her parents came back to her as raw as ever. She hurried past them unable to offer any consolation, afraid to.

Emmelina wasn't sure what to expect when she arrived at the Booth Hall. She guessed it might be a fairly stuffy and unfriendly affair. She wondered whether Severin would be at the meeting. It would be the first time they had seen each other since they had lain together. She wondered how she would feel seeing him. Wondered whether anyone would be able to tell something had passed between them. She worried he might become a victim of the disease and where that would leave her. The pain of grief and loneliness returned but she pushed them away, forcing herself to feel nothing and trembling from the effort.

As she walked into the main hall, heads turned and the hum of chatter tailed off. Undeterred and well prepared she walked past the gathering of men and sat down in a seat at the front of the hall. Gradually, the talking began again, getting louder. No doubt most of it was about Emmelina. She sat upright in the chair, her breathing rapid and her face slightly flushed. There was no sign of Severin.

Humphrey had been an important member of the guild. He had held the position of master until his death. The purpose of tonight's meeting was to elect a new master before any other business was discussed. As she sat waiting for the proceedings to begin, she recalled Humphrey's words when she asked him whether she would need to be a member of the guild to carry on the work she was doing for him. She had asked him in all innocence and the force of his response had upset her. He said he never wanted to see the day when a wife of his would attend a guild meeting and it would be "over his dead body" and here she was, attending a guild meeting, and Humphrey dead and buried. How truly strange life could be, terrifying one moment, joyous the next.

Emmelina listened attentively whilst the chairman explained the procedure for voting in the new master. He had hardly finished when Garlick stood up and addressed those assembled.

Looking directly at Emmelina, he began, 'Before we proceed. May I seek clarification on a matter?'

The chairman of the meeting, Gonzalo Bolante was a native of Cordoba, having travelled to the city on business some years ago, he had met and married a local girl and settled in the city. He was a short man with black, oily hair and swarthy, pitted skin. He spoke with an accent Emmelina rather liked.

'You may,' he addressed Garlick.

'Should a woman be allowed to attend or vote in these proceedings?'

Garlick glared at Emmelina. Her neck flushed with heat, the colour rising to her cheeks the heat intensifying as others turned to look her way. The question unleashed a barrage of discussion. A singular voice could be heard above the noise. It was Severin. Her heart lurched at the sound of his dark brown voice. She turned her head to look at him. They held each other's gaze for a second and then out of embarrassment or self-consciousness, she wasn't sure, she dropped her gaze. With her heart still pounding she listened to what he had to say, hoping all the while that what had transpired between them had gone unnoticed. It was only days since she had buried her husband.

'There is no rule in the guild's articles, which expressly forbids a woman from attending or voting. I suggest we get on with the meeting and allow Mistress Pauncefoot to remain. She has knowledge of the guild's work, through her marriage to the late Humphrey Pauncefoot and will make an important contribution, I'll vouchsafe.'

Severin had gained a good deal of respect in the city since he spoke up at the town meeting on the handling of the

205

Black Bane outbreak. Traders and burgesses alike listened to him when he spoke. A few of the guildsmen shouted their agreement. The chairman, who had been consulting his handbook whilst the discussion took place, agreed with him and ordered the meeting to get under way. Garlick, sat down, muttered something under his breath and shot a thunderous look at Emmelina.

The guildsmen listened intently as each candidate's name was read out. Severin's was not amongst them, however, Garlick's was, along with another name she did not recognise. Bernard Durandos, a cordwainer from the St John's area of the city was standing against Garlick for the position of master.

'I nominate Severin Browne,' shouted one of the men from the back of the hall.

A resounding cheer went up.

'I object,' yelled Garlick above the noise.

'On what grounds?' the chairman enquired.

'On the grounds that he is a mere journeyman and not qualified to hold the position.'

The chairman considered this point, checking his handbook once more but before he had reached the relevant section, Severin came to the front of the hall.

'Master Garlick is right. I am unqualified for the position. I thank you for the nomination but I am unable to accept.'

He bowed his head, took a side glance at Emmelina and walked back to his position at the back of the hall.

'Very well,' said the chairman, 'let's proceed to a vote.'

The vote was a show of hands.

'All those in favour of Bernard Durandos?'

Severin's hand went up. Emmelina, not wishing to vote for the despicable Garlick, raised her hand.

'And those in favour of Gilbert Garlick?'

From the number of raised hands it was inconclusive whether Durandos had won.

The number of hands looked even. The chairman instructed two of his assistants to count the vote. For the second time, Emmelina raised her hand. The two men went amongst the members and counted.

'Twenty one, chairman,' the assistant called out.

Hands were then raised for Garlick. The counters, counted.

'Twenty, chairman.'

Garlick had lost by one vote. He fixed his piercing eyes upon Emmelina. No doubt he would blame his defeat on her, she thought, almost regretting her involvement, Dulcina's words ringing in her ears.

The chairman announced Bernard Durandos had been duly elected. Durandos, a gaunt looking man, took his seat as the new master next to the chairman and the meeting continued. The main business on the agenda was that of the bridge repairs. The flood had undermined the brick arches and swept away the wooden walkway that formed part of the bridge, making it impossible for anyone to cross either to leave or enter the city. The repairs were being paid out of the city's coffers but were proving expensive and the coffers were running low. The burgesses were unable to collect their usual tolls from the users of the bridge and this was making them nervous. A heated discussion took place about their concerns that traders might go elsewhere, to Worcester or to the market in Bristol. The fear was they may never return.

The cattle sickness, which had now spread to the city's human population had taken many more lives since Young Will's. How many more would die was not known but this also was an area of great concern and another reason why traders were not coming to the markets. The fear and hysteria raged on amongst those in the community who had begun to believe a murrain had been sent to punish them. The fact remained that it unnerved visitors and kept them away in significant numbers. The chairman reported on the efforts of the bailiff and his men to eradicate the disease. He was confident they were winning the battle.

Another problem was the trows, which journeyed from the docks in Bristol down the River Severn to Gloucester. They were unable to dock in the city because of the damage to the river bank and the pontoons. Instead they had to dock in Bristol and transport their leather goods by road to Gloucester. The mood in the room was edgy.

Emmelina listened as the men spoke. Again, as in the town meeting, the men were complaining but no-one was coming up with any real solutions or helpful suggestions. She decided to make one of her own. She knew she had at least one ally in the hall and hoped she had one more in the form of the new master she had just voted for. She raised her hand to speak.

Chairman Bolante addressed her. 'Mistress Pauncefoot, you wish to speak?'

'Yes, Mr Chairman. I was wondering whether it might be prudent to raise the necessary funds through an additional levy on all guild members.'

The meeting dissolved into chaos at her suggestion. Chairman Bolante brought them to order.

'Let her speak,' he demanded, smiling warmly at Emmelina.

She cleared her throat. 'It seems to me as long as the bridge remains closed, everyone's business will suffer so it's in all of our interests to contribute to its repair. To not do so would be foolish and short-sighted, in my opinion.'

She smiled back at the chairman.

'I think Mistress Pauncefoot has a point.'

Gilbert Garlick's thunderous mood had not improved. He stood up and beat his hand on the table. 'I for one do not agree. We should not have to dip into our own pockets to sort out this problem. The hundred court should be able to help through pontage.'

Emmelina had no idea what 'pontage' was. She had never heard the word used before. She was out of her depth. Perhaps she should not have been so bold as to put forward her proposal without knowing the full facts. As if her thoughts could be heard, Chairman Bolante obliged by explaining the meaning.

'For those members who are unaware of the term "pontage", it refers to a toll that can be granted by the King for the repair of, or building of, bridges. I believe a "pontage" helped to build the bridge at Staines across the River Thames in London if I am not mistaken,' he added smugly.

Durandos, who had not yet spoken, leant forward. 'But we would need to seek the King's approval for such a toll and he would have to issue letters patent. The whole process could take years and we don't have time to wait. I have to say, I personally think Mistress Pauncefoot's suggestion is an inspired one.'

Durandos nodded at Emmelina. Garlick's eyes narrowed and he took a sideways glance at Durandos but said no more. Durandos had made himself a powerful enemy and an unimportant ally.

'I suggest we put Mistress Pauncefoot's proposal for an extra levy to a vote. Do you agree chairman? Durandos proposed.

The chairman nodded.

'All those in favour.'

One by one, hands were raised. The counters were not needed on this occasion. Garlick and a few other burgesses voted against her but it was clear her proposal had been carried. Emmelina could not believe it. She had triumphed once more.

A few more minor business matters were discussed before the meeting came to an end. Emmelina sat through these listening and trying her best not to look across at Severin who had returned to the back of the hall. She didn't linger afterwards as others did to chat and discuss the evening's business more informally. Instead she made her way through the throng of men, who stood aside to let her pass. She looked up, once or twice, to see if Severin was still in the hall but she couldn't see him. Her instinct was to hurry outside in the hope she might bump into him.

The evening had turned chilly. She was glad of her thick brocade. A blanket of stars filled a cloudless, black sky. Members of the guild were milling around outside but there was no sign of Severin. It was probably for the best. West Gate Street was empty, not even a drunken reveller in sight as she walked back. On the corner of Holy Trinity church, she stopped, detecting the sound of footsteps gaining on her from behind. The footsteps also stopped. She turned round hoping to see Severin. He hadn't looked at her directly while in the meeting and she had avoided his gaze for obvious reasons but she thought he might have tried to follow her surreptitiously after the meeting. To give her a sign, some hope that what had transpired between them had been more than a single moment in time. Perhaps he still thought it too soon. She had to keep telling herself to be patient.

But to her dismay it was not him. It was Gilbert Garlick. He approached her with the swiftness of a hawk and before she could get away he was standing over her.

'Are you following me?' she questioned him.

'A quiet word,' he whispered to her, swanning his neck to her level. 'Don't think your little foray into the workings of the guild this evening will do you any good. Just remember what happened to your mother.'

Emboldened by his recent defeat at her hands, she stared back at him defiantly.

'What did happen to my mother? Was she murdered? Did you have a hand in that?'

'It was an unfortunate accident,' he said, as he turned round to walk back towards the Booth Hall.

'Is that what you have in mind for me? An unfortunate accident?' she shouted after him.

He did not reply. Emmelina scowled at his back as he retreated towards the Booth Hall.

'What a loathsome man,' she said to herself.

She turned and carried on walking past the church. It was not long before she sensed she was being followed again. She swung round fully expecting to see Garlick trailing behind her. A black cat flew out of St Michael's Lane, mewling balefully and scurried across the street ahead of her. For a brief moment Emmelina thought she saw the flash of a monk's habit diving into the same lane the cat had emerged from. She stood for a few moments staring at the corner waiting to see if anyone showed themselves.

No one did. She quickened her step.

Chapter 40

The argument with Dulcina and her hasty exit from the house had played upon Emmelina's mind all night. Dulcina was more than a servant. She had become her good friend, along with Maud. She told herself she must apologise first thing in the morning and so on waking she dressed and joined Dulcina in the kitchen.

Her friend had already lit the fire and made a start on breakfast. Dulcina looked up when Emmelina walked in but did not speak. Emmelina could feel the unfriendly atmosphere and it made her feel uncomfortable in her own house.

'I'm sorry Dulcina,' she said.

'Sorry for what, miss,' Dulcina asked her, still not looking up.

'My behaviour last night. It was unkind of me to speak to you that way. I don't know what got into me. I know you've only got my best interests at heart.'

Emmelina sat at the table. Dulcina looked up and smiled.

'That's all right, miss. You've had a lot on your mind what with the master.'

Emmelina winced at the sound of his name.

'I'm sorry Dulcina but I really don't wish to hear my husband's name mentioned ever again in this house.'

'I understand, miss,' Dulcina promised, bowing her head again as if she had, once again, upset her mistress.

Emmelina stood up and went round the table to Dulcina.

'Here let me help you with that,' Emmelina offered.

'That's all right, miss. I can manage.'

Emmelina realised she would have to do more to gain Dulcina's friendship. She sat back down at the table dejected. For now, it was best left alone. Dulcina was not giving ground. Perhaps if she told her about how she had thwarted Garlick's attempt to be elected chairman Dulcina would have a better understanding of why she did the things she did. She also hoped Dulcina would forget about her outburst and they would be back the way they were. Dulcina listened in an uninterested way and made one comment, which instantly dampened Emmelina's spirits.

'It wouldn't be good to make enemies, mistress,' Dulcina said in response to the part when Emmelina told her she had out-voted Garlick.

Emmelina sighed inwardly. She knew Dulcina had no idea how her thinking affected the people around her, how she brought down their spirits. She knew Dulcina meant nothing by it but sometimes she wished her friend would be a little more encouraging. She decided not to tell her about Garlick's threatening behaviour or the feeling of being followed. She would probably tell her it was all in her imagination. Still she had a point it wouldn't help to make an enemy of Garlick. She would only be playing into his hand if she wasn't careful. He had a good deal of influence in the city and he seemed to be very close to the sub prior of Blackfriars.

She ate her breakfast and then informed Dulcina she was going for a walk. The walls of the house were closing in around her, like they were suffocating her. She needed some fresh air. The city was not as busy as it had been since the collapse of the bridges. A temporary quay had been built down river so that supplies could still reach the city traders. Emmelina ambled along the street, looking at the various wares displayed on the merchant's stalls. Her thoughts inevitably drifted towards Severin. It was crazy the way she had reacted to the sound of his voice. As if life were echoing her thoughts she heard his voice behind her and swung round to find Severin standing so close she could smell him.

'I had to see you,' he began.

Emmelina was so surprised she found she could not speak but instead stood gawping at him like some mute imbecile.

213

'When I saw you at the meeting last night I didn't know how to behave. I wanted to speak to you afterwards but it was too risky...After what happened to Humphrey.'

He grabbed her by the elbow and led her down Bull Lane away from the bustle of West Gate Street. The lane was quiet and empty of people. She could see in Severin's eyes the hunger he had for her, the need to take her. Once more, the physical beat of an invisible thread pulsated between them. It seemed to bind them together. Her body ached to touch him. She could tell he felt the same way. He went to touch her face, to pull her towards him but stepped back when someone walked by.

'We can't do this, not here. It's too dangerous. If anyone saw us...There would be talk.'

'I wasn't sure how you felt...after that morning. I wasn't sure whether you were avoiding me because you didn't want to see me again...'

She let her words tail off, not sure what the right words to say were.

'I wanted to see you again but after I heard what happened to Humphrey I thought it best I stay away.'

Emmelina knew he was right although she was aching for his touch. The frustration inside her was like a boiling cauldron of desire but one that must not be allowed to boil over. She had to be patient and exercise self-control. Her dreams of being free were not far away.

She was free of Humphrey. She was free to run his business the way she wanted. She was free to attend the guild meetings – and, ironically, it had been just as Humphrey predicted when he had said it would be over his dead body. And now that she knew how Severin felt about her she was free to pursue a relationship with him. In time.

A group of journeymen using the lane as a short cut to the river pushed past them. As they passed, they made a few crude remarks and joked amongst themselves.

'We can't be seen here like this. I just wanted you to know how I feel. I didn't want to leave things the way they were. Unfinished.'

'When will I see you again?'

'Soon. I hope. Very soon. Should I call on you?'

'Make it late. After Dulcina has retired. After midnight.'

Emmelina's heart was bursting with joy. All her fears about Severin, her suspicions about being used by him had vanished. He had been staying away out of respect for her and to give them a chance at being together.

'I want so much to kiss you right now,' she confessed.

'I'd like to do more than that,' he replied, his cocky smile re-surfacing. Another group of people went past them. The lane was no longer quiet and they had stayed there too long. Someone was bound to notice. 'We must go our separate ways. It wouldn't be good to be seen coming out of the lane together. I'll go this way' he said, striding off in the opposite direction of West Gate Street.

Emmelina walked away from Severin with a renewed feeling of exhilaration. Not dissimilar to how she had felt the day she had lain with him. But that had been short-lived. This time round her exhilaration was mixed with hope.

Hope for the future.

Chapter 41

Gilbert Garlick entered Blackfriars Priory from the main Scrudde Lane entrance. He demanded to see Sub Prior Gervaise at once. Osburne, the novice monk, asked him to wait by the entrance but Garlick was having none of it. Since the guild meeting, the night before, when his plans to be voted in as the new master were thwarted by Emmelina he had been incandescent with rage. Still consumed with rage and a growing hatred for the woman he saw as epitomising all that was distasteful in the opposite sex he had decided something must be done to stop her. Since his quiet word with Gervaise, he had heard nothing more from him. Today, he was determined to put something in place, something that would rid him of this meddlesome woman for good.

He pushed Osburne out of the way and stormed into the cloister, intending to make his way to the prior's private lodgings. The young monk ran after him, pleading with him to stop. Osburne knew he would be in trouble with the Sub Prior for letting him pass. The cloister was unusually busy. Brother Enoch had begun the building work in earnest on the priory. He now stood in the middle of the cloisters talking with the Sub Prior about his plans for the north transept window, holding up a large drawing, which he was showing to Gervaise. Gervaise turned round at the sound of raised voices. He was about to bellow across the cloister when he saw Garlick.

'Sub Prior,' began Garlick, 'I'm sorry for the intrusion but I must speak with you as a matter of urgency. In private.'

Gervaise dismissed Brother Enoch and Osburne and beckoned Garlick to follow him to his private lodgings. Once inside, Gervaise closed the door and sat down at his usual place, squeezing his corpulent frame into Prior Vincent's chair.

'What is so urgent you need to speak to me?'

Garlick removed his hat and clutched it tightly in his hand, crumpling the fine woollen felt. 'That woman. Emmelina

Pauncefoot. Remember we spoke about her after the burgesses meeting.'

'Yes, yes,' Gervaise waved his hand at him, impatiently, indicating for him to continue.

'You told me to leave it with you and I haven't heard anything from you since.'

'It's in hand. Why so agitated? What's happened?'

'Thanks to her I'm not the new Master of the Guild.'

'How is that possible?'

'She was allowed to vote at the guild meeting last night and as a result I lost. By only one vote and that was hers.'

Gervaise knew only too well how it felt to lose out to another. His bitter experience with Prior Vincent came back to him and his resolve to seek revenge was given vent. The animosity he felt towards prior Vincent was, in an instant, transferred to Emmelina.

'I know how you must feel. The injustice of it. How dare she,' he said.

'I tell you she's got them all under some kind of hex. They listen to her. She must be stopped. And another thing...'

Garlick thought of the questions Emmelina had been asking about what really happened to her parents and to Fayette and wondered whether he should tell Gervaise. He hesitated. He wasn't sure. Gervaise was waiting for him to finish.

'Yes?' Gervaise asked, his attention piqued.

He needed Gervaise's support and couldn't take the chance of scaring him off. So he decided to say nothing of her irksome questions. 'She's becoming far too powerful for my liking, that's all.'

'I agree. It is not God's intention to have women act as men. It's unnatural.'

'It's more than unnatural, it's diabolic.'

'You may be right, Gilbert. I've been studying such matters in relation to that woman.'

217

'I'm not interested in your studies. I want something done now before she can do more harm. Have you done anything since we last spoke?'

'I have had her followed.'

'And what did that reveal?'

'Nothing. When I last spoke to Guido he had followed her to the market but apart from that she has done nothing, which would draw suspicion.'

'When did you last speak to him?'

'A few days ago, but I told him quite unequivocally to speak to me the moment he discovered anything suspicious.'

'The boy's a fool. He wouldn't know a suspicious act from a saintly act.'

Gervaise reluctantly had to admit to himself that Garlick had a point. He had been busy with the funeral of Humphrey Pauncefoot and the building works to chase Guido.

'I'll fetch him now,' he told Garlick. 'Wait here.'

Gervaise made his way with surprising celerity to the scriptorium where he expected to find Guido, only to find his study carrel empty. Becoming increasingly angry and not wanting to be found out a fool in front of Garlick he went in search of him in the next place he was sure he would find him. The dormitory. Using the night stairs, he climbed to the monks' sleeping quarters. Having walked quickly across the cloisters, he was now seriously out of breath. He heard his chest wheeze as each step became an effort. By the time he got to the top of the stairs, he was in a rage.

The dormitory was empty, apart from one body. He walked over to the bed and without checking to see if it was Guido, picked up the edge of the straw mattress and tipped it over. Guido landed with a thud.

'Get up, you lazy oaf,' Gervaise bellowed, landing a kick into Guido's side.

Guido shot up from the floor hoping to avoid any more kicks. 'Sub Prior, I have hardly slept for five days.'

'That's not my problem. Come with me now.'

218

He pushed Guido towards the stairs, following behind him, digging him in the back to hurry him along. When they entered Gervaise's lodgings, Guido was surprised to see Gilbert Garlick in the room. He could see immediately Garlick was in a bad temper from the way he was pacing around the room. Gervaise sat down again to get his breath back.

Garlick stopped pacing and addressed Gervaise. 'Well.'

Gervaise didn't answer. He was wiping the sweat from his forehead and breathing heavily from his exertions.

Garlick turned to Guido. 'Have you been following Mistress Pauncefoot like the Sub Prior ordered you to?'

'Yes, sir. I haven't slept for five days such is my obedience to the Sub Prior's orders.'

'That's very good of you. Now tell us what you've discovered?'

Guido scratched his head. His lack of sleep was making him more sluggish than normal and he had to search his memory to remember what he had done in the last few days.

Garlick pressed him. 'Come on boy. It's not hard,'

'I did follow her out of the city one night.'

Garlick shot a look at Gervaise. Gervaise looked surprised. Guido had obviously not informed him of this significant event. Proof that Guido was indeed a fool and that he couldn't leave important matters to others to sort out.

'Why do I not know about this?' Gervaise demanded.

Guido remained silent. He had learned it was best to say nothing when he was in trouble

'I thought I told you to tell me as soon as you saw something suspicious,' Gervaise bellowed, his jowls flapping and his cheeks beginning to turn a puce colour.

Guido stared at the patterned tiles on the floor and at the painted wall decorations, anywhere but look at either man.

'You are in a lot of trouble, Brother Guido. I suggest you don't make things worse for yourself and answer the Sub Prior when he asks you a question,' Garlick informed him, the tone of his voice calm, but all the more cold and threatening for it.

Guido lifted his head and looked at Gervaise. Gervaise scowled back at the boy.

'Well, where did she go?'

Guido spoke quietly and hesitantly. 'In the direction of Robin Hoodes Hill, I think,'

Gervaise was getting increasingly impatient with the slow-witted monk and his tone showed it. 'You think? Well did she or didn't she?'

'She went out of the city by the East Gate. Then I followed her at a distance across Gaudy Green. She disappeared down some forest lane and that's when I lost her.'

Gervaise groaned. He knew he should have given the job to someone else but there was no-one. Jacquemon could be trusted but he was old and increasingly infirm.

'You lost her?' Garlick raged, moving towards Guido.

Guido, fearing Garlick would set about him like the last time, ran across to Gervaise and knelt in front of him.

'I followed the path all the way to the top of the hill looking for her. There was no-one there apart from some drunkards pissing on a pile of stones. I didn't like the look of them so I didn't stay long. I went straight back to Mistress Pauncefoot's house but I didn't see her again till morning.'

'Doesn't that crone Maud Biddle live up that way?' Garlick asked.

'I don't know,' replied Guido, still crouching on the floor in a penitent position.

'I wasn't asking you,' Garlick spat back at Guido.

Gervaise had regained his breath and was mopping the sweat from his brow. 'I believe she does,' he offered.

'Could she have been visiting her?' Garlick was voicing his thoughts. The question was addressed at no-one in particular. 'What time did you say this was when you followed her?'

'I didn't, sir.' Guido replied, not offering any further information.

Garlick gave him a sharp slap across the top of his head. 'Are you an imbecile? What time did you follow her out of the city when she left her house?'

'It must have been after midnight.'

Garlick pressed his thin lips together. He was forming a plausible scenario in his mind but he did not want to voice it in front of Guido. 'I think we have all we're going to get from this half-wit, Sub Prior.'

Gervaise gave Guido the blackest of looks. 'I'll deal with you later. You may go. But don't go back to the dormitory. Attend to your studies in the scriptorium.'

'Yes, Sub Prior,' Guido replied, lifting himself up and backing out of the room.

He had got off lightly with a slap to the head but no doubt the Sub Prior would find some loathsome penance for him like cleaning out the latrines, which he despised. And now, instead of catching up on his sleep he was expected to go back to the scriptorium and work. It seemed to Guido, that nothing he did was appreciated. After all, he hadn't slept for five days and this was all the thanks he was going to get for putting himself out.

When he had gone, and Garlick could be certain Guido was out of earshot, he shared his thoughts with the Sub Prior. 'What do you think of that? Why else would a woman sneak out of her house at midnight and head over to the hill?' Garlick questioned. 'You know what they say about those woods?'

Gervaise nodded. 'That there are Lollards preaching against the Catholic faith.'

'I've heard worse,' Garlick snorted. 'That woman Biddle. Wasn't she a friend of Sabrina Dabinett? Remember the rumours about those two?'

Gervaise looked uncomfortable at the mention of Sabrina Dabinett. He hadn't heard her name mentioned in a long time. He recollected how the monks were jealous of her gift to heal the sick, apart from Brother Paulinus. He had wanted to learn from her. Gervaise grunted to himself at the thought. Learn from a woman.

'Are you listening to me?'

'Yes, yes, of course.'

'You seem to be somewhere else?'

'Yes I remember all too well. But we couldn't prove anything at the time…'

'Yes that's true but it didn't stop us dealing with the problem…'

Gervaise was in a reflective mood. Memories of that night when the Dabinett's house burned to the ground came to him. It was unfortunate that Edmund Dabinett had been inside but, he reflected, there were always casualties when fighting a holy war. 'I'm not going to make the same mistake again,' he told Garlick, surfacing from his reverie.

'You must speak to Constable Rudge and get him to organise a secret raid. If we catch her up there, that's surely the evidence we need?' Garlick declared in triumphant mood.

'Wait,' Gervaise shouted. He heaved himself out of the chair, and waddled over to the bookshelf in quick, short steps. His fat fingers picked out the book almost instantly. 'I have this…' he said, lifting a large leather-bound book.

'What do we need a book for?' Garlick scoffed.

His patience was running out. He had come to the priory to see the Sub Prior for one purpose and one alone. To formulate a plan to deal with the irksome problem of "that woman". Now he had a plan in mind he did not wish his time to be wasted by irrelevant, unrelated nonsense in books.

'If you will allow me, I will explain.' Gervaise walked back to the table and placed the book upon it and began leafing through its pages. 'I've been studying it since the Lord placed it into my hands the night of the burgesses meeting. It's quite clear to me, having read this book that we are dealing with something much more malevolent, much more pernicious than the threat of the Lollards. We are dealing with the crime of heresy. Moreover, we are dealing with a sorceress. This book will help us bring this woman and any of her accomplices to account for their heretical deeds.'

Garlick rubbed his chin. Another thought was forming in his mind. 'The crime of heresy, you say? Tell me Sub Prior; am I right in thinking that in cases of heresy the church has the power to confiscate all the assets of the accused?'

'That is indeed the case,' Gervaise replied, a half smile forming.

'Perhaps we could help each other?'

Gervaise was no fool. He was wary of Garlick and his intentions. 'What do you mean exactly?' he queried.

'If I help you to convict her of sorcery then you can seize her assets and relieve me of my financial obligation to the priory?'

'Why would I do that?' Gervaise asked.

'You will have no need of my money. Emmelina Pauncefoot has inherited a fortune for which there is no living heir, no male heir to pass it on to. The church would get all of it.'

Gervaise thought for a moment. Garlick could be useful to him in this matter. He knew Humphrey had been a very wealthy man and that his assets would more than provide the priory with the means with which to build his new lodgings and be more than enough to advance his interests within the church. But with both fortunes he could amass a personal fortune of his own. He also considered the obvious added bonus that a successful campaign against the perniciousness of heretical depravity, followed by a successful conviction would surely bring him to the attention of the Vicar General, the Bishop of Worcester's representative, which in time would lead to greater things.

'If we are to accuse her of heresy we need to gather evidence against her. You may be able to help me in this. It may take a few weeks but then we can establish what kind of evidence is required to meet our ends. I will let you know in what way you can be useful to me.'

223

'I think we need to gain support for our cause. Others need to know the church's view on the spread of heresy in this city and her central involvement in the crime. May I suggest we convene a meeting to be held in secret and invite a few carefully chosen people?'

'Very well. Arrange a meeting with the others. I trust you know who to invite. Once I've finished my deliberations,' he said, patting the book like a favourite pet, 'and established what kind of evidence we require to meet our ends we may begin.'

Garlick smoothed out the creases in his hat and put it back on his head adjusting it to fit. 'I won't let you down.'

'In the meantime, I'll speak to Constable Rudge and have him organise a raid on the hill. If we are to catch anyone, we must act in the strictest of secrecy. Speak to no-one of this.'

Garlick looked relieved. He had already handed over the first instalment of his bequest and it would not be long before Gervaise asked him for the next. He turned to go.

'By the way, I'm curious. What's the name of this book that promises to deliver us?'

Gervaise, his smile fully formed now, patted the book affectionately.

'Its name in Latin is *Malleus Maleficarum*. In English it is known as The Hammer of Witches.'

Constable Rudge marshalled his men outside the gates of the castle. It was well past midnight and the night sky was ablaze with stars. Such a clear night meant it was bitterly cold and the men's garb reflected this. They stood before him, wearing dark clothing with leather boots, some with thickly woven balaclavas over their heads along with a woollen snood pulled down over their shoulders to keep out the cold; others wearing hauberks, a piece of armour which covered only the neck and shoulders. Each man had a weapon ranging from a heavy sword to a smaller more manageable knife tucked into their waistband.

Constable Rudge was an experienced constable. He had been present, as a young man, when Constable Beauchamp prevented Queen Margaret's men from crossing the River Severn at Gloucester in 1471, forcing them up river towards Tewkesbury and into the hands of the Yorkist army. Now well into his forties, he had seen more than most in the city and was well known for telling stories in the Booth Hall Inn, usually after the assizes. He now issued orders for the men to climb Robin Hoodes Hill, splitting them into two groups. One group of about thirty men would approach the hill from the west side; the other group of around twenty men, led by Bailiff Bliss would approach from the north. Sub Prior Gervaise had told him Lollards were practising their heretical faith somewhere on the hill. He was to arrest them all and imprison them in the castle until their trial. This order had come directly from the Sub Prior himself as he wanted to make an example of these heretics to prevent the further spread of any heretical pollution. Constable Rudge took a different view. He would sooner see them killed on the spot. But orders were orders and he did not dare displease the Sub Prior.

The men crossed the wooden drawbridge, their sturdy boots thundering into the blackness of the night. They marched to the South Gate, across the old Roman Bridge and out into the green fields bordering the city's walls. Once outside the city,

Constable Rudge ordered the men to split up sending one across Gaudy Green and the other directly south along Lower South Gate Street. Constable Rudge joined the second group. The noise from the men's boots was now softened by the grass and the soft, damp ground underfoot. They made their way up the hill, along the worn path Emmelina so often took. As they got closer to the summit, the path narrowed and they were forced to carry on in single file. Constable Rudge led the way. Half way up the hill a strange dense fog settled, covering the ground. Constable Rudge looked down at his boots. The fog was so thick he could not see them. He slowed the pace; raising his hand to indicate to his men that they also slow down and be as quiet as possible. The night was so calm the only sound was the occasional crack of a twig beneath their boots. There was not even the sound of wind rustling through leaves. Constable Rudge signalled to his men to stop. He had given them strict orders to keep silent so that when they reached the top of the hill they would be not be able to warn the heretics of their presence. Anyone who disobeyed this order would be dealt with severely. The element of surprise was key to the success of the task at hand. That was to arrest everyone they found, whatever their business.

Ahead of him, he could make out a glow from a fire or a brand of some sort. The dull sound of chanting, like the sound of the monks in St Peter's Abbey, reached him. Constable Rudge signalled to his men to fan out and surround the circle. The other group, led by Bailiff Bliss should, by now, he hoped, be in position on the other side.

Constable Rudge approached the clearing with stealth. He was expecting to find an errant, but pious group of people, holding a church service of some kind in the open air. He had not expected to see the sight, which now greeted him. A circle of men and women, but mostly women, naked and practising vile sexual acts on each other, man to woman and woman to woman presented itself. The glow from a bank of candles gave off enough light to make out the shape and position of their naked bodies. For a moment he did nothing but linger on the bawdy scene before him. He would not dream of doing those things to a whore, in private, what these people were doing in public. He felt defiled and debauched, like an unwilling participant in an orgy. At the same time lustful thoughts began to surface. These impure thoughts fuelled a fire within him of depravity but his church upbringing caused him to feel only self-loathing and disgust. This conflict of emotions sparked an explosion of fury against these offenders of God, which had to be sated.

'Attack' he roared, puncturing the expectant silence of his men.

They surged forward, smashing through the bushes they had hidden behind and roaring with equal intensity they bore down on the assembled worshippers, their weapons poised to strike. The attack was both frenzied and brutal. A battle axe hurtled through the air and landed in the back of the head of a young woman trying to escape. She dropped to the floor, without a sound, her head split open like a spatchcocked chicken. Constable Rudge could not help feeling a certain pride at the precision of the aim. He had given orders to capture anyone they found alive but their blood was up and his orders and those of the Sub Prior were forgotten in the melee. What would it matter if he was a few prisoners short, he considered. Besides, there was not enough room in the castle's goal for so many. He was not averse to cramming them in to a cell if needs must. It was of no consequence to him. A woman's terrified scream caught his attention. He turned to see one of his men wielding a falchion sword above his head and charging after an escapee. The falchion was a heavy broad-bladed sword designed for hacking blows, which caused the greatest damage to flesh and bone. With expert timing, the man raised the falchion and struck a blow to her shoulder, felling her to the ground. She lay on her front, her agonising screams silenced by another blow, which took her head from her shoulder.

The clearing groaned with the sound of metal hacking into bone as the constable's men, their taste for blood set ablaze, bore down on those trying to escape. The rousing sound of his men, thrashing about in the clearing melded with the chorus of high pitched shrieking coming from the women. Constable Rudge thought it wise to order his men to round up those that were left before he had nothing to show the Sub Prior.

Naked bodies were still scrambling around, searching for their clothes when Constable Rudge made his way towards a white-haired man standing next to a woman with a mass of long, wavy hair. It was Finn and his companion, Damiana. They both made a grab for their clothes, before heading towards the cover of the bushes on the other side of the clearing. Constable Rudge was not a young man and nowhere as nimble as his quarry. He was only half way across the clearing by the time Finn and Damiana ducked out of sight into the darkness of the bushes. His instinct told him the white-haired man was an important part of whatever he had stumbled across. He was determined to catch him. He followed them but before he could reach the bushes, two of his men from Bailiff Bliss's group emerged dragging the white haired man by his hair. Finn had a gash on the side of his head, which was bleeding badly down his face and onto his bare shoulders and chest. He had been coshed with the hilt of his captor's sword. Shortly after Finn's arrival, Damiana followed. She was holding her cloak in front of her in an attempt to conceal her nakedness. Constable Rudge noticed her full breasts and the curves of her body. His attention was brought to a stirring in his loins, which surprised him at his age. He quickly suppressed the feeling and turned his attention to the mayhem that was still taking place in the clearing.

Naked bodies lay on the ground, felled before they could make their escape. Constable Rudge took in the damage and satisfied not everyone was dead ordered his men to tie them up and corral them back to the castle.

The prisoners put up very little resistance as they lay there semi-conscious, moaning and dazed. First of all, their hands were tied together, and then a rope was tied around each person's waist, looped through with a metal ring. Then a metal chain was threaded through each ring so they were shackled to each other in a long continuous line. Constable Rudge counted them as they were dragged past him on their way back down the hill. They looked a sorry sight, he thought, as they filed past him but they would look even sorrier when put to flames.

***

The next morning Garlick arrived at the goal to inspect the constable's quarry. The whole ground floor of the keep had been given over to the prisoners. A low moaning from the twine of bodies covering every inch of the damp stone floor greeted Garlick as Constable Rudge opened the cell. Garlick stood by the door, reluctant to walk in.

'Is she in there?'

Constable Rudge looked puzzled. 'Who?'

'That woman, Emmelina Pauncefoot. You were supposed to arrest her on the hill. Is she in there?'

'I've no idea. Why don't you take a look for yourself?'

Garlick stepped into the cell. The floor had patches of congealed blood in places and the smell of defecation was unbearable. As he carefully stepped in between the bodies, a small thin person took hold of his boot. It was Rowan.

'Help me, please help me,' she begged, her voice weak and barely audible.

Garlick looked down into her pleading eyes. Her face was grey with pain. He felt nothing. He shook her off as he would a dog giving her a vicious kick. She let go of him, flopping to the floor like a skinned rabbit. He did not linger and, having satisfied himself Emmelina was not amongst the prisoners, he left the room.

'Did you let her go?' he asked Constable Rudge once outside.

Constable Rudge took affront at the suggestion he had not done his job thoroughly. 'I am not in the habit of letting go of any of my prisoners. If she's not here she might be amongst the dead outside in the bailey.'

'Whereabouts?'

'In a cart waiting to be buried. Just follow the smell.'

The dead had been loaded onto a cart and transported back down the hill. It didn't matter to Garlick whether she was dead or alive just that she was out of his way. He hurried over to the cart, like a desperate man, looking for lost valuables. The bodies were piled high on top of each other, much like the diseased animal carcasses being trundled through the city's streets. They lay uncovered, waiting to be buried outside the city walls in un-consecrated ground. He circled the cart looking through the slats but could not see the body of Emmelina. In desperation, he mounted the cart and, with his bare hands, started to turn the bodies over. Constable Rudge had never seen Garlick so wild eyed and demented. He was acting like some of the lunatics in his goal. He seemed unable to accept Mistress Pauncefoot was not amongst the dead.

'Satisfied?' he shouted at him.

Garlick grunted, kicked out at the pile of bodies and jumped down from the cart.

'The Sub Prior will not be pleased.'

'I've already spoken to the Sub Prior. He is quite satisfied with the way I have handled matters and pleased he has so many heretics to prosecute.'

Constable Rudge looked smug. Garlick was beginning to annoy him and he wanted rid of him. He had bodies to bury and prisoners to torture. Garlick just grunted at him and went away cursing under his breath.

***

Sub Prior Gervaise insisted on swift justice. He was keen to make an example of these heretics and stop the spread of heretical depravity. When Constable Rudge told him what he had witnessed on the hill, Gervaise realised he was not dealing with Lollards but something much worse. He insisted the trial take place the next day.

Gervaise was not disappointed Mistress Pauncefoot had not been amongst those arrested. Something would still need to be done about her and he was confident the brothers' good book would serve him well. But first he must turn his attention to the latest threat to the church's authority. He was sure the swift and decisive treatment of these heretics, followed soon after by the trial of a sorceress would certainly bring him to the attention of the Bishop of Worcester. Prior Vincent was not expected back for another few months but knowing Prior Vincent, as he did, he would likely put a stop to his plans so he must press on with the trial.

Gervaise was eager to have these two triumphs under his belt before his return.

Chapter 43

Emmelina heard the news of the arrests the next morning from Dulcina. She had woken in a good mood after seeing Severin but any remaining elation was swiftly extinguished as Dulcina gave her gory detail after gory detail.

'Everyone's talking about it, miss. They say they were found up there naked.'

Emmelina's legs buckled underneath her. She reached out for the chair back to steady herself, then sat down and listened as Dulcina recounted the brutal and upsetting details of the arrests. With each revelation her insides tightened like a knot. She could feel the blood drain from her face and the inevitable dizziness, which accompanied it. Dulcina knew about her comings and goings in the middle of the night after she had caught her on the stairs in her outdoor clothes the night Humphrey was calling her name but they had never talked about it. The incident had never been referred to, nor would it but she couldn't help wondering whether Dulcina had connected the arrests and what they found on the hill to her. For the first time in her life Emmelina thought she might be exposed and unprotected. For all his faults, Humphrey had sheltered her from the outside world. She never thought she would wish to have back the type of protection a husband could afford her.

Her thoughts were running away with themselves. What if they tortured those who had been captured and what if, under torture, they revealed her name? But then she remembered that was why Finn had insisted they be given faith names – to keep them safe.

If it had not been for her encounter with the monk a few nights ago she might easily have been one of those arrested and could at this very moment be languishing in a damp cell with Finn and the others. Or worse, she might be dead. It had taken that incident for her to finally heed Maud's advice and stay away from the hill.

Emmelina was absolutely sure Dulcina would not tell her secret to anyone. After all, she was the only thing keeping Dulcina from a life on the streets. Surely, she had considered that, hadn't she?

When Dulcina had finished telling all she knew she asked Emmelina whether she could attend the trial. She seemed to have an unhealthy and morbid interest in the fate of these unfortunate people. Emmelina had other reasons for wanting to be there.

'I'll come with you,' she told Dulcina.

***

Much to the annoyance of Dulcina, they arrived late. Emmelina deliberately made them late as she wanted to sit at the back and out of sight of the accused. She had asked Maud to come with them but Maud had refused saying it was ghoulish to want to witness such barbarity.

Emmelina spotted Finn immediately, his white hair standing out amongst the sea of heads in front of her. He was shackled to Damiana, along with Tegan and six more members of her faith. She couldn't shake the feeling she should be there, standing up for her faith, ready to pay the ultimate price. But she knew she was not brave enough to die for her beliefs like her heroine, Marguerite. She was a follower, not a leader and for that she was ashamed.

Gervaise approached Finn and began asking him questions as to what he was doing on the hill on the night in question. Finn could not feel the same way about his mortal life in the same way Emmelina did, for his testimony was unceasing, like morning birdsong. Emmelina's guilt increased as she sat listening to him.

In reply to Gervaise's question about what part of being naked and committing sexually deviant acts had to do with holy and sacred worship, he replied in his lilting, hypnotic voice

233

sounding more like he was giving a sermon than giving testimony.

'The soul annihilated in love can for the love of the Creator, behave without reprehension of conscience or remorse and concede to Nature whatever it demands or desires. Love tells the soul to express her desire nakedly. In this way we honour God.'

Finn was quoting directly from the Porete book. He had smuggled a copy out of France where it had been condemned as heretical.

Before Finn could go further, Gervaise cut him off. 'And where does it say you have to fornicate to honour God and be in His family?'

'Fornication is the word you choose to use but you lack understanding. You are nothing but a one eyed donkey...'

The Booth Hall erupted into raucous laughter. It was almost as if they were warming to Finn for having the courage to insult the Sub Prior. This did not help Gervaise's mood.

Finn continued. 'You seek God in creatures, in monasteries for prayer, in a created paradise, in words of men and in the Scriptures. You, and those like you, insist God be subject to your sacraments and your works. But God is here,' Finn fanned his arm outwards, indicating God was in the hall with them. 'He is in all places, in all of us. He is part of us and we are all one.'

He was getting the better of Gervaise and she could see by the deep crimson patches upon the sub prior's face and neck he did not like the way things were going. Despite the seriousness of the situation Emmelina was thrilled at the spectacle Finn was providing. The passion and earnestness he displayed for his faith left Emmelina in awe of him. She marvelled at the way he sparred with Gervaise. When Gervaise tried to twist his meaning, Finn twisted it right back.

'Are you calling me a donkey?' protested Gervaise, fuming with undisguised rage, yet unwittingly offering himself up for greater criticism.

Finn was deriding the Sub Prior in front of his flock, ridiculing him and his church. The crowd, still laughing and disorderly, were finally called to order by the mayor who hammered his gavel upon the wood block with the force of an axe man.

Finn explained. 'A donkey is a person who has not the intellect or the illumination to understand the higher realms of belief. You will remain miserable as long as you have such customs and practices. Your intellect is bestial. You leave the kernel and take the chaff.'

'You insult the Holy Church?'

'I insult no-one. I speak the truth. God's teachings surpass the Scriptures of the Holy Church.'

'Are you saying you do not believe in the sacred Scriptures?'

Gervaise needed to turn Finn's testimony to the church's advantage. If he were to draw Finn into speaking directly against the church and what it stood for he would be able to sway his flock back into the fold.

'I believe in God. I serve God. I would give my life for God.'

The passion and earnestness in Finn's voice was evident to anyone listening. No-one could question his obedience and love for God. There was tenderness and love in his voice, not harshness and hatred. The atmosphere in the Booth Hall changed. A pensive calm settled. No-one spoke, muttered or coughed. It was as though they had all fallen under Finn's glorious spell. All except Gervaise. He turned round to face those present. His face was bloated with rage. He scowled at anyone he could catch the eye of. His flock must fear God. If they didn't social order would disintegrate. Heretics would triumph. The world would surely come to an end if the Devil was allowed to prosper and that is exactly what the Devil was doing; working his evil way into the hearts and minds of these feckless souls. Gervaise needed to say something that would bring them back to their senses. He needed to put the fear of God into them.

'The Devil is at work in this court today. This heretic has entered into a pact with the Devil. He has renounced Christian worship in favour of the devoted worship of Satan himself. He does not love God. He offends God.'

Gervaise looked about him. His words were having the desired effect.   The crowd were crossing themselves and uttering prayers. Dulcina was amongst them.

'I think I have heard enough of this man's perfidious testimony and apostasy.'

Gervaise turned to Mayor Rawlings. He said nothing to him but as if on cue the mayor, wearing his purple Cap of Maintenance, picked up what appeared to be a pre-prepared speech.

'It has been repeatedly and reliably reported to us in this trial that these heretics act as if possessed with madness. They are nothing but creatures of pollution, preaching lies and heresy about our articles of faith and the sacraments of the church. They spread opinions that are contradictory to the Catholic faith. They deceive many simple persons in these things and lead them into various errors; they also do and commit, under the veil of Holiness, much else that endangers their souls.'

Emmelina listened to him defile her faith with his sordid interpretation and his accusations of heresy.

'You practice what is nothing short of sexual deviance, which is at the high end of the scale of contamination and which must be punished by the severest of methods. You insult our sensibilities and mask your deviance with a perverted sense of sacredness.   You pose a threat, omnipresent and highly contagious. You purport to worship God but your actions are nothing short of sexual menace. You are a bunch of seemingly wandering and rootless people confined by no boundaries, subject to no restraint of custom or kin, without visible means of support or a settled place in society. As such you pose a grave threat to the good people of this city.'

236

Finn sat silently, patiently awaiting his fate. He knew what was to befall him and in his acceptance there was great dignity. Despite her best efforts Emmelina's tears spilled out onto her cheeks. She wiped them away as quickly and discreetly as she could, fearing someone would spot her and deduce her unfaithfulness to the church.

Mayor Rawlings summed up. 'Fornication is sinful. Fornication without remorse smacks manifestly of heresy. I therefore find all present here today, accused of heretical depravity, guilty of such a crime and under ecclesiastical law I submit that you shall be excommunicated from the church and taken from here to a place of execution where you shall be burned to ashes. May God bless your corrupt souls.'

There was an outpouring of grief from the accused, all apart from Finn. Emmelina could see he was meditating on a Beguine text, going within himself, so he could bear his suffering and await the glory he knew would be his eternally when his soul finally left his body.

The guards were instructed to take them away. Dulcina stood to follow them. She had sat through the proceedings with a permanent startled look upon her face. She was a simple girl who had led an innocent life until she arrived in the city. Emmelina followed her. Outside, in the grey light of the afternoon, the procession gathered in numbers. An execution site had been prepared that morning, in the usual place, on the green in front of St Mary's Gate, just beyond the Abbey's precinct. A procession of onlookers followed the line of chained captors across West Gate Street to the execution site.

When they reached St Mary's Gate, Emmelina could see three huge pyres had been built, each with a central stake, substantial in girth so that three persons could be tied to it. Finn, Damiana and Tegan were dragged up a makeshift set of steps and tied to the stake at their waist and at their ankles. It was all Damiana could do to stand upright, such was her suffering. They were asked to renounce their sins and seek confession lest they should linger and rot in hell for their eternal lives.   Finn was the only one who remained calm and untouched. The faggots were lit and it was not long before the well-seasoned wood took hold and burned with very little smoke. Finn looked skyward and began to recite passages from his beloved teachings.

'Our souls have not earthly shame nor honour, nor fear of anything, which might come. Our souls have neither fear nor anxiety, nor are we fearful of the tribulations, which are to come. Fear not, for we are at the glorious seventh stage, of that we know not how to speak of. The gentle Farnearness is upon us.'

His words gave them solace as they repeated every word he spoke.

'Behold the aperture is opening and we shall experience true freeness, true annihilation. The presence of God is in everything,' he shouted above the roaring flames licking the faggots below his feet.

Taking comfort from his words and ceasing their sobbing and their cries they repeated the holy chant.

'The presence of God is in everything.'

The pale sun was momentarily eclipsed by an expanse of dark grey cloud casting a melancholy shadow upon the green. A sudden darkness came upon them, the glow from the burning pyres the only illumination. The green fell eerily silent. Dulcina crossed herself as did others. Sub Prior Gervaise had a worried look upon his face.

Emmelina could bear no more. She turned away and ran as fast as she could leaving Dulcina behind. She had to get far away from the smoke and the pungent smell of burning flesh. When she reached home, she was violently sick and took herself to bed for the rest of the day.

Chapter 44

Gervaise was true to his word and convened the meeting he had promised Garlick. He convened it in The Tolsey on The Cross. He had thought about holding it at the priory but decided he needed to distance himself as much as possible from the business at hand. Although significantly bolstered by his recent success with the routing of the heretics, which he saw as a straightforward affair, he was mindful this matter may be somewhat trickier. The Tolsey was used by the burgesses for town business and, if anything should go wrong, he did not want it to reflect badly on the church. Gervaise arrived with Jacquemon at his side. Already, sitting at the oak table was Gilbert Garlick, Bailiff Bliss, Alderman van Eck, Mayor Rawlings and lastly, Physician Teylove. The men stopped talking when Gervaise entered. He walked over to the top of the table and sat down. A pewter jug of ale and several tankards were on the table having been fetched from the Fleece Inn round the corner from The Tolsey. Gervaise reached over and poured himself and Jacquemon a draught of ale. Jacquemon took his seat in the corner of the room, taking his tankard with him and set out his parchment, inks and quills, whilst Gervaise addressed the meeting.

'Good evening, gentlemen. As you know, we have successfully crushed the spread of heretical contamination in this city but this evening I want to talk to you about something of a more serious nature. I have been made aware of the heretical activities of two women in this city, a matter of such concern to me I made it my business to talk to you all this evening. We must rout out all forms of heretical depravity and keep the faithful free from such pollution. We cannot allow this sickness to spread further and we must be diligent to see it does not. Do you agree, gentlemen?'

'Aye,' they all concurred.

'As I said, it has come to my attention that two women, namely, Emmelina Pauncefoot and Maud Biddle have carried out acts of sorcery in the name of the Devil and I fear their powers are growing. If we do not stamp out this sort of behaviour we shall see a preponderance of it and it will spread to our own families. That is why I have asked you all here this evening to discuss what is to be done about them.'

'What sorcery do you accuse them of?' asked the mayor.

'I think Master Garlick has the details.'

Garlick cleared his throat. 'I first became suspicious when the honourable master of the Cordwainer's guild, Humphrey Pauncefoot, became ill. I called to see him on several occasions and was not once allowed across the threshold.'

Teylove added, 'I attended Master Pauncefoot when he first became ill but those two women questioned my methods and my services were terminated.'

'That's correct,' Garlick nodded his approval at Teylove, 'and when I questioned the maid servant, Dulcina Sawyer, she told me the old woman treated him by the laying on of hands and the mixing of potions. It is my belief that between them they poisoned Master Pauncefoot, who you know, was a highly respected and upstanding member of this city.'

The men nodded their heads and muttered agreement at each other.

Garlick continued. 'She was also seen driving her husband's cattle to higher ground on the day before the flood. Everyone here in this room has suffered a loss as a result of the flood but not Mistress Pauncefoot. Her cattle were safe grazing on common land up on Painswick Hill. Not one cow has the sickness. She has even had the impertinence to suggest we pay more taxes for the bridge repairs and people are listening to her.'

'So you think she and that old woman caused the flood?' Alderman van Eck, a merchant who had settled in the city from the Netherlands asked in an accent Garlick found harsh on the ears.

240

Before Garlick could answer, Gervaise intervened. 'They do so by throwing rotting sage into a spring, and this stirs up miraculous storms in the air, which is what happened in this instance causing the terrible flood. The spring in question was Rolla's spring. It is a well-known heathen site.'

Garlick added his own opinion on the matter of the flood. 'The Sub Prior will speak in more detail on how these things are invoked. But for my own mind, I am convinced Mistress Pauncefoot caused the flood and, having only her own interests and furtherance at heart, made sure her cattle were taken to a safe place.'

Physician Teylove, still piqued at the dismissal of his services, added. 'And is it not true that sorceresses cause the birth of stillborn children?'

'That is so,' Gervaise confirmed.

'I attended the birth of Mistress Pauncefoot's first child and that child, a girl, was born dead, stillborn,' Teylove stated, nodding his head in agreement with his own statement.

Gervaise was pleased with the way the discussion was going. He needed to corroborate each person's contribution, speaking as he did with the authority of the church.

He said, 'She obviously brought about the death of the child because she knew it would be a good angel and therefore would have increased the numbers in heaven. The Devil knows unbaptized children are not allowed into the Kingdom of Heaven. Instead they linger in limbo on the border of heaven and so, by reducing the numbers admitted, she is helping to postpone the day of judgement that will see the Devil cast into eternal perdition. I suspect she has been working to increase the Devil's numbers for some time.'

'Of course, her mother was troublesome. There were rumours at the time the mother was a sorceress,' interjected Teylove.

'Yes, but if you remember that was dealt with some years ago,' Garlick reminded him. 'I have spoken at length with the

Sub Prior on this matter and he has come here tonight to give us his wisdom in these matters.'

Gervaise looked up from his tankard of ale.

'God has the answer,' he proclaimed, placing the leather-bound book he had been holding in his lap onto the table and patting it gently.

Everyone stared at the book. No-one spoke. Garlick cleared his throat again. Please, tell us about the book,' he invited.

'I believe God himself has placed this book into my hands to guide us.'

'What is this book and how can it help us?' asked the mayor.

'It was written a few years ago by my brother monks, Jacobus Sprenger and Henricus Institoris to stamp out the heresy of sorcery.' Gervaise scanned the room for a reaction before he continued. 'Having studied this book and hearing your testimonies tonight, I believe this is exactly what we are dealing with here.' He paused again. 'This woman, Emmelina Pauncefoot, like her mother before her, has made a pact with Satan. She must be stopped.'

He paused and looked around the table at the faces of the silent men. They were nodding in agreement. He was well rehearsed in whipping up emotions in his congregation. This was no different.

'And this,' he concluded, patting the book affectionately, 'tells us how to deal with the problem decisively.'

He sat back in his chair and this time waited for one of them to speak.

Mayor Rawlings emptied his tankard and poured himself another. 'And that is how?' he asked.

Gervaise sat forward, spurred on now he had their full attention.

'As you know, the Devil uses women to carry out his work because they are weaker than us and easily influenced.

Some have invited these demons to possess them. They are the wickedest of all. They are evil beyond imagining.'

The men nodded and a muted sound of agreement went amongst them. Gervaise knew he was winning. Another broadside and he would be finished.

'Yet they are cunning. They bewitch us with their charms, their wanton body, and their eager smile. Do not be taken in by their pleasant demeanour. Look to their actions. They are evil personified and must be stopped before we are all under the wing of Satan.'

Gervaise looked around the room. It remained silent.

'Go on,' said the mayor, sitting back in his chair, cradling his tankard in his lap.

'What we have not been aware of before is Satan is now more active than ever in our community. His demons are possessing women in greater numbers. These are the very women in your city.' Gervaise pointed at each of the men in turn. 'Your mother, sister, daughter, niece. It is for your own good you denounce them for you will be relieving them of their sins and evil doing.'

'Tis true Mistress Pauncefoot is a most comely woman,' Bailiff Bliss remarked,

'But not that old crone, Biddle,' Alderman van Eck added.

The men laughed. Gervaise did not. He leafed through the book until he found the page he wanted.

'Brothers Sprenger and Institoris recommend three approaches. The first is when someone accuses someone else before a judge with a charge of heresy or abetting it, then offers to prove this, and writes himself down for the penalty of retribution if he does not prove it.' Gervaise looked up from the text, momentarily to check he had everyone's attention. Apart from Brother Jacquemon, who was dozing in the corner, everyone was listening to him.

'The second method is when someone denounces someone else without offering to prove it or being willing to participate, and instead states he is making a denunciation through his zeal for the Faith or on account of the sentence of excommunication.' The words 'retribution' and 'excommunication' were spoken in graven tones. Again, Gervaise looked up from the quoted text. Satisfied he still held their attention, he continued. 'The third method is by inquisition, that is, when there is no accuser or denouncer, but the general rumour in a certain city or place is worked up about there being sorceresses.' Gervaise placed his hand flat upon the page and addressed his captive audience. 'It is this third approach I personally favour and the one which I recommend in this case.'

'What is wrong with the first two?' enquired the mayor.

'The book guards against the use of the first method because as it so rightly points out, if the sorceress practices her acts in secret, then if the accuser, for arguments sake let's say was Alderman van Eck, he would face the penalty of retribution if he failed to make good the proof.'

Alderman van Eck shuffled on his seat at the thought of suffering the intolerable and eternal pain of retribution as he remembered the church's teachings; that retribution was needed in order to satisfy the need of God to ensure such violations be paid for with pain.

'And the second?' the mayor persisted.

'For the same reason, the denouncer is liable to be excommunicated if the proof cannot be found.'

Excommunication was seen as a last resort. Because the church taught that everyone was born in sin and so the only way to get to heaven was through the church, then it followed anyone who was excommunicated would surely go to the eternal fires of hell when they died.

The mayor replied, 'Ah, yes, I see. So if we choose the third option, no-one is at risk of excommunication and no one person has to prove the allegation. You have researched this very well, Sub Prior. Excellent work.'

'But what if this woman turns her sorcery against us?' asked Alderman van Eck, still fearful of the eternal pain of retribution.

'Yes, what is to stop her?' the mayor threw in.

'That is why we must act quickly before her powers become too strong to overcome. Her house must be searched for images and objects of sorcery such as dried sage or the skin of a dead snake. The snake was the first tool of the Devil and as such sorceresses hide the skin or the head under the threshold of the doorway to a room or house. We must search for all these things when we arrest her and remove them from her. This will weaken her. And we must have her accomplice arrested at the same time and throw them both in the city's gaol.'

'So what is my role in this?' the mayor asked.

'I believe sorcery is exempt from the usual legal procedures,' Garlick prompted. 'I believe the correct term is "crimen exceptum", mayor.'

The mayor nodded his agreement.

'Your role is to act as judge in the proceedings and pass sentence on them,' Gervaise added.

'Very well,' said the mayor, standing up to go. 'If that is all?'

'Not quite. I have taken the liberty to have Brother Jacquemon draw up the necessary documents to take this matter further.' He turned to Brother Jacquemon whose head was resting on his chest, half asleep. 'Jacquemon,' he called, waking Jacquemon with a jolt.

The old monk shuffled over to the table from his seat in the corner of the room, holding a scroll of parchment. He rolled it out onto the table.

'The first is a notice we must affix to the priory doors and also the doors of the Booth Hall.'

'Read it out, Brother.'

Jacquemon's voice, shaky and croaky with age, read out the document Gervaise had asked him to prepare.

'We, the representatives of the Bishop of Worcester, yearn with all our desires and with all our heart that the Christian people entrusted to us should be comforted in the unity and serenity of the Catholic Faith and in their bowels should be removed from every plague of heretical depravity, and it is for the glory and honour of remembrance of the name of Jesus Christ, for the exaltation of the Holy Orthodox Faith and the suppression of heretical depravity, especially in connection with sorceresses, that the office imposed upon us makes us responsible for these matters. Therefore, to each and every person within the City of Gloucester, of whatever condition or status or dignity they may be, to whose notice these commands have reached, by the authority we enjoy in this regard, by virtue of holy obedience and under penalty of excommunication, we order, command and advise that within the next twelve days counted from now, whoever knows or has seen or heard that some person is reputed or suspected to be a heretic or sorcerer and, in particular, follows practices that can result in harm to humans, domestic animals or the fruits of the earth and in damage to the common good, they should inform us.'

'I have taken the liberty of drawing up two more documents to expedite matters.'

'You seem to be much organised, Sub Prior,' the mayor commended.

Gervaise puffed out his flaccid cheeks and smiled unctuously. 'I don't want anything to go wrong. It is imperative we take swift action against such heretical depravity.'

'Can I just clarify something?' Alderman van Eck asked.

'What now?' Gervaise barked, his moment of praise diminished.

'Am I to understand by just starting rumours about these two women, without any proof of wrongdoing, we are at liberty to lock them up in the castle gaol?'

Fearing he was losing the ground gained through his skilful sermonising, Gervaise fixed van Eck with a solemn look.

'Alderman van Eck, may I remind you that in the perennial struggle against sin man found himself helpless until Christ, armed as the heavenly warrior came to fight on man's behalf and free him from sin by submitting willingly to the fatal wounds of the crucifixion. The decisive victory having been achieved, man must still gird on his own spiritual armour or don his pilgrim's garb or prudently sail the turbulent sea on his way to salvation. We rely on God's mercy as long as we can remain mindful of God's justice. This will guarantee that we will never fall prey to the last and most dangerous snare of the Devil, despair.'

Alderman van Eck fiddled with his fur lined cap, no doubt regretting his question. He was no match for the Sub Prior and Gervaise could see from the anxious look upon his face he was once again winning the good fight.

'Jacquemon, finish reading out the documents so these good gentlemen may sign them and we can all retire for the night.'

Jacquemon unfurled the parchment he was holding and began reading in his faltering voice.

'In the year from the birth of the Lord, fourteen hundred and ninety seven, on the twelfth day of the twelfth month of December, it came to the ears of Mayor Rawlings through the report of general rumour and the evidence of clamorous notification, that Emmelina Pauncefoot and Maud Biddle from Maverdine Lane and Treadworth House respectively did such things pertaining to acts of sorcery in violation of the Faith and the common good of the State.'

Jacquemon paused for breath. Gervaise, impatient with him, snatched the document from him and finished reading it.

'That on the eve of All Hallowes, Emmelina Pauncefoot with the aid of the Devil did strike down her husband with an ailment, so grievous, it caused him long and painful suffering, which ultimately took his life. On the same evening, she caused the disappearance and subsequent drowning of her faithful servant, Fayette Cordy…'

'I thought the Coroner found an open verdict for her death?' the mayor interrupted.

'Quite so,' replied Garlick, 'All that means is he could find no real cause for the death but I find it an unnatural co-incidence on the same night her husband takes ill, not only does her servant go missing but she is then found dead, by the woman herself I might add.'

Mumblings of agreement went amongst the men.

'We know this night is the one night when the souls of the dead walk upon the earth and the Devil is at his greatest mischief,' Gervaise reminded them.

More mumblings and nodding of sombre faces.

'I'll continue,' Gervaise said, wiping his sweaty face with a cloth. 'That Emmelina Pauncefoot used the old woman known as Maud Biddle as her accomplice to poison Humphrey Pauncefoot with potions they mixed in the kitchen of his own house. That she further whipped up the storm by the use of dried sage, which caused the flood and the harm to animals and the good citizens of this city. That she gave her stillborn child to the Devil so he might increase his numbers in the fires of hell. These transactions were conducted on the twelfth day of the twelfth month of the year, 1497 in the presence of my scribe, Jacquemon de Bezille, who assisted me in the capacity of record-keeper and of Mayor Rawlings, Bailiff Bliss, Alderman van Eck, Physician Teylove and Gilbert Garlick, the witnesses summoned and requested for this purpose.'

Gervaise looked up from reading the document.

'Sign it.'

Jacquemon brought the ink well over from the small table he had been sitting at and handed it to the mayor.

'Just one more thing,' Gervaise said. 'I will be preaching a specially prepared sermon this Sunday on the subject of heretical depravity. I expect to see you all there.'

The men mumbled their assent. Garlick looked across at Gervaise, a self-satisfied look upon his face.

'I have one more question,' the mayor asked as he held the pen in his hand. 'What is the name of this book?'

Gervaise answered him in Latin. *'Malleus Maleficarum.'*

Mayor Rawlings scowled at him in annoyance. 'And in English, that means what?'

'The Hammer of Witches.'

One by one, the men scratched their signatures onto the parchment document solemnly sealing the fate of two women in the firm knowledge their actions would stop the pernicious spread of heretical depravity, which if they were not to act swiftly and decisively, would spread throughout the city.

Chapter 45

After the excitement of the trial, Dulcina relapsed into her silent and uncommunicative ways. She had changed since the distressing incident with Garlick from which Severin had rescued her. She was less chatty, more reserved and less inclined to go out of the house, even to go on errands, which she had previously been happy to do. Emmelina had tried to talk to her about what had happened with Garlick but Dulcina refused to open up so she had decided to wait until Dulcina mentioned it. The atmosphere in the house had also changed. A deep melancholy, foreshadowed by the absence of Dulcina's cheerful smile and her endearing habit of humming whilst she worked, invaded the house and was the source of much unease for Emmelina. She couldn't quite give these feelings a solid form but she found herself fretting about them, a nagging worry in the back of her mind. Her visits to the hill were well and truly over. She could not risk jeopardising the happiness she would find with Severin. They were destined to be with one another she felt sure of that.

Since the terrible deaths of her friends, she now looked for other things to occupy her mind. It was still too soon, she told herself, to be seen publicly with Severin. She did not want to attract unwanted attention. There was a jittery atmosphere amongst everyone in the city since the crackdown on heresy, led by the Sub Prior. Anyone who did not follow, to the letter, the principles of the Catholic Church were being routed out and severely punished. Emmelina thought it best to lay low and at least give the appearance of being a good woman, a grieving widow and a fervent follower of the faith.

Her efforts to gain some respite from the morbid atmosphere inside the house were fated. Beyond the city walls enormous pyres had been built to cope with the growing number of livestock affected by the strange and sudden disease, which caused them much suffering and left them dead within a matter of days. They burned unceasingly giving off the smell of burning flesh, which reminded Emmelina of the human burnings. They were accompanied by palls of black smoke, which drifted across the city's skies, blocking out the wintery sun and giving more credence to Jacquemon's prediction of a vengeful plague.

Not only were the cattle affected but people's horses, pigs, sheep and goats were also afflicted. The bailiff's men made frequent sorties around the city's streets rounding up any animal, which showed signs of being infected. Cartloads, piled high with the stiffened carcasses of rotting dead animals were trundled through the streets at all hours. There was much talk in the city's streets and taverns about the end of the world nearing. The preachers from Whitefriars, Greyfriars and Blackfriars for once had a common objective. They seized upon the fears of the city folk and used it to preach of sin and atonement and the retribution of God. They stood on street corners quoting passages from the bible and urging people to change their ways. Jacquemon had suggested at the meeting that the sickness affecting the cattle was the same plague as predicted in Exodus known as the fifth plague when all of Egypt's cattle died. Within a few days, the city was enveloped by a mass hysteria, whipped up by the religious community.

Emmelina, sympathetic to Dulcina's feelings and certain her mood would pass, happily took on her errands. It gave her an excuse to get out of the house.

Market days were always a pleasurable experience in Gloucester. The town would have an almost carnival feel to it with travelling troubadours singing for money and jesters entertaining the crowds. Then there was the usual traders buying and selling all manner of goods and the taverns full of people making money, their spirits high. Today, however, was different. The bridge had still not been repaired and the city was rumoured to be running out of money to finish the repairs needed. This meant visitors from the west of Gloucester had no way of crossing the river into the city. Those traders from Bristol and Oxford who were able to gain access by road did so in much fewer numbers for many of them feared they would catch the sickness.

Emmelina sauntered around the few stalls in West Gate Street before making her way toward the Kings Board. The structure was old, having been presented to the city by King Richard the Second in 1398, not long before he died. The roof was an unusual pyramid shape with a cross at the apex. On days when there was no market, people used it as a preaching cross and lay preachers could often be found, bible in hand, preaching from beneath the spandrels depicting the life of Jesus Christ. Today was no exception.

Dressed in his grey garments, tied at the waist with a thick rope, his uncovered head showing his distinctive tonsure and barefoot on the cold stone, a monk from Greyfriars was giving a sermon. The Greyfriars were zealous preachers against heresy and the importance of repentance. His sermon, which could be heard clearly above the noise of the market traders, was on the subject of heresy and, in particular, the heretics caught on the hill. Emmelina listened as he praised Constable Rudge for bringing them to the justice of the Lord. Cheers rose up from those listening. Emmelina looked at the faces of those around her. They were full of hate.

As she got nearer to the monk she noticed people were moving away from her. Those with small children held them close when she walked past making the sign of the cross and muttering a prayer under their breaths.

She stood for a moment looking around her to see if anyone else was receiving similar treatment. Perhaps it was a religious ritual she wasn't aware of but she could see no-one else on the receiving end of such behaviour. She caught the eye of a young mother. The woman spat on the ground in front of Emmelina and dragged her children away. The monk became aware of the reaction Emmelina was having on the crowd.

'What have we here? A sinner?' he cried out.

Everyone's eyes were burning into her like a pack of attacking wolves, their aggression bearing down upon her, crushing her. Perhaps her visits to the hill had been discovered. Did they all know? That thought terrified her. She turned and ran hearing the monk's words as she went.

'Repent. Repent. It is not too late.'

When Emmelina reached home she found Dulcina plucking a pheasant at the kitchen table. Emmelina took the few vegetables she had bought from her basket and placed them on the table.

'Dulcina...'

She carried on plucking the plump bird and didn't even look up when she heard her name mentioned.

'When did you last go out of the house?'

'Last Wednesday, miss, on market day,' Dulcina answered, her concentration on the task at hand.

'Did you notice anything strange?'

'Like what, miss?'

'Did anyone look like they were avoiding you?'

'No, miss.'

Dulcina had never been good at keeping a conversation going. Her one word answers and her reluctance to engage irritated Emmelina at times.

'I've just been accosted in front of the King's Board and called a sinner.'

'What do you mean, miss?'

'One of the Greyfriars monks was preaching on the Board and his flock, if you could call them that, turned on me.'

'I don't understand, miss?'

'Well they didn't exactly turn on me. But they were looking at me funny and pulling their children away when I went near them. Don't you think that odd behaviour Dulcina?'

'Perhaps you were imagining things, miss,' Dulcina replied, picking up a small axe and chopping off the pheasant's neck with the deftness of an executioner. She continued to cut the bird into four equal pieces, then scooping the pieces up in her plump hands, she tossed them into the blackened pot bubbling over the fire.

"I wasn't imagining anything. Have you been listening to what I was saying?"

Dulcina was stirring the contents of the bubbling pot. She stopped for a moment as if she was going to say something, then carried on stirring. She could be so irritating at times thought Emmelina but said no more about it and instead made a start on preparing the vegetables. The two women worked on in silence. It was at times like these Emmelina missed the company of Fayette. They carried on working, chatting about nothing important until a knock at the door interrupted them.

'I'll go,' announced Emmelina, welcoming the interruption.

It was Maud. She hadn't seen much of her since Humphrey's funeral. Pleased to see her friend, Emmelina gave her a hug. Maud stiffened and, pulled back. Emmelina wondered what was wrong. Maud looked troubled.

'Are you all right?' she asked her.

'I need to speak with you,' Maud answered.

Dulcina looked up when they both returned to the kitchen, greeting Maud with the same taciturn manner.

'I'll finish up here, miss and get on with cleaning upstairs,' she said, wiping her hands on her apron and giving the pot one last stir before replacing the lid.

Emmelina waited until Dulcina was out of earshot until she spoke. 'She hasn't been the same since that incident with Garlick. I can't seem to get through to her.'

'That might not be the only thing bothering her,' Maud said, placing her basket on the table.

'What do you mean? What's wrong, Maud?'

Maud fixed her with an inquisitive look. 'Haven't you heard?'

'Heard what?'

'The rumours.'

'Rumours?'

'About us.'

Emmelina stared at Maud. In her mind she linked the strange behaviour of the morning and the news that rumours were circulating about her and Maud. Her stomach knotted and the feeling of dread she used to feel at the sound of Humphrey's voice returned with sudden force. It was as though he had risen from his grave to haunt her. Feeling unsteady, she reached for the back of the chair. The fire crackled and flared, spewing out sparks. Emmelina tightened her grip on the chair.

'What are they saying about us?'

'There's a notice on the Booth Hall door asking all citizens to report anyone they suspect of sorcery.'

'But what has that got to do with us?'

'They're saying we caused the flood and the disease in the cattle.'

'But that's nonsense,' Emmelina began, but even as she spoke, Garlick's words on the day of the flood and following the guild meeting, came back to her. A sudden chill of death-like quality ran through her bones.

'What else are they saying?'

Maud took a deep breath in. 'They're saying we murdered Humphrey.'

Chapter 46

The nave of Blackfriars Priory was filled to capacity. Emmelina pushed her way through the tightly packed throng to stand at the back where she hoped she would not be seen. She had pulled the hood of her cloak over her face, obscuring it completely. She fixed her eyes on the floor, not wanting to be seen but curious to learn more of the rumours circulating about her and Maud. Dulcina had been tight lipped when she asked her.

An icy drizzle had begun on her way to the priory and by the time she reached the nave her cloak was damp. The nave, now humid from the warm bodies of the damply clad worshippers, smelt rank and mouldy. An air of expectation hung in the congregation, making Emmelina feel uncomfortable. She was surrounded by a group of unkempt, raucous men and women who smelt like wet dog. The children were dirty and their noses were streaming. They coughed and spat on the floor as they waited. She wished the monks would get on with the service so she could go home and dry herself by the fire.

Gervaise emerged from behind the pulpitum. He cleared his throat, commented on the greater numbers and thanked them for their faithfulness. Then he began his prepared sermon.

"Every heretic can be called a coiling, poison-spitting snake but he is actually the wicked foe of our human race, the Devil and Satan. With the subtlest rushing about, they cause storms which ruin crops and livestock and with the strongest assault they alight on and light it, and scatter and destroy it, subtly and damnably undermining the integrity of the Holy Catholic Faith"

Gervaise's voice bellowed out, in sharp tones, across the nave. He looked up occasionally from his sermon to be sure he had everyone's attention. He needed to see the fear in their eyes.

"My mission is to root out heresy and heretical depravity. Our world is divided between opposing and equal forces of good and evil.

256

There is a constant and titanic struggle between God and his arch enemy Satan."

Emmelina's ears pricked up when she heard the word Satan. Satan, she believed only existed in the minds of those who had evil thoughts. She looked around at those nearest her and wondered how many of them were thinking evil thoughts.

'God will have no hesitation in exacting his severest of punishments to anyone who commits acts of evil against him. We have witnessed such a threat in our midst as of late. What can we do to stop the spread of this evil?' he asked his God fearing congregation.

Gervaise scanned their faces. They gazed back at him in fearful awe but no-one dared speak up.

'I say this...Look into your communities, the streets you walk, the taverns you frequent, the homes you live in, the people you know, the people you live with and those you love. Look at them in a different light. May God grant you the power to see the evil in their ways. Root them out, expose them. For they must be brought to justice in the eyes of the law and God,' Gervaise continued, fervently. He was expertly whipping up fear and hysteria amongst those gathered and he was not finished yet.'God demands absolute loyalty from you. You are charged with seeking out evil. Are you up to the challenge I lay before you?'

The entire nave erupted.

'Aye,' they chanted in unison, eager to please and eager still not to be singled out for a lack of piety.

'There are those amongst us who are already infected with the sin of sorcery. I charge you to cast them out from amongst us and quickly before Satan triumphs.'

Sickened by the sentiments, fearful of what might happen next and worried she might be recognised, Emmelina slipped out of the nave.

Chapter 47

In the peaceful moments of dusk, Dulcina knelt at her father's grave and prayed. The painful memory of his death still haunted her. She prayed to God to keep her safe. Her violent encounter with Gilbert Garlick had rocked the foundations of her narrow world. She had no experience of boys, let alone men. She felt dirty. She prayed to God to forgive her. Her prayers were interrupted by a voice, which she immediately recognised and which sent a sword of fear into her stomach.

'Mistress Sawyer.'

It was Gilbert Garlick. Dulcina jumped up from the graveside.

'I think an apology is in order for my behaviour the other night. A momentary loss of control, I fear, brought on by the fine cider they serve at the Fleece.'

Dulcina's worried expression softened as she nodded her acceptance. Still, she did not want to remain in his company for any more than was polite. She turned to go. Garlick followed her.

'I must be getting back. I shall be missed.'

'What's the hurry?' he asked, grabbing hold of her arm.

'Please, sir.'

She tried to pull away from his grip.

'I think you should be a little nicer to me, Dulcina. I could, if I wanted to, get you into a lot of trouble.'

She couldn't look at him. The terror that entered her soul at the sound of his voice and those piercing eyes fixed her to the spot. She dropped her gaze to the ground, fearing he might put her under some kind of spell.

'What do you mean? I haven't done anything,' she cried, keeping her head down.

'You know what they're saying about your mistress, don't you?'

'I don't listen to gossip,' she replied.

'You should, when it involves you,' he said, softening his voice.

The tenderness she detected in the tone of his voice frightened her even more.

'When what involves me?' I don't understand you?' she said, this time looking him straight in the eye.

'Your mistress and that old woman, Maud, are in a lot of trouble.'

'That's no business of mine.'

'Oh, but it is,' he answered, twisting her arm and pulling her closer to him. 'You live under the same roof. You're tainted by that very association. No-one would believe you're innocent of the same accusation.'

'I don't know what...'

He touched her lips; his fingers were cold and bony and smelt vaguely of something unpleasant. 'Such pretty lips. Such a pretty girl.' His finger traced her face, moving down to her chin and continuing towards her neck, settling on her collar bone. 'But a very stupid girl if you can't see the rumours extend to you.'

Like a cornered animal, paralysed with fear, she could not move. All she could think of was that the prayers she'd offered up to God, to keep her safe, had not been heard. Garlick's light touch upon her flesh, was like a branding iron, pressing against her fast beating heart. Beyond her control, her chest rose and fell with each booming beat, attracting the attention of Garlick. Her panic shot to new heights.

'It would be a shame if someone so pretty, and so innocent, suffered needlessly.'

'I don't understand your meaning, sir?'

His eyes were fixed upon her heaving chest. He tucked his finger inside the deep cleft between her breasts. Dulcina blanched.

'I can help you, keep you safe. Make sure nothing bad happens to you.'

'How?' Dulcina asked, pulling away from him.

'I'll let you go. But first you must promise to do something for me.'

He removed his hand from her cleavage but kept his grip on her arm and began to rummage in the inside of his jacket. Dulcina tried to free herself.

'Please, sir,' Dulcina pleaded.

'You misunderstand me, Dulcina. No need for that,' he said, re-tightening his grip on her arm.

He produced what looked like a long piece of leather and held it up in front of her. It was grey with a distinctive black zig-zag pattern. She recognised it as the dried skin of an Adder.

'I simply want you to place this snakeskin beneath the threshold of your mistress's house.'

'Why?'

'Don't ask questions,' he snapped back at her, 'just do as I ask and I promise no harm will come to you. If you don't do as I ask I cannot guarantee your safety, nor avert the inevitable consequences.' He pinched her cheeks together, so tightly they hurt, and, raising her face to his. 'You know the punishment for sorcery?'

Unable to speak, she nodded her head.

'Here, take it and say nothing to no-one.'

He shoved the snakeskin into her hand. Dulcina stared down at it.

'Well, go on, go home. Before I have a change of heart and take you in those bushes over there.'

He put his hand on the belt of his trousers, in readiness. Dulcina ran from him as fast as her short legs would take her.

When she arrived back at the house, Emmelina was in the kitchen. Not wanting to see her, she crept up the stairs.

'Is that you, Dulcina?'

Dulcina stopped. She had the basket in her hand with the snakeskin hidden in it. It was the basket they both used for market.

'Dulcina?' Emmelina called out again.

260

Dulcina could hear her mistress moving towards the hall. It would look strange for her to be taking the basket upstairs. It was always kept in the larder.

'I'm coming,' she shouted, hoping to stop Emmelina from entering the hallway.

Dulcina whipped out the snakeskin and left it on the stair. With any luck, Emmelina would not notice it.

'Ah, it is you. I thought I heard someone.'

Emmelina spoke from the doorway of the kitchen. Dulcina had reached the bottom of the stairs, somewhat breathless.

'Are you all right, Dulcina? You look a little pale.'

'I'm fine,' she replied, forcing a smile.

Dulcina walked past her mistress, drawing her away from the stairs and into the kitchen. She walked to the larder and put the basket back in its place.

'I think I'll have an early night, miss.'

'Are you sure you're all right. Is that business with Garlick still troubling you?'

Dulcina could hardly meet her mistress's gaze.

'I said I didn't want to talk about that.'

Emmelina gave her a supportive squeeze of the shoulder.

'Sorry, I know. I'm just worried about you.'

'I'm just very tired.'

'Very well. If you're sure.'

'Good night, miss.'

Dulcina hurried out of the kitchen and back towards the stairs, praying with each footstep her mistress would not follow her. Reaching the step where the snakeskin lay, she deftly swept it up in her hand and carried on up to her attic room. Once alone in her room, she threw the snakeskin on the floor, undressed and got into bed. But sleep was not her companion. On the stroke of four, she heard the Curfew Bell from St Michael's church tower, its monotonous daily toll reminding everyone to light their fires. She had spent most of the time tossing and turning, drifting in and out of fitful sleep and

261

wrestling with her conscience. Emmelina had been kind enough to give her work as well as a home. She was the closest thing to family she had. How could she do what Garlick asked? She had been flattered by his attention at first and couldn't understand why the mistress was so against him when he seemed so charming. But she could see now that Garlick was no gentleman. How could she have been so stupid as to fall under his spell and now he was using her for his own ends. The self-reproach at betraying her friend had been gnawing away at her insides like the poison from a Death Cap mushroom. Garlick had threatened her with the fire and that terrified her. Since witnessing the burning of the heretics Dulcina was well aware of the agonising death she would endure if she did not do as Garlick had asked. It was this thought that was now driving her every step upon the wooden stairs.

All was quiet. Emmelina was asleep. Unearthing the snakeskin from the folds of her skirt, she lifted the straw from the threshold and, placing the skin on the floor, covered it back up. Even with the covering of straw, the snakeskin was visible and obvious. Anyone walking past would notice it. Garlick had told her to put the snakeskin under the threshold but she couldn't take the risk Emmelina would find it. Her life depended on it. She decided to place it on a narrow shelf just above the door. Taking a small, three-legged stool from the kitchen, she stood it in front of the door, taking care to make sure it was on even ground. She stood still for a moment, listening for any sounds. Certain her Mistress was still asleep, she stepped onto the stool. Being small in stature she had to stretch herself to reach the shelf. The stool wobbled and, for a moment, she thought she was going to fall off and make an unwanted noise. She steadied herself with her other hand and reaching again, placed the dead thing on the shelf, pushing it as far back as it would go so no-one would notice it. Disgusted by the feel of it, she replaced the stool and washed her hands, drying them on her skirts, then made her way back up the stairs, treading cautiously as she passed Emmelina's bedroom.

Sleep was no friend to Dulcina that night. She spent the time she had left till morning, kneeling by her bed, praying to God to forgive her.

Chapter 48

Emmelina woke to the sound of impatient hammering at her door. Whilst dressing hurriedly, she shouted to Dulcina to answer the door. There was no reply.

'What is happening to that girl these days?' she said to herself out loud, 'she never seems to be around when I want her.'

The hammering continued. She rushed downstairs to answer the door and stop whoever was making the noise. Opening the door wide, she was surprised to see a gathering of men, including the Sub Prior from Blackfriars. Before she had time to speak the Sub Prior began crossing himself. Emmelina noticed the rest of the men also crossed themselves.

'In the name of the Lord,' he began. 'It has come to the ears of the mayor of this city through the report of general rumour and the evidence of clamorous notification...' He sounded as though he had memorised some legal text. '...that Mistress Emmelina Pauncefoot of Maverdine Lane did commit such things as pertaining to acts of sorcery in violation of the Faith and the common good of the city.'

Emmelina could not take in what she was hearing.

Constable Rudge moved forward. 'We are here to search your house for evidence of the deed. Stand aside.'

Before she had time to act upon the instruction Constable Rudge pushed his way past Emmelina followed by several of his men. They spread out like cockroaches moving from room to room and running upstairs. Emmelina could hear the sounds of drawers being pulled out, chests being opened and slammed shut. She tried to follow them but was prevented from doing so. Dulcina appeared at the top of the stairs, accompanied by two of the constable's men. She looked tired and nervous.

Emmelina watched as Gilbert Garlick scrabbled around on his hands and knees by the threshold searching for something. When he didn't find whatever it was he was looking for, he turned his head to look up at Dulcina. With a slight incline of her head, she motioned to the shelf above the door. The gesture did not go unnoticed by Emmelina. Garlick stood up and effortlessly reached to the shelf from where he pulled something that looked like a shrivelled piece of leather but with an odd colouration.

'Here is the proof,' he exclaimed, holding up the object.

Gervaise crossed himself once more saying, 'It is well known the first tool of the Devil is the snake and sorceresses conceal such objects within their homes. This is most definitely the evidence of the deed.'

Emmelina looked up at Dulcina. 'Dulcina, is this you're doing?'

Dulcina did not answer. Instead she lowered her gaze and held onto the banister. Emmelina turned to Garlick.

'This is your doing, isn't it? You made her put that thing there.'

Garlick stared at her defiantly, breaking into a sardonic smile. He held the snakeskin out in front of him. He said nothing.

'Why are you doing this?' she demanded when he didn't answer her.

'It is God's work,' interjected Gervaise. 'Silence the sorceress before she can call upon the Devil and have us all cursed.'

Constable Rudge drew forward, holding an iron branck, another of his guards held a pair of rusty shackles. Emmelina backed away from them and headed into the kitchen in a futile attempt to escape. She bumped into the dresser behind her, upending the bottle of mead from the top shelf. It smashed onto the unyielding flagstone, spilling its unctuous contents across the floor.

'Seize her immediately before she causes any other objects to fly across the room,' Gervaise commanded, again crossing himself and holding up his crucifix.

Emmelina's knees gave way beneath her as the constable's men grabbed hold of her arms. She struggled but soon realised the pointlessness of that. Constable Rudge's men were strong and determined. Her hands were tied tightly together in front of her with a rough twine of rope. Constable Rudge and his men advanced towards her. Emmelina struggled even more, panicking at the thought of the ordeal that was to befall her. She was outnumbered and outmatched but while she still had the power to speak she vented her anger.

'Is this what you do to women who don't behave as you would want them to?' she shouted. 'Is this what you did to my mother?'

There was no answer. She looked across at Dulcina who was sobbing into the hem of her skirts. Despite her own predicament, Emmelina could still feel sorry for her. She was certain Garlick had played a great part in her betrayal, probably threatening poor Dulcina. Whilst she could still speak she shouted across to her.

'I know they made you do it Dulcina. I understand. Please don't...'

Constable Rudge held her head firmly with his large hands. She tried to press her mouth shut but he pushed his grubby thumbs in between her lips and prised open her jaw. In his firm grasp Emmelina's jawbone became like the delicate skull of a small bird, ready to cave in. For fear of broken bones and with a fatalistic resignation she allowed the branck to be fitted. The rusty metal tongue forced into her mouth tasted bitter. The guards, holding onto the chain attached to the branck, tugged at it violently and pulled her forward.

Outside in the lane a mob had gathered. Gervaise delivered an impromptu sermon.

'*Whatever we do in word or work, let it all be done in the name of our Lord, Jesus Christ. Amen.*'

'Amen,' the mob repeated reverently.

Gervaise held up the dead snake in triumphant victory. The mob cheered loudly and shouted obscenities at Emmelina. Their religious fervour had been whipped up, first by the burnings and then Gervaise's Sunday sermon. Thus began her

266

ordeal as she was dragged along the lane and into the busy streets of West Gate Street. It was market day and so the streets were packed with traders and buyers. Once people realised what was happening they joined in with the shouting and threw whatever rotten fruit and vegetables they had to hand. Strangers spat at her. A chorus of 'whore', 'hell hag' and 'sorceress' echoed behind her as she stumbled her way through the milling crowd.

Only a small group of hecklers remained when they reached the entrance to the castle. The wooden drawbridge spanning the moat clattered as the constable and his men with their stout boots tramped across. Once inside the bailey, they dragged her to the entrance of the keep. Still being dragged by the branck they led her up a circular stone staircase to the top of the tower. Several times she stumbled on the narrow steps only to be yanked to her feet by the man holding the chain. At the top of the stairs Constable Rudge opened a small wooden door inlaid with iron studs, a small barred window at its centre. Once inside they removed the branck and untied her hands. The rope had left welts where it had been fastened too tightly. She could still taste the rusty metal in her mouth but at least she was able to breathe easier. They pushed her to the wooden floor where her feet were fastened into a pair of leg irons, which were bolted to the base of the outer wall leaving her hands free. Constable Rudge checked the irons were securely fastened, stood up and walked to the door. Remembering tales of poor souls languishing in prison till their death, panic swamped Emmelina.

'Wait,' she cried, struggling to her feet, 'What's going to happen to me now?'

'That's for the judge to decide,' he said, without turning.

'When will you be back?'

Constable Rudge ignored her question. The door slammed behind him and she heard the key turning noisily in the lock. She listened as the sound of their footsteps grew distant until she was left in silence and alone with her thoughts.

Standing there, shackled to the floor and full of despondency she sank to her knees, placing her hands together in prayer. Never before had she experienced such an urgent need to ask for help from a higher authority, such was her desperation.

'Heavenly Father, I know I am close to despair. Bring home to me that I am never alone, but that You are with me even in the depths of my despair. Remind me that no matter what I may endure now, an unending joy awaits me. Heavenly Father, in my present need, help me to believe that you are with me and will do whatever is best for me. Give me the strength to trust You and put the present and future in Your Hands. Grant this through Christ, our Lord. Amen.'

She repeated her prayer, like a mantra, over and over until she drifted into a trance-like state and, mentally exhausted, fell asleep.

Chapter 49

Maud sat by the fire in her kitchen sipping peppermint tea. Pomfrey stretched out on her lap and began stredding.

'Now stop that, your claws are too sharp for that nonsense,' she admonished.

Pomfrey took no notice of her. She stroked his warm fur and he purred in response. The purring sound instantly relaxed Maud as she warmed her old bones by the roaring fire. She closed her eyes and sank further back into her favourite chair, thinking of the busy day ahead of her. First, she had to visit Hannah Coprun, wife of Isaac in the Jewish quarter, a once thriving community down East Gate Street. No-one else would attend her on account of her being Jewish but this did not concern Maud. She had just given birth to her sixth child and was feeling very weak. Maud had made up some fresh tonic that morning from the herbs she grew in her garden. Then she planned to visit Emmelina to see how she was coping after the death of Humphrey. She was worried about her friend. It was obvious she was not grieving from the death of her husband but her reaction to his death that day in the kitchen had not been natural. That was not her only concern. The rumours she had heard regarding his death disturbed her greatly. She needed to talk to Emmelina and explore what could be done about them. After that, she would spend the afternoon at the market and stock up on herbs and spices she was not able to grow in her garden and perhaps call in at the New Inn for a small glass of cider as a treat.

She heaved her weary frame from the armchair, tipping Pomfrey onto the stone flags. He stretched again and slinked off to his spot on the windowsill. Maud was packing her things into a basket when she heard loud thudding on the door. Alarmed, she looked across at Pomfrey. He was arched and alert. She hardly ever had visitors, living as she did outside the city walls and preferring to keep herself to herself. She walked over to the door. Before she reached it, there was more insistent thudding and this time she heard voices shouting. Maud's heart beat faster and her breathing became laboured. Her sixth sense told her this was not a friendly call. She took in a deep breath and opened the door. Bailiff Bliss and his men stood in front of her. Bailiff Bliss held an official document in his hand, which he read out to her.

Maud's mood changed from one of alarm to one of resignation as she heard the charges read out.

It had only been a matter of time.

Chapter 50

Dulcina sat on the bottom step of the stairs in the empty hallway of the house she had come to look upon as her home. The noise of the baying crowd had long since gone and the house had taken on an eerie quietness in the early morning gloom. Visions of Emmelina being dragged out of the house by the constable's men haunted her as did the look on Emmelina's face when she realised who had planted the snakeskin and sealed her fate. She remembered the many kindnesses of her mistress and the old woman Maud, who had become like a mother to her.

The enormity of her betrayal consumed her and, like the sudden force of a wave, she was struck with a queasy feeling in her stomach accompanied by a metallic taste in her mouth. Knowing what was about to happen she ran to the door and out into the lane where she was violently sick. Steadying herself by the doorway, she heard footsteps. She turned to see Constable Rudge and his men marching with haste towards her. Fearing her imminent arrest, she dropped to her knees and began praying.

'Out of the way,' one of the men shouted, pushing her aside.

They marched past her into the house. Still feeling sick and holding onto her stomach, she leant against the doorway. She could hear Constable Rudge shouting orders and lots of loud banging. Afraid to enter the house, she peered into the hallway just as Constable Rudge emerged from the kitchen. She ducked back into the lane but he had seen her.

'Are you Dulcina Sawyer?'

'Yes, sir,' she replied, her stomach lurching at the sound of his voice.

'This house is no longer in the possession of Mistress Pauncefoot. It has been appropriated on the orders of the Sub Prior.'

'Sorry sir, I don't understand?'

271

'It means you can't stay here. I'll give you five minutes to collect your belongings or I'll arrest you for trespass.'

'But where will I go?'

'That's no concern of mine. If you don't hurry up and stop asking questions I'll arrest you now for obstructing me in my official business.'

He made a move towards her. With the speed of a hunted animal, Dulcina shot past him and ran up to her room. She hurriedly stuffed the new clothes Emmelina had bought for her into her basket along with a few personal items of her father's and ran back down the stairs and out of the door.

Once again, Dulcina found herself sitting on The Cross, clutching her basket, facing an uncertain future. Homeless, hungry and fearing for her safety she sat for some time in a daze. As the streets got busier, people walked past her but she was barely aware of them. She had neither eaten nor drunk anything since the previous evening and the hunger in her belly was gnawing away at her insides. As if by some primal trigger of self-preservation, she stood up and headed for the only person she thought could help her.

The New Inn was busy as usual with visiting pilgrims, the atmosphere jolly and comforting as she entered the bar in search of Thomas Myatt. He was standing by the beer barrels, talking to a young kitchen maid.

'And to what do we owe this unexpected pleasure so early in the morning, Mistress Sawyer?' he asked, his booming voice carrying over the room.

Before she could answer him, a strange feeling overcame her. She collapsed onto the stone flags and passed out. When Dulcina opened her eyes, Thomas and the maid were standing over her.

'Here drink this,' Thomas said, placing a cup of warm ale to her lips.

She took a few sips then pushed the cup away and tried to get up.

'Just sit there for a while and take a few more sips, then we'll get you up and sorted.'

She took a few more sips, thanked him in a weak voice and again tried to get up off the floor. This time Thomas helped her to a nearby pew by the still unlit fire.

'Now then, what's brought this on?' he asked, sitting down beside her.

'My mistress was arrested this morning.'

He didn't look surprised at the news.

'I did hear rumours,' he replied, offering her the cup.

Dulcina took it from him and took a few more sips. The young girl had followed them to the table and was standing by it.

'Is it true, then?' she asked Dulcina.

'Is what true?'

'That your mistress murdered 'er 'usband and...'

Thomas interrupted her. 'That's enough, Mae. Get back to work.'

Mae looked offended. 'Huh,' she said, throwing her head back and leaving them alone.

'I'm sorry to hear about your mistress. She seemed like a nice young woman.'

Dulcina's face crumpled. 'She was...and I've sent her to her death.'

Thomas put his arm around her shoulder to comfort her. This only made her worse. Thomas said nothing, only squeezing her gently and drawing her close to his barrel chest.

Chapter 51

Severin was working on the trinket box he planned to give to Emmelina using a technique the French call 'cuir cisele'. He had learnt it in France while working his way to England. First of all, he created the outline of the pattern he had designed, using a pointed tool, and then dampened the leather. He was now bringing the design into relief by depressing the background, and stamping a succession of dots into the leather very close together by means of an awl.

He was thinking of Emmelina and their brief but pleasurable time together. Since their brief meeting in the gate street they had not seen one another. It had not been for want of trying but each time he had approached her house after midnight one of the Blackfriar monks had been skulking outside as if keeping guard. He couldn't risk it. He had to content himself with his memories of her. He had surprised himself at the intensity of feeling he had for her. It had come upon him like the strike of a bolt of lightning. No other woman had had such an effect on him. She possessed a mixture of vulnerability and strength, qualities he found so exquisitely arousing in a woman. At the guild meeting she had displayed a certain feistiness managing to vex Gilbert Garlick. And when he pulled her into the lane, how vulnerable she became. How he wanted to take her by the hand and lead her through the streets of Gloucester to his bed and experience the pleasure all over again.

She had looked more beautiful than ever that day, her careworn features brighter and more relaxed. He had known many women but none were like her. Emmelina was different and he found himself thinking about her at the oddest of moments. His shock at finding out Humphrey was dead had been tinged with hope. Maybe it was time to settle down and make an honest woman of her. The constant frustration at not being with her was driving him insane with desire. How he had kept his hands off her, he would never know. It was so acute it was affecting his work. He had made several mistakes whilst working on the box and had made several false starts. Just thinking about her now, naked next to him, in his bed...

He threw the metal awl against the wall. It struck with such force the wooden handle snapped off. Annoyed at himself, he bent down to pick it up and to see if he could fix it. Tools were expensive and he could ill afford to damage them in such a way. He knew if their union was to be a success there would have to be a period of mourning but if only they could sneak the odd moment together without anyone knowing and then, after a respectable amount of time had passed, perhaps they could court each other, and then...

His thoughts were interrupted by a rapid bout of knocks at his door. He opened it to find his friend Thomas standing there with a pale looking Dulcina.

'What's the matter?' he asked, thinking Dulcina had taken ill in the street.

'It's Emmelina. She's been arrested.'

Severin still had the wooden handle of the awl in his hand. He was vaguely aware of the metal point digging into his palm. Still, he could not ease his grip.

'Sit down, you look like you could do with a drink,' Thomas said, taking hold of his friend's shoulder and guiding him towards a chair.

Severin slumped into it, dazed and in shock, his heavy brows knotted into an expression of disbelief.

'Arrested,' he repeated, as if it would make more sense if he said it again.

'Yes. This morning. Maud as well.'

'What for?'

'Heresy and sorcery,' Thomas replied, flatly.

'Heresy and sorcery,' Severin repeated, bewildered.

Thomas leant over and gently eased the awl from his fingers. The point had pierced his palm and a pin prick of blood seeped from the wound.

'What has she done?' he asked, running his fingers through his thick black hair.

Thomas was no fool. He could see there was more to Severin's concern for Emmelina than friendship.

'They say she killed Humphrey, amongst other things,'

'Killed Humphrey? Who says?'

'The Sub Prior and the burgesses. Constable Rudge arrested them early this morning. They've been taken to the castle gaol.'

'They?'

'Maud has been arrested with her.'

Severin was so shocked he was lost for words. He pressed his hands against his cheeks, dragging them slowly down his face in a gesture of sheer disbelief. Eventually, he stood up.

'I must see her,' he said.

'Wait a moment. We need to talk,' Thomas said, pressing down on Severin's shoulder and forcing him to sit. He pulled a chair over and sat opposite his friend. 'They have evidence against her,' Thomas began.

'What possible evidence could they have?'

'The only solid evidence was a snakeskin they found hidden above the door at Emmelina's house.'

'I don't understand. How is a snakeskin evidence of sorcery?'

'Something about how a snake is the first tool of the Devil and how she was able to kill Humphrey by using its powers.'

'I don't believe it. Any of it. It's nonsense.'

Dulcina broke down. 'I'm sorry, I'm so sorry. I didn't have a choice. He told me he would burn me for sorcery if I didn't do it.'

'What's she talking about?' Severin looked at Thomas for the answer.

When Thomas didn't say anything he turned on Dulcina.

'What have you done, Dulcina?' Severin demanded.

Dulcina couldn't speak such was her distress. Thomas intervened.

'Dulcina has explained it all to me this morning. Gilbert…'

Severin shot a thunderous look at Thomas. 'That toad! What's he got to do with this?'

'Gilbert Garlick threatened Dulcina last night. He said if she didn't hide the snakeskin he gave her, he would accuse her of sorcery along with the others. She had no choice.'

'Of course she had a choice,' Severin snapped.

Thomas tried to placate him. 'Can't you see? She's only a girl.'

Severin rubbed his eyes vigorously with the palms of his hands.

'What I see is a foolish young girl who has sent two innocent women to their deaths,' he shouted.

Dulcina cowed in her seat, still pleading forgiveness.

'Just stop her making that noise Thomas. It isn't helping.'

'Look, you can see how bad she feels about it. Now is not the time to scold the poor girl. We need to think about how we can make this right.'

'Well, we'll have to confront Garlick, get him to admit he forced Dulcina to plant the snakeskin and get them out of gaol.'

'It's not that simple.'

Severin glared at his friend. Thomas explained.

'They're saying they killed Fayette as well, *and* caused the storm *and* the outbreak of the Black Bane through means of sorcery.'

'But that's ridiculous. I already explained to them the illness was caused by the flood.'

'They say they caused the storm by throwing rotted sage into Rolla's spring.'

'But Maud uses sage in her healing potions. That's what she gave to Humph…'

He stopped in mid-sentence, realising how that sounded. People could be very superstitious and easily frightened by such things. He could see with uncanny clarity how a story

277

could be concocted out of nothing but still be believed. No doubt the church had a large part to play in denouncing Emmelina and Maud and stirring up feelings of fear in the burgesses. He had long held the notion Garlick was no good, even before he caught him molesting Dulcina in the porch of St Mary de Grace church. He looked at her now, her head leaning against the ample chest of his good friend Thomas, her body juddering with sob after sob.

'Is there nothing we can do?'

'It doesn't look good. Short of breaking them out of the castle gaol, I fear not.' Thomas walked over to Severin, put his arm over his shoulder and took him aside. 'I have a favour to ask, my friend,' he whispered. 'Dulcina has been thrown out of Emmelina's house. The church has confiscated the property. She has nowhere to go.'

Severin pulled away from his friend.

'Oh no,' he countered. 'What about yours?'

'I only have room for staff and I just took someone on yesterday.'

Severin looked at Dulcina. She was wiping her eyes with the hem of her skirts. She looked very young and acutely vulnerable.

'She's been a good servant and friend to Emmelina since Fayette's death. I'm sure she would do a good job looking after you.' He slapped his friend's back. 'What do you say?'

Severin hesitated. He must be getting soft in his old age, he thought, as something tugged at his conscience. 'Very well. But she'll have to sleep down here.'

'I'm sure she'd prefer that to the cold ground outside,' Thomas grinned, acknowledging his friend's acceptance of the situation.

'Garlick will have to pay for this,' Severin said with menace.

'No good can come of that kind of talk. You'll only end up in the next cell. No, that won't do. We must pray and hope something comes along to change things.'

278

'I don't pray,' Severin snapped.
'Then perhaps you should start.'

Chapter 52

Maud sat on the floor of her cell, her back resting against the dank coldness of the stone wall as she watched a family of dormice scurry in and out of a hole in the wall dragging lengths of corn to build a secret nest somewhere beyond the walls that encased her. There was a faint smell of boiled cabbage mixed with the smell of mushrooms, which she took to be coming from the trails of green slime running down the walls. Her old bones ached more than ever and she missed her cat Pomfrey. The enforced separation from her dearly loved pet had caused her more anxiety than her arrest. She worried whether anyone had thought to rescue him or feed him. She missed feeling his warm body on her lap, the warmth from her roaring fire and her morning tisanes.

The dormice kept her amused whilst she reflected upon her life. Her marriage had been a happy one. Her husband had been good to her. Sadly, no children. But she was old now and the best of her life was behind her. Lately, she had been feeling very tired and the tonics she took every day to keep her healthy seemed to be having less effect. Since her arrest, her health had deteriorated quite rapidly. She had a hacking cough and now and again her heart beat with such rapidity it left her breathless. She knew she would not last long in this cell.

Emmelina was a different case altogether. She was young and healthy and had all her life to look forward to. Perhaps marry a nice young man. She had noticed how Emmelina looked at that young leather worker, Severin Browne although she was not sure about his suitability.

In the weeks of her incarceration, she had spent interminable hours thinking how she could save Emmelina's life. The only way she could think to save her was to confess to the crimes of heresy and in so doing exonerate Emmelina. She owed that much to her good friend, Sabrina Dabinett. The only true friend she ever had. Her life was as good as over. Her time was running out. She had nothing to lose.

She struggled to her feet and yelled at the guards. At first, they ignored her but she continued to shout. After some time, she heard the rattling of keys and heavy footsteps outside her door. A young guard, looking more like a fellow prisoner but for his uniform, his beard straggly and his face smudged with dirt, stepped into her cell.

'What do you want?' he barked.

'I demand to see the Sub Prior.'

He laughed. 'Who are you to make demands, you old hell hag.'

Maud, having made her decision, was not about to be wrong-footed by this impudent, rude young man. 'He will want to hear what I say. If he finds out you have kept vital information from him you'll be in trouble.'

The young guard looked uncertain. From the dim expression upon his face, Maud could see he was not very bright.

'Bring him here and he will thank you. You might even profit from this.'

The guard's expression brightened and a greedy grin appeared on his face.

'I'll see what I can do,' he replied, closing and locking the cell door behind him.

Several days passed and Maud had given up hope of ever being heard, despite her daily prayers. She had just finished praying when the cell door opened and in walked the Sub Prior and old Brother Jacquemon.

'What do you want to tell me, old woman?' the Sub Prior demanded.

'I want to confess my guilt to all the charges.'

Gervaise raised his straggly eyebrow.

'The guard said you had information for me that was vital.'

Maud sat up.

'That's what I need to tell you. Emmelina Pauncefoot is innocent of all charges against her. It was not her. It was all my doing.'

'That's for the court to decide, not for you. As to the charges laid against you, I will see that your confession is duly noted.'

He nodded to Brother Jacquemon to make a note. Maud, unskilled and artless in matters of negotiation, could see she was at a disadvantage. 'But I will withdraw my confession if you do not lift the charges against Emmelina.'

'You are a foolish woman to think by confessing your own guilt you will somehow manage to save your friend from a similar fate. The court will decide your guilt - and your punishment. As for your friend...she will be tried with you. You may even have sealed her fate by so graciously confessing your own guilt.'

'You have no evidence against her.'

'On the contrary, we do have evidence. That is enough. Come Jacquemon, we are wasting our time in this filthy hovel.'

'You can't have. What evidence?' Maud asked, somewhat bewildered.

'The snakeskin she kept by her door with which she was able to exert such enmity upon her victims.'

Maud almost laughed, out of disbelief, not merriment. 'That cannot be so. I know Emmelina. She is no sorceress.'

'As I said. That is for the court to decide. You've wasted my time long enough.'

Gervaise turned to go. 'Unless, of course, you wish to denounce your accomplice as a sorceress and give evidence against her?'

Maud looked away from him, sickened by his suggestion. She did not answer him.

'So be it,' Gervaise announced.

They left and once again Maud was left alone to wait out the days. The palpitations in her heart increased. She placed her hand on her chest in an attempt to calm them. To no avail. The irregular beating in her heart was accompanied by a throbbing beat in her head. She was struggling to breathe. Her chest compressed, void of air, as if someone were standing on it, preventing her from taking breath. She retched, but brought up only bile from her empty stomach. Struck by utter despair, she realised her attempt to save Emmelina had backfired.

Chapter 53

Severin sat in the New Inn drowning his sorrows. Since Thomas had knocked on his door to tell him of Emmelina's arrest he had been unable to think of anything other than how he could get her out of gaol. There was no point in doing any work. He couldn't concentrate. All he could think about was Emmelina. How she looked, how she smelt, how she smiled, her hair, her yielding flesh. How he ached to touch her.

His bitterness at being cheated of his happiness was matched by his anger towards the people responsible for her imprisonment. She was innocent. He had no doubt of that.

His first reaction had been to visit Emmelina in gaol but Thomas had advised him against this. He didn't always accept the advice of others but on this occasion he had. Emmelina was newly widowed and, so far, their relationship was only known to each other and now Thomas, since he had confided in him. The old fox had known all along. His visit would only draw unwanted attention to him and may cause more trouble for Emmelina. He couldn't take that risk. In any case, the guards had been given strict instructions not to allow Emmelina or Maud to have any visitors for fear they might corrupt others and make them their accomplices in sorcery.

Severin had thought of speaking to Lord Malverne. He was well connected and might be able to influence matters. But then why would such a high-borne wish to help a woman accused of heresy. He could think of nothing else other than how he could get them both out of gaol. It seemed whatever idea came to him there was a drawback of some kind or another. As each idea entered his head, another came swiftly on its heels to persuade him it wouldn't work or he would think through the consequences and come to the same conclusion. His thoughts looped endlessly until he could take no more and the only way to stop them was to drink them away. There was another reason.

Being alone in the house with Dulcina as evening drew on did not sit well with him. He could see she was nothing more than a simple, sweet girl who had been placed in an impossible situation. The real culprit in all this was Gilbert Garlick, hiding behind his position and the church. He had thought about whether Dulcina should make it known Garlick had forced her to hide the snakeskin but then who would believe her. The word of a maid against an influential burgess. Garlick was a nasty piece of work. Severin could see Dulcina was terrified just by the mention of his name. He would think nothing of carrying out his threat of accusing her of sorcery, then, all three would be in gaol.

He wasn't entirely happy with the arrangement but he could see Thomas's point – she had nowhere to go and didn't deserve a life on the street. Emmelina, he felt sure, would not want that fate for Dulcina. Besides, he had a sneaking suspicion Thomas was sweet on Dulcina and that's why he brought her to him. The arrangement was bearable during the day as he could get on with his work and Dulcina could keep out of his way doing domestic chores but as darkness came, he became ill-at-ease with her company. It was then he sought sanctuary in the convivial surroundings of the New Inn.

He sat alone, drinking heavily, his thoughts swirling around in his mind, a dull pain forming between his eyebrows. No amount of cider would ease the aching in his head or his heart.

'You're not doing yourself any good,' Thomas reproached him as he pulled up a stool and sat down next to his friend.

'Leave me alone,' Severin snapped, knowing full well Thomas's meaning.

'Brooding on it won't do no good.'

'Nothing else I can do,' Severin responded sullenly, hanging his head in his hands.

'There might,' Thomas replied.

Severin straightened up. 'What do you mean?'

'I know a guard from the castle, look. 'E comes in 'ere, now and again. I might be able to persuade him, look…'

Thomas raised his tankard to his lips and took a long swig, waiting for Severin's reaction.

'But you said it would be risky?'

'Officially, but not this way. It'll cost yer. He likes a drink or two,' he said, a cheeky, almost boyish grin forming.

He had no doubt Thomas would be able to sort something out. He was a resourceful, sly old fox. His position as landlord made him a useful person to know and people would be more than happy to do him favours for a few free drinks.

'I need to see her, Thomas.'

'I knows you do. I'll see what I can do,' he said, standing up. 'You need to go home. You've had enough.'

The thought of being able to see Emmelina lifted his spirits. 'You're right, my friend, I've had enough. Time I went home.'

He drained his ale, wiped his mouth with the back of his hand and gave his friend a solid slap on the back before lurching towards the door of the inn.

He walked home that night, unsteady on his feet but in a much better mood.

Chapter 54

It was hard to tell how long Emmelina had lain there. It could have been days or weeks. Food was brought to her by a sullen old man who never spoke and seemed to be frightened of her when she tried to speak to him. A kind of malaise had overtaken her, whereby she drifted in and out of dreams and her mind wandered. In one, she saw herself in church. Severin was beside her and they were being joined together in matrimony. Tears of joy were falling down her cheeks. She woke to find she was actually crying. The joy she experienced in the dream quickly turned to wretchedness as she became aware, once more, of her predicament.

She had discovered if she stood up her leg irons would allow her to walk as far as the window in her cell where she spent long hours looking out over the river to the fields beyond remembering her freedom and regretting everything that had ever happened to her in her life. In her darkest moments she remembered the burning of Finn, Damiana and Tegan and wondered if she was to suffer the same fate. Their excruciating cries still echoed in her dreams and her waking thoughts and the smell of burning flesh would return like a memory.

There were moments of the deepest and most unshakable despair when she thought she could not bear her situation any longer, when she longed to die, to be struck dead so she couldn't feel anything, anymore.

On one such occasion, she was kneeling deep in prayer when the door to her cell opened. Constable Rudge entered with two men. They unfastened her leg irons and helped her to her feet. Thinking her prayers had been answered and that she was being released she thanked them. They gave her a queer look. No-one spoke. They led her back down the stone staircase and down into an underground vault. Her joy at thinking she was being released ended there.

Three women stood in the chamber, their sleeves rolled up. A tub of water stood on the floor and beside it, a whetstone and a thin bladed, iron razor. The women looked strong and savage. The guards pushed her inside and shut the door behind her.

Two of the women took hold of her arms and held her tightly. The third woman, taller than the other two and more muscular, picked up the blade and began slicing at her clothes.

'What are you doing,' Emmelina screamed, struggling to free herself.

'If you struggle this will hurt more,' said the woman with the knife.

They stripped Emmelina bare. The blade was then sharpened on the whetstone, the noise of it grating on Emmelina's nerves and making her wince. Having sharpened the knife, the woman came behind her, yanked her head back and began hacking at her hair. Her long ebony locks flounced to the floor like the shiny feathers of black crows. When the hair was short all over, the blade was re-sharpened. This time they shaved her head closer to the skin until only shadowy dark bristles could be seen amongst the numerous cuts that were now bubbling with blood. Emmelina wept silently as the weight and feel of her hair upon her shoulders was no more.

'Get her on the floor,' the knife woman directed.

Emmelina was pinned to the floor by the other two women. One held her arms above her head, the other held her ankles.

'Check under her skin. See if she has any devices for sorcery sewn under there,' the woman in charge ordered.

After checking her armpits and finding nothing there, the knife woman re-sharpened the blade on the whetstone, the grating noise filling Emmelina with such fear. When she had finished the woman knelt down beside her and started shaving the hair under her armpits. The blade cut into her flesh, drawing blood. When she was done, the woman wiped the knife on her filthy skirt and still on her knees, crawled towards Emmelina's feet. What else could she be going to do now, thought Emmelina, with renewed dread. The answer came swiftly with the forcible opening of her legs.

Before she was led out of the room, the women tied long lengths of paper around her neck, which only just managed to cover her body and upon which had been written the seven sacred words of Jesus Christ, thought to be a means of protection against the evil of sorceresses.

"Pater, in manus tuas commendo spiritum meum."

(Father, I commend my spirit into your hands)

Naked, apart from the strips of paper covering her private parts, chained, shorn of all hair and stripped of all dignity, Emmelina was led into the next chamber.

Chapter 55

The pious men sat in the darkened shadows of the chamber. A fire raged in the corner but its purpose was more for burning than for warmth, although on this cold morning it served both. Light came from a few tallow candles flickering in iron sconces. The smell reminded her of the tannery. No-one spoke. As Emmelina was dragged in front of the row of men she could feel their dark energy.

Sub Prior Gervaise, Mayor Rawlings, Constable Rudge, Bailiff Bliss, Alderman van Eck, Physician Teylove and Gilbert Garlick sat in a line behind a long table, upon which had been sprinkled Blessed Salt, a device to ward off evil spirits. Jacquemon sat apart from them, a desk with writing implements in front of him. He was to act as scribe. Opposite them a single chair had been placed. The stone floor had been newly scrubbed and vervain, known as the holy herb, strewn between her and the seated men. Emmelina stood upon dried stalks of Fennel which was commonly used in households to ward off evil spirits. Wax candles, taller than a man, stood at each end of the table, another means of protection against the sorceress.

The guards left Emmelina standing in front of her inquisitors. Despite her barely concealed nakedness, she stared defiantly at the men sitting opposite her. Bailiff Bliss and Alderman van Eck looked embarrassed, Gilbert Garlick had a different look upon his face, like someone who had successfully cornered and killed an innocent animal for sport. Mayor Rawlings cleared his throat. The gravelly sound echoed around the vaulted chamber.

'You must first swear on the four Gospels of God that you shall tell the truth about yourself and any others we may ask questions of you.'

Jacquemon rose and shuffled towards her, a bible in his wrinkled hand. Shakily, he held it out for Emmelina to swear on. She placed her left hand on the bible.

'Look,' Gervaise pointed out, 'how she uses her left hand, she is a sinistral.'

Emmelina quickly withdrew her left hand, placing her right hand on the bible.

'To be noted as evidence that the denounced is a sinistral,'

Mayor Rawlings instructed.The oath given, Jacquemon returned to his desk and began scribbling.

'Please state where you were born,' the mayor continued.

'Here in Gloucester, sir,' Emmelina answered.

'And who were your parents and are they still alive?'

'My father was Edmund Dabinett of Maisemore and my mother was Sabrina Dabinett of the same place. They are both dead,' she added.

'And did they die of natural causes or were they burned to ashes because of acts of sorcery or had they been considered suspect?'

Mayor Rawlings appeared to be reading from a list of questions in front of him. Why was he asking that particular question? Maud had expressed her suspicions to her but now was not the time to explore the truth of their deaths.

'I think you all know they were burned to death in their home under suspicious circumstances. I know nothing of accusations of sorcery.'

Emmelina glared across at Garlick. He glared back at her with sullen dislike.

'Just answer the questions as asked,' the mayor retorted, 'or we will have to conduct this inquisition under less than salubrious conditions.'

He nodded at the constable who in turn motioned to one of his men. The guard walked over to a contraption, which resembled a wooden pulley to which was attached a thick rope. He swung the pulley so the end of it hung high over the fire. Leaving it in place he stoked the coals, releasing orange flames that flickered across the blackened stones of the vast hearth.

'I believe there were some concerns your mother was a heretic but the fire in question was nothing more than an unfortunate accident. Make a note to this effect, Brother Jacquemon.'

Emmelina thought differently but she knew the brutal purpose of the pulley and she did not wish to be suspended from it. She remained quiet.

'Do you believe sorceresses exist and that they can conjure up storms and contaminate domestic animals?'

'No, I don't.'

Gervaise turned to the mayor and whispered in his ear. 'The book says she will deny this and her denial will be further proof of her guilt.'

Mayor Rawlings nodded and scribbled something on the parchment in front of him. 'Do you know that the common people fear you, that you are universally hated and that you have a bad reputation?'

'If that is so, it is others who have caused this to happen and not of my doing.'

'It is my duty to put to you all the charges of acts of sorcery you have committed. Witnesses have sworn on oath you have committed the following acts of sorcery...'

'What witnesses?' Emmelina demanded, cutting in.

'They are not to be revealed to you on account they could be seriously endangered.'

'Endangered? How?'

'You have been warned to answer only the questions put to you.'

'But am I not to know who accuses me of these things so I may defend myself against them?'

The mayor's expression hardened.

'Guards,' he shouted, 'tie her to the strappado.'

The constable's men grabbed Emmelina and dragged her over to the pulley whilst another guard lowered the rope. She began to struggle, through fear than from any real hope she could escape. The rope was tied around her wrists and she was hoisted upwards. When her bare feet reached almost a foot above the fire, the pulley was swung across so that her feet hovered over the smouldering coals, the heat searing their soft soles.

Mayor Rawlings read out the charges against her.

'That on All Hallowes Eve, in the year of fourteen hundred and ninety seven, you conjoined with the Devil to afflict your husband with an illness. That you, along with your accomplice, Maud Biddle, administered the Devil's potion to your husband, which poisoned him and caused his death. And that, on the same evening, you being a jealous woman, sought the Devil's help in dispensing with your maidservant, Fayette Cordy. That you conspired with the Devil to cause the great flood by the tossing of rotted sage into Rolla's spring, a well-known place where heathens gather to worship against the teachings of the church. It has been further witnessed that on the day before the flood you herded your cattle through the streets of this city to higher ground to protect them from the murrain that you, with the Devil's help, inflicted upon the cattle and the people of this City. And finally, and perhaps most cruelly, that you lay with the Devil and, by way of sacrifice, gave up your first born to him, causing the child to be stillborn.'

The pain in Emmelina's shoulders from the weight of her body could not match the excruciating pain of the fire roasting the soles of her feet. Her only thoughts were of the secret she carried within her. She felt the baby move.

'I confess. I confess to everything,' she screamed. 'Stop, please stop,' she begged them.

For several days, she had not felt the baby move and believing it had died inside her like her last child she had lost the will to live. She had told no-one about the pregnancy, fearful of the consequences and so far she had been able to keep it a secret. It was a blessing that she did not show. Not yet anyway. But she couldn't keep her secret for much longer. It would not be long before someone noticed. Miracles were possible if you prayed hard enough. She must pray harder.

On the orders of the mayor, the guard swung the pulley away from the fire and she was lowered to the ground. Not able to stand on her feet, she collapsed onto the cold flagstones.

'Let it be noted the accused has confessed to her acts of sorcery. Take her away,' ordered Mayor Rawlings.

The guards dragged her across the floor. A number of times she tried to get to her feet but the strength had left her.

Chapter 56

Severin approached the castle by way of Castle Lane, across a fortified bridge, which spanned a deep, water-filled ditch. The stone walls were forty feet in height and six feet deep. There would be no escape. Thomas had managed to persuade his contact in the castle to let Severin in to visit Emmelina and Maud. He carried with him two sacks of food and ale, wrapped in some warm clothes, one for each of them. Thomas told him who to ask for and when to go. The best time was late in the evening, at change of shift when he would not draw too much attention.

As he approached the gatehouse, a guard on duty emerged from a side room, brandished his sword and shouted 'halt'. Severin was startled for a moment until another guard appeared from nowhere and cut in.

'I'll deal with this,' said a burly young man. 'Follow me,' the young guard barked at him without introduction.

Severin did not answer but followed him as ordered. They crossed the bailey and went towards the keep, which appeared to be in poor repair. The light was poor but Severin could see the castle had seen better days. He followed the guard up the pitch black, narrow stone staircase, searching for each tread in the darkness. At the top was a heavily reinforced door, lighted by a single tallow candle which flickered on their arrival.

'You got it?' he asked, holding his hand out.

Severin fumbled inside the sack. His heart was racing at the thought of finally seeing Emmelina. He brought out several coins, which he placed into the guard's large and coarse hands. The guard walked over to the candle, held his hand under the light to check the amount and, satisfied stuffed the coins into a leather purse he had secreted underneath his uniform. He then removed a set of keys from his belt and unlocked the door with a very large key.

'In there,' he pointed, as he stood aside to let Severin pass.

Severin hesitated for some unknown reason. He wasn't sure what to expect.

'You 'aven't got long. I'll be back soon.'

The cell was no more than six foot square. He could feel a cold draught as he walked through the door, which was slammed shut behind him and re-locked. Although the light was poor, lit by moonlight alone coming through the window opening, he soon detected a shape in the corner of the cell, lying half propped up against the damp stone wall. He approached slowly, clutching at the sack. The shape stirred.

'Emmelina, is that you?'

A chink of light coming from a small opening beside Emmelina cast some illumination as he drew near. He had not known what to expect. His stomach turned at the sight before him. Emmelina looked like something he would have walked past in the gutter. Her clothes were dirty, her face blackened and her feet were bare, apart from some filthy rags that had been tied loosely around them. Worst of all, was the sight of her hair. In place of her long, black shiny hair were uneven tufts like the hide of a wild boar, matted in places with dried blood. Severin composed himself. She would not want to see his true reaction to her appearance. She hardly seemed aware of his presence. He knelt down beside her and, without saying anything, put his arms around her and drew her close. She stiffened at first and then she relaxed into his arms. The feel of her warm body brought back memories of their time together but there was no arousal on this occasion. Only deep concern.

'I've brought some food and some warm clothes,' he told her, trying to focus on practical matters. He took out a heavy woollen shawl, which he wrapped around her shoulders.

'Thank you,' she murmured.

Her voice was croaky and weak. Severin emptied out the contents of the sack onto a clean cloth he laid out on the dirty straw. There were chunks of freshly baked bread, cheese, some cold meat and a flagon of ale. He prised off the cork and held the flagon to her lips.

'Here, have some of this.'

Her lips were dry and cracked. She took a few sips and this seemed to revive her a little.

'It's so good to see you,' she breathed, an eager smile appearing on her sad face. 'I have something to tell you.' A spark had appeared in her dull, dark eyes. She took hold of his hand and placed it on her stomach. 'I'm having your child.'

Severin stared for some time at his hand enclosed in hers, not able to take in what she had told him. The joy at hearing Emmelina was having his child was marred by the torment inside him. He laid his head on the swollen bump, taking care to keep the full weight of it from the precious life, which thrived beneath. He lay there a while, letting his silent, secret tears fall. She ran her fingers through his hair, like his mother had done when he was a child. He would have liked to stay there, feeling her touch for an eternity. He heard the rattle of keys and knew he had only moments left. He raised his head and kissed Emmelina, holding her face in his hands.

'I will come back for you. Do you understand?'

'Promise me, you'll come back,' Emmelina implored, hanging onto him and not wanting to let him go.

'I promise.'

The guard stood at the door, rattling his keys. 'Get a move on,' he growled, becoming impatient.

Severin stood up quickly in response to the guard's tone and walked out. He could not bear to look back. Outside the cell, the taciturn guard locked the door and started down the staircase.

'What about Maud?' Severin asked.

'No time for the old woman,' he answered, making his way quickly down the narrow stairs.

'But…' Severin began.

'No buts. Out now.'

Once outside in the bailey, Severin pushed the remaining sack intended for Maud, into the hands of the guard.

'If you won't let me see her, the least you can do is give her this.'

The guard opened the sack and looked inside. He said nothing but carried on to the gatehouse. The same guard as before emerged from the side room, holding his sword, in a challenging stance. The taciturn guard waved him away. At the exit, Severin stopped to look back. The guard was already walking back to the keep, ferreting through the sack.

Chapter 57

The constable's men led Emmelina and Maud the short distance from the castle to the Booth Hall. Spring and summer had come and gone since their incarceration and now late autumn sunshine and a clear blue sky greeted them as they made their way across the city. Emmelina had barely been aware of the seasons but now she filled her lungs with the cool morning air and tilted her head towards the cloudless sky. She could feel the warmth of the sun upon her cheeks. It had been a long time since she had enjoyed the simple bliss of Mother Nature. The months of confinement in her cell, the pain of torture and the lack of nutritional food had all taken its toll. Her small frame, swollen from the child she was carrying, struggled to walk. Her back ached and the burns on her feet had not healed properly. Her swollen ankles were covered in weeping sores where the leg irons had been. The short walk was more like an ascetic pilgrimage as she struggled along, breathing heavily and stumbling several times.

Maud walked behind her, separated by a phalanx of guards. They were not allowed to talk to each other. Emmelina noticed Maud had lost a lot of weight since her arrest. She looked ill and ashen faced.

A huge crowd had gathered outside the Booth Hall, lured by the morbid spectacle of a trial and the fact it was market day in Gloucester. As the two women entered the hall, a ripple of murmurs went along the rows of seats. The hall was crowded, bristling with anticipation.

The new incumbent Mayor van Eck, having been elected mayor on the sudden death of Mayor Rawlings sat in the middle of a long table. Constable Rudge, Bailiff Bliss, Gilbert Garlick, Sub Prior Gervaise along with several more prominent burgesses sat either side of him. The jury of twenty four men sat opposite the witness chair.

Emmelina's first thought when entering the hall had been whether or not Severin would be there. She had not seen him since his clandestine visit to her in gaol when he had promised to return. Hollow promises. Had he ever felt the same intense feelings for her that she felt for him? Would they be joined forever in eternity as soul mates? She would never know. She scanned the hall, looking for him. Just knowing he was there would make her feel so much better but she couldn't see him. The guard pushed her into the seat opposite the mayor and although she tried to turn to see into the crowd she was hampered by her swollen belly and the chains, which remained around her hands and feet.

Sitting opposite the jury were Physician Teylove and Dulcina, both summoned to give evidence. Dulcina looked like she had been crying, her eyes were red and her face blotchy. Physician Teylove sat with his mouth pinched together, looking mean-spirited as usual. A young steward appeared, no more than a boy, holding a copy of the bible. Emmelina raised her shackled left hand awkwardly to place it on the bible. Gervaise jumped up, wafting his hands impatiently towards the steward.

'Take that away. No sorceress can touch the book of God. No holy oath can be relied upon in these circumstances.'

The Booth Hall erupted into a show of fearful piety. People were either making the sign of the cross or whispering sacred prayers under their breath. The young steward looked bewildered for a second then returned to his seat.

Clearing his throat, Mayor van Eck spoke in his deep basso voice. 'Emmelina Pauncefoot and Maud Biddle, you are aware of the charges against you?

The two women nodded.

'How do you plead?'

He pointed first at Maud. Maud swallowed hard. She knew she was about to lie before God.

'Guilty, sir,' quickly adding. 'I did it. Emmelina had nothing to do with this. She is innocent. I am the one...'

'Silence, silence woman. You are only required to answer your plea. Nothing more. If you continue to speak I will have the branck placed upon your shrieking mouth.'

300

His rebuke was severe and effective. Maud realised the futility of her words and sank back into her chair. The branck would just be one more public humiliation and she could see she wasn't achieving anything. The mood was against her. She could feel the hostility, like a dark and heavy entity smothering her.

'And how do you plead?' he asked, pointing at Emmelina.

Emmelina placed her hand upon her swollen belly as if she were protecting her unborn child from the lie.

'Guilty, sir.'

Mayor van Eck smirked. 'I see you have no wish to wear the branck and have been mindful enough to keep your answers short and to the point, unlike your accomplice.' He shot a fiercely disapproving look at Maud. 'Sentence will be pronounced following the evidence of the witnesses who will attest to the said sorcery. Sub Prior Gervaise, you wish to question the witnesses?'

'I do indeed, your honour.'

Gervaise, clutching his bible to him, approached Physician Teylove who took the oath.

'You were the physician of the deceased were you not, Physician Teylove?'

'I was,' Teylove replied.

'Were you dismissed from these duties?'

'I was.'

'Did you think the two women were in a conspiracy with the Devil when you were dismissed?'

Teylove had been told in advance the questions he would be asked and instructed as to how he should answer them by Sub Prior Gervaise.

'I did, sir.'

'Do you think Humphrey Pauncefoot would be alive today if you had been allowed to continue his treatment?'

Teylove looked across at Maud, a hint of a smirk upon his face. 'I do, sir,' he replied, emphatically.

There were a few murmurs amongst the assembled throng, which only seemed to add weight to Teylove's testimony.

'And if I could cast your mind back to some four years ago when you were called upon to deliver Mistress Pauncefoot's baby?'

'Yes. I was in attendance at the birth.'

'And what happened?'

'When I arrived it was obvious to me there were complications and, after a much laboured birth, the baby was eventually born dead.'

Emmelina sat quietly, the tears rolling down her dirty face, as the memories of that traumatic day re-emerged. She had not been allowed to see the child and was only told it was a girl later that night when Humphrey visited her with the smell of beer on his breath and told her not to worry as it was only a girl and there would be plenty of time for her to bear him a son.

Gervaise addressed the jury. 'It is my contention this woman did conspire with the Devil to take this baby into the bowels of hell so that its gentle soul did not ascend to heaven.'

Members of the jury conferred with each other and in the momentary lapse in proceedings, the crowd became unruly and Mayor van Eck was forced to slam his gavel upon the sounding block. The noise reverberated throughout the cavernous edifice of the Booth Hall whereupon order was restored.

Gervaise, having made his point to the jury, continued questioning Teylove.

'More recently, Physician Teylove, you were alerted to Humphrey Pauncefoot's illness by his wife on the eve of All Hallowes, last year. Can you tell us more about that?'

Physician Teylove straightened his back in an attempt to look more important than he was.

'Mistress Pauncefoot called on me that morning to tell me her husband had taken ill. When I arrived at the house Master Pauncefoot was lying in bed. His face was contorted into a grimace, his hand was twisted and shaking and his speech was impaired.'

'Had you seen anything like that before in all the time you have been a physician?'

'No, sir.'

'Did you think that he had been struck down by the Devil?'

'Yes.'

Emmelina listened to Teylove's testimony and noted, with bitter resignation, how the Sub Prior was leading him to answer in a certain way. They were guilty before being proved innocent.

'Thank you, Physician Teylove.'

Teylove stood down; a satisfied and supercilious smirk upon his face. He made a point of looking, first at Maud, then at Emmelina as he walked past them in the dock. His meaning was clear.

Garlick Gilbert took the stand.

'Can you tell the jury what you found at the accused's house the day we arrested her?'

'A dead snakeskin.'

Gervaise walked over to a table where documents, books and various artefacts lay. He picked up the dead snakeskin and held it aloft. 'This was found above the threshold of the accused, which in the opinion of the church is the most significant evidence and proves, beyond all doubt, her guilt.' He pointed it at Emmelina. 'Placed there by the sorceress herself.'

The crowd exploded. People stood to hurl insults, shaking their fists at the prisoners. Again the mayor had cause to hammer his gavel against the wooden block. It was barely audible above the tumult.

'Order. Order. I insist you respect this court or my guards will have you all put in irons,' he threatened.

Still the crowd could not be hushed. They could hardly contain themselves. Shouts of 'hell hag' and 'guilty' were hurled at the women. Gervaise looked pleased with himself. He had done a good job so far. They were as good as dead.

'Mayor van Eck. I have completed the questioning of this witness.'

Emmelina sat, looking tired and defeated. When she heard Gervaise mention the snakeskin, she looked over at Dulcina. Dulcina did not return her gaze.

'I now call Dulcina Sawyer as a witness.'

Dulcina approached the chair, visibly trembling. She had been summoned a few days after Emmelina's arrest and interviewed by Constable Rudge and Gilbert Garlick. The threat of arrest by Constable Rudge had been enough for her to attend and answer all of their questions in full. They had twisted her answers and forced her to sign a confession, which damned the two women. Her statement was now amongst the documents in the Booth Hall.

'Mistress Sawyer. Tell us what happened when Maud Biddle first came to the house?'

'She was very nice, sir…'

'Get to the point woman,' Gervaise snapped.

Dulcina's lip quivered but she managed to pull herself together enough to answer the question.

'She took hold of the mistress's hand and read the lines.'

'For the benefit of members of the jury, the witness is referring to the practice of hand divining where the heretic makes predictions by somehow divining the meaning of the lines appearing on that person's hand,' Gervaise informed the jury.

'Did you see her bring jugs of poison which she then administered to Humphrey Pauncefoot?'

Dulcina twisted tighter on the cloth she held, the ends of her fingers turning white.

'I don't know if it was poison, sir. I thought it was an 'erbal mixture meant to heal the Master.'

A few members of the jury found Dulcina's ingenuous testimony amusing and an infectious titter passed among them.

Fearing the jury might veer away from the gravity of Dulcina's evidence he changed tack.

'It's of no consequence. The witch has already confessed to his poisoning.'

How strange, thought Emmelina, how the most innocent of acts could be misinterpreted by those who had evil in their hearts.

'And one last question. How did Mistress Pauncefoot behave on hearing the news her husband was dead?'

Emmelina stared at Dulcina. She knew her friend had to tell the truth and the truth, on this occasion, was damning. Dulcina looked petrified.

'Was she upset?'

'Not as such,' Dulcina stammered.

'Come on now; tell the court what she said that day in the kitchen, the day her husband died?'

'She said,' glancing at Emmelina before answering, 'She said, "may he rot in hell", sir.' There was uproar in the Booth Hall. This time they vented their hatred by throwing missiles at Emmelina. A rotten egg narrowly missed her. It splattered onto the tamped earth in front of her, giving off its chokingly sulphurous odour. The mayor was not impressed with this lawlessness. He dispatched two of his guards to deal with the offender. The woman was seized upon by the guards and dragged out of the hall, still screaming abuse and obscenities. The action had the benefit of calming a crowd who were by now baying for Emmelina's blood. The mayor set his stern expression on a few individuals at the front who were being particularly vociferous. Eventually order was restored.

'I have no further questions, mayor,' Gervaise ended, pleased with his efforts and satisfied he had carried out God's work to a satisfactory conclusion. 'I believe that concludes the evidence against these two women.'

The mayor, looking grave and imperious addressed the jury. 'You have heard the evidence against these two women. How do you find?

There was a brief discussion, much nodding of heads and then the head of the jury stood. Their deliberations could not have taken more than four short minutes.

'We have reached a verdict, sir. We find both Maud Biddle and Emmelina Pauncefoot guilty of sorcery and the crime of heresy as charged.'

Cheers went up from the crowd. Hats were thrown into the air as if a celebration were under way. Shouts of 'guilty', 'burn them', and other, cruder, obscenities were hurled at Emmelina and Maud. Maud reached for Emmelina's hand. The two women sat, their hands clasped tightly together, waiting to hear the mayor announce their sentence. Mayor van Eck, took out his ermine lined, purple Cap of Maintenance and delivered the sentence in a courtroom that had become as silent as a grave.

'Sorcery is Satan's assault on the very fabric of God's creation. We can only thwart Satan's evil purposes through the physical destruction of his evil minions. Let this be a lesson to all present here.' The mayor looked up from his notes and surveyed the silent court. Satisfied, they were all listening attentively, he continued. 'On this day of the None of September in the year, fourteen hundred and ninety eight and in the presence of Constable Rudge, Bailiff Bliss, and Sub Prior Gervaise...' The mayor paused, looked up and gave a reverential nod towards the Sub Prior, 'and the burgesses of this town, Emmelina Pauncefoot and Maud Biddle are condemned and judged this day to be burned until their bodies be consumed to ashes in the place accustomed with the confiscation of all their moveable goods and heritage. This sentence delivered in justice and set to be carried out on the tenth day of September.'

Unusually, the mayor did not bring them to order by hammering his gavel but allowed the mob to jeer and taunt the women. Hysteria spread through the Booth Hall as shouts of 'murderer', 'sorceress' and 'heretic' bellowed out across the hall.

Emmelina heard the mayor's words and, although she had expected the worse, on hearing she was to be burned to ashes, she dropped to the floor. The noise in the room became muffled and distant; the faces zoomed in and out of her blurred vision. A crushing sensation upon her chest squeezed the air from her lungs, constricting her heart. With help from Maud she picked herself up, twisting round to search the faces of the hostile mob, hoping to see Severin one last time. She spotted him standing at the back of the hall. He looked lost.

It was then she felt the baby. A strong, healthy kick. Instinctively, her hands went to the spot. A hard lump, like the small heel of a child stretched her skin. She could see it protruding through her thin woollen smock. Then her waters broke and warm amniotic fluid trickled down the soft flesh of her inner thighs. The sound of water pittering onto the floor caught the attention of the steward. The young steward looked out of his depth. He stared, transfixed at the steaming puddle of wet earth on the floor, the smell of grassy, damp straw rising up.

A strong pain, like a steel knife, ripped into her lower back. She cried out in pain. Momentarily, the crowd stopped their ranting. All eyes were upon Emmelina. Then a shout went up.

'It's the Devil's child!'

There were further cries of 'burn them now' and 'burn the Devil's child'. The atmosphere in the hall was turning lawless. Fearing the crowd would take the law into their own hands, Mayor van Eck decided to act with speed to avert any spectacle of public disorder.

'Take them away,' he ordered Constable Rudge. 'Get them out of here.'

Chapter 58

Emmelina arrived back in her cell, half carried, half dragged by the constable's men. They threw her down on the straw covered floor as if she were vermin, slamming and locking the door in haste, leaving Emmelina in her cell to face the birth of her child alone. When she realised she was to give birth unattended, she panicked and began hammering on the door, screaming to be let out and taken to the infirmary. After a while, when she realised no-one was listening she sat down on the festering straw and waited for the contractions to consume her.

She prayed to God to allow the baby to be born alive and healthy. She desperately wanted to hold it and hear its first cry. Not have it taken away from her, blue and lifeless. She tried hard to remember the instructions Teylove had given her. It was important not to upset herself. She remembered that. It would only distress the baby. She remembered being told to breathe deeply to help with the pain and to sit upright rather than lie down. She propped herself up against the cold stone wall and waited for the waves of pain, which she knew would come.

She wished she could have seen more of Severin. In between painful contractions, she wondered whether she would ever see him again and what would happen to her baby. She howled with the pain of each fierce contraction but this did not compare to the mental anguish within her when she remembered the shouts in the Booth Hall. Would they throw her baby onto the fire with her? She wept at the thought of her innocent child, Severin's child, thrown onto the flames. The vision was vivid and harrowing in her mind. It was too much to bear.

After what seemed like an eternity of pain, the contractions became more regular and more frequent. She could feel the pressure of the baby's head in that space between her legs. The pain was intense and relentless, draining her of the little energy she had left and making her delirious. With each contraction, more powerful than the last, her strength ebbed away. The delirium, mixed with exhaustion and terror gave her a sense of floating outside of her body. It was as though the pain, the birth, the baby, all of it was unreal. Her fingers searched down below for the baby's head. It was there, just the top of it. She knew it wouldn't be long now.

She imagined Severin kneeling by her side, stroking her forehead and whispering her name.

'Emmelina...'

Her eyes fluttered open. She saw him kneeling in front of her. She reached out to touch him.

'Are you real?'

He took hold of her hand and kissed it. 'I'm very real, Emmelina. I'm here, right here by your side.'

He squeezed her hand tightly.

'I thought I was dreaming,' she said, widening her eyes and trying to focus on him.

'It's not a dream and you need to help me.'

Hot tears rolled off her cheeks. His rough fingers wiped them away.

'Emmelina', she heard him say, softly, 'Emmelina.'

'Severin,' she heard herself say.

'I'm here, Emmelina. I'm going to help you have this baby.'

'Thank you,' she breathed.

Emmelina was aware of the gentle pressure of Severin's hand squeezing her cheeks, shaking her head from side to side.

'You need to wake up. You need to push this baby out.'

She opened her eyes. 'I don't think I can. I haven't any strength left to push. I'm sorry.'

'You have to find the strength.'

He took a jug of boiled water from a sack he had brought with him, which he uncorked and poured over a clean cloth. He wiped her face and then her hair using the wet cloth. She rallied a little. Severin parted her thighs. He could see the baby's head, covered in thick black hair.

'Come on, Emm, you're nearly there. One more push. I know you can do it.'

The urge to push overtook all sensation. She took a deep breath and pushed down hard. It took all her strength. The pressure of the baby's head was more than she could bear.

'Push again. You're nearly there.'

'I can't,' she screamed, 'I can't do anymore.'

Severin took hold of her hand. 'Just one more push, Emmelina. I know you can do it.'

Emmelina gritted her teeth. Somewhere from the depths of her being she drew upon a hidden seam of untapped strength. Like the swell of a Severn Bore, a powerful energy rose from somewhere inside her, at the core of her being. She pushed again, arching her back and bearing down as hard as she could. There was a sudden release from pain and she collapsed back onto the wooden floor. Her eyes were fluttering, drifting in and out of consciousness, dipping in and out of the dream world she seemed to be inhabiting.

'Emmelina, look, you have a baby girl.'

Severin was holding a bundle of bluish white flesh, a twisted purple cord still attached to it.

'Is she alive?' Emmelina asked, emerging from her dreamlike state.

'Yes. And she's beautiful.'

'Is there anything wrong with her?'

'No. She's perfect. Hold her. I need to cut the cord.'

He placed the baby on her stomach. Her naked body was warm and slimy to the touch with a bluish tinge. She looked down at the black haired bundle on her chest. Wide, dark blue eyes stared back at her. She was tiny and perfect. Gathering her skirts, she wrapped the child as best she could and watched while Severin took the knife from his belt. Skilfully, he cut through the umbilical cord. The child filled her lungs and let out a healthy cry. Something inside Emmelina contracted. Again, acting on pure instinct she put the baby to her breast. The child latched on and began to suckle.

'How did you get in?' Emmelina asked, bewildered.

'I bribed the guard,' he replied, concentrating on the task of tying a knot at the end of the cord.

He worked quickly and confidently as if he had done this kind of thing before. Tears rolled down Emmelina's cheeks with a mixture of relief, joy and sadness; relief at having given birth, joy at seeing Severin again and sadness wondering how much time she would have with her baby given the death sentence hanging over her. Severin stroked her hair, and pressed his hand on her still swollen stomach.

Emmelina winced. 'What are you doing?'

'I'm feeling the womb sac. When I tell you, you must start pushing down again. Can you do that?'

'I think so,' she said, becoming much calmer.

Severin placed both his hands on her stomach just underneath her rib cage and applied gentle pressure. 'Did you feel that?'

Emmelina winced. 'Yes, like something inside was giving way.'

'It's time, Emm; you must push out the sac.'

Exhausted and weak Emmelina gave one last push. There was a gushing sound and then a plopping sound as the placenta successfully expelled itself from her womb. Severin took some cloths from the sack and cleaned up the mess as best he could. Emmelina lay quietly with the baby who had fallen asleep. When Severin had finished, he took out a large, clean cloth and folded it to make a triangular shape. He draped it over his outstretched arms.

'Give the baby to me now, Emm,' he said, softly.

'You're taking the baby?'

'I have to. I can't leave her here,' he answered, holding her gaze.

'Not yet. Let me have a little more time with her?'

311

She knew before she even spoke it was futile. She looked down at her baby, peacefully asleep on her chest.

'Before you take her, I want to give her a name?'

'Of course,' he said, stroking her hair, trailing his fingers across her shoulder and onto to the baby's soft cheek.

'I want to call her Sabrina, after my mother.'

'Sabrina Browne. It suits her.' He looked down at the small baby sleeping contentedly. 'I have to go now. The guards will be coming for me.'

Emmelina handed him the baby. He wrapped the tiny bundle in the cloth. He gave Emmelina a long and tender kiss. The key turned in the lock and an impatient guard stood in the doorway.

Emmelina gripped Severin's arm. 'Take good care of her.'

'I will.'

The tears spilled down her cheeks as she watched him leave, carrying her daughter away from her. Just like before. He disappeared behind the door without looking back. Emmelina heard the dull thud as the door was slammed shut. The key turned in the lock. She was alone again. Her heart was an aching hole. Her swollen stomach felt like it had been ripped out so great was the loss she felt. If someone would take her life now she would be glad of it. Anything to stem the pain of immutable loss.

Chapter 59

Maud had requested she be left alone to pray and prepare herself for the ordeal she was about to face. She spent the night in deep prayer and meditation and by morning when the constable's men came to collect her she was ready. Quietly, and with great dignity she left the castle by the main entrance, and began her short walk to the place of execution. The crowds had gathered in the streets of Gloucester to watch this graceful old woman take her last steps, the baying crowd in stark contrast to Maud's tranquil mood. She looked untouched and unmoved by the cruel taunts accompanying her solitary walk down Castle Street to Abbey Lane where the stake and neatly piled faggots lay awaiting her arrival. Shackled and oblivious to the taunts she shuffled along the street looking ahead of her and averting her gaze from the hateful people who lined her route until someone from the crowd ran up to her and crashed into her almost knocking her over on her unsteady feet. It was Dulcina.

'Here Maud. Take this. It'll help.'

Dulcina thrust a handful of seeds into Maud's hand before she was hauled away by one of the constable's men. Maud looked at the offering and putting it to her nose to smell immediately recognised it as the seeds of the Hemlock plant, which she kept in her store room of herbs. She quickly stuffed the seeds into her mouth before the guards had time to take them away from her. Although she had prepared herself mentally and spiritually for her ordeal she had no doubt this would help to numb the physical pain when it inevitably came. Her life had been spent easing the pain of others in their final hours and so she was thankful to Dulcina for showing her the same consideration. She only hoped there was enough time for the herb to take its effect on her.

'Bless you,' Maud shouted after her.

When Maud entered the grassy space in front of St Mary's Gate she looked up at the great elm that grew there and smiled. It was as though the tree represented a friendly face amongst the misguided throng she was surrounded by.

Mayor van Eck stood by the tree dressed in his official garb, along with the other dignitaries and, of course, representatives of the church, headed by Sub Prior Gervaise. The mayor read out her sentence, then Gervaise followed by asking for her salvation.

'Maud Biddle, you have confessed and been found guilty of the heretical crime of sorcery. Repent now for your sins and you will be spared the iniquities of an eternity in hell.'

Maud stood before him and looked him directly in the eye. Unblinking, and in a strong, unwavering voice, she spoke.

'Whoever has taken from this Soul, honour, wealth and friends, heart and body and life, still has taken nothing from me, as long as God is with me. I am not in need of your salvation. God is with me,' she repeated.

Gervaise shifted on his feet. He hadn't expected that from the old woman. He was visibly shaken by her gentleness and strength of spirit. It unnerved him. He regained his composure and his steely determination to set an example to all those who would question the church's authority.

'You refuse to receive the salvation of the Lord and repent of your sins?'

'The salvation of every creature is nothing other than the understanding of the goodness of God,' she said proudly, a serenity falling upon her countenance.

Gervaise was further troubled by her strange outburst. Her manner was disarming. He straightened, and puffing out his barrel chest, he delivered a withering speech.'

"Salvation shall not be yours. You will toil in the everlasting flames of hell and eternal damnation without the favour of God's good grace. You will dwell forever in the bowels of the earth, hearing the screams of agony and torment of lost souls. There you will abide, hideously deformed and tormented physically, mentally, and spiritually. You will suffer for the rest of your unending days with the wrath of God and the scourge of an unquenched thirst of titanic proportions. The bible says, "And the Devil that deceived them was

314

cast into the lake of fire and brimstone, where the beast and the false prophet dwell, and ye shall be tormented day and night for ever and ever. Amen."

Maud did not respond. She looked upwards to the puffy white clouds above her. A hawk circled in the thermals, a graceful sight, mesmerising and other worldly. Nature was indeed a spectacular and wondrous thing, she reflected. To soar above the scenes before her. To be free of the hatred of sick souls. She had confessed to save Emmelina. That was before she knew about the baby. She would have done anything to save them both but it was too late and regrets were of no use to her now. She saw no need to repent for a sin she had not committed and for a life she had spent without sin. She had done nothing wrong. Some people in the crowd, on hearing Gervaise's rallying speech to the faithful, cried out to Maud to repent and save herself. Maud seemed to be already in another world, far from the baying crowd.

Mayor van Eck, eager to get the proceedings underway motioned to Gervaise to hurry along.

'Very well. You have made your choice. We, therefore, commit your body to the flames and your soul to the everlasting flames of hell.'

A wooden box had been placed next to the pile of faggots for her to step onto so she could be tied to the stake. On seeing the still green faggots piled high around the stake, Maud's resolve wavered. She faltered and fell against the arm of the young steward who had unshackled her. He steadied her. Maud held onto his arm and looked into his startled eyes. She begged him to fetch dry faggots to make a strong fire so she might not suffer a long and excruciating death. The young steward nodded his assent and in return she gave him a most angelic smile. For a moment he was transfixed by her gaze.

'Hurry along,' shouted Constable Rudge. 'Tie her to the stake and be quick about it.'

The steward shook his head as if he were shaking off Maud's spell. Fearing punishment and not wanting to appear

315

weak in front of the constable, he dragged her onto the box and roughly tied her hands and feet to the stake. Jumping down from the box and without hesitation, he seized the firebrand from another steward and walked round the pile of faggots setting light to them. Being green, the faggots did not light but instead gave out flumes of white smoke, which billowed upwards towards Maud. Her eyes reddened and acrid tears streamed down her cheeks and yet still, she seemed serene, almost saintly. Amidst the choking smoke she cried out with joyousness in her heart.

'My Soul is no longer fearful for I am illuminated by the dazzling brightness of the sun's rays in my Soul. Forgive them Lord, for they know not what they do.'

On hearing this, the young steward approached Constable Rudge and asked if he could fetch dry faggots. Constable Rudge agreed.

'We will have a better spectacle of it no doubt,' the constable gloated.

The faggots continued to smoke without flame until the dry wood was fetched and a fiercer fire took hold. The effects of the Hemlock was beginning to take hold. Her breathing was restricted and she couldn't feel her hands or her feet. A deathly coldness had fallen upon her despite the heat of the flames. Still choking on the thick smoke Maud raised her scorched and blackened face to the sky.

'Thank you Lord. I am ready. My soul is yours to keep and I shall have life ever after.'

As the smoke and flames consumed Maud, burning the grey hair from her head and melting her finger nails, she continued to pray. No scream came upon her lips even as the flames grew fiercer.

The crowd fell silent and many were moved to compassion for her piety and their watching eyes turned to tears as Maud endured the excruciating agony of the fire through the power of prayer. The smell of burning flesh pervaded the Abbey green. Though black in the mouth with her tongue now swollen greatly and her hair and skin burnt entirely from her skull, she continued in prayer.

Increasingly agitated, Gervaise turned to the crowd. 'She feels no pain. The Devil dulls her pain. She could be torn, limb from limb and still she would feel no pain, such is the Devil's deception.'

Still Maud prayed on, repeating the same words.

'I am God, for Love is God and God is Love, and this Soul is God by the condition of Love.'

Her words of love and God alarmed him. He could see the crowd were finding sympathy for this heretic. He renewed his hateful preaching hoping to find support amongst the more loyal and fervent of his flock.

'Have no mercy upon this woman. She is a heretic and has refused the Sacrament of Confession. She will not be reconciled with God or with the church nor recover His state of Grace. She will be eternally punished and abide forever in the bowels of Hell for committing the gravest of mortal sins, *"peccata mortalia"*. Her sins have created a rupture in the spiritual link between her and God. Peace and serenity of conscience, and spiritual consolation shall not be hers. Her soul will be dead for eternity.' Gervaise held his crucifix heavenwards. 'So shall it be. Amen.'

The onlookers who had appeared sympathetic to Maud's plight were renewed in their faith. They spat, jeered and swore at her, condemning her to a place of everlasting hell and damnation. Gervaise went amongst the throng and blessed those who were most vociferous in showing their commitment to the church.

Maud was oblivious to the scene before her. She had prayed her way to a higher consciousness, separating her physical body from that of the spiritual. She was not in pain. Hardly able to speak she continued to pray.

'Though my physical presence on this earth be destroyed, my soul lives on forever in your Kingdom and in your Love. For Thine is the Kingdom, the Power and the Glory, for Ever and Ever. Amen.'

She opened her eyes and looked directly into the eyes of the Sub Prior. She mouthed something to him and although her words were not spoken they were understood. 'Bless you,' she mouthed, 'I forgive you.'

Gervaise shot his hand to his heart. A pain, so fierce, like a piercing through the heart from the Devil's sword itself. He was suddenly gripped by an irrational fear. Stunned by the force of feeling, he looked on, speechless, with a rising fear deep in his soul.

As the fire raged around her fragile frame, burning the clothes from her body, blood and subcutaneous fat began to drip from the ends of her fingers. After almost forty minutes in the fire Maud's scorched and blackened head finally dropped to her chest, a blessed sign her gentle soul had departed this cruel world forever.

Chapter 60

Jacquemon lay very still upon his sick bed in the infirmary, his only movement the gentle, rhythmic rise and fall of his chest as he breathed. Brother Paulinus had made him as comfortable as he possibly could, having administered a medicinal potion of Henbane to ease his restlessness. It was now just a matter of time. Sub Prior Gervaise had visited him following Nocturnes but had retired with firm instructions to Brother Paulinus if there were any developments in his condition he wanted to be woken.

The infirmary smelt of incense and wood smoke. All was quiet apart from the occasional cough or moan from the patients. Brother Paulinus worked diligently, tending to the sick with the dedication of a saint. That evening, he sat by the bed of his old friend Jacquemon and reflected upon their years of friendship, saddened they would never work, side by side again. Jacquemon was dying of old age and there was nothing he could do about it except ease his old friend's passing and pray for his soul. He knelt, once more, on the cold stone flags of the infirmary floor, feeling the familiar pain shoot up through his right knee. He winced slightly. Placing his hands together in prayer and, leaning on the side of the bed to steady himself, so as to take the weight off his painful knee, he began to recite passages from the Ars Moriendi in a quiet monotone. He felt sure Jacquemon had led a good and Christian life and truly believed this was the best preparation he could give his old friend for a good death.

"My Lord God, most benign Father of Mercy, do Thy mercy to Thy poor creature. Help now Lord his needy and desolate soul in his last need, that hell hounds devour him not. Most sweetest and most lovely Lord, my Lord Jesu Christ, God's own dear Son, for the worship and the virtue of Thy most blessed passion, admit and receive him within the number of Thy chosen people."

His prayers were interrupted abruptly by Jacquemon's fevered grip around his wrist.

'Fetch Guido,' the old man breathed, his eyes a ghostly glaze.

On hearing Guido's name, Paulinus recoiled as if Jacquemon had spat upon him. He detested the young monk. Even the mention of Guido's name was distasteful to him. Perhaps the henbane had caused his friend to become confused.

'Would you rather I fetch Sub Prior Gervaise to you, Brother?'

Jacquemon had not relinquished his grip and on hearing the question he pulled Paulinus nearer him.

'Fetch Guido now. I don't have much time,' he insisted.

With some difficulty and a heavy heart Paulinus lifted himself from the floor. 'Very well.'

Guido should be asleep at this time of night in the dormitory with the other monks thought Paulinus but he was not always where he was supposed to be. Picking up a lighted candle, he left in search of him and found him asleep on his mattress. Paulinus tiptoed across the wooden floor. When he reached him he placed his hand over Guido's mouth before shaking him awake. Guido's eyes opened wide, and realising he was being restrained started to struggle. Paulinus forced him back on the mattress. Signalling to him to be silent before he removed his hand from Guido's mouth, he spoke in whispers.

'Brother Jacquemon is asking for you.'

'For me,' Guido whispered.

'Yes. You must come now. He's dying and hasn't much time.'

The two monks walked back to the infirmary in silence. When they reached Jacquemon's bed it looked like they might be too late. Paulinus reached out and touched his friend's hand. It was still warm.

'Brother Jacquemon. I have brought Brother Guido to you. He's here by your side.'

Jacquemon opened his eyes, a look of relief appeared on his heavily wrinkled face.

'Leave us, Paulinus. I must speak with Guido alone.'

Reluctantly, Paulinus left them alone. Jacquemon waited until Paulinus was out of earshot, and then beckoned Guido toward him.

'Sit. I have something to ask of you.'

Guido pulled up a stool and sat by his bed, looking bewildered and half asleep.

'You must go and fetch Severin Browne to me. I must speak with him. Tell no-one where you are going. Make sure you leave by the slype and do not let anyone see you. Go straight there and come straight back. Do not return without him.'

The old monk's face had taken on the look of a death mask, unnerving Guido. Despite his weariness, he jumped up from the stool, fearful of disobeying the old monk.

'I will return with Master Browne,' he assured the old monk.

Guido slipped past Brother Paulinus and left the priory by the slype as instructed and ran through the empty streets of Gloucester. By the time he reached Severin's house he was out of breath and his lungs hurt from the exertion. More afraid of the curse of a dying old monk than waking the neighbours, he hammered on Severin's door, shouting his name.

A bleary eyed and tousled Severin opened the door. The strong cries of a baby could be heard coming from the upstairs room.

'What the Devil...'

'Begging your forgiveness, Master Browne but Brother Jacquemon has sent me to fetch you,' Guido rattled out before Severin could finish his question.

'Why?' he asked, rubbing the sleep from his eyes.

'I don't know Master Browne. I only know he's dying and he hasn't much time. He insisted I fetch you and said I was not to return to the priory without you.'

Unsure why Brother Jacquemon should want to see him at this hour, but curious to find out, he told Guido to wait for him while he got dressed. He disappeared inside, re-emerging moments later, fully dressed. Guido set off at speed back to the priory. He was keen to get back to his bed before attending Lauds. Severin hurried after him. Once inside the priory Guido showed Severin the way to the infirmary excusing himself at the entrance. Sleep beckoned and he did not want to be given any more jobs.

Severin crept into the infirmary, checking each bed in search of Brother Jacquemon. Lavender scented candles, which the monks used to fumigate sickrooms, burnt by the bedside of every patient, giving off a dim flickering light and adding to the calm. He found him at the end of the hall nearest to the altar.

'You wanted to see me, Brother Jacquemon?' he whispered, not wanting to disturb the other sleeping patients.

Jacquemon opened his weary eyes and beckoned Severin to come closer.

'Yes. I have something to tell you. Something you should know.'

Severin leaned in closer to hear more clearly.

'You like Emmelina Pauncefoot, don't you.'

Severin thought this a strange question to be asked and in even stranger circumstances but he answered the dying monk.

'I do, Brother Jacquemon.'

'Is it your child?'

Severin could see no reason to deny it. The man was dying. What harm could he do?

'It is Brother,' he confessed.

'Emmelina has been wronged. She has been falsely accused by the Sub Prior and Gilbert Garlick.'

Severin's heart beat quickened. 'How do you know that?'

'Gervaise asked me to witness the signing of a document by Gilbert Garlick.'

Jacquemon paused to get his breath. Severin could hear the hollow rattle of his chest.

'And?' Severin pressed, eager to hear more.

'The document promised all his wealth to the priory when he died.'

Severin thought Jacquemon must be losing his mind.

"What's that got to do with Emmelina?'

'Garlick killed that young girl Fayette.'

The candle by his bedside flickered. A patient in the bed, opposite, sat bolt upright, screamed out something unintelligible and collapsed back down on the mattress. Severin had, up till now, always believed Fayette had met her death by some tragic accident. His mind went back to that night when he left her at The Cross.

His friend Thomas, the inn keeper, had behaved in his usual bawdy way whenever Severin brought women to the inn. He had winked and made vulgar hand gestures behind Fayette's back making Severin squirm with embarrassment. The evening had gone as well as could be expected. She had let him kiss her as they stood by The Cross but when he tried to feel her breast she had pushed his hand away, giggling under the influence of a few cups of cider. He had offered to walk her home but she had insisted he leave her at The Cross. Her mistress, she said, would not approve of her staying out late, not being married and all. That was the last time he had seen her.

'Fayette was murdered?' he inquired, rhetorically. His mind worked quickly, slotting pieces of information together to form a more cohesive thought. His blood pulsed as he realised the significance of what Jacquemon was confiding in him.

'Go on,' he urged Jacquemon.

'He came to the priory that night to ask for help. He told the Sub Prior he had killed her by accident and begged him to help him cover up the murder. Brother Gervaise agreed to but only on the condition Garlick bequeathed a large sum of money to the priory and the rest when he died.'

'Why didn't you say anything of this before?'

323

Jacquemon shook his head. 'When I became a monk I took a vow of obedience to the order. My whole life I never broke that vow.' He paused, his watery eyes fixed on Severin. 'Now my vow of obedience is to God.' Jacquemon grabbed hold of Severin's sleeve, a determined look upon his face and pulled him closer. 'Listen,' he whispered, 'the document is also a signed confession by Garlick of the murder of that young girl.'

'But how does that help Emmelina?'

Jacquemon's breathing had become raspy and laboured. He was weakening. 'Those charges were false. Garlick and Brother Gervaise made them up.'

'But why would they do that?'

'The Sub Prior is an ambitious man. He has designs on becoming the next prior. He hopes the trial will bring him to the attention of the Bishop of Worcester and this will further his career. He wants to get his hands on her money so he can build new lodgings for when he becomes the new prior.'

'But he had Garlick's money?'

'Brother Gervaise has become greedy. He has succumbed to, and been defiled by, *Avantia, Septum Peccata Montalia.*'

Severin thought Jacquemon must be delirious. He did not understand him.

Brother Jacquemon smiled weakly at him. 'My apologies. Old habits die hard for a Latin scholar. Gervaise has succumbed to one of the seven deadly sins, that of avarice. Not content to further his career, he intends to amass great personal wealth on his way there.'

'So, it's all been about money to satisfy Gervaise's greed.'

Jacquemon started coughing. Severin poured out a small amount of liquid from a bottle by his bed.

'Here drink this.'

Jacquemon raised his head and took a sip, flopping back onto the bed, exhausted.

'And what about Maud?'

324

'When he realised the old woman had property and lived alone…'

Severin finished his sentence. 'He saw the opportunity to take her wealth.'

'I'm afraid so.'

'How do you know all this?'

'I've lived in this priory since I was fourteen years of age. I know many secrets. There's no time to explain. You must trust me.' Jacquemon grabbed hold of his tunic with his bony fingers. 'Do you want to help Emmelina?'

'Of course I do,' he answered with passion.

'I can help you.'

Severin looked at the old man. He was dying, his body wizened with age, his eyes hollow and sunken. The shadow of death was upon him. This was the dying confessional of an old man needing to make peace with his maker.

'Where is the document now?'

'It's in the Prior's private lodgings.'

Severin's hope waned. How could he possibly get his hands on it?

As if Jacquemon had read his thoughts, he continued, 'You must tell Brother Paulinus I have need of him. While he is with me, make your way to the nave. Wait there. When Paulinus comes to me, I will send him to bring Brother Gervaise. While they are with me enter Gervaise's private lodgings. No-one will see you. The monks are all in the dormitory and Lauds is not till daybreak. You'll find a chest he keeps under his bed. The key is kept in the top drawer of the table by his bedside. Retrieve the letter and leave the priory by the same entrance Guido brought you through this evening. It's very rarely used, and, if you're quick, no-one will see you at this hour. Now go and tell Paulinus I want him. Remember; wait there until Paulinus and Gervaise both leave. Now hurry, and may God go with you.'

Jacquemon relaxed back on his pillow, his confessional almost over, his face took on a more serene glow.

'But won't the Sub Prior notice the document is missing?'

'No. He very rarely looks in the chest. Now fetch Brother Paulinus. It's not over yet. You must get the document away from here and take it with you tonight.'

'Why are you telling me this now, Brother Jacquemon?'

'I am dying, young man. It's important for me to repent of my sins so I may clear my path to the everlasting bliss that awaits me.'

'But you have not committed any sin?'

'To keep something to yourself when you know that very thing is an act of evil is to sin. I cannot, with good conscience, meet my maker without trying to undo the harm caused by my omission.'

Severin's throat tightened with emotion. Was it possible he could save Emmelina? He had little time. The guards had told him she was to be executed later that day. He fell to his knees and thanked Jacquemon.

'Your thanks to me are not necessary. Thank God.'

Jacquemon smiled and closed his eyes. It was a contented smile, like the smile of a man well fed.

The cloister was empty apart from Paulinus standing by the lavatorium, splashing his face with water to keep him from falling asleep. He told Paulinus that Brother Jacquemon wished to speak with him urgently. Paulinus eyed him with distrust.

'What did Jacquemon want with you?' Paulinus enquired.

'He didn't make any sense. He's delirious.' Severin replied, approaching the stone sink and splashing his face with cool water to mark time.

'Are you coming?' asked Paulinus.

'No. I must go.'

He watched Brother Paulinus walk away. Once out of sight, he ran along the cloister and entered the nave. Making his way to the monks' private chapel he opened the door that led to the Chapter House. Checking no-one was in the corridor he left the door ajar so he could hear Paulinus approaching. His

326

heart beat rapidly as he listened from behind the chink in the door willing Paulinus to hurry to Gervaise's chambers and depart.

Presently, he heard the soft clacking of the monk's sandals as he walked along the stone flags of the corridor that led to the sleeping Sub Prior. Severin tensed and held his breath. He heard the door open and then muffled voices. The voices grew louder. Then the door closed shut and the voices grew distant.

Satisfied Gervaise and Paulinus had left; he let himself into the Sub Prior's lodgings. Severin had expected to see something more luxurious like the rooms he'd seen at Lord Malverne's but the room was simply furnished with one window to the east letting in a little moonlight. In the dimness, he made his way over to the bed and looked underneath. No chest. He scrambled further under the bed, his whole body disappearing apart from his boots. He searched with his outstretched hands in the dark but the chest was not there. Backing out from under the bed like a dog from a rabbit hole he stood up and looked around. His eyes had adjusted to the dimness of the room and he now noticed a huge cope chest, made of oak, in the shape of a half circle. He lifted the lid. It was full of ecclesiastical vestments. Was Jacquemon mistaken? Was there ever a chest or a document? Doubt and despair descended upon Severin like a shroud. This was his last and only chance to save Emmelina. Muffled voices in the corridor halted his search. It was Gervaise returning from the infirmary. Severin looked around the room for somewhere to hide. There was only one place. Under the bed. He hurried to the far side where a thick damask curtain hung protecting the sleeper from draughts. There, on a bedside table, was the chest previously hidden from view by the curtain. The metal latch on the door clicked as Severin dived under the bed. Gervaise was muttering to himself. Something about 'old fool Jacquemon'. He was out of breath, having walked the short distance from the infirmary to his lodgings. Severin heard the bed give way and the wooden frame creak and crack as Gervaise heaved his considerable bulk back into bed and settled himself. Severin hoped Gervaise would fall straight to sleep. He lay there, perfectly still, trying to keep his breathing even and shallow. The bed creaked above him once more as Gervaise rolled over and got out. Severin could see his thick, shapeless ankles from his hiding place underneath.

This is it, thought Severin. In a moment Gervaise would kneel down and discover his presence. There would be no other course of action, but to knock Gervaise out by some means, hope he stayed unconscious while he found the document and flee the priory before any alarm was raised. While Severin was planning all this in his head, he watched Gervaise's feet as they turned to face the bed, then heard Gervaise wheeze as he bent down. Any moment now, he would be face to face with him. Gervaise's hand appeared under the bed, groping around in the dark for something. Severin spotted a chamber pot towards the head of the bed. Gervaise located it and pulled it from beneath the bed. A sigh of relief uttered by Gervaise was accompanied by the sound of gushing water. Gervaise was relieving himself and it sounded to Severin like a horse pissing. Eventually, the pot was pushed back under the bed, wafting the fresh smell of piss under Severin's nose. Relieved Gervaise had not discovered him under his bed he waited till he could hear Gervaise snoring loudly. His snores were accompanied by his dewlaps flapping and making a noise like the sail of a trow sailing down the Severn in high winds.

Severin crept from under the bed and with only a curtain between him and Gervaise; he slowly lifted the lid of the chest. A bundle of papers lay inside. He fingered through them as quietly as he could. Each time Gervaise stopped snoring Severin stood deathly still and held his breath. The first two sets of papers contained church business from Rome. Severin then spotted a hand written scrawl that looked different from the official church letters. He opened the folded page. His eyes were drawn to the statement written in Garlick's hand, which began:

"I, Gilbert Garlick, do hereby confess to the murder of Fayette Cordy."

The rest of the document continued in a forgiving tone asking that his bequest to the priory be recognised as just compensation for the absolution of his sins. It was witnessed by Jacquemon de Bezille. Severin put his hand to his stomach to quell the rising sickness at the thought of Fayette dying at the hands of a man like Garlick. His mood turned murderous and the urge to kill the Sub Prior to avenge Fayette's murder and Maud's wrongful execution came upon him, extinguishing all other thoughts and feelings. He could easily do it. He had his knife on him. Gervaise had stopped snoring and was moving around in his bed. The bed creaked each time his heaving bulk moved. His fingers caressed the hilt of his knife, the cold steel re-assuring.

Then the image of Emmelina holding Sabrina entered his head and he knew he wouldn't be of any help to them hanging at the end of a noose. He could think of nothing else but to get out of the priory with the document without being seen. He held the key to all he desired in his hand. It was time to go.

Gervaise started snoring again. Severin removed his boots and inched out from behind the curtain keeping his eyes on the undulating mound of flesh sleeping in the bed. He did not wait to see if he woke. Tiptoeing to the door, he opened it and without looking back, closed it behind him.

Jacquemon had been right. No-one was around to see him take flight across the cloisters.

As he fled down the slype and out into the lane he heard the doleful knell of the priory's bell, signalling the death of old Brother Jacquemon.

Chapter 61

Severin slumped in the chair by the fire at the back of his workshop, holding the stolen document tightly in his hand. As he stared into the embers of the fire, he couldn't stop thinking that, had he known about the document sooner, he might have been able to save Maud's life. A dragging weariness overtook him, brought on by the relief of tension in his body from lack of sleep and concern for Emmelina. His eyelids were heavy, weighted by fatigue. His head nodded a few times, each time, jolting him awake. Finally, his chin lolled onto his chest as he fell into a deep sleep. As sleep took a firm hold, his body relaxed, loosening his grip on the document he still held in his hand. Sabrina's cries woke him and he lurched forward with a start.

The papers flew out of his hand and fluttered onto the greying embers of the fire. The edges curled and turned brown almost immediately. Emmelina's freedom, his daughter's future happiness and that of his own were contained in the pages about to be engulfed by flames and destroyed forever. He leaped out of the chair and snatched the scorched papers from the burgeoning flames, singeing his fingers as he did so. Although scorched, there was no serious damage to the parchment and the writing could still be seen clearly. Unnerved by the ease with which he had almost lost the evidence, he folded the papers with great care and tucked them into the inside pocket of his jacket.

Sabrina's cries grew louder. Flustered and anxious for his daughter, he called up to her as he ran up the stairs. He had left her asleep with, Meg, the wet nurse. Meg was asleep on the mattress. Sabrina lay on her back in the small crib he had made for her, screaming and distressed. There was a smell of stale ale in the room. He picked her up and attempted to soothe her. She was hungry and no amount of soothing from Severin would calm the child. He nudged Meg. She grunted and turned over. Severin dug her in the ribs. Sabrina, now howling with hunger, was trying to suckle against Severin's woollen shirt. Angry now, Severin lifted his boot and gave the woman a kick, knocking her off the bed onto the other side.

Meg pulled herself up from the floor and hauled her large frame back onto the mattress, grumbling under her breath. She motioned to Severin to pass Sabrina to her. Opening her top, she placed the child to her equally large breast and Sabrina began to feed hungrily. Peace returned to the room, the only sound Sabrina's contented suckling. Severin stood for a moment over the two of them and watched his daughter lying in the arms of a stranger. His heart ached at the thought of her mother lying in her fetid gaol awaiting execution. It was a cruel world that kept a mother from her child. He thought about how he would face telling his daughter when she grew older about what happened to her mother. He took a deep breath to dispel the corrosive feeling of despair welling inside him. Meg fell back to sleep as easily as she had woken, only to be woken again by Sabrina demanding the other breast. Her cries had woken Dulcina who had been asleep on a straw mattress on the floor in the corner. The arrangement had worked out well. Meg as wet nurse and Dulcina as housekeeper.

'What's wrong?' she whispered.

'Everything,' Severin replied.

He looked once more at his sleeping child and satisfied she had settled, went back downstairs. A few moments later, he heard footsteps on the stair and Dulcina joined him by the fire.

'Where have you been?' she asked, stoking the embers into life.

Severin related the events of the evening to her. Dulcina sat and listened. When he had finished she spoke.

'What are you going to do?'

'I don't know. I don't think it's enough to save Emmelina,'

He buried his head in his hands and leant forward. Dulcina touched his shoulder.

'Thomas Myatt has a wise head on his shoulders and gives good counsel. Why don't you go and see him?'

It was still only four in the morning and Thomas would not be best pleased at being woken at this hour but he knew Dulcina was right. He was sure his friend could help. He stood to leave.

'I'll come with you,' she said, rushing to the coat hook and grabbing her shawl.

Severin hammered on the door for several minutes before an untidy and weary Thomas opened it.

'Can't a man have some peace,' he muttered, scratching his distended beer belly.

Severin and Dulcina stood side by side. Severin held out the scorched paper to Thomas.

'I need your help,'

Thomas brought them into his private room at the back of the inn. There was a small fire in the room with a roughly made table and bench seats. On the table was a barrel of ale, a couple of flagons and several cups, some with their contents half drunk. Thomas made an attempt to clear away the mess. He brought clean cups for his visitors and poured them both a cup of ale. For himself, he re-used an empty cup and waited for his friend to speak.

'Garlick killed Fayette,' Severin said, flatly, placing the document on the table and pushing it towards his friend.

Thomas picked it up and studied it. 'Is that what it says?'

Severin looked embarrassed, forgetting Thomas could not read. 'Yes.'

'I knew there was more to that young girl's death,' he said, placing the document back on the table and taking a large draught of ale. 'Never took to the man. A crafty *coillon*, if you ask me. Something about his shifty eyes. Where did you get this?'

'From Brother Jacquemon. I stole it from the Sub Prior's private room.'

332

'You stole it?' Thomas asked, wiping his mouth with the back of his woollen nightshirt.

'I had to. There's more...'

Thomas raised his eyebrow and waited for further revelations.

'Jacquemon told me the charges against Emmelina and Maud were made up.'

'Why?'

'They didn't like her meddling in their affairs so they accused her of sorcery to get rid of her and get their hands on her money. They knew if she was found guilty of heresy the church were at liberty to confiscate her money and property.'

'The church doesn't like women and a woman of independent means...Well, they wouldn't like that,' Thomas replied philosophically. 'But the old woman. There was no need for that. What are you going to do?' he asked Severin.

'I don't know,' he said. 'That,' pointing at the document, 'isn't enough evidence, on its own, to free Emmelina. I only have Jacquemon's word the charges were false.'

'Surely, he will testify?'

'He's dead.'

Thomas poured another drink. 'Oh,' was all he said.

The three friends sat in the small back room in silence. Only the sound of collapsing embers in the fire grate accompanied their thoughts.

'How is Emmelina...and the baby?' Thomas asked.

'The baby is fine but if I don't do something quickly her mother will be executed later today.'

'Surely, we can do something to save her?' Dulcina asked them, having sat quietly up till now.

Severin looked down at the table.

'It's not enough.'

'Garlick must know something. He and that Sub Prior have been behind this from the start. I say we pay him a visit,' Thomas suggested after a few more moments in silence.

'He's not going to talk to us,' Severin shouted, kicking the chair leg in frustration.

'He'll talk to me,' Dulcina replied in a quiet but determined voice.

Thomas and Severin stared at her.

'I'll go and see him,' she added.

'No,' Thomas protested, 'I don't think that's a good idea. It's too dangerous. He's already attacked you once and now we know he killed Fayette.'

'Please Thomas,' she pleaded, placing her hand upon his, 'I owe it to Emmelina. I should go.'

Severin agreed. 'I think she's right, Thomas. She's got more of a chance than either of us of finding something out...And we don't have much time.'

Thomas was not at ease. 'I don't like it. You can't just go and talk to him. No. We need a plan.'

'I could take some dwale with me and put it in his drink?'

'By Christ's blood, what is dwale?' Thomas barked.

'Maud told me about it. She used it when a sick person was dying. It takes the pain away but it also makes them sleepy and unable to move. Maud told me it was a very powerful potion and could kill a person if too much is given. I was thinking if I could slip some dwale into his drink and wait till he's asleep, then I could look for the document.'

'What's in this stuff?' Thomas asked her, his interest piqued.

Dulcina recited from memory exactly as Maud had told her. 'Equal parts, that's three spoonfuls of bile from a barrow swine, hemlock juice, wild neep, lettuce, pape, and henbane. Mix them all together and boil them a little and put them in a glass vessel, well stopped and put three spoonfuls into a potel of good wine and mix it well together.'

'That should do it,' Thomas quipped. 'But where in hell and damnation would we get such a thing at this time in the morning?'

Dulcina looked sheepish. 'I have some,' she said quietly.

'Just curious, but why do you have such a thing?' Thomas asked her.

'I asked Maud for some.'

'Why?' Thomas pressed her, becoming more curious.

'I was going to give it to Garlick.'

Thomas gave out a hearty laugh. 'I like a woman with spirit. So you were going to finish Garlick off, eh,' he added, scratching his head with an expression of mild amusement.

'That's all very well,' Severin pointed out sharply, 'but even if you could get him to drink the stuff you still wouldn't know what to look for.'

'Yes, but you would,' Thomas countered. He gave his temples a few vicious knocks with his fists as if to bounce the thoughts out of his head. 'I think it might work. If Dulcina goes there first, you follow and wait outside. Dulcina gives him the dwale, waits till he's asleep, and then lets you in.'

'What if he wakes?' Severin asked.

'Give him a wallop. That should do it.'

'That's settled then,' Dulcina announced, rising from the table. 'I'll go and change.'

335

Chapter 62

Wearing the clothes Emmelina had bought her, Dulcina set off to Garlick's house. Severin followed close behind. It was still early morning but already a few traders were setting up in West Gate Street. Ahead of her, the spire of St Nicholas's church stood tall, dwarfing Garlick's house, which was tucked in by the side of it. It was a fine timber-framed, merchant's house, which had recently belonged to the de Whittington family of Pauntley. She crossed herself for the umpteenth time as she turned down the side of the house into the alley adjoining the church's cemetery and knocked on the rear door. As she waited for the door to open, she nervously adjusted her smock, just as Severin had suggested, to reveal a little more flesh than she would normally be comfortable with and to check the ampoule of dwale was still in position. Almost immediately, she lost her nerve and wrapped her woollen shawl tightly across her chest. She had tucked the small ampoule inside her tight-fitting chemise. Hopefully, in that position, it would remain undetected until she was able to sneak the dwale into Garlick's drink when he wasn't looking. Maud told her the correct amount to administer was three spoonfuls in a potel of ale or wine. The problem was Dulcina had no idea how much a potel was. A potel was the equivalent of four gallons. Dulcina intended to empty the full contents of the ampoule into Garlick's cup. After a few knocks, Garlick answered, already dressed in his fine clothes.

'What do you want?' he asked in a surly tone.

'I don't know who else to ask, sir. .'

'You'll have to come back. My wife's away at her mother's,' he answered, his gaze still on her chest.

She gave him one of her most comely smiles. He looked her up and down before settling his gaze upon her ample chest, still covered by the shawl.

'I had heard she was away, sir. It's you I've come to see.'

336

Garlick's demeanour changed in an instant from hostile to predatory.

'Is it now? Then perhaps I can help. Step inside and let's talk.'

He opened the door wide and stood back to let her step past him into the kitchen, closing the door behind her. Unlike Emmelina's house the kitchen and fore hall were one large room, supported by oak beams. The remains of Garlick's breakfast were still on the kitchen table. An empty jug of ale, a half-eaten round of bread and some cold meat. He picked up the jug and looked like he was going to offer her some, then he changed his mind.

'It's not often I entertain a young lady at this hour of the day. Let's have some wine.'

Dulcina had never drunk so early in the morning, but Garlick's suggestion fitted nicely into her plan. However repugnant this task was, she would need to go along with everything Garlick suggested to gain his trust. He came back with an unopened bottle of Gascon wine.

'Please, sit,' Garlick invited.

Dulcina perched herself on the edge of the chair. She could feel the ampoule pressing against the soft flesh of her breast, her heart pounding so fiercely beneath it she feared it might dislodge her secret.

'Why are you really here?' he asked, uncorking the bottle and placing two fine wine goblets on the table.

He poured two full measures, emptying the bottle. He passed the goblet to her. Dulcina took hold but did not drink from it. Garlick drank his.

'Well?'

She watched him closely, thinking all the while how she could slip the dwale into his drink.

'I came to ask you for work, sir, since I am no longer in the employ of Mistress Pauncefoot.'

He studied her face. 'You're not drinking.'

Dulcina took a sip. She had never tasted wine before. It tasted bitter to her and she couldn't understand the fuss that was made of it. She would much prefer a glass of sweet cider. She took another sip, even though it drew the inside of her mouth because she needed to settle her nerves. Her whole body was trembling and she didn't want Garlick to see how nervous she was. He would suspect her and knowing him as she did he would turn nasty.

'What kind of work did you have in mind?' he asked, curling his mouth into a suggestive smile.

He pulled a chair towards him and sat on the table facing her, placing his booted foot on the seat of the chair. Garlick kept hold of the goblet and, tipping his head up, drained the rest of his wine and placed the goblet back on the table. His cock, though hidden by the cloth of his pants, was now at eye level. Dulcina could not help noticing a substantial bulge. The bulge twitched slightly and appeared to get bigger. She suppressed an urge to flee. Instead, she sat further back in her chair in an unsuccessful attempt to put some physical distance between her and Garlick. Perhaps if she talked about his wife it would break the palpable tension in the room.

'I thought, perhaps your wife might need some help with the children. I hear she's pregnant again.'

Garlick shifted himself nearer to her. 'Indeed, she is. Which is why she's not here. Gone to her mother's again,' Garlick replied, his displeasure showing clearly by his tone and the look on his face.

'If you took me on I'd be close by...to attend to the children of course,' she added.

'You could attend to me?' he said, taking hold of her hand and placing it on his bulging cock.

Dulcina had not expected him to make a move on her so suddenly. Taken by complete surprise she cried out and tried to pull her hand away but he had an iron grip. To her utter disgust, he used her hand to rub himself. His cock twitched and stiffened beneath her forced hand. Garlick groaned. This was

338

not how she had planned it. He was moving too fast and, repulsed as she was by his behaviour, she knew she had to go along with him. At least until Severin arrived. Then she realised, with rising concern that Severin would not be coming. He would be waiting outside for her to let him in once Garlick was asleep. At least that had been the plan. Her heart beat like a pair of bellows underneath her smock and she could taste the raw panic at the back of her throat. She swallowed hard. 'Please, Master Garlick; you haven't finished your wine.'

'You haven't finished yours,' he replied, releasing his grip on her hand and pressing the goblet to her lips.

Her throat had contracted to the size of a bird's. She sputtered as he poured the drink down her, watching her all the time. He had placed his other hand on the back of her neck, preventing her from moving and, keeping the goblet to her lips, invited her to drink more.

'Have some more,' he coaxed in his threatening way, tipping more wine down her throat.

Dulcina choked. The wine spurted out of her mouth, dribbled down her chin and trickled down in-between her breasts. Garlick's eyes followed the claret trickle. Before she had time to stop him, he tore the shawl from her shoulders and made a grab for her.

'Ah, the sweet soft breasts of a virgin,' he moaned.

Dulcina, terrified he would discover the dwale concealed there, grabbed his hands and tried to prise them off her. 'No, please,' she protested, trying to stand up and get away from him. Her plan had seemed so perfect, so easy, and so flawless. If he found the dwale now, her plan to save Emmelina would be thwarted and there was no telling what he would do to her. He was a sick and angry man. She understood that much.

'What's this?' he said, fumbling with something.

'Nothing. It's nothing,' she cried, the panic rising in her voice. She tried to wriggle free but it was no use. He was not going to let her go.

Garlick pulled out the ampoule and pushed her back down on the chair. He prised out the stopper and put the neck to his nose.

'This smells vile. What is it?'

'It's nothing,' Dulcina repeated. 'Give it back to me,'

'It can't be "nothing" if it is secreted here between these beauties.' He grabbed hold of her hair and pulled her head back. 'Tell me what it is?' he demanded.

'Let go of me,' she shrieked. 'You're hurting me.'

'I'll only ask you one more time. What is it?'

She hated her hair being pulled and Garlick was much rougher than the girls in her village. She winced as he pulled tighter hoping to elicit an answer from her.

'I told you it's nothing. Just some medicine. Please, let me go,' she pleaded.

'I'll do more than that, you little minx.'

He spun her round; pushing her onto the hard surface of the kitchen table, face down. Dulcina struggled but she was no match for this monster. She was aware he was struggling with his belt to undo his trousers. She heard them drop to the floor. Still pressing the side of her face into the table he lifted her skirts, and fumbled with her undergarments.

'What have you really come here for? Not for a job. That's for sure. Want some cock?' he asked her, thrusting his groin into the soft flesh of her naked behind.

Dulcina tried to jam her legs tightly together but Garlick had the advantage and was already forcing them apart. His hand explored the soft place between her thighs. She could feel the sharp edges of his long fingernails inside her.

'Moist little cunt for one so cock-shy,' he mocked.

His swollen member slid between the cheeks of her arse.

'That's what you've come for, isn't it? That's what they all want. Cock hungry bitches. Like it rough, do you? That bitch you replaced liked it rough.'

He pulled back, momentarily and for a moment Dulcina thought he had changed his mind. Still pinning her to the table, he bent down to pick something up. It was the leather belt from his trousers. He pulled on her hair to raise her head from the table and slipped the belt around her neck. The belt tightened. Her whole body went weak and her lungs emptied of air. She could see stars in a blackened sky. Gasping for breath, she prayed to God to save her.

'Get off her,' a familiar voice yelled.

The belt loosened around her neck. The pressure on her lungs eased. She wrenched the belt from her neck and, falling to the floor, scrambled under the table to get away from Garlick. She saw Severin advancing on him, a murderous look upon his face. Hampered by his trousers, which were still around his ankles, Garlick made a clumsy move towards Severin. Although slightly smaller in stature, Severin was quick and nimble. He jabbed Garlick in the face several times, drawing blood. Undeterred, Garlick lunged again at Severin. Severin dodged out of his way and grabbed hold of the leather belt, which Dulcina had managed to untie and left lying on the table. He lashed out at Garlick and caught the side of his head with the metal buckle. Garlick cried out, raising his hand to his temple. When he looked at his hand it was covered in blood. Severin, in a frenzy of revenge began whipping Garlick, repeatedly, with the leather belt. After several lashes Garlick fell to the floor, groaning, his face streaked with blood. His trousers were still around his ankles but thankfully, thought Dulcina, his undershirt covered his groin area. Severin had the advantage and he was not going to waste time. He quickly grabbed a length of rope that hung on the back of the door and with some effort dragged Garlick's pummelled body over to one of the beams. With quick movements, he lashed him to it, wrapping the last of the rope around his shoulders and waist, making sure he was securely tied.

Garlick lay slumped against the beam, semi-conscious and trussed up like a wild boar for roasting. His face was badly cut and bleeding, his right eye was barely open, and already turning a deep purple.

It was only then Severin turned his attention towards Dulcina who lay on the floor, coughing. He found some weak ale in the larder and propping her up against him made her drink some. This only made her cough more.

'I'll be all right,' she rasped, her voice hoarse from the ligature around her neck.

Severin left her with the cup of ale and went back over to Garlick. 'What did you do to Fayette? She was alive when I left her at The Cross that night,' he demanded.

Garlick scowled. 'What are you talking about?'

'I know you murdered Fayette. I have your written confession.' Severin produced the document from the inside of his jacket. Garlick's expression changed. His eyes narrowed as he watched Severin. 'The confession you signed to save your wretched soul,' he shouted, brandishing the document at Garlick.

'Where did you get that?' Garlick demanded.

'I stole it from the Sub Prior.'

Garlick's eyes flashed with astonishment. He remained silent.

'I asked you what you did to poor Fayette.'

Garlick sneered. 'Why so concerned about that quean?'

'She was not like that.'

'They're all like that. Acting like they don't want it when they do.' He looked across at Dulcina who was still crouched on the floor, coughing. 'Just like that jezebel over there.'

Severin slammed his boot into Garlick's face. Garlick's head snapped back, accompanied by the sound of crunching bone. He howled like a pig having its throat cut. Through gritted teeth Severin asked him again. 'What did you do to Fayette?'

Severin's boot was firmly pressed into Garlick's chest, constricting his breathing. Garlick could see no way out of his predicament. Severin had his written confession and he could not imagine Sub Prior Gervaise would stand up for him.

'I saw her walking home on her own. I mistook her for a street walker. When she refused my advances I dragged her into the alley for a little amusement.' He smirked to himself, his swollen bottom lip oozing blood. 'She struggled. That only made it sweeter of course. I was just getting down to business when her whole body went limp.'

For a second, Severin detected an element of sadness in Garlick's voice.

'It was an accident. I must have pressed my arm against her throat in the struggle. I panicked and went to see the Sub Prior. I begged him to help me. He said he would but only if I gave him money. I had no choice but to sign that document.'

'You had a choice... to kill her or not.'

Garlick raised his head. 'I don't know how she ended up in the river.'

'But you didn't care, did you?'

Severin removed his boot from Garlick's chest but not before giving him another kick. He walked away returning the document to the inside pocket of his jacket.

'How are you feeling now, Dulcina,' he asked, crouching beside her.

'Don't worry about me. You haven't much time. See if you can find something, anything that will help the mistress,' she urged him.

Pacing the room, his attention was brought to a small oak chest in the corner. He hurried across to it and tugged at the lid. It was locked. 'Where's the key?' he shouted at Garlick.

Garlick raised his bloodied head and slurred. 'Go to hell.'

Severin looked around for something to prise open the lid. Garlick's sword, in its leather sheath, was hanging from an iron hook. He unhooked the sheath and, withdrew the sword. Returning to the chest, he inserted the tip of the blade into the space between the lid and the box.

'What are you doing?' slurred Garlick, struggling to free himself of the ropes.

'Looking for something that will help me save Emmelina.'

Garlick huffed. 'You won't find anything in there.'

Severin placed his foot against the wooden chest and levered the sword. There was a sharp sound of wood splitting and the chest snapped open. Inside, Severin found hundreds of documents. He picked up a document, glanced at it, and threw it on the floor. More followed.

Once the chest was open, Garlick became increasingly agitated. 'There's nothing in there. I told you, you're wasting your time.'

Frustrated, and unable to free himself, he shouted at Severin, in a barely understandable slur. 'Those are my private papers. You have no right to look through them.'

Severin ignored him. He picked up a pile of documents and threw them across the floor at Dulcina who had propped herself against the table leg, keeping well away from Garlick.

'Dulcina, help me look through these. We don't have much time.' he directed, furiously discarding document after document.

'I can't,' she replied, her voice still hoarse.

Severin turned on her and glared.

Dulcina's lip quivered. 'I can't read.'

He returned to searching the chest. It seemed an impossible task. He didn't even know what he was looking for. As his resolve waned, he noticed a tightly rolled scroll tucked into the back corner in an upright position. All the other documents had been stored flat. He snatched the scroll and read out loud the tiny script on the attached tag.

"To my sons. Only to be opened in the event of my death."

Garlick writhed vigorously trying in vain to loosen his bonds. 'Give that to me. That's private.'

Severin tore at the wax seal, snapping it in two and unwound the scroll. Garlick renewed his attempts to free himself whilst Severin studied the document intensely.

'What does it say?' Dulcina asked, her voice infused with optimism.

She raised herself from the floor and came to Severin's side.

'It's his last will and testament,' Severin told her, all the while searching the document for any mention of Fayette.

'Well,' asked Dulcina, tugging at Severin's arm.

After a few more moments Severin scrunched the brittle parchment in both hands and threw it on the floor. 'It doesn't help us. There's no mention of his conspiracy against Emmelina.'

He fell back on his knees, and searched the rest of the documents until the chest was empty. Nothing. There was nothing. Severin stared at his captive. He walked over to him and stood in front of him. 'What did Emmelina ever do to you?'

Garlick wrestled with his bonds once more without success. 'That woman was insufferable. She meddled in affairs that were none of her business. I would have been Master of the Guild if she hadn't voted against me. She would have opposed me at every opportunity. She had to be stopped.'

'No, *you* have to be stopped. Perhaps the Bishop of Worcester will be very interested to find out what his Sub Prior has been getting up to. Come on Dulcina.'

'Where are we going?' she asked, somewhat bewildered at the turn of events.

'To see the bishop,' Severin replied, already making his way out.

Dulcina picked up her shawl from the floor and ran after him.

'What about me?' Garlick shouted after them. 'You can't leave me here like this.'

'You can rot in hell,' Severin shouted back as he slammed the door shut, leaving Garlick to wrestle with his bonds.

Chapter 63

Dulcina tried to keep up with Severin who was marching back towards The Cross.

'What are we going to do now?' she shouted after him.

Severin appeared not to hear her. He kept up the pace. Dulcina had no option but to follow behind. When he reached the High Cross, he stopped and dropped down onto the stone steps, putting his head in his hands. Severin's anger had turned to despair. Dulcina could find no words to comfort him. She sat down beside him, feeling his silent pain.

'I've failed her,' Severin lamented.

'I am the one who has failed her,' she confessed. 'If I hadn't hidden that snakeskin she'd still be with us.'

'I don't think she would. I think they would still have arrested her. Garlick hated her and the Sub Prior wanted her money. In a strange way, Humphrey protected her. Once he was dead, she was exposed.'

Dulcina began to sob. 'What's going to happen now? What else can we do?'

Severin pressed the heel of his palms against his eyes and rubbed vigorously, to wake himself up and to rub away the despair that was bearing down on him like the shadowy wings of a demon. His thoughts turned to Sabrina. She would be waking and Meg, the wet nurse, would be waiting for Dulcina to take over the care of his daughter.

'You better get back and see to Sabrina,' he said.

'What are you going to do?' she asked him.

'I don't know. I need time to think.'

'What about the bishop?'

'I just said that to make him think. There isn't enough time to get to Worcester and back before...'

His voice trailed off, not wanting to say out loud what he knew to be the inevitable.

'Will I see you back at the house?'

Severin didn't answer. He was bent forward, his head back in his hands. He looked a broken man. Dulcina quietly slipped away and made her way back to his house.

Severin sat for some time on the steps of The Cross. A crazy plan was forming in his head. He would break into the goal and rescue Emmelina and along with Sabrina they would leave the city forever. Live abroad and start a new life. It was all he could think of, all he had left. A desperate plan.

'Severin?' a voice cried out.

He looked up to see Lady Alice standing before him, looking bright and carefree.

'How delightful to bump into you…Are you all right?' she asked, seeing the grey circles beneath his bloodshot eyes.

Severin had lost all interest in other women and the usual charm he applied when talking to pretty women was absent this morning. Lady Alice took his hand.

'I've never seen you looking so sad. What has happened?'

'You haven't heard?'

'Heard what?'

'That Emmelina has been found guilty of heresy and is to be burned at the stake today.'

Lady Alice dropped his hand in shock at hearing the news. She had been staying, at the insistence of her father, in London with her uncle and aunt since the outbreak of the sickness and had only recently returned to the city. It seemed her father had not thought it necessary to tell her of such matters.

'But why is that of such concern to you?'

'Because…'

Severin struggled to explain. Alice did not need any explanation. She could see from his pained expression that he had strong feelings for the woman she had been so jealous of.

'I thought there was something between you both but I put it out of my mind. I didn't want to think badly of you. After all, she's a married woman.'

'Was,' Severin added.

'Oh. She's no longer married?'

'Her husband died some months ago. That's when all this nonsense started.'

'All what nonsense?'

'The rumours and accusations of sorcery. Emmelina is no more a sorceress than I am a Lord.'

Lady Alice giggled but seeing Severin's irritation she stopped.

'But how did this all come about? It seems so sudden.'

Severin told Alice everything. The more he blurted out the better he felt, like digging out a festering thorn from an old wound. He told her about Garlick's signed confession.

'Then surely that is enough to exonerate her?'

'That's only one of the charges they've levelled at her. It doesn't clear her of the crimes of sorcery she is supposed to have committed although I know, but can't prove it, that Garlick and the Sub Prior have invented the rumours so they could get their hands on her money. Garlick even threatened her servant with the fire if she didn't hide a snakeskin in the house.'

'There must be something else you can do…'

'The only thing left is to show the signed confession to the Bishop of Worcester but I don't have enough time to get there and back.'

Lady Alice flashed a look of concern.

'What is it?' Severin asked.

'I'm afraid even if you could get to Worcester and back it wouldn't do you any good.
The Bishop of Worcester is an Italian. He's never set foot in the country, let alone Gloucester.'

Severin's last hope had gone and with it the life he had imagined with Emmelina and their daughter. He'd always known there was no point in praying. Bad things always happened. It was almost as if God wanted to punish him because he had finally found happiness. Was he being

348

punished for his callousness towards women, for all the women whose hearts he had broken in the past? He would never know. He stood up to go.

'Where are you going?' Lady Alice asked him, touching his arm out of concern.

'I'm going to fetch my daughter, Sabrina and take her to Emmelina...'

'You have a child?' Lady Alice asked, startled at the news.

'Yes. A little girl. I want Emmelina to see her daughter one last time before...'

'Before what? Lady Alice asked.

'Before I break into the castle and free Emmelina.'

Severin started walking in the direction of his house. Lady Alice ran after him. 'You can't do that. You'll be killed.'

'I don't care. I might as well be dead.'

Lady Alice could see Severin was not thinking straight. He was beside himself and likely to do something foolish. She hadn't much cared for Emmelina but while she had been away she had fallen in love with a young suitor who her father approved of and was to be married soon. Her feelings for Severin were no more than a young girl's crush and she knew that now. His love for Emmelina was obvious. He was prepared to die for her. She had to help him.

'Have you asked my father for help?' she shouted, running by his side to keep up with him as he strode along North Gate Street, pushing people out of his way.

'What's the point? Why would he want to get involved in my problems?'

'Well he might not but he would if I asked him?'

Severin stopped abruptly and grabbed hold of Lady Alice's shoulders. His eyes were wide open with rage, with the dangerous madness of a deep love.

'This isn't some silly childhood game. Don't say things you don't mean.'

'But I do mean it. You'll have a better chance of saving Emmelina and re-uniting her with her daughter than some foolhardy, half-cocked plan to break into the castle.'

Severin squeezed her shoulders tighter, not realising his strength. Lady Alice squirmed with the pain but now was not the time to complain.

'Why would you do that? I thought you didn't like Emmelina?'

'I confess to being a little jealous of her but that was then. Things are different now. I would never allow an injustice to be carried out on anyone... if they were innocent...' she gave him an enquiring look. Then because she couldn't help herself, added. 'Even if she has stolen you away from me.'

Severin detected a little flirtation in Lady Alice, which normally he would have found amusing and responded to in the same vein but he could not shake off his sense of doom.

'Would you really do that for me...for her?'

'I have a strong sense of justice passed onto to me by my father. I am not the silly little girl you think I am.'

Severin regretted thinking of her in that way. He could see now he might have misjudged her. She had a more serious side to her nature than he ever thought possible.

'My father is loyal to the King but no lover of the Pope. He has great influence in this city and beyond. I'm sure he can do something. And he hates injustice of any kind. Besides, my father is very fond of you. I think he views you as the son he never had. I'm sure he can help if what you say is true.'

Severin still holding her shoulders, searched her face as though he were looking for something, a hint that she was being serious. 'May the devil strike me dead. I've told you the truth. Emmelina is innocent of all charges.'

Lady Alice stared back at him. She could see his pain etched into his weather-beaten face. He seemed to have aged since she last saw him.

'I believe you.'

Severin let go of her shoulders and looked away from her.

'Listen,' she said, sounding in charge of her emotions. 'It will take me some time to speak to my father and time is something we don't have too much of. You said you went to Garlick's house looking for a written confession of sorts to prove he and the Sub Prior were in collusion. Yes?'

Severin was not thinking straight. He had had no sleep and was exhausted from his fight with Garlick. Any energy he may have had had been drained from him when he realised the hopelessness of Emmelina's situation. Now he was running on hidden reserves of energy but it was not helping his thinking. Why was Lady Alice going over old ground? Why wasn't she making her way to her father's house?

'Well,' she continued. 'Why don't you let the Sub Prior think you found Garlick's confession?'

'That won't work. He'll just go to see Garlick and ask him.'

She thought for a few moments, a frown appearing on her pretty face. Then her expression changed and a small smile appeared on her lips.

'I know. Can you get into the castle goal to see Emmelina?'

'Yes. I need only bribe the guards.'

'Go to her. Tell her you have a signed confession from Garlick that proves her innocence.'

'But...'

'You must give her hope,' Lady Alice said, with the understanding of a woman's heart.

This was not the silly, flirtatious young girl he had met before. She was sharp and intuitive and Severin was beginning to believe God had sent her to him in his time of need even though he didn't believe in such things.

'Tell her she must summon the Sub Prior to her cell. She must tell him she wants to confess.'

'What?'

'Don't worry. He doesn't know the real reason he is being summoned. Once he gets there, she can convince him she has Garlick's confession. That will make him nervous and nervous people who are guilty often make mistakes. Besides, it will give me time to fetch my father.'

Severin's brain was working on slow time. He tried to think through her plan but his thoughts moved like sludge. He was at the end of the road. There was nothing else he could do. He could only hope Lady Alice's plan would work.

'Go to her now. I'll fetch my father.'

She turned him in the direction of the castle and pushed him forward. His legs were as heavy as a war horses' as he took his first few steps. He turned to say thank you but Lady Alice had already set off towards the North Gate. She was running.

He hurried as fast as he could towards Castle Lane, the signed document still in his inside pocket. First, he would have to bribe the guard on duty. Since his first visit, he had learned it was common practice to bribe the castle guards. He didn't recognise the guard on duty today but as soon as Severin took out his leather pouch, the guard approached, his hand outstretched. Severin tipped out the last of his money.

'Follow me.'

Severin followed him across the bailey where two guards sat in the sunshine playing a board game. They both looked up as he passed, and uninterested, carried on with their game. Inside the keep, Severin climbed the stone steps. Each step seemed to take an age. The gaoler unlocked the cell door and held it open.

'Don't be too long now. Theyms coming to fetch 'er before long.'

Severin entered the chamber. Emmelina was curled up in a ball. She didn't move at the sound of his footsteps approaching.

'Emmelina,' he said softly, 'I have good news.'

She stirred and lifted her head. He dropped to her side and smudged away the dirt from her face.

'I can prove your innocence.'

Dazed and exhausted, she moaned.

'Emmelina, I need you to wake up. This is important.'

He propped her up against the damp, stone wall. 'Listen to me. I need you to summon the Sub Prior to your cell.'

'What?' she murmured, half asleep.

'I need you to tell the guards you have something you must confess to the Sub Prior before you go...before they...' He struggled to finish the sentence.

'Why?'

Severin explained what he wanted her to do and why and with each revelation, Emmelina's strength grew.

'Do you think you can do this, Emmelina? Are you strong enough?'

'I want to do it,' she said, gripping Severin's arms.

'I thought you would,' he said, kissing her forehead.

She smiled. 'You kept your promise'

'What promise?'

'To come back for me.'

Chapter 64

Sub Prior Gervaise entered the dungeon that had been home to Emmelina for the past eight months. He carried a bible in one hand and a perfumed cloth in the other. Emmelina sat on the floor with her legs outstretched; her body slumped against the damp stone wall with her chin resting on her chest. She barely raised her head to see who her visitors were.

'You wanted to confess something?'

Gervaise stepped toward her through the rotting filth, which covered the floor. He had brought Guido with him whom he knew could be relied upon to deal with the more ungodly business of the priory now faithful Jacquemon was dead. When she didn't respond Guido gave her ankle a sharp kick. She stirred and opened her eyes. Gervaise recoiled from her, stepping in a mound of festering straw, almost losing his balance. He reached beneath his cassock and pulled out a crucifix. Kissing it, and saying a prayer under his breath as if warding off an evil spirit, he regained his composure. Guido stayed close by.

'Well?' Gervaise pressed.

Her dark eyes had taken on a maniacal quality. She stared at the two men before her as though they were the Devil's messengers.

'I have a proposal to put to you.'

Gervaise laughed, mocking her. 'You're not in any position to put forward a proposal, and,' he added, 'in any case I have no interest in hearing anything you have to say.'

He turned to go.

'Wait. You'll want to hear this.'

'What could I possibly want to hear from the Devil's assistant?'

'Hear me out. I promise there is something of benefit to you in what I have to say.'

Gervaise stopped and half turned. 'Benefit to me? In what way?'

354

'What I have to say is strictly between us. I will not speak with anyone else present.'

Gervaise said nothing for a moment or two. Emmelina could tell he was considering her proposal.

'Wait outside for me,' he told Guido.

'But…'

'Outside,' he barked.

Guido left, closing the heavy door behind him. They were alone except for a few large rats nibbling on the remains of an ear of corn. They could be heard scratching in the corner.

'What is this proposition and what makes you think I would be interested?'

Emmelina, though physically weak had regained her spirit since Severin's visit. Emboldened by her faith and her renewed hope, she spoke with conviction.

'Renounce all charges against me, return all confiscated assets and resign your post as Sub Prior. In return you will be allowed to leave the priory a free man.'

Gervaise laughed with contempt. It sounded hollow. The rats scurried off through a hole in the wall.

'Resign my post. Leave the priory. Are you mad as well as evil?' You have nothing of benefit to offer me. You're wasting my time.'

Emmelina growled at Gervaise like a feral dog bearing its teeth. 'I wouldn't leave just yet. You haven't heard all I have to say.'

Gervaise raised his crucifix again and kissed it.

'I don't need to hear any more. You're not offering me something I don't already have. Your late husband's money is mine to keep.'

'Not if I'm proved innocent.'

Gervaise laughed again. 'That isn't going to happen.'

'How can you be sure of that? You know as well as I do I'm no sorceress. It suited you to make other's think I was. It fitted very nicely into your plans.'

355

'I have no plans concerning you. My allegiance is to God and it is to him I look to for the divine plan.'

Emmelina managed a weak but derisive chuckle at his mock piety. 'I have new information from Gilbert Garlick exposing your plans.'

'What plans? How does Garlick know of my plans? Is this more sorcery?' Gervaise moved closer. His plans to build new lodgings for himself and dispatch Prior Vincent might be in jeopardy. He needed to know what she knew and more importantly whether anyone else knew. 'What plans? I have no plans that involve Gilbert Garlick.'

'I know different. I know you have secrets.'

'What do you know?' he demanded.

'I know you covered up Fayette's murder on the understanding Garlick donate a substantial sum of money to the priory.'

Gervaise had not expected that revelation. How could she possibly know that? He decided it was fruitless to deny her accusation on the grounds he needed to know who else knew. It was important there were no loose ends.

'Who else knows about this?'

Emmelina smirked. Gervaise was fishing.

'No one... at present.'

She concentrated on his face, looking for any sign that told her she had created enough uncertainty to throw him off his guard. There it was. A quick flash of his eyes.

'Huh! Don't waste my time...' he began.

Emmelina held up her hand to interrupt him. 'There is a letter.'

He moved closer, stepping carefully on the rotting straw. 'What letter?' he demanded.

'The letter I wrote to the Bishop of Worcester.' She saw his eyes widen. 'Don't worry. It hasn't been delivered...yet.'

'Who has that letter?'

'You don't think I'm going to tell you that?'

'I suppose your lover Severin has it in safekeeping?'

Emmelina was surprised to hear Severin referred to as her lover but she supposed people had worked out Humphrey could not be the father of her child. Severin's visits and his attendance at the birth was probably common knowledge. She was past caring what people thought about her. She looked directly at Gervaise, giving no acknowledgement to his barbed comment.

'I think not. That would be too obvious. It's already in the hands of someone I trust waiting to be delivered to the Bishop should my sentence be carried out.'

Gervaise paced up and down the small cell, nervously twisting the crucifix around his neck. 'I don't believe you. In any case you have no proof. It's simply your word against mine. Who is going to believe a woman accused of sorcery?'

'I have proof.'

He stopped pacing. 'What possible proof could you have?'

'The document you made Garlick sign.'

Gervaise raised his straggly eyebrow and calmly asked Emmelina what document she was referring to.

'The document you asked Garlick to sign confessing to the murder of Fayette. The one you insisted he signed to save his soul.'

'How is that going to harm me? I have not committed any crime. You're wasting my time. You have nothing.'

Gervaise turned to leave.

'On the contrary. Your crime is covering up a murder for financial gain. How would the church view that behaviour? Besides, I have more damning evidence against you. Not only do I have that document, I also have a signed confession by Garlick, which exposes the false accusations against me.'

He stopped abruptly. Without turning he asked, 'And...?'

'It says he colluded with you to charge me with the crime of heresy in exchange for release from his financial commitment to the priory. It further says he offered to place evidence that would ensure a conviction and that this evidence was the snakeskin you told him to hide. You see, he also needed an insurance policy.'

Gervaise could not contain his anger. He swung round to face her, throwing his bible at the wall. It slammed into the stone, breaking the spine. The thin parchment papers loosened from their binding and fluttered to the floor settling amongst the dirt. Emmelina wasn't finished with him.

'Garlick never had any intention of handing over his money to the priory? He always intended to keep it for himself.'

Emmelina watched him but said nothing. She had said enough. Gervaise looked defeated. She hardly dare feel the fragile stirrings of victory.

Stretching the loose skin of his face until he resembled a bloated fish and after several moments of contemplation he finally spoke. 'Very well,' he replied, abjectly 'I shall speak to Mayor van Eck and make the arrangements for the charges to be dropped and for your release.'

'And your resignation?'

He glared at her. 'I will speak to the Bishop.'

'One more thing...'

Gervaise looked back, his face red, bloated and turning purple, the anger emblazoned on his face. He was obviously not used to being given orders by a woman.

'Yes,' he bellowed.

'You must leave the city and never come back.'

As weak as she was, she could not help but feel a sense of triumph. She collapsed onto the stone floor, her strength sapped by the effort it had taken to play her part. She hoped it was enough.

Chapter 65

Gervaise was not about to give in to a woman's demands. Who did she think she was? He had been right to accuse her of sorcery. Women like her were dangerous.

He had not told her of the absence of the bishop for it was obvious she had no knowledge of such things. Even if she sent the letter to the bishop he would not receive it. It would be delivered to the bishop's representative – the Vicar General - who Gervaise knew supported him in his efforts to rout out heresy. He was sure he could persuade him the whole thing was a conspiracy against the church. But he couldn't take any chances. Nothing must stand in the way of his plans to become the next prior. Garlick's document was a loose end. Something which he had no knowledge of. Until now. In that respect his meeting with the sorceress had been worth his while. He could not afford to leave any loose ends at this critical stage.

He found Guido sitting outside the keep in the early morning sunshine leering at a young servant girl delivering ale to the gaolers.

'Get up,' he shouted, kicking him forcefully on the soles of his sandaled feet. 'I have some matters to attend to in the city. You must go back to the priory and attend Terce. Brother Paulinus will have to conduct the service in my absence. Be sure to tell him I have extremely urgent business to attend to which has prevented me from returning. I'll be back later.'

'How long will you be?' Guido asked innocently.

'That is none of your concern.' Gervaise snapped back.

They left the castle in a hurry, Gervaise striding ahead at a rapid pace. Guido watched Gervaise turn in the opposite direction to the priory towards the quay and wondered where he was going. For a minute he thought about following him but decided against it. Trouble followed him. He didn't need to seek it out.

As Gervaise approached Walker's Lane, he turned to check Guido was not following him. Seeing that he was not and checking further the road behind and ahead of him was clear he ducked into the lane. He cursed Emmelina as he thought about her lying there in the dirt still managing to cause trouble and meddle in his affairs. Garlick was right. The sooner they were rid of her, the better. By the time he reached West Gate Street he was sweating and wheezing. It was a cloudless, blue sky and the heat of the late summer sun was proving tiring for him. He stopped for a few moments to regain his composure. He took a perfumed cloth from under his thick woollen cassock and wiped the sweat from his reddened face. Having taken care not to be seen, he didn't want to attract attention to himself when he walked down the busy thoroughfare to Garlick's house. Putting the cloth back in his pocket, he turned the corner and walked at a more measured pace towards St Nicholas' church, which was only a short distance away.

Garlick's house was set back from the road slightly, nestling in the shadows of the twelfth century church. Gervaise could not resist looking up at the church's tall spire admiring its coronet and the metal cross at its zenith. He crossed over and stood in the porch a few minutes and waited for a group of journeymen to pass. They were probably making their way to the bridge to work on the flood repairs, which had not yet been completed. He could not take the chance someone might see him entering the house. When all was clear, he scurried up the side alley and entered the back door without first knocking.

The kitchen looked empty but signs of a recent struggle of some kind were evident. Pewter plates and cups were knocked over and the contents spilled onto the wooden table. The house was unusually quiet. He heard a low moan coming from the fore hall. He noticed Garlick slumped and tied to a timber post. Garlick looked up as Gervaise approached him. His face was a swollen mess.

'What happened to you?' he asked Garlick, keeping his distance and making no attempt to untie him.

'That swine Severin burst in here whilst I was engaged with a young maiden,' he informed Gervaise, squirming to free himself. 'Thank God you're here. You can help get me out of these.'

'I'm afraid I can't do that, just yet.'

Garlick looked confused. 'What do you mean?'

'What did Severin want with you?'

'He was looking for something.'

'What?'

'Something that would prove that woman's innocence.'

'And what did he find?'

'Nothing. There is nothing other than the document you made me sign to get your hands on my money. He did have that with him. Did you give him that?'

'Don't be absurd. I have no idea how he got hold of that. Are you sure it was the real document and not some fake? Did you get a good look at it?'

'Not closely but he knew the contents of it.'

Gervaise cut him off. 'Don't think me a fool. I know why he was here. He was looking for your document.'

Gervaise studied him for his reaction. Garlick looked more confused than anything.

'What document?'

Gervaise could tell Garlick was being evasive. 'Don't waste my time. I know about the document. The one you foolishly wrote exposing my role in the false accusation of that meddlesome woman.'

'I don't know what you're talking about. There is no such document. Who told you there was?'

'Well? Where is it?' Gervaise demanded, ignoring Garlick's protestations.

'Whatever anyone has told you, it's a lie. There is no document other than the one you made me sign. Now untie me and let's talk about this over a bottle of my best wine.'

He struggled with his restraints. Gervaise ignored him. Spotting Garlick's sword on the floor, he walked over to it and picked it up.

'What are you going to do with that?'

361

Gervaise smirked. Finding Garlick trussed up and helpless had been an unexpected bonus. God was on his side and helping him to carry out His work. It was all for the greater good.

'I don't believe you. Tell me where the document is and I'll untie you?' he said, approaching him slowly, a bountiful smile upon his face.

'How many times do I have to tell you? There is no document.'

'Who has it?' Gervaise demanded, thrusting the tip of the sword into Garlick's throat.

'I've told you I don't know what you're talking about. All I know is Severin Browne showed me a document in which he said I had confessed to the murder of Fayette. It looked like the same document you made me sign. He said he stole it from your lodgings.'

'That's impossible. How could he have got in to my private lodgings and how did he know of the existence of the document? Unless you told him?'

'Why would I do that?' Garlick cried, his voice sounding strangulated from the pressure on his windpipe. 'Untie me now and stop all this nonsense.'

Gervaise considered Garlick's response. Why would he tell Severin? It didn't make sense. 'Where is Severin now?'

'I don't know.'

Gervaise pressed the sword harder against the taut skin of Garlick's throat.

Gervaise asked him again. 'Where is he?'

'He said something about going to the Bishop of Worcester,' Garlick replied with difficulty, his throat constricted by the cold metal of the tip.

Gervaise could see only one way out of his predicament. He couldn't afford to let Garlick's letter get into the wrong hands. Garlick had betrayed him, lied to him and double crossed him. He might be telling the truth but Gervaise could not take that risk. He had become a liability.

'You have been very foolish and ungrateful, Gilbert.' He addressed him by his first name, something he very rarely did. His tone was polite but the meaning menacing. 'I'm sorry, Gilbert.'

He raised the sword and with all his force drove the tip into Garlick's throat. Garlick looked surprised. Gervaise pulled out the sword. Blood gushed from the gaping tear in his throat in rhythmic harmony with his still beating heart. Gradually the flow stopped. Garlick slumped against the timber post, his expression still of surprise. Gervaise threw down the sword. It clattered onto the stone floor where it became smeared in Garlick's blood, now pooling before him.

It seemed there was one more loose end that needed to be cleared up. Severin. He had been going over in his mind what Emmelina had said. She mentioned a letter she had written to the Bishop of Worcester exposing his role in the murder of Fayette and the false accusations. He thought it through. Perhaps she had been bluffing him and there was no letter. He couldn't take that chance. He had to find Severin before he showed anyone the document. If it got into the wrong hands it would require a good deal of thought to put forward a plausible defence. Emmelina was no longer a problem. She would not be around to defend herself. Neither was Garlick. He was no longer around to give evidence against him and he could easily blame his murder on Severin. They were no longer a matter for concern but he had to get hold of the stolen document from Severin. He looked at the limp body of his former benefactor slumped against the post, his swollen head lolled to one side. He was satisfied he had carried out God's work by removing a sinner. He must go on in order to do more of God's work. He walked out of Garlick's kitchen muttering to himself and kissing the crucifix around his neck.

'Take pity on me, Lord, in your mercy; In your abundance of mercy, wipe out my guilt.'

Chapter 66

Gervaise composed himself before leaving Garlick's house. He took several deep breaths, patted down his cappa and stretched his corpulent, squat body to its full height. Checking he would not be seen leaving Garlick's house, he walked in the direction of Abbey Lane. Skirting the Abbey precinct, he came upon Severin's house through the cramped and noisy back streets of the burgages of St John's. Craftsmen were toiling at their trade whilst small children ran around playing and mothers hung washing out to dry in the yards at the rear. Gervaise tried to appear calm as he dashed along the dusty lane. He stopped outside the wooden gate that led to the back door of Severin's workshop. Taking out his linen cloth he wiped the sweat from his florid face and neck and once again composed himself. He was hoping to catch Severin before he left for Worcester. Worcester was a day's ride away and he would need to pack provisions. He entered the courtyard, cautiously, taking care to close the gate behind him. The back door was open. Gervaise's spirits lifted.

'God is on my side,' he whispered.

From inside he could hear a woman's voice. As he crept through the door, he saw Dulcina soothing a baby in her arms, swaying from side to side.

He crept up behind her with the stealth of a fox. 'Where is he?'

Dulcina swung round at the sound of his voice. 'He's not here, sir. Only me and the babber.'

Dulcina took a few steps back, clutching baby Sabrina to her chest.

Gervaise moved toward her. 'Don't waste my time. I know he's here.'

'As God's my witness, sir, I swear on this babber's life, he's not here,'

'That won't do you any good if that's the Devil's child you've got there.' He took a few more steps towards her. 'It should have been killed at birth.'

As if alerted by an innate fear of danger Sabrina whimpered. Dulcina rocked her to settle her.

'I can still have it thrown on the fire to burn to ashes along with its mother. Give it to me?'

He reached out and snatched Sabrina from her arms. Sabrina let out a shrill cry. Holding her at arm's length like she was a rancid piece of meat, Gervaise walked out.

'Please don't harm her,' Dulcina pleaded, running after him.

'Tell him if he gives me the documents I will spare the child.'

'I don't know where he is.'

'I suggest you find him,' Gervaise replied, fixing her with the chilling stare of an ecclesiastical despot.

Chapter 67

Paralysed by despair, Dulcina stood in the middle of Severin's workshop. Severin had entrusted the care of Sabrina to her and she had failed him. Emmelina was her friend and she had betrayed her. And Severin? He had taken her in when she was thrown out of Emmelina's house by Constable Rudge and his men. She had failed them all. Her family, cruelly taken away from her. There was no-one left. A heavy sadness, like a dark and heavy shroud swamped her. Then like the lighting of a candle inside her head she remembered Thomas Myatt from the New Inn. He would know what to do. He would help her.

She ran out into North Gate Street, past the throng of traders and journeymen, bumping into anyone who got in her way and not even apologising, which was so unlike her. Even at this time of the morning, the New Inn was busy with visiting pilgrims. A group of journeymen blocked her way. She stood for a moment to let them pass but they remained in the doorway. In desperation, she pushed past them.

The youngest man in the group, no more than a boy, had obviously been drinking and was full of false bravado. He grabbed hold of Dulcina's arm.

'Here, what's the rush, my pretty?'

She tried to wrench herself from his grasp.

'Hold on, now. I likes 'em wi' a bit o' spirit,' he added, leering at her breasts, making a grab for her other arm. His breath had the stale smell of ale, rank and sour.

'Let go of me,' Dulcina shouted at him, struggling to free herself.

She pushed the young drunk as hard as she could. Not expecting to be pushed, he fell against one of the others and the two of them, unsteady on their feet from the drink, fell over each other. In the fall, the boy lost his grip on Dulcina. The frustration at losing Sabrina and the revulsion she had towards all men like Garlick bubbled to the surface. She still had to push past the others to get inside and she was in no mood to back down.

'Get out of my way,' she demanded, shoving against the rest of the men. One of them grabbed hold of her between the legs.

'I bet she's ripe for the taking,' he leered.

Memories of Garlick's assault surfaced. The panic returned as she tried to push the man's hands away. Then a familiar and welcoming voice shouted out from behind her.

'What the Devil's going on here?'

Thomas Myatt was striding towards the group, his large frame, full of threat.

'Let go of this young woman and be off wi' yer. I run a well ordered house here. Now be off,' he yelled, as he cuffed the nearest man to him.

The men recognised Thomas as the landlord and seemed to sober up. Thomas went over to pick up the other two from the floor.

'We were only 'aving a bit 'o fun. No harm done,' said an older man, holding up his hands to Thomas in a gesture of bonhomie.

'Get off wi' 'yer and don't think of coming back.'

The men cussed under their breath as they made their way quickly out of the courtyard.

'Thank you Thomas,' Dulcina said, straightening her skirts. 'I don't know what would have happened if you hadn't come along.'

'You looked like you were getting the better of 'em,' he grinned, winking at her.

'I need your help, Thomas. I don't know who else to turn to. Severin has lost his mind and…'

'Come with me, lass. I think I can help.'

Thomas gently placed his arm around Dulcina's shoulders and guided her towards his private quarters at the back of the inn. He opened the door and gave her a light push into the room.

'Severin!' she exclaimed, so relieved to see him. 'I'm so glad you're here.'

'Why are you here?' he questioned, standing up from the table. 'Where's Sabrina?'

Dulcina looked around her as if she might find the answer to his question somewhere in the room.

Severin asked again. 'Dulcina, where's Sabrina?'

Again, Dulcina looked from Thomas to Severin and back to Thomas, a silent entreaty for help. When none came and all she got back was blank stares she blurted out her confession. 'Gervaise has her. He came to the house and took her.'

'What?' Severin shouted, pushing the table away from him in anger.

'He said I was to tell you to return the documents and he would give Sabrina back. He took her away with him.'

'Where's he taken her?' Severin demanded.

'I don't know. He just left and didn't say.'

'Where did he take her?' he yelled, taking hold of her shoulders and shaking her.

Dulcina was so upset she was beyond speech. Severin realised his anger wasn't helping. He held her face firmly with both hands and tilted her heads backwards, forcing her to look at him.

'This is very important, Dulcina,' he spoke in a slow staccato. 'Where has he taken her?'

Dulcina's plump cheeks bulged under the pressure of Severin's large hands. She looked at him, wild eyed, with the fear of a hunted doe when it senses the end.

'Did you ask him?' he pressed, becoming impatient with her.

Cowed, she replied. 'No. I didn't think.'

'Severin,' Thomas shouted, coming between the two and prising Severin's hands from Dulcina.

Severin let go and turned away from her like a hunter who has lost his taste for blood. Dulcina's face crumpled.

'I'm sorry.'

Thomas glanced across at Severin. His expression had hardened. He had seen that look many times on the faces of men down on their luck.

'Do you have a sword?' Severin asked.

Thomas did not reply but left the room, returning with a heavy sword in its leather sheath. Severin wrapped the belt around his waist and tied it securely. He then rummaged in his inside pocket and took out the document.

'Here, take this from me.' He pushed the document into Thomas's hand. 'Make sure you place them safely into the hands of Lord Malverne. He knows me and if anything happens to me he'll know what to do with them.'

'What are you going to do?' Thomas asked. 'You can't kill a man of the cloth?'

'He has my child and he's threatened to kill her. He can no longer hide behind the cloth. I'll do whatever needs to be done to protect my family.'

He left Thomas to tend to Dulcina who had dropped to her knees and was praying feverishly, crossing herself over and over whilst holding up her crucifix to an invisible higher realm.

Severin hesitated at the door. He appeared to be thinking of something else to say.

'You've been a good friend Thomas. Guard those papers with your life.' He turned to go, then added, 'And look after Dulcina.'

'Don't worry I have some strong ale that will sort her out,' Thomas quipped.

Chapter 68

Prior Vincent sat on the stone-arcaded seat in the Chapter House facing a circle of monks who looked surprised to see him. He had returned from church business in Rome without sending word ahead and he was not best pleased.

'Can anyone tell me where Brother Gervaise is?'

The monks remained silent. Prior Vincent scrutinised each of their faces for anything, which would tell him someone knew something. He had arrived back from Rome to find his Sub Prior missing and old Brother Jacquemon dead. His instincts told him something was seriously wrong. His gaze settled upon Guido. Guido shifted in his seat and looked down at the tiled floor, studying the pattern in the hope Prior Vincent would forget about him and not ask him any more difficult questions.

'Brother Guido, do you know where he is?' Vincent asked, raising his voice. Guido, he knew, was a troubled soul. Out of all the monks at the priory he would be involved in some way. Vincent had looked for a sign and Guido's unwillingness to look him straight in the eye was enough to tell him his instincts were right. Guido knew something.

'If you know something, it would be best to tell me now,' Vincent pressed.

The other monks all turned to look at Guido waiting for his answer. He knew their eyes were upon him even though his own were firmly fixed at a point in the pattern on the tiled floor. He had not had time to speak to Brother Paulinus and give him Gervaise's message about Terce. Instead, by the time he returned, Prior Vincent had already arrived back and was demanding to know where his Sub Prior was. Guido would have had no difficulty in telling Paulinus Gervaise had important business. Paulinus would not have questioned the orders of his superior. But now he was faced with telling Gervaise's superior and Prior Vincent would not accept any half-truths or vague replies. He would want to know the nature of that business and more. Guido kept quiet in the hope Gervaise would arrive back in time to give his own account of where he had been and what he was up to. There was nothing more he could do. Gervaise was not back and he could not remain silent much longer. He would just have to accept whatever punishment Gervaise decided to mete out to him later.

'Am I to take your silence as an admission of guilt?'

Guido looked up. 'Brother Gervaise had important business in the city,' Guido replied, without giving more detail.

'What possible business could he have?' Vincent asked, eyeing Guido suspiciously.

'I don't know the nature of his business, Prior Vincent,' Guido replied, avoiding the Prior's stare.

'How have you come by such information?'

This was what he had been dreading. An inquisition from the Prior. Gervaise would be furious with him when he returned but here he was faced with the rising anger of the Prior, Gervaise's superior. It would be simpler if he could just have one brother in charge of him then he might not get into so much trouble.

'He told me to tell Brother Paulinus he had important business in the city and to tell him to conduct the service at Terce in his absence.'

'What could possibly be so important he would miss Terce?'

Guido clasped his hands together almost in prayer. 'I don't know, prior.'

Vincent sat in his prior's seat. He looked diminutive in comparison to Sub Prior Gervaise being a small, slim man, in his early fifties. His features were drawn with the weariness of his long journey but otherwise his face was tanned and glowed, unlike the lardy pallor of Gervaise's portly frame. A tense silence fell upon the Chapter House, broken only by the sudden entrance of Severin wielding Thomas's sword.

371

Vincent stood up. 'What the Devil is the meaning of this? Who are you?'

'I'm looking for Sub Prior Gervaise. Where is he?' demanded Severin, ignoring Vincent's question. Vincent shot a glance at Guido. This could not be a coincidence.

'This is a place of holy worship and quiet contemplation. You cannot come here bearing arms and making demands.'

'Is he here?' Severin continued to ignore the Prior's questions, scanning the circle of monks and settling upon Guido.

'What business do you have with him?' asked Prior Vincent, noticing his interest in Guido.

'He has my daughter.'

Prior Vincent laughed, a reaction brought on by a mixture of disbelief and tiredness. 'And what would Brother Gervaise want with your daughter?'

'He means to kill her.'

Prior Vincent fell back onto the stone plinth. The Chapter House fell silent. The early morning sun shone through the east window and landed on the shaft of Severin's sword sending shards of glittering light across the shiny tiles of the Chapter House floor. Out of the silence came a faint cry, a baby's cry. It was coming from the cloisters. Severin spun round.

'Who are you?' Vincent shouted at Severin as he retreated from the Chapter House.

Severin turned round to look at Prior Vincent. 'My name is Severin Browne, my daughter is Sabrina and her mother is in the castle gaol thanks to Brother Gervaise and your benefactor Gilbert Garlick.'

372

Chapter 69

Severin emerged into the cloisters just in time to see Gervaise disappear into the store room next to the monks' refectory. He knew the slype led directly onto the street, which in turn led down to the monks' private quay. Severin unsheathed his sword and ran after him. A fierce south westerly wind greeted him as he stepped out into the lane. He could see Gervaise ahead, his head bowed, struggling against the wind, his cassock wrapping itself around his legs. Gervaise reached the wooden pontoon and loosened the rope to which a small boat was tethered. He turned slightly and Severin caught sight of his daughter's tiny body still wrapped in her coverlet, nestled in a large leather shoulder bag Gervaise had slung across his chest.

Severin battled through the gusting wind and caught up with him. He could see he was sweating, his hands were shaking and he was having difficulty untying the rope.

'Give me the child?' Severin asked him in a calm and soothing voice though his heart thudded like a trebuchet beneath his woollen shirt.

Gervaise redoubled his efforts at the sound of Severin's voice.

'Give me the documents and you shall have the Devil's child,' Gervaise shouted back above the rising noise of the wind.

Severin realised Lady Alice's plan had partially worked. Gervaise had accepted there was more than one document. Emmelina must have been convincing.

He could hear Sabrina's muffled cries, each one twisting at his already pounding heart. Gervaise clambered down onto the wooden steps just as another forceful gust of wind battered the rickety pontoon and knocked Gervaise off balance. He was thrown backwards but managed to grab hold of the top of the pontoon to steady himself. His tiny captive let out another heart wrenching cry.

'She's no Devil's child and you know that. She's an innocent child of God. Give her to me and you can have the documents,' Severin offered, edging towards Gervaise and hoping he could put off having to present them.

He was now standing on the pontoon. With each step it creaked and groaned beneath him, swaying dangerously in the wind. The flood waters had no doubt undermined the footings and the pontoon was no longer safe underfoot. Gervaise, still struggling to hold onto the pontoon such was the force of the wind, lowered himself, one step at a time. With each of Gervaise's heavy steps, the wooden structure yielded. The step gave out an audible crack and once more Gervaise lurched and almost fell.

'Show me the documents,' Gervaise insisted, pausing for a moment to take a breath.

Severin had given the documents to Thomas for safekeeping. He had nothing on him with which to trick Gervaise.

'Leave Sabrina behind. I promise I will destroy the documents. No-one need know. You can start a new life somewhere else.'

Sabrina's muffled cries had turned into shrill shrieks, audible above the roaring wind.

'You'll have to do better than that,' Gervaise fired back, the sweat dripping from the folds of his chin.

Another voice from behind Severin cut in. It was Prior Vincent.

'Brother Gervaise. What is the meaning of this? Have you gone mad?'

At the sound of Vincent's voice, Gervaise's expression changed from one of defiance to one of derision and enraged scorn. Prior Vincent walked past Severin with Brother Guido following close behind. Still clinging onto the side of the pontoon and seeing Vincent's fast approach Gervaise lifted Sabrina out of the leather bag and held her high by the neck of her gown; one which Dulcina had lovingly sewn. Sabrina wriggled, howling in terror.

'Don't come any closer or I will pitch this Devil's child into the river,' he shouted.

Vincent stopped abruptly and held his hands out in a gesture meant to calm Gervaise.

'Please Brother Gervaise, what has happened here in my absence. Surely you don't believe this innocent child is the product of the Devil?

Gervaise made no attempt to hide his antipathy towards the prior. His eyes became wild like those of the mad men kept at St Bartholomew's Hospital. It was as if a life-time of obedient service under a man he despised had finally come to an end. There was no need for any more pretence.

'I have listened long enough to you, Brother Vincent. Too long. The monks may have elected you all those years ago but I have never accepted your authority as prior. *I* should have been the prior not *you*,' he shouted, shaking Sabrina at prior Vincent as if she were a stick. Sabrina wailed in response.

'I'm sure we can work something out Brother Gervaise. All is not lost. You are a good man. God will forgive you if you stop this now.'

But Gervaise was beyond help. His mad eyes darted from Severin to the prior, all the while his grip upon the flimsy coverlet. Sabrina hung precariously over the increasingly choppy waters of the River Severn. Her fate lay in the hands of a deranged monk who had lost his mind.

'Still believing in the goodness of people. Your naivety sickens me. You think you are saving the souls of these wretched sinners in this city of Gloucester...' he derided. 'You don't see the wickedness, the putrefaction, the insidious perversion of these people, the Lollards, those heretics on the hill, the women of the night. You think you are doing God's work by preaching to these malefactors. There's no point. They cannot be saved. They are doomed to perish in the burning fires of hell and that is what we must make them understand. That is what we must preach.'

'Then surely that is where you will find yourself Brother Gervaise. You have lost your way. I can see that now. God will forgive you if you repent now and give this man's child back to him.'

Severin was painfully aware of the precariousness of Sabrina's situation. One wriggle too many and she would slip out of the loosely made linen gown. He had taken the opportunity, whilst Gervaise was distracted by Prior Vincent, to edge forward. Severin looked down at the small boat, bobbing about vigorously in the water. The roaring of the wind had reached a deafening level followed by an equally tumultuous sound of rushing water.

Something, a feeling or instinct made him glance up river. A wall of water, higher than the Booth Hall, was hurtling towards them with terrific speed. He had seen bore tides before and witnessed the destruction they were capable of but he'd never seen anything of such magnitude. The bore was ripping into the river bank on both sides tearing huge chunks of earth, which were collapsing into the brown sludge of muddy water. Logs, whole trees, their roots visible in the churning waters were being propelled along in a terrifying, swirling vortex. He cried out to Gervaise to warn him. Gervaise was still holding Sabrina who was no longer wriggling but hanging limply from the chubby hand of the Sub Prior. He turned his bloated face slowly to look in the direction Severin was pointing. His expression was one of surprise, like the face of a man who doesn't see the executioner's sword.

Severin had one chance to save Sabrina. He reached for the sharp knife he kept sheathed on his belt and with the alacrity of a circus tumbler, he lunged at Gervaise, slashing at his wrist. Gervaise squealed in pain, loosening his grip on Sabrina. Severin yanked Sabrina away from him, using his boot to push himself backwards against Gervaise's shoulder. Gervaise lost his balance and fell backwards. He grabbed for the pontoon to prevent himself falling into the river and, by sheer luck, managed to hold on. He shouted at Guido to help

376

him. For an instant Guido was unsure what to do. Gervaise pleaded with him. Guido glanced at Prior Vincent then stepped forward to help Gervaise.

The weight of the men on the pontoon had weakened the wooden struts further. The entire structure began to give way beneath them. With Sabrina held firmly in his grasp, Severin picked himself up and made a dash for solid ground. Prior Vincent was quick to follow, his nimble frame crossing the pontoon and reaching safety before the water hit.

As soon as Severin reached solid ground, his first thought was for Sabrina. Cradled in his arms, Sabrina had cried herself to sleep. Her pink face, stained with tears, had the angelic expression only a babe could display under such perilous circumstances. Satisfied she was in no distress he turned to look back. Gervaise was still gripping the edge of the pontoon, struggling to pull his heavy weight onto the platform. Guido was close by. A mighty whooshing sound accompanied the deluge of water, which engulfed the frightened Sub Prior. He disappeared from sight, re-surfacing moments later some way down river. Guido, as always, a little slower than the rest, stood open-mouthed until the wall of water smashed into him, sweeping his body high up into the air and pitching it into the maelstrom.

Severin watched as their limp bodies were carried along with the rest of the detritus the bore tide had annihilated in its wake.

Chapter 70

Emmelina lay curled up in a fetal position on the festering straw. Two rats nibbled at the sores on her ankles where the leg irons had been tethered. She gave her leg a feeble twitch to shake them off but they returned when she settled.

Her months of confinement, the torture and the birth of her daughter had all taken their toll on her health. The removal of her baby, minutes after giving birth, had destroyed her spirit. Despite the fitful fever of her heart, she had rallied for her confrontation with Gervaise. Just the thought of seeing the look on his face when she told him she knew about the documents had buoyed her spirits. That now seemed a long way off. No-one had arrived to free her. Gervaise was a slippery maggot and had probably found a way to save himself. She had nothing left to give. The rats at her shins were bothering her but she had no more strength to shake them off. What would it matter? She would be dust and ashes by the end of the day.

An image of Sabrina entered her mind. Soft, warm and pink. She could hear her making contented noises, so vivid was her vision.

'Emmelina?'

She could smell Sabrina's skin. So soft.

'Emmelina?'

Something touched her. Not the rats this time. Something else.

'Emmelina? Sabrina's here. She wants you to hold her. She's missed you.'

'Oh, I've missed her, too,' she murmured to herself.

Opening her eyes, she looked up and focused. A heavenly image of Severin kneeling at her side, holding Sabrina appeared before her. She reached out to touch the vision. She heard a voice, the cadence of tenderness.

'Here, she needs you.'

Soft lips touched against hers. Warm tears ran silently down her cheeks. Severin knelt beside her, he was holding her hand. His touch was warm. Sabrina's touch soft.

Such rapture.

Emmelina's despair lifted like a celestial cloud, her heart filled with love and her spirit soared.

'I'm free. I am finally free.'

Chapter 71

It was an odd procession that made its way from the keep, across the bailey towards the castle's moat bridge. Severin carried Emmelina in his arms, her wasted body curled, arms hanging limply. Dulcina held baby Sabrina, escorted by Thomas Myatt. Lady Alice walked by the side of her father, Lord Malverne who was holding the document Thomas had placed into his hands.

Prior Vincent had ordered Constable Rudge to release Emmelina. He had questioned Guido in the Chapter House after Severin made his dramatic exit. Determined to get to the bottom of the chaos he had arrived back to he had succeeded in prising out a confession from Guido. Guido, honouring his vow of obedience and realising Gervaise had gone too far had confessed all to Prior Vincent. He was able to tell Prior Vincent about the document Garlick signed confessing to the murder of Fayette and he also knew about Gervaise's involvement in the concealment of her death. It had been Gervaise who had instructed him to dispose of her body. He had also been listening at Gervaise's door long enough to hear the conversation between Garlick and Gervaise the day the confession was signed and he was able to tell how Gervaise had forced him to follow Emmelina but that he had seen nothing to suggest she was a heretic. But the most damning evidence Guido had been able to give Prior Vincent was how he had sneaked back to the Sub Prior's lodgings and overheard Garlick suggesting the church was at liberty to confiscate Emmelina's assets if proof were found of her sorcery and how Gervaise would then have her wealth and would no longer need his. Prior Vincent did not need to know more to be convinced Emmelina had been the victim of an unholy plot to steal her money. He had hidden the Malleus book because he had read evil in its very pages. But Gervaise had been foolish enough to allow the book to see the light of day and so had brought upon himself and the city the darkest of times.

Constable Rudge was no fool. He had been acting on the orders of the Sub Prior but Prior Vincent was his superior. At first confused by the reversion of the order he soon realised why when Lord Malverne informed him of the Sub Prior's death. The death of the Sub Prior had changed matters. Prior Vincent was back in charge of the priory and Lord Malverne was a powerful man in the city who had influence with the King. With the look of a man who had lost sight of his prey whilst out hunting he escorted them out of the castle. There would be no execution today.

'Bring your men and follow us,' Lord Malverne ordered.

'For what purpose?' Constable Rudge asked.

'To remove the timbers blocking Mistress Pauncefoot's front door and allow her to return home.'

The constable muttered something under his breath then shouted orders to three guards who were walking across the bailey.

The strange troupe walked through the city attracting the attention of everyone they passed. By the time they reached Maverdine Lane, Severin was struggling to walk and keep hold of Emmelina but despite offers of help from Lord Malverne, he would not let go of her. The constable's men were ordered to remove the planks of timber across the door. Once safely inside, Lord Malverne ordered the men to leave. Without waiting to be thanked, he and Lady Alice left.

Dulcina led Severin upstairs to Emmelina's bedroom where he laid her tenderly upon the bed.

'I'll go and light the fire and boil some water. You best come and help me,' she said to Thomas, nodding her head towards the door.

Thomas nodded back, understanding her meaning. They left taking the baby with them.

Severin sat on the edge of the bed and stroked Emmelina's face. Her skin was pale and yet she was hot to the touch. He spoke her name but she seemed hardly to notice him. He removed the filthy rags from her frail body. Her swollen stomach had already shrunk back to its normal size despite just having given birth. Her skin was almost transparent where it stretched across her protruding hip bones. He wondered how she had managed to give birth to Sabrina in such a feeble and emaciated state. Perhaps it had been sheer will, knowing she had another life inside her. He covered her body with the clean sheets, which still lay on the mattress and took hold of her hand. It lay in his hand, limp and unresponsive. Severin feared for her life. He was at a loss as to what to do to save her. Maud was not there to advise or help him. Then he did something he had not done since a child. He prayed. He slipped from the edge of the bed onto his knees and pressed his palms together. The tears came, hot and salty.

'Please don't let her die. Please. I'll do any penance, anything. Just don't take her from me,' he pleaded. He kissed her hand and buried his head into the mattress, sobbing. 'Please Emmelina, please don't give up now. Think about Sabrina, she needs you...I need you.'

The last three words sounded strange to him. His voice sounded strange. He had never needed anyone. He had never allowed himself to need or care for anyone. He knew why now. The anguish of loss was so achingly painful. He heard footsteps on the stairs and, wiping his eyes with the sheet, sat back on the bed.

Dulcina opened the door, carrying a pail of warm water and some clean cloths under her arm.

'There's not much you can do now. Go and sit with Thomas downstairs and get some rest. You'll be no good to either the mistress or Sabrina. I'll give her a wash and make her look decent. I'll call you if I need to.'

Dulcina was right. There was nothing he could do. All that could be done, he had done. He heaved himself off the bed. Dulcina walked round him and set the pail on the floor and began ringing out a cloth.

'You will call me the moment anything changes?'

She turned to him and gave his arm a squeeze. 'Of course.'

The crackle of the fire was a welcome sound when Severin joined Thomas in the kitchen. The two men looked at each other but nothing was said. Thomas busied himself stoking the fire and boiling some ale.

'Here, drink this. Dare say you're in need of it after the day you've had.'

Severin slumped into a chair by the fire and took the cup offered to him by his good friend. He drained it in one and sat back looking into the fire. Severin broke the silence.

'I think I'm going to lose her, Thomas.'

'Don't say that. There's always hope.'

'Do you think God is punishing me for ignoring him all these years?' he asked, continuing to stare into the fire.

'Now don't be going there with that talk. That's not like you,' Thomas replied, pouring his friend another drink.

Severin took the cup from him but did not drink from it. 'This reminds me of the day Young Will died. I sat in the tavern with his father and got drunk while his son lay dying.'

Severin shot out of his chair and thrust the cup back at Thomas. 'Here, you have it,' he said, walking out of the room at a pace. 'Tell Dulcina I'll be back soon.'

'Where are you going?' Thomas asked, startled at his friend's sudden change of mood.

'To fetch the prior.'

Chapter 72

Severin returned with Prior Vincent. His face was grey with exhaustion and anxiety. He climbed the stairs with the strength of a man much more senior than his years. Dulcina and Thomas were stood by the bed in the failing light of the early evening as he showed Prior Vincent into the bedroom. Candles flickered on each side of the bed, sending restless shadows around the walls of the room. Sabrina lay swaddled and asleep in a makeshift cot; a drawer lined with soft woollen cloths. All that could be seen was her plump little face, pink and cherubic. Emmelina lay motionless, her face had been washed and she had been dressed in a clean linen nightgown. Beads of perspiration covered her forehead. She looked a deathly colour.

Prior Vincent took stock of the scene and without speaking produced from beneath his cassock a bible. Holding the book in one hand, he approached the bed, crossing himself and in a solemn tone began.

"Father, hallowed be thy name. Your kingdom come, thine will be done, on earth as it is in heaven..."

Severin, Thomas and Dulcina joined in. Emmelina stirred. Severin took hold of her hand.

'I'm here,' he said, playing with her delicate fingers.

'Shall I administer the last rites before it's too late?' murmured the Prior.

Severin looked up at Thomas. Thomas nodded. Keeping hold of her hand, Severin leant over Emmelina and kissed her forehead. A lingering kiss. He muttered something softly to her, as he kissed her cheek. Both candles, the only source of light, guttered and went out, plunging the room into darkness and filling it with the smell of burnt candle wax.

Severin felt a slight pressure on his hand. In the dark he could not see Emmelina's face. He squeezed her hand. The gesture was returned. Dulcina found and lit a fresh candle. The light from it illuminated Emmelina's face. Her eyes were open.

She tugged on Severin's hand and tried to speak, her voice barely audible. Severin leant in closer.

'Marry me,' she whispered.

Severin swallowed hard. Still holding onto her hand, he straightened up. 'Prior Vincent, will you marry us?'

The Prior smiled a benevolent smile. He knew of the child. Unlike Gervaise, Prior Vincent was a true Christian. The child would need a name.

'Very well,' he announced.

Dulcina cried silent tears. She wiped them away with the edge of her skirts. Thomas, standing next to her, placed his arm around her shoulders and drew her to him. She rested her head against his shoulder. There, in the candlelight and amongst the dearest of her friends, her daughter and her soon to be husband, Emmelina was married.

"O Eternal God, Creator and Preserver of all mankind, Giver of all spiritual grace, the Author of everlasting life; Send thy blessing upon these thy servants, this man and this woman, whom we bless in thy Name..."

'Amen,' they chorused.

Prior Vincent took hold of the couple's hands.

'Those whom God hath joined together let no man put asunder.'

'Amen,' they whispered to each other.

Severin bent down to kiss his cherished new wife.

"God the Father, God the Son, God the Holy Spirit, bless, preserve, and keep you; the Lord mercifully with his favour look upon you; and so fill you with all spiritual benediction and grace, that ye may so live together in this life, that in the world to come ye may have life everlasting."

385

Chapter 73

God did not call for Emmelina's soul that night.

Her recovery was in large part due to the loving care Dulcina gave her. Shortly after the wedding service, she sent Severin to fetch fresh willow bark. Maud had told her about its healing effects, particularly in cases of fever. When Severin returned she took a clean pan and soaked the bark overnight. Early, the following morning, Dulcina administered the first of the bitter tasting concoction to Emmelina. Severin lifted her head while Dulcina put the alder cup to her dry lips. Emmelina retched as soon as the liquid passed her lips. Every hour a small amount was given. By the afternoon Emmelina's fever had broken and she seemed more comfortable. Once the fever had broken, Dulcina began to feed her small amounts of boiled frumenty mixed with eggs to build up her strength.

Emboldened by her success, Dulcina set about making a tonic for her mistress. The hours spent with Maud in the kitchen had not been wasted on her. Watching her mix up tonics for Humphrey she had asked about the different effects of each herb. Confident she could make up a suitable tonic with her scant knowledge, she began by mixing Quince for the fever, with Mugwort for fatigue and Nettle, which Maud had described as a cure-all.

Still, Emmelina lay for days drifting in and out of fitful sleep. Dulcina continued to administer the foul tasting tonic and willow bark infusion every few hours. Finally, there was a marked improvement in her condition. She was still very weak but there now seemed hope she would pull through. Every day baby Sabrina was placed by Emmelina's side so she could hold her in the hope this would give her the mental strength to carry on. It seemed to work. Whenever the baby was close, her countenance brightened and her spirits improved.

At last, it seemed the worst was over. The house took on a homely atmosphere. The oppressive gloom pervading it when Humphrey was alive had lifted. Laughter and infant sounds filled the rooms.

Emmelina could not have been happier. Since being orphaned and placed in the care of Humphrey all she'd dreamed about was being free. Free to live her life on her own terms. To not live in fear. To not cower when her husband spoke to her. To not have to endure her wifely commitments. She was, of course, still a wife but a wife to someone she loved and who loved her back. But the sweetest part of her new life was baby Sabrina. Emmelina could not have imagined how much joy a small person could bring. She loved being a mother. Loved holding Sabrina's sweet-smelling face to her own and kissing her sweet, adorable face.

Her mother had often told her as a child, usually when she was administering some foul medicine to her when she was ill, that whatever didn't kill you made you stronger. After what she had been through she had to admit there was some truth in the saying. She had learnt from her months of internment that true freedom came from within for although she had been trapped by the four walls of her prison she was free. When she was near to death, rather than feel afraid, she had experienced release, an inner sense of intense joy, a sense of freedom in its purest form. Her epiphany had led to the realisation she need not visit the hill in search of freedom or escape. It had been there all along. She just hadn't understood its meaning. And now she had Sabrina and Severin she didn't feel the need to visit the hill.

It was late autumn when Emmelina finally ventured out of the house. With Dulcina to help her and baby Sabrina asleep and in the care of Meg, the wet nurse, who had been kept on and moved into one of the attic rooms, she walked down Maverdine Lane. Her leg muscles had almost wasted away having been incarcerated for so long. Months in gaol, when her movements had been restricted from the shackles and then weeks of being bed-ridden had weakened her. Each step was an enormous effort, like she was climbing the steepest part of Robin Hoodes Hill.

Slowly, the two women made their way to West Gate Bridge. The city was buzzing with activity. Emmelina breathed in the air. The sounds and smells of the city were so familiar to her but somehow so new. It was as if she experiencing them for the first time. The vibrancy of the city was palpable, melding into her soul, enlivening her spirit. With each small step, she was getting stronger.

Finally, they reached the Foreign Bridge. Emmelina was exhausted and had to sit down on a stone bench, which had been placed by the side of the road for weary travellers entering the city. Much had changed since she was last here. The king had granted pontage, in letters patent, for the repair of both bridges damaged by the flood. Emmelina had not known at the time what it all meant but she was pleased to see she had in some way contributed to the flourishing of this fine city. Work was well under way. Stonemasons, carpenters, labourers were hard at work re-building the bridges so the much needed trade could return. The city had suffered a lot and so had she.

She looked up at the sky. It was clear and blue with a few wisps of cloud scudding along. She closed her eyes and felt the warmth of the autumn sun on her face. Something inside her awakened, a stirring of life. The beginning of her long recovery back to health. A few days later, Emmelina and Dulcina went in search of Pomfrey, Maud's much loved cat. Dulcina found him in the garden of Maud's old house, emaciated and hungry. They brought him back, fed him and he lived contentedly at Maverdine Lane till the end of his days. Dulcina also took the opportunity to bring back the various herbs and potions Maud had stored in her house and re-installed them in the kitchen at Maverdine Lane. Emmelina could never forget her friend. When she gave birth to a second daughter she called her Maud in memory of her dearest friend and on the anniversary of Maud's death and every year thereafter, the family laid a posy of herbs by the elm tree where Maud had met her cruel death.

Building on the legacy of her mother and Maud, Emmelina set herself the task of becoming a healer. With the help of Dulcina and the support of Severin she filled her days with the study of books brought back from Severin's business travels and the experimental mixing of potions. Her early successes with her own children gave her the courage to treat others. In time, she built a solid and respectable reputation as a healer, one which her mother and Maud would have been proud of.

Severin turned out to be a loving husband and devoted father. Together, they took over the running of the business becoming well-respected members of the Cordwainer's guild. Emmelina continued to attend guild meetings much to the continued annoyance of some of the burgesses. She never told Severin about her visits to the hill. She never told him or any other living soul but took that secret to her grave.

Sabrina grew up to be a strong and independent woman, much like her mother. Emmelina made sure her daughter was well educated and taught her to read and write so that, one day, when Emmelina was long gone she would not meet the same fate she had endured when her own parents died.

Dulcina helped Emmelina look after the children and continued to live at the house until Thomas the innkeeper summoned up the courage to ask her to marry him. They were married at St John's church soon after and went on to have six children, four boys and two girls.

It was years before Dulcina found the right moment to ask Emmelina what Severin had said to her the day Prior Vincent was brought to administer the last rites. They were sitting in the kitchen at Maverdine Lane, as they often did, reminiscing and drinking peppermint tea. The children had been washed, fed and put to bed. Emmelina looked up from her needlework and smiled wistfully.

'He told me not to give up because he loved me.'